CASUALTIES OF WAR

AUTHOR'S NOTE

All characters in this book are characters from the author's mind and imagination, and bear no relationship to any persons, either living or dead.

The island in this book is purely fictional, and is only there for the purpose of entertainment.

For Georgia Groome

'A penalty! The referee has awarded England a penalty!' the reporter almost spluttered into the microphone sat on the table in front of him. The information would be relayed through the radio to the thousands of listeners unable to attend the match.

The noise inside the stadium died from what had been pandemonium to a hushed silence within moments.

England versus Scotland. A packed Old Trafford. A cold rainy afternoon. Some 40.000 spectators stood speechless.

The score was currently level at 0 – 0, and with three short minutes left in the game, a loosely timed tackle by John Harmon, the Scottish full back, had floored George Harris, the tall English centre forward.

Willie Herbert made to walk over to pick up the ball.

'What a chance!' the reporter continued. 'Go on Willie Herbert!'

Herbert, dressed in a long white shirt, tucked into black, knee length shorts, walked across and took the ball from the referee, and nodded politely. He breathed in, and looked across at the goalkeeper, who returned the greeting nervously.

Herbert turned, and to the bewilderment of the thousands of supporters packed inside the ground, threw the ball across to the debutant, Tommy Adams.

The crowd broke from their silence to raucous disbelief. Man turned to man in incredulity. Even the supporters, having made the long journey from Scotland stood aghast, and slight smiles slowly crept across their faces. From the gloom, and inevitability of a penalty from Hall, there was suddenly a chance. If only of maintaining the draw. They rubbed their hands together, as much in glee as to bring feeling back to their frozen fingers.

Tommy Adams looked as perplexed as the majority of the crowd. He looked down at the ball in his hands, then once more to Willie Herbert.

'Have a poke, son,' Herbert winked at him. 'You've deserved it.'

Tommy Adams was not the only one stunned by the decision. Several seasoned England players looked across in disbelief. Tommy looked at them with a bewildered expression on his face, seeking approval, as several of them turned their backs on both he, and then Herbert.

'Don't worry about them. Just take the thing, son,' Herbert reiterated, nodding towards the goal.

Tommy took the ball and placed it gingerly on the penalty spot, and carefully readjusted its position so that it sat just right, the laces sitting proudly on top of the ball.

He looked up and stared into the eyes of the Scottish goalkeeper, stood resolutely inside the frame of the goal, brushing the dirt from his gloves. He smiled and winked at Adams, then brushed aside the tousled hair the rain had plaited onto his head.

The spectators had resorted to silence once more, and stared at the new boy, England's fate in his hands. One way or another, Tommy Adams was going to make a name for himself.

He stepped two measured steps back from the ball, and looked once more towards the goal. The goalkeeper stood, feet apart, arms stretched wide with hands the size of barn doors. The goal seemed to be getting smaller and smaller the longer he looked at it.

'Dear God!' Tommy thought. 'There's more room to score than that, isn't there?' He took a deep breath, and looked aside to the referee, waiting for the seemingly endless penalty preparations to finish.

Tommy nodded across to him and watched as he licked his lips, and finally, sniffing, raised the whistle to his mouth and blew.

The whistle sounded for what seemed an incessant time. Tommy waited for it to stop, but its shrill blast continued, unrelentingly.

He looked across, but the referee's face was set fast. The whistle, far from stopping, changed first its pitch, then resonance, and slowly it turned from what had been a clear shrill tone into a loud, droning blare.

Tommy shuddered as he found himself being roughly shaken by the shoulder, and turned to see exactly what was happening. He shrugged violently against the assault, trying to concentrate, but his eyes became bleary, and slowly he heard a voice, shouting. Garbled words. He shook his head, trying hard to comprehend its meaning.

'Get up, you lazy good for nothing. Get up, and get yourself downstairs.'

Tommy blinked and finally opened his eyes. The sound of the whistle had materialised into that of a siren. An Air-Raid warning. The voice was that of his father. He had spent little more time or care than was necessary to do anything more than simply rouse the youngster from his slumber before hurriedly departing the scene of the crime.

'Get your lazy arse down these stairs before...' his voice receded, the farther he walked away from Tommy's room.

Tommy yawned, rubbing the sleep from his eyes, returning him to reality. He slowly climbed out of his bed muttering to himself. He grabbed at the bedclothes that moments before had held him in a world of his own in front of a packed Old Trafford, and sharply dragged him back into the real one. He shook his head, and turning to drop his feet to the floor, forced his feet into his ice-cold, ill-fitting shoes. With bedclothes still draped around his shoulders to best maintain some semblance of heat, and now something resembling a creature from a swamp, he grabbed at the cylindrical box beside his bed containing his ever-present gas mask, and felt, rather than saw his way downstairs.

The crisp night air soon drew life into Tommy Adams as he exited the house into the cold night air of the garden, and he shivered despite the loose cladding heaped around him. He shook his head again and finally brought to his senses, he struggled as he looked through the darkness, and staggered off in the direction of the Anderson Shelter.

The Anderson Shelter, a confined space of some six and a half feet long by four and a half feet wide, was far from a welcoming confine. Little more than a garden shed, it consisted of a marriage of fourteen sheets of corrugated iron, somehow knitted together to provide shelter. Built to a standard depth of four feet, and covered in some 15 inches of soil, it was the difference between surviving a sustained night's bombing, and not. Or so it was rumoured. Whether it would survive a direct hit from a bomb was in the lap of the Gods, and something that could be argued out with the afore-mentioned, soon after, if it did not.

Tommy clambered down the muddy steps into the confines of the shelter, and still in a trance, carefully picked his way round a large puddle that had gradually formed in its centre. He nodded his presence in the direction of his father, who was currently curled up on one of the two bunks they had erected inside, and was already away with the fairies, snoring loudly. He planted his backside onto the remaining bunk, and heaving the bedclothes, somehow still draped around his shoulders over the top of him, did his best to settle in for what was left of the night.

Despite the cramped conditions, the shelter was that much roomier due to the absence of Mrs Eve Adams. She had walked out on the pair of them when Tommy had been only four years old. Now thirteen, he remembered little of her, and but for a misty memory of her face lodged somewhere deep in the back of his mind, he comforted himself that her absence was at her discretion, and not enforced by the Luftwaffe. Such was the case with many other poor unfortunates whose journeys to their various shelters, Anderson or otherwise, had not been quite so successful.

Now curled into a ball, he and his father both slept out another expectant onslaught from the Luftwaffe. It was 1940: The Year of the Blitz

Tommy was awoken by another hard juddering welcome to the new day from his father. He mumbled something, almost incomprehensible in response in return. He rubbed the night from his eyes once more, and climbing from the warmth of the bunk, sank his feet into the now sodden shoes that sat, surrounded by the puddle that had grown measurably since his last inspection of it. Despite being late summer, the puddles in the shelters had to be swept clean regularly, but clearly neither he nor his father had bothered, at least recently.

He shivered as the cold of the dirty water made contact with what warmth there might be in his feet, and he wished that at whatever ungodly hour he had come down last night, he had been awake enough to think to put them on a shelf. Or even sleep in them.

His father shouted something inaudibly in his direction as he made his way off into the day to discover whether the Bus Garage, at which he worked as a conductor - and occasional driver - had survived the night's bombing. The last Tommy saw of his father's pleasant, 'Good morning,' was the departure of his huge, proudly polished, black work boots.

Tommy grabbed roughly at his bedclothes and dragged them in the general direction of the two-storey house the pair of them called home. He looked up to check that he still had a roof, much less house into which to take them, and that he hadn't slept through a direct hit. But seeing it stood proudly, he offered a quick, *'Thank you, God,'* up in the direction of the heavens. He was not a religious sort, but as the current climate tugged on all resources, he didn't mind hedging his bets. Just in case.

Tommy roughly threw the bedclothes down onto the bed, and clumsily gathered what was left of his school uniform, discarded the previous night. He roughly clothed himself, grabbed at his school belongings, and within minutes of getting up, set off to see if the school had survived the night. He had seen many dreadful sights since the sustained spells of bombing, but like everyone else, he had quickly had to come to terms with everything that went with them. For all that, he and his friends joked, *The 'Jerries' couldn't hit our school if we lit it up for them, and put a Bull's Eye on the roof.* St Peter's Church of England School was obviously not a number one on Mr Hitler's list of priorities.

Another relatively uneventful school day, finished with the bell sounding throughout the classrooms. The children exited the building excitedly, showing little or no care or attention to the welfare of the room left behind in their wake. What Mr Hitler couldn't do with a bomb externally, they seemed far better able to do so from within. Chairs were left flung against desks and tables, and all decorum was set to one side for another day.

'Don't forget your gas-masks,' the teacher called out, despairingly.

The pupils barged their way carelessly past one another, and admonishments from members of staff were left to be acknowledged the following day. School, at least for today, appeared to be out.

Tommy snatched at his satchel and draped the gas-mask round his shoulder, and no better or worse than any other pupil, joined the rush to see who could relieve themselves of the school buildings first.

'You should try being this quick during air-raid exercises,' the exasperated teacher muttered to himself, and watched as the classroom cleared of the last of his charges.

'Night, sir!' an unseen voice shouted back, but the donor was long gone before a polite reply could be returned.

As the ensemble exited the school, en masse, they finally reached open ground. It was as if all physical restraints had been released, and from what had been a unified scholastic assembly, they now scattered to all points of the compass. Loud, raucous voices suddenly filled the air.

Tommy, emancipated, quickly wished well to one of his fellow pupils who had turned down the opportunity to join him for an hour or two's further company and watched him disappear around a corner. He looked around him, suspiciously, and finally, resolved to his solitude, turned left, out of the school gates, and made off, alone.

Time now on his side. His father not due home from his work for a good while yet, he quickly ran through a hundred different options open to him. He sniffed, and almost kicking his heels, opted for an evening down by the river. The previous night's bombing seemed to have passed him by, but he was sure it was likely to have hit somewhere in the near vicinity. Someone else's demise was sure to be another man's opportunity. An evening scavenging through fresh properties seemed most suitable, and he would certainly need to get there before anyone else beat him to it, and no stranger to the surrounding area, quickly set off in the direction of the Thames. Signposts were unnecessary. Indeed, most had been removed – to confuse an invading force - and any venture outside one's own manor, the greater the chance of becoming lost. Any foreign army would have to find its own way to Buckingham Palace.

Tommy, a grey shirt, sleeves rolled up, a pair of shorts which came to an end just above the knees, and usually knee-length socks, now scrunched around the ankles, came to an abrupt halt at the end of the road. He quickly looked around him to check he was still alone. He stood shiftily, in the event that he was being observed by an unseen foe. He scratched at his cropped brown hair, ruffled on the top of his head, and quickly determined his next move, and who he might have to fend off in his efforts to better line his pockets. He thought carefully, and looked up to the sky in the event that rising smoke which had not been fully extinguished by the exhausted fire services the night before might better guide him to his goal. Nothing obvious, he opted on chance and turned away, along what had once been Netheravon Road, further towards the river.

Tommy ran down to the corner of the road and looked down towards the river. He drew up, puffing, and quickly turned over the options of abandoning his pillaging for an hour on the eyot, sitting barely a hundred feet away in the centre of the river. The eyot, a stretch of land barely small enough to quantify as an island, was accessible only when the tide was out, and offered plenty of opportunity to explore. Better still. The tide was out.

Tommy carefully walked down to the water's edge, and touching the toe of his school shoe into the mud, quickly adjudged the journey across too parlous. Despite the probability of the tide turning, unannounced – the strength of the river certainly too strong for all but the strongest of swimmers – the thought of explaining away the mud on his shoes and uniform to a father who forbade him unaccompanied access to the river in the strongest of terms, was too much to bear. His backside would be sure to smart for the best part of a week.

The river, now an afterthought, Tommy resumed his journey with intent. He quickly scurried along various back roads, seeking out his prey, trying his hardest to avoid the attention and suspicion from anyone at home who might question his exact purpose in being there.

Arriving at the end of the road hopefully offering the best opportunity of illicit gains, he looked along it to see if there were any hopeful signs. The road had not been closed, but that was nothing to Tommy. Roads were usually closed the morning following a raid, to better search out any survivors, or check on gas leaks. At this time of the day, the worst of the damage would have been dealt with.

Tommy steered his attention away from the main road, and like an otter along a riverbank, quickly scurried away through the gardens to the rear of the properties.

Quickly clambering over walls and fences, almost as if they weren't there, he set about covering the length of the road as fast as he could, until…

Tommy looked up as smoke and dust rose up in the air ahead of him, and he eagerly eagled in on his prey.

The wind blew unexpectedly, and his attention was caught by a large barrage balloon flying high above one of the houses. It darted furiously through the air against its mooring, and for a moment looked sure to break free. These preventative measures were certainly of little importance to those whose houses had already been struck, but it was said they were there for a reason. Whatever, they were now part of the furniture, and never failed to attract his attention.

The wind died down and the balloon, still tethered, finally, and assuredly settled back into its purposeful attitude, and Tommy's attention returned to the task in hand.

Working his way carefully along the bottom of the gardens he finally reached his target. He looked up towards the rear of the house to check that there was no one to stop his purpose, or divert his intent any more than had already become necessary.

He scrunched his eyes and peered from some distance through what was left of the small taped windows to the rear of the house. The tape that had been stretched across the windows – to better prevent the glass shattering or imploding on the occupants if hit from a nearby blast – deflected, but could not disguise the fact that the house appeared to be empty.

6

Time now pressing, Tommy quickly leapt through the scrubby bushes at the bottom of the garden, and hurriedly across the open ground between he and his intended target.

The fire, as he expected, had been suppressed long before now, but small plumes of smoke still ebbed their way defiantly into the sky from resilient embers that had refused to be doused as Tommy approached the house of the unlucky recipient of a stray 200-pound bomb. What turned out to be the last of the houses in the road had clearly had the rear wall blown out of it, exposing what was left of the upstairs of the house, and what looked to have been the kitchen on the ground floor. And more to the point, there was now no one around. Tommy had the place to himself.

The large hole in side of the house revealed what was left of the kitchen, and as bombed out houses tended to go, this was no Spanish galleon. Tommy tentatively stepped over the threshold and edged his way inside the confines of the house. Time was short, and taking care to avoid any dangerously loose floorboards and stonework, it was time to go to work.

Tommy foraged quickly through the scant kitchen, and stopped only occasionally as he turned over various portions of the rubble, now spread across the floor. The familiarity with which he rummaged enabled him to discard anything of worthlessness with just a casual toss to one side, and as much as knowing a bargain, rationing had brought new value to what had once been everyday goods. Despite his apparent blasé nature, his hurried exploration had to be carried out quietly as there were now constant patrols, and an A.R.P. Warden would certainly give chase on sight. Air Raid Personnel now had the same effect on errant youngsters as policemen patrolling their beat. Certainly best to be avoided at all times.

Tommy scrambled across the last of the loose rubble, being careful not to stumble. He watched carefully where he put both his hands and feet as the broken bricks and debris from the building, despite being sharp to the touch, still held some of the heat from the fire of the previous night. He also had to be careful that the ground did not give way beneath his feet, the foundations of the building having been disturbed.

Tommy's practiced eyes suddenly snapped onto something, like a hawk spotting prey on the ground beneath. He crawled across a large piece of masonry into the centre of what would the day before have been the working kitchen. Something glistened in the early evening light. He lowered his head beneath the jagged edge to an exposed beam, and cautiously worked his way across the rubble-strewn floor. He crouched down and rested his arm on the remains of the crumpled gas cooker. With the finesse of a trained rescue team, he sniffed quickly to ensure there was no gas in the air, and satisfied, bent down to move two shattered bricks.

The concealed object revealed itself as a penknife. The glare appeared to be coming from an exposed blade, as dusty as everything else in the room appeared to be. It was a large penknife with two functional blades, one slightly smaller than the other, still buried into the body of the knife. On closer examination, the blade appeared to be razor sharp and he winced as he drew a spot of blood through the dirt on his now grubby hands, testing its quality. Tommy turned it over and over, and examining it more and more carefully with all the skill of a shrewd rag-and bone man. Placing a brisk value on it, he readily folded the revealed blade back into the body, and proudly pocketed it. A result!

His first piece of business accomplished, he quickly put thought of the acquisitionto the back of his mind, and returned to the business in hand. He looked up and around him inquisitively, and smiled happily as something else caught his eye. He hurried across, as best possible, and picked up a packet of cigarettes from a small shelf that had somehow held its place, and opened them. Hopefully. It was a packet of *Players*, and only one missing from the full packet, at that. But, more importantly, as valuable as the illicit goods may at first have appeared, beside them, lay a brass cigarette lighter.

Tommy drew one of the cigarettes from the packet, and greedily forced it into his mouth. He pulled back the cover to the waterproofed lighter, and pulled hard at the striker. It lit. First time.

Tommy smiled that both the cigarettes and lighter had survived both the bombing, and the attempt of the water to put out the ensuing fire.   He drew hard on the cigarette, and coughed as the smoke entered his mouth, then drawing in, filled his lungs. He was not a hardened smoker, more an opportunistic one. He sat down in the midst of the ruins around him, and once more examined the penknife, his other ill-gotten gain, and dreamily finished his smoke.

A sharp noise quickly brought Tommy back to his senses, and his attention was drawn to children's voices coming from the direction of the front of the house. Taking avoiding action, scrambling to his feet, he clumsily stumbled and fell, grazing his knee. He winced, but muffled the expletive as he ensured he had extinguished the cigarette, as if with all that had happened the previous night, the smell of a cigarette might betray his whereabouts.

He rapidly regained his feet, and then, carefully, and a quietly as possible, made his way into the back garden, searching quickly for some form of shelter. Somewhere to hide. The chances of there being anything still big enough inside the kitchen behind which to hide had been greatly reduced by the previous night's visitor, and as the voices grew louder, all he could find for the time being was an unwelcome, prickly bush.

As the voices in the house started to grow louder, Tommy struggled to get his body behind what there was of the prickly bush and the rickety fence behind it. Oblivious to whom the voices might belong, he had to assume they were both bigger, and probably fitter than he. He would just have to put up with the discomfort.

As he better adjusted his position, the thorns of the bush fully announced their presence. A particularly large thorn seemed to have imbedded itself deep into his shoulder, and it was all he could do not to yell out. He bit down hard on his tongue, and somehow maintained his silence.

As uncomfortable as he may have been, he now adjusted his position slightly to better see exactly who had come into the house.

Three heads emerged from the rear of what was left of the kitchen and quickly surveyed the garden.

Tommy scowled as he identified the blue uniforms worn by the boys. They were

8

from the St Paul's School, and archenemies of his own - the apostolic unity of the Saints lost in a schoolboy rivalry. Though they were some twenty yards away, Tommy held his breath as if they were right on top of him and continued to watch.

Two of the boys were taller and somewhat stouter than Tommy, and he was now pleased he had chosen to hide. They escorted the third, smaller boy, through the ruins. It was clear from the little Tommy could hear, that the smaller boy lived here. Or at least seemed to have done, prior to the previous night's bombing.

The two larger boys now appeared to be assisting him in a search over his - or what had been his parents' property. They picked noisily through the rubble, far less worried about their discovery than Tommy had been, and eventually came out into the back garden their arms filled with the goods they had managed to pick out. They stood with their backs towards Tommy and surveyed the house.

Tommy glanced at his watch. He seemed to have been concealed there for hours, but it was evident from the minute hand on his watch, that it had indeed been only minutes.

'You were unlucky, Harris,' one of the larger boys said. 'Could have been worse.'

'Worse!' Harris replied. 'How could it have been worse?'

'Well,' the other larger boy said, 'If it hadn't been for Mick and me, you might not have been able to save all this stuff.'

Harris grimaced, but perhaps wisely held his silence, as it was evident he was not going to be the recipient of any of the spoils the visiting boys had, clutched in their arms.

'And what have we got here?' Mick barged Harris out of the way. 'Look at this, Danny!'

Tommy froze, thinking he had been spotted, but Mick had clearly seen other spoils lying somewhere nearby. He bent over in the hope of further increasing his ill-gotten gains.

Tommy could see the smaller boy shrink slightly, realising that what little possessions the bomb had left in the house seemed to be diminishing by the second. Despite the fact that Tommy had already had his limited share of booty tucked away in his shorts, he had only picked his way through the empty house. Regardless of his affinity to St Peter's school, he did not like the idea of the two bullies stealing it in front of their victim's eyes. He smouldered angrily and shifted slightly as another thorn made its presence known. For all his bravery - or was it fear of being discovered - he was now unable to avoid a slight yelp, and looking up, he suddenly stared straight into the eyes one of the equally startled trio.

Tommy glanced down at the grey St Peter's jersey he was wearing, then up at the smaller boy, to whose defence he had been about to leap. The just reasons for anyone's presence there were now simply reduced to a school rivalry, and the differing colours of their uniform.

The three St. Paul's boys, originally oblivious to Tommy's presence, took slightly longer to assess the situation. Albeit, only by a second or so. Tommy just had the edge on them, and took instant advantage of it. He rapidly extricated himself from the bushes, and frantically searched for a way out. The ruined wall at the back of the garden was it,

9

but whether he could reach it before any of the others was open to question.

There was however only one way to find out.

'St Peter's! You thieving… Get after him!' Mick cried out, as his two cohorts stood momentarily transfixed. 'Go on. I'll get the road.'

Time was no longer a luxury. The question of scaling the wall at the bottom of the garden that he had so easily surmounted entering the garden, seemingly only minutes before, was now a different matter altogether. He was now under pursuit.

Harris, bemused by the whole series of events, a bystander in the hunt, stood back in the middle of the garden, still mesmerized by everything that was happening around him. He watched as Mick took off in the direction of the front of the house, and Danny eagerly eyed Tommy.

Tommy and Danny's eyes met, each looking for a jump on the other.

Tommy jumped first. He leapt away, and somehow managing to keep his feet on the wet grass, pushed away, and made for the wall.

Danny, caught off-guard, took off in pursuit a second or so later, but the advantage was currently Tommy's.

Tommy was only a few feet ahead of his assailant, but reaching the wall first, he leapt it with ease. He landed solidly, and blindly ran into the open space in front of him.

Danny, slower off the mark, and desperate to avoid letting him get away, met the wall at a slightly different angle and pace. His leap to breach the wall was ill timed, and the supporting foot with which he pushed off slipped ever so slightly in doing so, altering his balance. The heel of his leading foot caught on the top of a loose brick and his equilibrium was thrown completely. He never stood a chance. The shin of his trailing leg struck the top of the wall and an excruciating pain shot through his body. He collapsed in a heap, and grabbed at the spot where the pain seemed the most severe. He looked up at Harris, who had inquisitively hurried down to the bottom of the garden to observe the ensuing fracas, and stood looking down at him.

'Well don't just stand there. Get after him, you idiot.'

Harris, far from the stature of the two larger boys, gingerly picked his way over the wall, and arrived at the now incapacitated body in front of him.

'Go on, you fool!'

Desperate not to disappoint Harris smiled, and looking off in the direction of Tommy's departing figure, quickly started off after him.

Harris, far less up for the pursuit that his larger mentors seemed to be, stumbled, and in trying his hardest to regain his balance, rested his foot directly on top of Danny's exposed leg.

From the language that burst from Danny's mouth, it was apparent that it was the exact spot at which his leg had come into contact with the wall moments before. The resultant knee-jerk reaction caused Danny's leg to kick out furiously, catching Harris hard in the ankle, and in seconds, the pair were one in a heap.

'Aargh!'

Tommy caught the tail end of the mayhem behind him with a quick glance, and afforded himself a laugh. In so doing, he also lost his footing, but though he stumbled, he recovered his balance much sooner, and without so much as a further backward glance, took off into the evening.

Air Vice-Marshall Lord Belvoir lowered the binoculars from his eyes. It was clear through the early morning mist from the balcony of the War Office that another night's heavy bombing from Goering's Luftwaffe would do little to raise waning spirits.

He brushed at a crease that had appeared in his uniform, still immaculate after another night's unbroken spell at his desk. He prided himself on the reasoning that though the German air force may be able to destroy much of the city, they would never be able to damage their pride.

A sudden knock at the door quickly brought him back to his senses. He briskly walked back inside his office, and placing the binoculars onto his desk, called, 'Come in!'

His secretary, Corporal Wallace appeared in the doorway. A bright, young, fair-haired girl of no more than nineteen or so, her normally shoulder length hair tucked up under a hair net, and away under her uniformed hat.

'Tea, sir?' she offered, proffering a steaming cup and saucer.

Lord Belvoir smiled politely and nodded in the direction of the battered desk behind which he usually sat.

'Thank you, Alice,' he said, dispensing with her rank.

The office, on the top floor of the building was the Air Chief Marshall's normal abode during daylight hours, affording a panoramic view of the centre of London. Air raids, and innumerable nights demanding his attention, took business down into the confined converted cellars and specially erected bombproof shelters, prepared specifically for the purpose to enable work to continue uninterrupted.

Corporal Alice Wallace, noticing the binoculars around his neck, nodded in the direction of the window. 'Another bad night, sir?'

'The usual,' Belvoir replied, tiredly, answering in a matter of fact way, speaking as if he were with one of equal rank. He coughed, resuming his status slightly. 'Did you get home safely last night, Alice?'

Alice pointed beneath her eyes, indicating dark bags, and said, 'I stayed with a friend, sir. I didn't get away till late, and I didn't get much sleep at that.'

'We'll catch up when they give us a break - sometime. They can't keep this up forever.'

'Yes, sir!' she replied.

'Thank you, then. For the tea.'

Wallace smiled politely.

'Is it true, sir? Mr Churchill was out, watching the bombing last night?'

Belvoir frowned. 'It's worrying, sir. Why can't he just use the shelters like everyone else?'

Belvoir coughed, pointedly, and indicated a pile of papers on his desk.

'Ring if you need anything, sir,' Wallace said, shyly, realising his discomfort, and made for the door.

As Wallace reached the door, another knock superseded her departure.   She stood back and allowed a second corporal, carrying a small pile of papers through the door. He brushed past her shoulder, and saluted to the Air Chief Marshall.

'The latest figures on casualties and bomb damage sustained last night, sir,' the corporal said, placing the papers on the table in front of him.

He backed away, and both he and Wallace saluted, and left the room, closing the door behind them.

Belvoir walked to his desk and picked up the cup of tea in his right hand, and turned over the top cover of the folder with the other. He looked down onto a photograph of a child's body lying on stretcher, covered in a bloodstained blanket. He replaced the cover without addressing the figures beneath, and reached across the desk to a framed picture. He picked it up and took it with the tea across to the window, and holding the picture in front of him, he studied it with a cold London montage as its background.

He looked to the picture showing himself with his wife and two children, and then, raising his head, looked out at distant smoke rising high into the air. He thought of his two children, Catherine, a young lady, just turned sixteen, and his young son Phillip, '*Ten but nearly eleven*,' as he would remind everyone. Belvoir smiled, and then thought back to the photo lying in the folder on his desk. He sipped at the tea, sighed, and having turned around, walked back to the desk, sat himself down, replaced the cup in the saucer, and re-opened the folder to review the remaining papers.

The Golden Harp was busy. The Public House was full of those finished with work for the day, and in need of refreshment before returning home to whatever the night might bring. The sound of a piano - long since requiring the delicate hands of a tuner - echoed around the bar, with a raucous accompaniment to the tune. Though neither the tune, nor the accompaniment gave any real clue to the purist as to its originality, or the composer's identity. The bar was littered with glasses, all drained. Beer was not at the top of the list of commodities that required rationing, and any rationing that took place at all, was usually the amount that one could consume before leaving. Or being asked to leave.

A huge body walked from the bar and wandered across to the piano. He physically lifted the would-be pianist from his stall, and taking his place, started to place his own fat fingers randomly onto the piano keys. In comparison to the music from the departing pianist, there was now no tune or rhythm at all. Just a drunk, sat on a stool.

'Time to go home,' the voice of the proprietor of the pub called across. The body mumbled something indecipherable, and slumped over the keys, breathing heavily.

'Get him out, before we have to have him dragged out,' the manager called across to the body's colleagues. 'Better he go peacefully. Go on George. Get outside and sober yourself up. I'll keep a barrel on tap for you for tomorrow, don't worry.'

Three swarthy figures shook their heads reluctantly, drained what was left of their ale, and marched across the bar to pick up the body, and somehow, together, heaved him out through the pub doors.

The last the barman saw of him was his polished black work boots staggering away, as the door shut firmly behind him.

Tommy finally turned the corner to his road at pace. Only then did he slow his velocity. He took a last look behind him to ensure the St Paul's boys had really given up pursuit and that he was finally safe. He sighed, and wiped the sweat from his forehead. That had been close. In his previous forays into bomb sites, his only worry had been coming across an A.R.P. Warden, and his youth had always had the better over any aging pursuer. He made a mental note to be more careful, and certainly more selective next time.

Tommy walked slowly up the road, looking guiltily, either side of the road, still laden with the stolen goods, and nimbly fingered the penknife, the cigarettes and the lighter. He eased slightly as he reached the gate to his house. He looked across to the house next door, and caught the eye of Mrs Smedley, who peered over the adjoining fence, looking Tommy up and down, suspiciously. Though a neighbour, neither Tommy nor his father had ever had anything to do with her more than a grunt if they had happened to pass in the street. She always dressed in black, though for no reason it was assumed. She had a working husband, and a son, albeit away in the Armed Forces. His father had once said, *She should keep her miserable bloody nose out of everyone else's business*, though this was thinking out loud, and not especially for anyone else's ears, and discovering he had caught Tommy listening to him, he had warned him against ever repeating one word of what he had heard. It had however been like red rag to a bull. Not just stored away, but available at a moment's notice. Unfortunately. One evening having returned from a particularly stern telling off at school, he had been so angry, that on seeing her prying eyes peering through her curtains, he had blurted out his father's words, almost to the letter. It had felt good at the time, but his backside had paid for the pleasure when she had reported the incident to his father later that night.

Tommy resisted the opportunity to poke out his tongue, and merely smiled, making her even more suspicious. Tommy laughed out loud, irrespective of what she thought, and walked through the gate, along the path, and through the door leading into the back garden. He shut the door behind him, and kicking at a stone on the path, made his way down the alleyway into the back garden.

As he turned the corner, and now comfortable in his own surroundings, he let out a huge sigh, and relaxing for the first time, breathed freely. He once more fingered the cigarettes in his pocket, and checking either side into both of the next-door gardens, walked in through the rickety toilet door, and closed it behind him.

The toilet was no more than a small wooden shack, with a small ceramic bowl. An aged wooden seat sat on top of it, a slight crack off centre at the back, demanding the user's attention. The recipient only sat down on it once and ignored it, a pincer motion trapping the skin in its clutches.

The wooden door to the toilet was no more than four planks of vertical wood, held together by two horizontal cross sections and a dozen rusty screws. This was further held on to the shack by two corroded hinges. During winter, and cold days, visits for ablutions were never for pleasure, but wholly necessity.

Tommy carefully sat down on the seat, leaned forward and fiddling with the lock, ensured the door was bolted. He rubbed his hands together to regain some feeling, and reached into his pocket removing the now crumpled packet of cigarettes. Fumbling, he opened the box and reached inside, slowly drawing out one of its contents. He had wanted a cigarette for some time now, and after his escape from the St Paul's boys, finally felt he had earned it. He looked down at the cigarette with relish, raised it to his nose, smelt along its length before finally putting it between his lips. He dug further into his pocket and removed the lighter, and in seconds, it was lit.

Inhaling the smoke, as if he had smoked all his life, he sat back, enjoying the moment.

Tommy's breathing was only just returning to normal, and his heart still beat at ten to the dozen. The effect of the smoke on Tommy's body, momentarily created a bout of light-headedness, and he shook his head to clear it. He was not an addict to smoking, and did so more as a statement. The first couple of puffs on a cigarette always had the same effect, but by the end, he considered himself hardened to it. His attention to details was such that he failed to hear the front gate opening into the garden. Nor indeed, the gate leading into the back garden.

15

The gap along the bottom of the door afforded only a slight view along the garden path. Seated on the toilet, anything visible from the slight gap at the top was usually sky related. Though it comfortably hid the occupant, it did little to conceal the presence of smoke. This was the first thing a slightly refreshed George Adams saw on turning the corner into the garden.

The first thing a dreamy Tommy knew of his father's arrival was when the weather-beaten door was wrenched off its hinges in one movement, leaving behind a shattered lock, hanging lamely from the door with one remaining rusty screw. The second, what was left of the cigarette being violently wrenched from his hand and thrown across the garden. He looked up, petrified at his seething father. They stared momentarily, face to face, and though holding his hands up in defence, he thought silence might currently be the best protocol.

'And what exactly do you think you're doing?' his father blurted, annunciating every word clearly for effect. The sight of Tommy seemed momentarily to have burnt off the earlier effect of the alcohol.

Tommy, smelling the alcohol on his father's breath, quickly judged the odds of barging his way past his father, to better receive his wrath at a later date. Despite his condition, the huge man blocking his exit seemed to have all the odds in his favour.

Tommy, sighed, guiltily, and looked his father in the eye. This was clearly not the first time he had had to do so over an exchange of views.

'Well?' his father re-iterated, the stink of alcohol, prevalent.

Tommy slumped back onto the seat.

A huge pair of hands reached inside the toilet, and grabbed at Tommy. He caught the breast of his clothing just below his shoulders, and physically lifted him clear of the toilet. Tommy baulked at the stale smell of alcohol on his father's breath, and turned his head away.

'Don't you turn your head away from me when I'm talking to you! You may be fourteen, but you're not too big to receive a hiding,' his father growled, lowering him to the ground with a thump.

'I wasn't...' Tommy began, spluttering for a reasonable explanation.

'Don't you dare answer me back, you hear!'

Tommy turned his head back just in time to see his father's clenched fist coming across.

The strong blow caught Tommy squarely on the jaw.

Tommy stood, momentarily transfixed, unable to fully accept his father's brutality. It was only for a moment, before the force of the punch registered and as all the energy in his legs deserted him, he fell to the floor.

Tommy somehow opened his eyes in what was now a semi-conscious state, and looked up despairingly at the hatred written across his father face. He started to mumble something, almost inaudibly as his father, far from ashamed at his actions, drew his foot back, and applied a hard kick, from his still polished working boot, deep into Tommy's ribs.

'No!' Tommy managed, just as the force of the kick took the wind out of him. He drew his knees to his chest and scrunched himself into a ball to avoid any further punishment.

George Adams took a last look at Tommy through bleary eyes, and either from any last minute realisation at what he had just done to his own flesh and blood, or simply due to the delayed affects of the alcohol, stumbled, collapsed, and finally passed out in a heap.

Tommy was the first to recover. He slowly managed to sit himself up and took stock of the lasting effects of the beating he had just taken. He licked at his dry lips, and tasted a salty residue inside his mouth. He spat out and looked down at the blood mixed in with his spittle. He painfully reached up and rubbed at his face, and pulling at his nose, soon found the cause of the bleed. He sniffed deeply, and then coughed, violently, as blood from the still bleeding nose caught in his throat.

Just managing to stop himself passing out again, he managed to sit himself up, and drawing down one of the sleeves of his shirt, spat on the exposed cuff, and carefully dabbed at his scarred face.

He shook his head, both for clarity and disbelief at his father's antics. Whatever their relationship had been, however angry he had been, he had never, ever, punched out at him. He looked down to his watch to check exactly how much time had passed. It was broken. The glass face had smashed, presumably, he imagined, from the force of the fall from the punch. The destruction of the watch was the last straw. This had been a present from his grandfather - on his mother's side - and for years it had been too big for his slight wrists. But now, it was getting to be just right. And to make matters worse, it was one of the few reminders of his mother that he had left.

He started to climb to his feet, but sat down again as a pain in his stomach reminded him of the state he was in. He winced, but was determined to stand up. He shook his head violently, fighting off both nausea, and an extreme desire to vomit. He edged his way onto his backside and with his hands splayed out beneath him, just managed to push himself up into a sitting position.

Slowly he edged his knees up to his chest and with what seemed to be the last of his energy, Tommy staggered to his feet.

He stood, still woozy, beside his father's prostrate body. He lay with his head lolling to one side, his mouth wide open, saliva dribbling down one side of his chin. Tommy stared at him in disgust. But for the sight of his chest heaving up and down, he could have been dead, and Tommy was not currently sure whether he would have felt any sorrow if he had been.

He stood for some moments, and stared down at the hateful face. Recalling previous altercations he had had with his father, and looking at the state he was in, everything seemed to come to a head in an instant. He had had it. He hated the man lying at his feet, and without any rational thinking, drew back his right foot to kick hard into the body lying in front of him.

Sensibility kicked in just before Tommy did, and as his foot came forward, he ground

17

his toe into the dust, and safely brought his foot to a halt, inches short of its target. He stared once more into the hateful face, and shook his head in disbelief. He turned his back, and started to walk away from his father, until some few steps later, he stopped and turned.

'You're not worth it,' he said to himself. 'You're just not worth it. All the nastiness in you, and I...' Tommy choked, and realised he was crying. Tears ran down the side of his face in streams. He rubbed at his eyes, heaving, finding breath difficult.

He finally steadied himself, until, with a final glance at his father's face, he said, 'You're on your own now. You hear? You're on your own. I'm off.'

It was early evening, and the Air Vice-Marshall Lord Belvoir had done as much work as he could possibly do for the day. Crisis or not, he had to sleep, and he had been ordered to go home for the first time in a week.

'Or was it longer?' he thought.

He checked around his office to see that all the papers he had to deal with were up to date, and finding himself yawning, put a hand to his mouth to cover it.

The best that could be said of the summer months was that it meant that the evenings were longer, and drawn out. The darkness when it came was not in for too long. This small benefit ensured that German bombing raids were kept to a relatively shorter duration of time. Any bombers caught in daylight ran a heavy risk of encountering Allied fighter coverage.

But as grateful as Londoners might collectively be for the benefits it might have brought about, it would be small change to those houses that were affected by the slightly shorter period of the raids.

The phone rang on his desk, and he picked it up. It was Corporal Wallace to tell him that his car was ready.

'Thank you, Alice,' he replied, and put the phone back down. He took a final look around at the papers on his desk, and convinced that there was nothing left he could not leave for the next day, he picked up his coat and gloves, adjusted his cap, and finally left the room for the night.

His exit into the outer office was met by many salutes, which he answered with slightly less enthusiasm.

'Good luck tonight, chaps,' he said, and catching sight of his Corporal, said, 'and you Alice.'

'Get some rest, sir,' Alice whispered for his ears only, and escorted him to the door.

Belvoir climbed into the rear of the car, sat down and draped a coat over his knees, and for the first time in many days, relaxed.

'Drive on,' he said to the driver, who ground the accelerator to the floor, and the car lurched forwards.

'Sorry, sir,' the driver said. 'Bit tetchy today, the car.'

'Aren't we all?' Belvoir thought to himself.

The car finally caught, and as it slowly took off, Belvoir settled back and looked out at the London he was going to be leaving behind. If only for the night.

The car jolted to a sharp halt, and Belvoir sat up sharply, realising he must have drifted off to sleep.

'Sorry, sir!' the driver called from the front of the car.

'The Germans are doing their best to kill me, Thomas. Let's not beat them to it, eh?'

As the car started up again, he looked out of the window to see if he could figure out exactly where they were, and how long he had been asleep. As the car drew off again and turned a corner, he caught sight of one of the newsstands:

Children Evacuations Continue

If it registered at all, it no more than barely caught his attention. He sat back quietly, and ignoring the drivers attempt at conversation, returned to thoughts of his own.

After a journey of some miles, Belvoir sat up straight. Behind them, and some miles off, the now familiar drone of the air raid sirens kicked into gear once more. He relaxed, guiltily, thinking of the staff and personnel he had left behind him to face the night's upcoming perils.

'I've got to go back into that, after I drop you off,' the driver broke the silence.

'Yes! Good luck!' was the best that Belvoir could manage.

The bombing raids had not shifted this far outside London yet, concentrating on the centre of the city. How much longer it might last was another thing altogether. He knew it was short-term, and certainly something the Luftwaffe would turn their attention to when the time seemed right, but for the moment he offered up a silent prayer of thanks. Whatever, he was now wide awake, and desperate to see his family.

Tommy was walking without purpose, angrily kicking at stones and any other objects that happened across his path. In his own mind, he had now left his house for the last time. Where he would end up was clearly in the hands of fate. He could not go to his mother. When she had walked out on his father, she had walked out on him as well, and there was never to be any reconciliation. Where she was now, or even if she were still alive at all, he did not know. With the years that had passed, he didn't care anymore. He was walking blindly, and had little or no interest in what was going on, or indeed, where he was going.

Finally, weary from both the beating he had received, and the journey he had covered thus far, he stopped and looked around him. He had come a long way. He was only vaguely aware of the area, and suddenly he realised exactly how far he had walked. He stood where he was for a moment or two, looking at the other passers-by walking around him, totally oblivious to his presence. Any attention to the now dried out blood on his clothing was only passing, and his welfare was never called into question.

He was suddenly unsure as to his next course of action. A return home was out of the question, and he suddenly felt very alone. He looked around him hoping for inspiration, but the immediate need was quickly taken out of his hands as an air raid siren sounded.

At the start of the war, the sound of an air raid siren had been treated with ultimate concern. The introduction of clumsy, uncomfortable gas masks had brought with it a fear, and united the nation. But as the war had started to settle in for the duration, it was now treated with a little less enthusiasm. In many cases at dead of night at its sound, many people it was reckoned weighed up the option of swapping a warm bed against that of another night in a cold shelter, and they simply rolled over and returned to sleep. Sometimes, for ever.

The siren was reaching its crescendo, and it appeared it was being treated with the same abject respect. It was almost a mixture of something that had become routine, and the excitement drifting out of it, was a chance to stick two fingers up to Mr Hitler.

Sometimes the alarms came to nothing, and even the relief of a bomb-free evening was mixed with grumbles about the time the whole charade had wasted. Many people now lived by the edict, *If there's a bomb up there with my name on it, it will find me.*

For all that, Tommy was now some good many miles from the *comfort* of his home shelter, and he now had to do something about it.

The sound of bombs falling, some way off in the distance, suddenly woke everyone from their sluggishness, and two fingers or not, in no time everyone was running, looking for the nearest shelter.

Tommy looked up sharply and realised he was unexpectedly bereft of ideas. He saw people running left and right, each with a purpose, while he, in his case, was lost.

Another explosion in the distance quickly made up his mind for him. He quickly watched to see the direction that everyone appeared to be running and decided to follow suit. He turned right, and his walk turned into a trot as he tried to keep up with those familiar with the surroundings. He stopped, as the person he had been following veered from the main road, and took off in the direction of private dwellings. He stopped, confused, and was unceremoniously shoved out of the way for his efforts.

'Sorry mate!' the voice called, as the owner disappeared as quickly as he had turned up.

Tommy looked around him, as the sound of the bombing appeared to be closing in. He found himself by an entrance to a small alleyway, and bereft of positive ideas, decided to carry on through it.

The speed at which the sound of the approaching bombs appeared to be coming in quickly hastened his journey. He ran as fast as his legs would carry him, but despite his youth, he was now tired. The day had already taken a lot out of both he, and his body.

Tommy spilled out of the alley into a larger road. The area had clearly been bombed before, and closely resembled a bombsite. Whether it was from the previous night, or some time before, he was not sure, but the knowledge was of little use now, anyway.

He ran across a road, devoid of cars, and stood beside a red telephone box, resting his arm on it, catching his breath. The bombing was coming closer by the second. He had heard bombing before, but not this close, or being this exposed to it. He looked around frantically. To his right were the remains of a large ornate building, the beaten wall held up only by good fortune. What must have been a smaller shell had created a large hole in one of the walls. It was not a bomb shelter, but at the moment Tommy saw it as haven.

He hurriedly ran across the piles of rubble blocking his way, and not before time, crawled in through the hole and disappeared inside into the darkness beyond.

Tommy crouched down with his hands over his head. He was shaking with fear, and slowly, almost unconsciously, he started to edge his way further and further inside the building.

As the sound of the raid seemed to fill the surrounding area, Tommy somehow managed to get to his feet and kick the remains of a dislodged door out of his way. He climbed over broken bricks, rubble and piles of dust and finally he found himself in a strange, large oblong room. The walls on three of the sides of the room had been destroyed and had crumbled in heaps on the floor. He circled, warily until in front of him stood the one remaining wall. It was untouched. It seemed preserved, as all around it had been all but obliterated.

In the unusual darkness, with the light of early evening its only source coming in through the gaps in the broken roof above, it looked somewhat beguiling. Tommy, caught up in the moment, momentarily ignored the sound of the bombs falling, and walked up to the wall, almost spellbound. He looked down at his feet to discover an array of broken frames and torn canvas scattered around him, dusty, and mixed in with the rubble from the collapsed brickwork.

A bomb exploded, sounding far too close for comfort, and Tommy swiftly sheltered himself against the sturdy wall, and held his breath.

He sheltered as the bombing continued, now shaking, curled into a ball, tucked into the apparent safety of the imperishable wall, and waited.

Slowly, ever so slowly the sounds of the bombing seemed to recede, and gradually Tommy allowed himself to move from his almost foetal ball. He breathed, heavily, and now less frantic, started to take in his surroundings.

He looked up at the wall, which still defiantly held its shape, and peered up at what appeared to be an oil painting, in a fine, ornate gold frame, transfixed.

As his foot shifted on an unsteady brick beneath his feet, he broke from the spell and looked around him, taking in the destruction the bomb that had previously hit the building had caused. Paintings of every description and size lay, canvasses torn, frames split. Shattered. Tommy looked up at the wall – his wall - and surveyed what seemed to be the only surviving painting. It was almost a sign. He was oddly - and totally out of character - fascinated by it.

The painting was compact, and no more than a foot by eighteen inches in size, and far from domineering in appearance. It was just that it appeared to be the only one that had survived. Tommy looked more closely at the painting, and took in the content. It was an oil painting depicting St George on a rampant white stallion, slaying a fierce fire-breathing dragon with his lance. It held his attention as if nothing else around him mattered. The artist, whose work it was, was anybody's guess, and the name had been scrawled and hidden away in the corner of the painting, not to detract from the content of the picture itself. It would have been little interest to any fourteen year old boy, least of all, Tommy. But the content - and its survival - was strangely something exceptional. He took the lighter from his pocket, and struck it. He held it up in front of the painting to try to further gain something from its illuminated beauty. There had clearly been many other paintings inside the room, some larger and far more imperious, but this one was intact, and seemed to have him transfixed. He snapped shut the top on the lighter, and standing on tiptoe, no mean feat on the unstable ground beneath him, reached up, and at finger tips, took the painting down off the wall. It was both heavy and awkward for its size. He stretched to get a firmer stance with his feet, but his foot slipped on a loose stone and the painting slipped from his grip. He saw the painting starting to fall, and as if it were glass, dived forward, and though unable to catch it cleanly, managed, somehow, to stop it falling onto anything too sharp.

He quickly scrambled to his feet and rushed over to see the state of his salvage.

The hefty frame surrounding the picture had taken the brunt of the fall, and he picked it up to examine it. Though the frame would probably no longer pass muster, the canvas appeared undamaged.

Satisfied, for the time being, Tommy slowly lowered the heavy article to a safer refuge.

The painting safely dealt with for now, he now set about looking after himself. He cocked his head and having listened carefully to ensure the immediate bombing had passed away, looked at the current state of the… *Gallery*, he thought. Whatever the other paintings had been – all of the canvases damaged beyond repair – he had no interest in their welfare. If studied carefully, minor details could perhaps be picked out, but the torn canvasses ensured the whole content was ruined. Forever.

Tommy, heaving the large frame into his arms once more, made to take it to a slightly safer surrounding when he once more stumbled on the uneven ground, and barely managed to keep his balance. No longer trusting himself with its welfare inside the uncomfortable frame, Tommy reached inside his pocket, and fumbled to see if his penknife had survived the journey thus far. He dug deep until its welcome shape manifested itself in his hand, and taking it out, carefully opened the larger of the two blades. Turning the frame so it firmly, and safely, rested on the ground, he carefully inserted the sharp blade just inside the surround of the frame, and started to cut the canvas free of its restraint. He cut carefully, and as closely to the inside of the frame as he was able, and having extricated the painting from its display, held it out in front of him. He didn't know if he was rescuing, or if he was in fact stealing it. At the moment, however, it really didn't seem to matter.

The worst of the air raid done, the Air Raid Precaution staff sprang into life. What with a mixture of A.R.P. officials, the police and various armed forces personnel patrolling the street, there was now quite a hubbub.

'Is there anyone there?' a loud voice called seemingly yards away from where Tommy was located.

He looked down at the canvas lying by his feet, and spotting the empty frame, quickly judged just how his situation might be viewed if he were found inside the gallery.

'Is there anyone there?' the voice repeated from slightly closer.

Tommy looked down at the canvas, and allowing for being discovered, weighed up the odds of taking the canvas with him, or leaving it where it was, perhaps to return at a later date.

'Hello!' the voice called, still considerably closer.

He looked down at the canvas, and in an instant, set about folding it up, to take with him.

Tommy quickly folded and unfolded the canvas in every way shape and form he could think of without damaging it, but nothing seemed suitable.

As the sound of footsteps, slipping on rubble nearby met his ears, sheer panic forced him to hurriedly roll the canvas up into a tight tube, and stuff it inside the waistband of his shorts, carefully pulling down his shirt to fully conceal it.

It was slightly uncomfortable, but Tommy thought if it had lasted this long, it certainly wouldn't mind roughing it for just a little bit longer.

A face appeared in the doorway through which Tommy had come. The white helmet with A.R.P. written on the front, sat on top of a squat, small, officious looking man, with glasses on. He looked across the hall and shouted. 'Anyone in here?'

Tommy was not sure whether or not he should answer. How would he implicate himself if he did? He said nothing, but shifted his position slightly. In so doing, he landed his foot on yet another pile of precariously stacked bricks. They crashed off to his right in an irritating clatter.

The A.R.P. Warden, in the process of continuing his search for stragglers elsewhere, turned back into the building.

'Is there anyone in here?'

Tommy was in no mood to argue his way out of a tight corner just at the moment, and decided to make a run for it. His pursuer had cut off his preferred exit through the doorway through which he had come, but there was another hole in a wall to his right that appeared to lead out into another street. He quickly, though clumsily clambered over all sorts of obstructions, and made for the hole in the wall.

The A.R.P. Warden, having taken stock of the state of the Gallery, and observing a body, disappearing at pace, quickly assumed the worst, and gave chase.

Tommy, the fox, had made little if no ground on the hound on his trail, but hoped youth and the little strength the day had left him, would save him. A quick glimpse of his pursuer had the fox as lithe and fit, and the hound as having sat around lazily on the farm for a little too long. Tommy had the legs on him. He was sure of it.

Tommy ran, diverting left and right along various roads and alleyways, never running in a straight line for longer than was necessary. He stopped, panting, and looked behind him, sure he had given the warden the slip, but just above his breathing, he could hear the loud footsteps of his shadow.

He took off once more.

Just as he was about to relax, there was the distant sound of aircraft.

'You haven't had the all clear,' an angry voice shouted from nearby. 'Get back inside!'

Tommy looked around, urgently, ready to take flight.

The warning wasn't for him. It was shouted in the direction of a small group of men and woman emerging from the tube station nearby.

The small group, listening to the advancing aircraft, quickly turned tail and scurried back inside.

Tommy looked up urgently. It made perfect sense to follow them inside the station, but he thought if he had been spotted by the A.R.P. warden, he would be walking straight into a dead end.

He took a quick look behind him, fairly convinced he had outrun his pursuer, but no. He could see the A.R.P. warden, some distance off, but still hot in pursuit.

The warden, his age against him, as Tommy had correctly judged, puffed heavily from the pursuit. His chest heaving, he clutched at a nearby lamppost for support. Raising his head he caught sight of Tommy and pointed in his direction, and somehow, started off after him once more.

Tommy felt the canvas working its way up, and caught between its safety, and his, hurriedly stuffed it deeper down inside his shorts, before turning to take off once more.

Where to?

'I've got you,' the hound growled from the distance, and the fox now had little or no

25

choice but to go to ground. He headed for the entrance to the underground.

It was wrongly assumed that any falling object could clearly be heard if one was stood close enough to it, no matter how big or small. Neither Tommy, nor the Warden, however, had heard or seen the bomb that landed between them. The force of the explosion blew the Warden clean off his feet, and his limp body landed a good twenty feet from where he had been stood.

Tommy looked back, hypnotized as the bomb detonated between them. The blast that accompanied it was like a mighty gust of wind hitting him square on. It knocked him backwards and he landed in a crumpled heap just short of the steps leading down into the station.

The staff car pulled into the drive just outside the front door of the house, which opened almost before the car had stopped. Lord Belvoir waited as the driver opened his door, and climbing out, thanked him.

'Will you be needing me again tonight, sir?' the driver asked.

Belvoir shook his head. 'No. You get going,' he told him. 'And for God's sake, be careful.'

'I will. Goodnight, sir,' the driver wished him farewell, saluting. He climbed back into the car, the engine still running, and drove off, out of the drive, and off into the night.

The housekeeper bobbed, and stood back holding the door open as Belvoir mounted the stairs into the house.

'Good evening, Mrs Broom.'

'Evening, sir.' she bobbed once more, taking the proffered coat from him.

'All well?' Belvoir asked over his shoulder, as he walked away into the house.

'Yes, sir. And it's nice to have you home, sir.'

'It's nice to be home,' Belvoir turned and smiled, almost familiarising himself with the house once more.

'Dinner will be served shortly, sir,' Mrs Broom informed him, and turned to go to the kitchen.

'No, Mrs Broom,' he replied stopping the Housekeeper in her tracks, she halfway down the hallway to start to deliver the meal. 'I want to see the children.'

'Now, sir?' she asked, puzzled. 'Why, I'm not sure if the…'

'Now,' he interrupted her flow of conversation. 'If you wouldn't mind. Please.'

The housekeeper nodded, still confused, and walked off in the direction of the stairs.

Lord Belvoir walked into the dining room, and picking up a glass from the sideboard, poured himself a brandy from a large cut-glass decanter stood on a silver tray. He rolled the brandy round the glass before sipping at the contents. He swallowed the liquid, relishing the taste, and stood waiting.

Belvoir was stood by the window, looking out into the drive, and looked up from the glass as some moments later, the door to the dining room quietly opened behind him. A pretty, dark haired lady in her mid-forties walked into the room. She wore a white blouse on top of a plaid knee length skirt, which she gently brushed down to remove any creases. She walked over to the window and kissed her husband on the cheek.

'Hello darling,' Lady Belvoir said quietly. 'Mrs Broom tells me you want to see the children. Is something wrong?'

'I haven't seen the children in over a week, and I want to see them now,' he explained. 'And I didn't realise I needed the permission from the housekeeper to do so.'

'She didn't mean anything, darling. It's just you wouldn't normally see them this late at night. You know she is a stickler over their bedtimes. Couldn't you just poke your head around their doors?'

'I just…' he started, aggressively, but stopped short as the door opened once more.

A pretty, dark haired girl, dressed in a smart cotton nightgown, walked into the room, shutting the door behind her. She was both tall, and lean. She adjusted the dressing gown draped over her shoulders, and smiling, was in the process of a curtsey, as the door burst open, knocking her forward, ruining her presentation completely.

A young boy, dressed in baggy pyjamas, shrouded in a thick woollen dressing gown, burst into the room, and ignoring his sister's welfare, forced his way past her, coming to a halt, standing proudly, almost to attention in front of his father.

'Huh-hum!' his father coughed.

The young boy checked himself, quickly, and frustrated, reached into the jacket pocket of his pyjamas, drew out a circular framed pair of glasses, and hooking them round his ears, re-adjusted his position.

'Better.'

'Father!' he beamed.

His sister, frustrated at his entrance, shuffled up beside her brother, and re-presented herself for his approval.

'Father!'

Lord Belvoir left his wife's side and walked in front of the pair.

'Straighten those shoulders, young man. That's it. And tuck in that tummy.'

'I haven't got a tummy, father.'

'No talking in the ranks. Hmmm! Yes! You'll do.' He looked across to his daughter, who tried hard not to smile. 'And you, young lady! I take it you haven't got a kiss for your father, then?'

The two children broke from the ranks and hugged their father.

The housekeeper appeared in the doorway, and coughed, pointedly, looking at a carriage clock sitting on a small table.

'It looks like I've broken all the house rules,' Belvoir feigned. 'And I suppose Mrs Broom is right. Go on. Go on! Off to bed, the pair of you.'

'But father!' his daughter begged.

'No! Go on, Catherine. You too, Phillip. I don't want to get on the wrong side of Mrs Broom, now, do I? Off you go.'

The two children slunk out of the room, and as the housekeeper shut the door behind them, the pair of them could be heard fighting each other in an attempt to climb the stairs.

Lady Belvoir turned to her husband, shaking her head, laughing quietly, and said, 'They've missed you dreadfully.'

'Let's eat,' Lord Belvoir replied. 'And I'll tell you what a horrid time I've had.'

The dust was slowly starting to settle at the entrance to the underground station, revealing a huge crater outside. Tube stations were not entirely safe from direct bomb blasts, but the mere fact that one was so far below ground was of some comfort.

Tommy shifted uneasily, and for the second time that day, checked his body, physically, limb-by-limb to ensure he wasn't badly injured. Relieved, he sat back against the wall and offered up another silent prayer.

His mind returned to the Air Raid Warden, and he anxiously looked out into the street. The dark of the night seemed to have quickly drawn in, and suddenly, wherever he was, or whatever condition he was in, as long as he was no longer in pursuit, it was of no concern to Tommy.

Assuming the worst, Tommy slowly edged his way down the stairs of the underground station. He could not avoid painful glances over his shoulder to ensure he was not being followed. He did not wish the warden any harm per se, but a little space between the two would certainly be welcome.

Tommy, his own safety confirmed, now checked on the condition of the canvas inside his shorts. He was worried it might have been damaged, or become dislodged in the recent blast. But reaching down, it seemed the canvas was made of sturdy stuff, and more satisfyingly, was in no mood to go anywhere else.

The sound of several bombs exploding somewhere in the distance reminded Tommy that the air raid was far from over, and now concern for his own safety foremost, he hurriedly made his way down the stairs into the depths of the station.

Tommy had not used a tube station as shelter before as he had more often than not been at home, and used the Anderson Shelter in the garden. He was slightly nervous, but having survived the worst of the brunt of the bomb outside the station, surely nothing could be worse down here. He had heard many different stories about the platform welfare as the less homely stories made their way through the classes at school. Stories of huge rats, no toilets, and the like. He slowed his pace, and started to walk, nervously.

Tommy reached the foot of the stairs, and as he turned to enter the platform, the whole milieu of the shelter expanded in front of him. He was amazed. He had imagined that the shelter was for use in emergencies only, yet the sight that greeted him made him sigh. What appeared to be whole families had set up camp, and far from avoiding the current raid, seemed to be happily settled in for the duration of the war. Bunks had been set up against some of the walls, and for others mattresses were lined along the platform, the occupants already covered up with blankets. These people seemed to have been here for hours already.

Tommy, still anxious about discovery - if the A.R.P. warden had miraculously survived - started to carefully pick his way through the throng of people. He stumbled several times in his attempt to find safe ground, somewhere in the middle of the fray, and despite the reported camaraderie the war had brought about, received many an ill word for his efforts. He did not feel comfortable in such large numbers, and as he stumbled through the masses, at one point, untucked his shirt to fully cover the protruding piece of the canvas that had been working its way into view. He certainly did not want it stealing, he thought. There was no honour among thieves, however, and he did not know any of the people here from Adam. Content, however, that it was safe for now, he edged his way further along the platform, and satisfied that his anonymity afforded him some security, began to look for somewhere to settle for a while.

Tommy had heard of tube stations, full of singing and happy people making the best of things. This was not such a tube station. People seemed satisfied keeping themselves to themselves, and singing certainly did not appear to be in their repertoire.

He looked to the platform, and careful not to be too close to the edge or in danger of falling onto the line, he tried to spot a place to settle.

'Are you lost, my love?' a voice called from nearby.

Tommy turned around, assuming for no other reason than it may well have been aimed at him, and caught the eye of an elderly, grey haired lady, covered in a blanket.

Convinced he was safe, for the time being, and now just another face amongst the masses, Tommy started to relax. It appeared from the state of the station around him that he was now here for the night. He was going to have to make the best of it. He looked back at the elderly lady, and nodded.

'Far from home are you?' You come here my love.' Tommy nodded. 'You stay here my pigeon, and let Edna keep you safe.'

Tommy eyed the options available to him, but there seemed nothing better open to him. Besides, fatigue was now starting to take its toll. The effects of the bomb, and any injuries that had not yet surfaced, had taken it out of him, and now unaware of the state of the city above him, he crouched down beside her.

As he settled himself in, he shivered, slightly, the cold registering for the first time that night. Edna noticed his reaction, and shifting across slightly, reached behind her and handed him a blanket, which he took and quickly snuggled into. It wasn't the warmest garment he had ever slipped inside, but it was certainly warmer than not. Looking up at Edna, he winked his thanks. Edna smiled, and putting her arm around his shoulders, gave him a hug.

Tommy could not remember the last time he had had a hug, and despite his independence, the feeling was not abhorrent. He looked up at her, and smiled. She rubbed his hair, and seeing that he had settled down, turned away to talk with a neighbour.

Above ground the shells continued to fall, and it was clear that the shelter and its inhabitants were there for the night.

In one small corner of London, a telephone box stood alone. The building beside it, what had been left of it, had taken a direct hit from a bomb. The glass on the telephone box had shattered, having been hit by flying debris. Just another casualty of a bombing campaign structured to put an end to Allied resistance against a German foe, hell-bent on world domination. Just another victim. But had one cast more than a wary eye through the rubble, the broken frames, torn, and burnt canvas would have offered some small hint as to the previous purpose of the building.

Tommy woke early the next morning, initially unsure of exactly where he was. The owner of a strange cough hacked away in the distance. He slowly sat himself up, and looked about him working out his logistics. Though it was dim, and there were scattered movements further along the platform, it was clearly early. He stretched out, rubbed his eyes, and attempted to sit up. The elderly lady, Edna, who had taken him in, so to speak, was still next to him. She lay, facing him, still fast asleep. Tommy could smell the familiar stench of stale alcohol on her, and his mind suddenly drifted back to his father. The hatred he had held the night before had not diminished in just one night, but he was curious about his welfare . Maybe!

Edna snored loudly, mumbled something in her sleep, and her eyes opened momentarily. It was an almost unconscious reaction, but in so doing, she turned her head away from Tommy, and returned to sleep.

Tommy smiled, and was ready to return to his own troubles, when he noticed Edna's bag, lying on her chest. It was as it had been the night before, except, on closer examination, the clasp holding it together had sprung open, revealing the contents hidden inside.

Tommy curiously peered inside the bag, scrunching up his eyes to try to make clear exactly what was there. He looked about him shiftily to ensure he was not being watched, and listened carefully. He observed how the bag moved to and fro with her breathing. Another more assertive look around to check his bedfellows were asleep, and he gently moved his right hand to the edge of the bag. He timed his work with an almost professional precision. As the old lady breathed in and her chest expanded, the bag offered itself to him, and retracted as she breathed out. He placed his hand in a position such that on the subsequent breath, the bag would encircle his hand rather than he enter it. After two or three such dummy runs, he clasped at some papers. *Ration books*, he thought, and as she exhaled, her chest deflated and the bag pulled away leaving him just a gentle tug, and the papers were his. He sighed at the exertions of his day so far, and quickly stuffed the papers into his pocket, before laying quietly for a while. The old lady was unmoved by the experience, and Tommy noticed her purse, now sitting proud, having been initially obstructed from view by the papers. This was going to be a slightly more difficult task due to the size and shape of the purse, but one more check on the sleeping neighbours, and he set about the new task in hand with vigour.

The method was no different to that of grabbing the papers, but he was suddenly scared. He had a long way to run if she awoke during the operation, and he was already ahead if he chose to leave now. The thought, *A good gambler always quits while he is ahead*, entered his mind, but he knew not from where. He considered it for a short while until the old lady suddenly moaned in her sleep, and making to turn over, would release him from any decision. Tommy watched, concerned, as she unconsciously shrugged her shoulders and started to turn over.

Luck appeared to be on his side this early morning. Gravity, or perhaps the weight of the handbag itself seemed to prevent the turn and keep her exactly where she was. Unconcerned, she merely snuggled into a slightly more comfortable spot.

Tommy decided it was now or never. He watched her breathing again, and now, with far less care, grabbed at the purse, and pulled it clear.

He lay back, guiltily, breathing hard. Readjusting his position, he hastily hid the remaining papers with the ration book, and stuffed the freshly acquired purse further beneath his blanket. He nervously turned to check Edna was still asleep, but needn't have bothered. The noise alone, emitting from her flaccid jaw, clearly indicated that she was.

Tommy rolled over, trying to make space in his pocket to stow his newly acquired acquisitions. He already had the penknife, the lighter, and a crumpled packet of cigarettes in the other. He spent so much time struggling with the pocket, he was sure someone would notice him and turn him in. Finally though, the goods were consumed. He placed the canvas, which he had carefully put to one side for the night, back inside the waistband of his shorts, and sat back letting things settle for a while, now planning his escape.

Lord Belvoir stood back, looking through the windows of his office on the ground floor of the Georgian House, out onto a fresh day. He sipped at a cup of freshly made tea, and thanked God that Goerring had not extended the bombing this far out of London, overnight. He turned back to the desk, and looked down at the headline of the newspaper, staring up at him:

Latest Convoys Safely
Through To North America

He stood quietly, as the door opened in front of him, and his wife walked in.

'We're still safe then?' she asked rhetorically, smiling, sweetly.

'For now,' he replied, shortly.

'Darling…? ' Lady Belvoir offered weakly, but turned, unable to finish.

Belvoir walked across to her, and turned her. 'What is it, silly?'

'I – I'm so scared that this beastly war is going to spread.' Belvoir looked down at her, and laughed. 'And I am worried about Catherine and Phillip,' she added.

Lord Belvoir drew her into him and peered over her shoulder. She had not been alone in the thought. He was about to offer his opinion, when she broke from his hold, and defiantly, carried on.

'I want them evacuated,' she muttered, and looked down at the floor, expecting a rebuke. 'I want them evacuated, so they can't be harmed.'

'Catherine is nearly sixteen…'

'She is sixteen, darling,' she reminded him. 'That's exactly it. You can't even remember small things like birthdays now.'

'Sixteen then,' he concurred. 'She could be working in the land army. She'd be away from London. And Phillip…'

'And Phillip would be siphoned off into the countryside, God alone knows where, to be looked after by God alone knows who. Do you want them split up? Do you?'

'No darling, of course not. It's just I thought…'

Lady Belvoir broke away from him and rushed over to look out of the window, hiding fresh tears.

'Look!'

'No! I won't look,' she blurted, turning to face him. She lowered her face, trying to hide the tears. She looked down at the headlines on the newspaper. 'Canada!' she announced. 'We can send them both off to Canada. My sister can look after them. Lots of convoys are getting through now. Use your connections. Let's at least get something out of this wretched war.'

'We'll see,' he said, bringing the conversation to a halt as the door opened, and

Georgia, the maid, and daughter to the housekeeper, entered the room. She stood, slight in stature, her dark hair tucked away under a white headband.

'Sorry, sir. Will you be taking breakfast?' she asked shyly.

Belvoir looked to his watch, and nodded his head. It would be over an hour before the car dispatched to collect him, arrived.

Georgia exited the room, and made her way down a small flight of stairs into the kitchen, where a cook fussed over breakfast things, and the housekeeper stood waiting.

'His Lordship will be having breakfast,' Georgia said. 'I saw him in the dining room. I didn't think he'd be up this early.'

'Never mind whether his Lordship is up or not,' the housekeeper reprimanded her daughter. 'Take these trays up to Miss Catherine, and Master Phillip.'

Georgia smiled. She did not mind the mild rebuke, and she always looked forward to the opportunity to take the breakfast trays up to the children.

There was a knock on the bedroom door, and Catherine stirred. She sat up quickly as Georgia entered with a breakfast tray. Georgia drew the blackout curtain to allow light into the room. Catherine patted the bed, and told Georgia to sit for a minute. Georgia was used to sharing the gossip with Catherine, and the two year or so gap in their ages was far from apparent.

'What sort of mood is papa in this morning?' she asked.

'I only caught a brief glimpse of him, Miss' Georgia said.

'He was in a funny mood last night,' Catherine confessed.

Georgia looked non-plussed, and shrugged her shoulders.

'Never mind, we shall find out this morning if I catch him before he leaves for the War Office,' she concluded, and with no further ado, set about her breakfast tray.

Georgia shared a few more polite words with Catherine, then left the room, and picked up the tray meant for Phillip. She walked outside his room, and knocked politely.

'Come in,' a bright voice called out.

Georgia entered the room to find the curtain already open, and Phillip sat up in bed with his eyes glued to a book opened in front of him. Seeing Georgia, he carefully put the bookmark in at the point at which he had reached, and laid it beside him. *Huckleberry Finn*.

'Morning, Georgia!' he said excitedly, dipping his head to look at her over the top of his glasses.

Cook was sharing banter with the delivery boy as the door to the kitchen opened, and Mrs Broom entered, tears welling in her eyes. Cook left her worries with the delivery boy immediately, and rushed to her side.

'Whatever is the matter, Mrs Broom?' she asked, urgently.

Mrs Broom sniffed strongly in a very unladylike manner to clear her nostrils, and slowly, composing herself, said, 'They're sending my Georgia off to Canada with Miss Catherine and Master Phillip.'

34

The scene in the dining room was no better. Catherine stood distraught, and Phillip simply stood beside her, speechless. Georgia, trying to put a brave face on things, smiled strangely as she looked to both Catherine and Phillip in turn, for support, then back to Lord Belvoir.

'I won't go,' Catherine said firmly. 'I am sixteen years old, and I do not need to be told what to do.' With that, she folded her arms and looked to her mother expecting her to rally to her cause.

Her mother tucked her chin in, and gave her an, *I'm sorry, I agree with your father* look, in return.

'Mother, No!' Catherine glared in her father's direction.

'I think in time, you will all realise that it is probably all for the best,' their father concluded.

Lady Belvoir straightened herself, guiltily, sorry that her husband was taking the brunt of the blame. She offered a weak smile in his direction. She coughed, pointedly, to gain their attention, and folding her hands behind her back, added, 'Now ready yourselves for your tutor, please.'

The two children turned as one, and marched out of the room, leaving an uncomfortable Georgia, stood facing their parents.

11

Tommy slowly managed to extricate himself from the blanket around his legs. Gently, and paying careful attention not to disturb the person to his right any more than the old lady to his left, he slowly, and carefully stood and stretched his legs. His legs felt as if all the energy had been robbed from them, and he violently scrunched his toes inside his shoes to try to get some feeling back into them. He looked further along the platform towards his target. The exit to the street, and escape.

His limbs, now in slightly better condition, he slowly started to walk away from Edna, at the same time trying to avoid anyone else's in his immediate vicinity. He was forced to smile politely at anyone else who also happened to be awake, and far more aware of his presence than he would have wished. He nodded respectfully, hoping he was not wearing a guilty face, and several times tried to adjust it in the hope that it passed as ordinary. He tentatively stepped over what seemed to be endless numbers of blankets and feet, and convinced that he had got away with it, was only some twenty yards from the exit when a loudspeaker sounded. He froze for an instant, and glanced over his shoulder in the direction of the old lady. She, as many others, had awoken at the sound, and it had taken her as little time as it had Tommy to look back to realise that her personal belongings had been stolen.

'Help! Thief!' she yelled above the sound of the loudspeaker. Her voice carried clearly above the others along the platform, who were themselves just coming round. She stood rather too swiftly for Tommy's liking, and certainly far too quickly for a woman of her age. He maintained the look in her direction just that moment too long. She looked up and meeting him eye to eye, pointed an accusing finger at him. 'That's him. Stop! Thief!' she hollered.

Tommy had waited too long already, and now spun towards the exit. There were only a few bodies between him and the exit, but far less than there had been from the other end.

The old lady had now attracted the attention of anyone who wanted to listen, along with most of those who didn't. They all looked in Tommy's direction, and slowly, heads started to focus in on him.

Tommy was far less careful with his escape now than he had been. He ran fast, across mattresses, blankets, bodies, bags and anything else that threatened to stop him reaching the exit. He did not look back once, and despite uncomfortable noises behind him, he made the stairs to the street in what seemed like seconds.

He paused at the top of the stairs, unsure of whether to turn right or left. A closing shout behind him, forced him to decide just that little bit faster.

He turned left, and ran through the early birds, milling around the underground exit, and in the same manner that he had adopted the previous night, he kept up a criss-cross pattern in his running, once more deciding to avoid keeping a straight line for more than a few hundred yards.

Despite his youth, he could still hear shouts close behind him, and he now had to be careful he wasn't doubling back on himself without his knowledge.

He turned up a sharp corner and made his way into an alleyway where he paused to draw breath. He reached behind him to rub at an irritation, and realised that the canvas was still on his body. He sighed, not having given it a second thought, moments before. He quickly repositioned it for safety. *Now what!*

He edged his way along the alleyway, and poked his head around the corner. He did not recognise anything. He wiped the gathering sweat off his forehead, and feeling the need to do something, decided to walk at a more leisurely pace, so as not to attract any more attention.

In spite of the fact that Tommy was well away from his stomping ground, it should not take have taken him too long to have worked out a route home. Normally, he would have used his common sense, but as he looked around him, he became aware for the first time, the full magnitude of the damage the heavy bombing had done to the city. Fire appliances remained manned as firemen tried to quell fires, still burning, and there were yet more taped off areas keeping the public away while searches were carried out inside ruined buildings. Desperate families stood, waiting for some sight or sound of someone close, still lost inside a number of the collapsed buildings. He was humbled, and for the moment, and standing for a while beside distraught families, momentarily forgot that he was on the run.

An urgent shout nearby, quickly jerked Tommy back into life. He imagined it was another of the people from the underground, who had somehow managed to catch up with him. He quickly took stock, though wondered at this person's resolve and energy to want to catch him that badly. The journey he must have led him on, he was not sure Sherlock Holmes himself could have found him.

He glanced in the direction of the shout, and quickly realised that it was not aimed at him, and as the beat of his heart finally started to return to normal, he decided it just might be best to make for home.

Home!

He waited for a moment. He had left home last night under a personal oath that he would never return there again. He pictured his father, beating the living daylights out of him once again, and reached to his mouth to discover the scab on the side of his lip, a reminder of events so little time ago.

He shook his head, trying to recover some of the hatred he had had the previous night, but was unable to do so. A night's rest, along with this early morning's antics, and yesterday seemed a million miles away. He would head home, God help him, and try to best see out another day.

Lord Belvoir climbed into the back of the staff-car, and looked back towards the front door. Lady Belvoir stood watching his departure with a bewildered look on her face. He noticed the wave that saw him off was not carried out with the usual passion. He would dearly have loved the children to be there to wave him off, and at the same time wished he had not left the burden of the day with his wife. But he had put on his other hat now, and the War Office was his main responsibility for the rest of the day.

'Damn it!' he cussed.

'What was that, sir?' the driver asked, turning his head.

'Nothing,' Belvoir answered, almost apologetically. 'Drive on!'

The children had had their parents' decision forced upon them. They had not liked it of course, and their refusal to come down to see their father off was a confirmation of this.

The car drew away from the front of the house, leaving its troubles with it, but Lord Belvoir was far from relieved.

Lady Belvoir closed the front door, and turned to face Mrs Broom. The housekeeper sighed.

'I will understand if you want to hand in your notice,' Lady Belvoir said quietly, looking down towards the floor, not strong enough to face Mrs Broom directly.

'I won't be going anywhere, ma'am,' she answered quietly, in her broad Nottingham accent. 'My place is here with you.'

'But I thought with Georgia…'

'Georgia is in as much danger here as your children, and I should be grateful to have the opportunity to get her away. And to remain with Miss Catherine and Master Phillip, well – she could be in worse company.'

Lady Belvoir regained some of her composure, and straightened herself up. 'We'll talk later,' and a quick glance at Mrs Broom, she returned to affairs in the dining room.

Tommy walked with a little more assuredness about him. He had found his locale, and appeared to have seen off any more of the trouble from this morning. He walked quickly through the streets and avenues, and despite the events of the previous evening, turned towards his street with a resolution to start afresh.

His heart sank as he looked up towards his road. Several uniformed personnel surrounded a roadblock which cordoned off the entrance to the road, and a large placard stood propped up with, **Bomb Damage, No Entry**, written on it, blocking his way.

He turned a nasty shade of grey, and rushed to the top of the road. He was just about to charge through the barrier, when a large hand caught his shoulder and spun him around.

'You can't go down there, son. It's not safe,' a strange, but calming voice said.

He jerked his body violently, trying to release the grip on him. He looked up petulantly into the eyes of a police officer who had grabbed hold of him, firmly, but with reason.

'But I live down there, and I...' Tommy blurted.

'In that case, you had better stay with me and we will find out exactly what has happened. And anyway, young man? Shouldn't you be at school? Just wait there a minute.'

Tommy was unable to see far enough down the road to discover the condition of his house, so he waited until the Policeman's attention was elsewhere, and what with the thought of school on top of his other worries, he had suddenly had enough, and ripped himself sharply from the authoritarian grip.

He could not fail to notice the entrance to the road in front of him completely blocked, so he turned and took off in the direction of the adjoining road, the yells from the Policeman echoing in his ears.

His attempt at approaching his house from the far end of the road was also doomed. It too was blocked. He stood, anxious now about the fate of his father. His house... His... Whatever it was, he wasn't going to get there this way. The only option open to him was to cut back along the road that ran parallel to his own, where he could then make his way across the gardens, and could...

Catherine was sat on her bed, sulking. She was dressed for the day. Her head swayed to and fro, her face drawn, and she was clearly livid. There was a knock on the bedroom door, and she shouted, 'What?' angrily, and then, despite herself, called in a slightly more ladylike manner, 'Come in.'

The door opened slowly, and a figure, more forlorn and lost than angry, walked into the room, and slumped itself onto her bed.

'What are we going to do?' Phillip asked.

Catherine looked across at him, and slowly put a sisterly arm around his shoulder, and drew him alongside her. He snuggled into her embrace. She looked down at his lost demeanour, and shook her head. 'I don't know.'

Shortly, there was another knock at the bedroom door.

'Go away, mother,' Catherine shouted. 'We don't want to talk to anyone, thank you.'

It was always her mother's way to try to repair the damage that father had done, and somehow try to put a good face on things. But on this occasion, Catherine was having none of it. Phillip looked up, amazed at his sister, if not, just a little proud of her.

The door remained shut, but soon there was another, slightly more urgent knock.

'Go away,' Phillip echoed, looking up to his sister for approval. Catherine looked across at him, angrily.

The door opened, and they both stiffened and looked over, worried about the bravado they had shown just a few moments before.

They eased slightly as Georgia, the maid, walked in, her head held down.

'Georgia!' Catherine said, noting her demise.

Georgia looked up, shyly, her eyes red, and face streaked from tears that had not yet dried.

'Oh Georgia!' Catherine released her brother and ran to her and threw her arms around her.

Georgia once more opened up, uncontrollably.

'I'm so sorry' Georgia wept, excusing her tears. 'I've tried to be brave. I'm so sorry.'

Tommy ran back along Somerset Road. The gardens to the rear of these houses lay flush against those of his road. He only knew a few of the residents in his own road, and did not know any of the owners of those houses that ran along the back of his. As yet, he did not know if any of those houses had suffered structural damage, but the road seemed to be open at least. And from what he could see, the fronts of the houses did not seem to have suffered any damage at all.

He ran down as fast as he could to the house that that he imagined stood in front of his own. Irrespective of anyone being home, he tore up the path beside the house, and despite a crude lock to keep the garden gate shut, it did not take a lock-pick to undo it.

Tommy charged on.

At this time of day, and as had been pointed out by the policeman, most of the children would be at school. And what with all the previous night's bomb damage and casualties in the surrounding area, Tommy thought chances of encountering anyone questioning his motives were likely to be remote.

He charged through the garden in front of him, regardless, and whether they were in or not, he did not cast a backwards glance to find out.

He reached the adjoining garden wall and leapt at it. Managing to somehow get both hands on top, and despite it being a good two feet taller than himself, he somehow managed to drag himself up.

A final heave and he managed to drag his chest over the summit of the wall, and onward until he could finally swing his backside around, and sit, his feet dangling over the reverse side.

He rested for a second, and then looked around to get his bearings. He had guessed well, but was in fact two gardens down from his own house, and…

Tommy went cold. He looked past the damage done to his neighbour's houses, and then further up towards the rear of his own. The energy suddenly drained from his body, and for the time being, all he could do was sit and stare.

The roof belonging to his house had gone completely, exposing what little was left of the bedrooms. And from the little he could see from this angle, all the remaining windows had been blown out as well.

He sat for, he didn't know how long, just staring in disbelief. Time had stood still, and only as another piece of masonry fell from the roof did he move. He somehow managed to get to his feet, and balancing as best he could, walked carefully along the six-inch width of the garden walls until he stood shakily, behind the small garden to his own house.

The toilet miraculously stood as it always had. Any damage appeared to have fallen either towards the road at the front, or inwardly. The falling roof had crashed through the ceiling inside the house, and Tommy, having managed to jump down off the wall found his access to the back door blocked by debris. There was a slight access through one of the windows, but barely enough for a body to squeeze through. He walked, still in a state of shock to the side of the house, and somehow managed to climb over mounds of rubble, along the side of what was left of the house, and up towards the front garden.

The wooden gate to the alleyway at the side of the house lay on its side, piled high on loose bricks and dirt. Through the gap into the street, he could see various people stood, looking on in anguish at the damage. A man with a red cross stencilled on his helmet walked past the front of the house accompanied by other concerned onlookers. Tommy edged his way to the front until he stood, and looked out onto the street.

'Oi! What do you think you're doing?' an angry voice called out. Tommy looked up in bewilderment. 'Get out of it, you idiot. Are you trying to get killed?'

'Don't you yell at me,' he shouted back, and charged towards the reprimanding voice. 'I bloody live here.'

He looked over the shoulders of the man and saw a few other youngsters standing by, watching. He angrily waved his fist at them.

'You touch one thing inside and I'll bloody kill you.'

A policeman ran along the road in the direction of the house, pushing various bystanders out of the way.

Tommy watched his approach, but any gusto he had had, had disappeared on seeing the house. He stood deflated, and waited.

As the Policeman approached, someone caught hold of his arm, and whispered something in his ear. The Policeman looked up from the conversation, firstly to the pavement outside the front of the house, and then to Tommy.

Tommy noticed the direction of his initial glance, and inquisitively looked off in that direction.

A stretcher sat on the floor, with a body, crouched over the top of it. The body, a nurse, was drawing the blanket over the top of the stretcher, covering both the head and the majority of the body, hiding its identity. She hadn't seen Tommy, and looked across at her colleague, and resignedly shook her head. Tommy watched, bemused, and slowly worked his way down the stretcher to the far end from which poked two feet. It was not the would be horror of a dead body that smacked at Tommy, as death was something people were sadly coming to terms with day by day. It was the huge polished black work boots.

Tommy was suddenly giddy and light-headed, and he collapsed to the floor, barely avoiding passing out. He sat on his haunches, and looking up forlorn, stared into the eyes of the nurse, who had now been made aware of exactly who Tommy was, and was now looking back at him. She bit on her bottom lip, and put her hand to her mouth.

A tear came to Tommy's eye as he sat where he was, and he wiped it away, creating a clean patch on what was now a grubby face. One tear, then another ran down his cheek, and he sobbed, furiously, trying to catch his breath.

As the Policeman walked towards the front of the house, Tommy had suddenly had enough. Shaking his head, so not wanting it to be true, he turned and rushed off towards the back of the house, through the garden, and by the time the Policeman had got to the same point, he had disappeared over the wall, and away.

Catherine, Phillip and Georgia were sat on the bed, and Georgia's tears had finally dried. They sat in shared silence, staring into space.

'Maybe we could…' Phillip began, but then stopped short as the others looked at him. 'No, maybe not.'

Catherine flopped forward to lie face down along the length of the bed, tucked her hands under her chin and sighed. She was also out of ideas. Despite the three of them having thrown fruitless ideas to and fro for some time, there certainly seemed no feasible way out of their predicament.

'It's no use,' she said. 'Short of running away, there is no way we can get out of it.' She thought on this idea for a moment, but the thought of roughing it on the streets was not something she fancied, even if just to spite her mother and father into submission.

'I can't run away,' Georgia said.

'No. None of us can,' Phillip confirmed.

They stared hopelessly into each other's eyes, looking for further inspiration, but none came.

'I'd better get downstairs,' Georgia said, realising she had been away from her post for far too long. 'They'll be wondering where I've been.'

'Why?' Catherine enquired lazily. 'What is the worst that they can do to you? Send you away?'

The house had been empty for weeks, and was no more than a bombsite. It had been evacuated weeks ago, and nowadays, nobody cast it more than a fleeting glance as they passed by. It was no longer of any use to anyone. The roof had been blown away taking the ceiling beneath with it, and what had been the front room was now open to the elements. A few sheets of wood blockaded the front door, and some bedraggled rags hung from the glassless windows. Inside the front room, what was left of the furniture was stacked in a pile, and scattered cushions lay amongst the waste.

It was from the centre of this pile of furniture that Tommy suddenly appeared, crawling up through a small, concealed hole, coming out from its bulk. He looked strange, dressed in a tweed coat that he had found. Although it was slightly too long for him, the unusual quality of the cloth at least ensured that it would keep him warm.

He quickly checked to see that he was still alone, and then crawled clear of his castle. He stretched, and yawned. His clothes were dirty, and it was clear from his appearance that he hadn't washed for some time. His greasy hair lay matted on top of his head.

He casually checked in his pocket to see that he still had money, which for some reason he had kept in the purse in which it had been stolen, and fingered what was left of the vouchers he had also purloined.

Tommy carefully extricated himself from the ruined house, and quickly checked the streets. He had to ensure that his sudden appearance from the ruin would not be spotted, as looting was both a criminal offence, and he had nowhere else in which to hide. Though he was currently just in residence inside what remained of the house, he was not really in a strong enough position in which to defend his innocence against any legal accusations.

Having exited the house, apparently unseen, he made every effort to blend in with the rest of London, and remain anonymous. The thought of being an orphan and taken into care, on top of everything else, was more than he could bear. He sometimes tried so hard that it was difficult to remember that just being himself would cover the job admirably. Despite that, he continued to walk everywhere under a cloud of suspicion.

The shop on the corner of the street looked as if it had been there for generations, and the shopkeeper had appealed to Tommy the second he saw the man. He had a glint in his eye, and so far the purchase of goods with the fraudulent ration book had not raised any questions. Ration books were usually registered with a shop local to the owner, but *business is business*, Tommy had been told on first handing over the vouchers.

Tommy waited outside the shop for a while and waited for the two or three customers already inside to complete their business before attempting entry. Despite the clandestine agreement with the shopkeeper, he was still wary of everything inside the shop. He knew that it would only take the shopkeeper to have a particularly bad day to turn on him, or try to trick him out of more than he was due.

He finally entered the shop. The doorbell jingled to announce his arrival, and he checked carefully that it was to be just him and the shopkeeper. He extracted the ration book from his pocket, and leafed through the remaining vouchers. Tommy realised that he was entitled to rations of his own, but his father had always dealt with those. Any attempt to return to find them would create far more trouble than he was already in. He realised if he was caught now, he would be handed straight over to the police, and would end up... It didn't bear thinking about. The ration book would obviously run out in due course, but that was a problem for later, and not now. Just for the moment, in a strange way, he felt secure. He was his own person, and for the moment did not have to answer to anyone.

The shopkeeper walked across, and winked at Tommy.

'All right, my son?' he asked. 'What can we do for you today?'

Tommy handed across the ration book, and watched as he leafed through the remaining vouchers. He took some cigarettes from behind the counter and left them on the counter beside the remaining vouchers as he walked away to see to the other items. Tommy walked across, and checking once more that they were still alone in the shop, slipped the cigarettes into his pocket. Despite their nefarious acquaintance, he did not think for one moment that the shopkeeper was in any way as friendly as he appeared. He did not think for one second that he was not being short-changed, but, on the run, he had to deal with anyone he could, and currently, this man seemed to be as good as anyone else.

Tommy started to look at the various items on the shelves with view to purchase as suddenly the doorbell rang. Someone else was coming into the shop.

Tommy immediately pocketed the book from the counter, and stood furtively, hands in pockets. He took a quick look in the direction of the door, and swiftly edged his way back behind a stack of boxes, which stood one on top of the other in the centre of the shop.

Finally, he cautiously poked his head around the corner of the boxes, and immediately returned to his hiding place. A policeman had come into the shop, and was making his way up the aisle towards the counter. Tommy felt flushed, and quickly reddened, guiltily.

The policeman stopped at one of the stands, picking up certain goods, carefully turning them over in his hands for inspection.

Tommy slowly edged his way around the various stacks of shelves, and assuming that his days in this shop were numbered, started filling the pockets of his recently acquired coat with anything he could lay his hands on - in the event that he needed to make a run for it.

Despite a lack of urgency on the policeman's behalf, Tommy suddenly had the impression that the man had not called in to the shop on the off chance, and had somehow been summoned by the creepy shopkeeper. As he made his way down the adjacent aisle in the direction of the door, he grabbed at still more and more items until his pockets could finally carry no more. If the Policeman was here to arrest him, or if he was able to get away safely, it was clear he would not be able to utilise the shopkeeper's wares again. He did not feel guilty in the slightest, and on balance, he was sure that he and shopkeeper were now just about on an even footing.

He reached the door in one piece, but realised in horror the greatest obstacle that he would have to overcome in his bid to escape safely, was just above it. Any attempt to exit through the door would cause the bell to ring, and he would be stood there, alone, and out in the open. He was either going to have to wait out the policeman's visit, and hope that he was merely on a social visit, or risk everything, and make a run for it.

He looked back in the direction of the policeman, and strained his ears, trying to listen to the conversation between he and the shopkeeper.

Unable to clearly gather any of the conversation, Tommy crouched down. He was caught between a rock and a hard place. But just as he thought his game was up, the shop door opened, and a grey haired old man walked slowly into the shop. Tommy abandoned any interest in the conversation he had been listening to, and as the old man had barely entered the shop, slipped majestically behind him, and out and away.

Tommy, having reached the safety of the street, walked off briskly without running or looking back, the consummate crook. His job was done.

It had been decided, and the papers had been all but signed, sealed and delivered. There was no turning back.   The date for their departure had been arranged.   The children's hopes of a reprieve had dissolved, and they were to depart on *The Maid of Orleans* in just two days time. All thoughts of escaping their demise had now vanished.

Catherine had wanted to pack several suitcases along with a trunk containing all the things she thought a girl needed to travel with.   What she had been provided with however, scarcely met with her expectations.   The three evacuees had been issued with one piece of luggage each and it was far from the quality Catherine had been expecting. The luggage was no more than a deep sack, made from a tough durable hemp-like material, and was purely for the purpose of transport of goods, and most certainly not fashion. Catherine had held hers at arm's length when she had first seen it, and declared it to be, *Dirty*.

Phillip had finally had his bag packed by his mother, after his own attempts at doing so were discovered, and with one large Teddy Bear taking up most of the room in the haversack, a repack was soon ordered.

Catherine, once resigned to going, had wanted to take her entire wardrobe with her, but her mother had pointed out that there would be others wanting to board the ship as well, and that she should leave some of her possessions behind for their eventual return. Catherine was quick to point out that if they were queuing up for places aboard the ship, she would happily swap her place with one of the others.   They could take the place of both she, and her luggage.

Her mother smiled, and set about unpacking Catherine's initial effort.

They had also all sadly been informed that they were not to be travelling first class as they might have assumed under better conditions, and worse still, would have to muck in with everybody else. The ship was purely a means to an end, and they would have been very lucky to find themselves boarding a cruise liner. Catherine had joked that it was the *Titanic*, but was quickly hushed, as they really did not want any more bad luck thrown their way.

Georgia's *sack*, on the other hand, was packed with virtually everything she had. It was decided that as the maid to the others, after their departure from the house, she would be excused duty until they all arrived, and were met in Canada. Catherine, despite her fondness for Georgia had complained vociferously at first, but eventually, and to save any more grief to her mother, had given in without too much more of a fight. They were going, they were going to have to rough it, and clearly, that was that.

Tommy was stood shiftily beside the grocers. After his unexpected exit from his usual place of purveyance, he had need of further supplies. Worse still, he now had the need to find pastures new. And, equally roguish traders with which to do business. Though still happily sheltered in the same bombed out location, he had had to broaden his areas of commerce, as he did not want to become too well known locally. Or more importantly, for his past to be examined too thoroughly by anyone that did get to know him.

He entered the chosen shop, climbing the three steps to do so, and as before, a bell rang as the door opened. *Dear God*, he thought. *Is there no trust in the country any more?* He laughed to himself.

There was a customer being served as he walked in, and he waved politely as the lady shopkeeper glanced across in his direction. She looked up, a little more concerned, and not a little wary as he entered, but was soon drawn back to a conversation she was having with the customer stood in front of her.

Tommy had now become a dab hand at filching goods, and as he watched, her attention drawn away once more by her customer, he immediately grabbed at whatever came to hand, and hastily put it inside his coat into one of the available pouches and pockets that had now been better packed. He kept an astute look to ensure he had not been spotted, and by the time he had reached the counter, there was little need for more. But he had to buy something, if only to remove any suspicion.

The previous customer dealt with and departed, the lady shopkeeper, middle-aged, dressed in an apron that had seen better days, brushed her hands and finally addressed Tommy. Tommy took out the purse from his pocket, and withdrew what little money he had left. The shopkeeper eyed the purse suspiciously.

'It's my mum's,' he said quickly, and smiled sweetly, better adding to the effect. It had worked well on previous occasions. He hoped she too was not averse to a little under the counter trade, but would need to butter her up before he finally revealed his intentions.

'Your mum's? Is it now!' she said doubtfully, in a manner leaving Tommy feeling most uncomfortable.

'Yes! Miss!' He tried to soften the incident quickly, hoping that the 'Miss' would impress the older lady. 'She'd like some cigarettes, and…' Tommy reached instantly for the ration book, and produced it to add some substance to his story. He went through a short list, insisting that he had to get it home quickly, as his mother was looking after his three brothers, and she herself was poorly. The shopkeeper raised her eyebrows, and looked closely at the ration book in his hands.

'All right!' she said, finally, taking the ration book from him. 'Give me a minute. I'll get your stuff together.'

She turned and walked away, and quickly disappeared out of sight.

Tommy stood uneasily, shifting from foot to foot. She now had the ration book, and she was in command. He wished he had stuck with his original supplier, and in stealing from him, not bitten the hand that fed him.

She had now been gone far too long for Tommy's liking, and all at once he began to feel more than uncomfortable at risk he was taking. Looking around the shop, he noticed that he was still alone. He cautiously edged his way up to, and behind the counter. He grabbed at a packet of cigarettes as he sidled his way towards the door through which she had gone. He nestled his head up against the door hoping he could catch sight of exactly where she had disappeared, and hoped it was to a storeroom of some sort, but could not see her. He listened carefully, trying to judge what she was up to. He could hear her talking, and hoped it was to her husband or another such relative, but as he listened more attentively, he heard her voice clearly. 'Yes, Officer,' he heard. 'It wouldn't do any harm to check it out, anyway.'

Tommy turned on a sixpence. He left the shop at a hundred miles an hour. He stumbled as he descended the steps, and fell to the floor. Several of the items he had pocketed fell from his pocket, and he wasted valuable seconds as he grabbed at them, stuffing them once more into any available pocket.

'And what's appears to be going here then, sunshine?' a voice called from slightly farther down the street.

He looked up, guiltily. Luck was not on his side. It was a policeman, who happened to be patrolling, and had seen his speedy exit from the shop. And his frenzied efforts to gather his goods together.

'There's... There's a burglar in the shop,' he shouted up the street, pointing up the steps he had just descended, 'and he...'

The policeman ignored the rest of Tommy's words completely, running past him, and leaping the steps to the shop in one. He charged inside the shop, and as the door closed behind him, Tommy jumped up, and without a second thought, jumped onto a nearby bus as it passed along the road.

Tommy moved quickly along the vehicle, losing himself among the other passengers, oblivious to his flight. He looked back to the shop to see the policeman exit it, and watched as he looked quickly up and down the street for him. He ducked, peculiarly below the window, and crawling along the bus, quickly found a seat, and settled back. He checked that he had enough money for a bus fare, its destination not one of immediate concern, and content that he had given the law the slip for now, settled back to enjoy the ride.

The interior of the train station was bustling with a huge variety of people, both professional and otherwise, going about their business. Cars, lorries, buses, and every other form of transport ferried goods in and out of the station forecourt, loading and depositing their goods, without a second glance or care about anyone else there. Vast numbers of drivers, passengers and private individuals added to the melee as they scurried around on foot, dodging through the gaps the vehicles had not yet occupied.

In one corner of the station, a large group of children were congregated. They stood, dressed in an assortment of clothing, from a distance, the only noticeable way to clearly distinguish one from the other. As they shuffled around, barely under control, fawn tags, hanging from the lapels of the coats they were wearing, flapped around loosely in the air.

In the midst of the children, several adults did their best to bully them into discernable lines, but it was not without much effort and a few raised voices from the elders there. Once settled, the burly middle-aged women walked up and down the lines, checking the names on the tags on their coats against those on clip-boards in front of them.

'That's enough of that, thank you,' one of the minders shouted across at one of the children, who was finding the experience far too dull.

'Andrew Stephens?' another voice called, trying to locate another victim.

One of the younger chaperones, clearly her first major assignment, fought with her list and the counting of the numbers in the lines, as the metamorphosis from line to group and back to line became far too much for her.

'Will you please all stand still,' another berated voice called.

Catherine, Phillip and Georgia had said a tearful farewell to their mother at the entrance to the station, and been handed over to the care of the chaperones to the children. Phillip had done his best not to cry, but at best, had only managed to restrict the number of tears he had shed. Catherine was more resentful than tearful, although as her mother had turned to go, she had relented, and rushed to her for a fonder farewell.

Georgia had said her goodbyes to her mother earlier, and her sadness had been left at Belvoir Manor, so to speak. She had had a polite hug from Lady Belvoir, and she had been told, *Take care of yourself*, and *Make sure Catherine behaves*. She had smiled, but was now a little more tearful. But true to her word, and in respect to the others, with a gentle rub at her eyes, she managed to suffer the departure of Lady Belvoir quite well.

Catherine nearly exploded as one of the chaperones took her by the shoulder and gently pulled her away from Phillip and Georgia towards a group of children more her own age. She angrily jerked out of her grip, and grabbing at them both, informed the lady in question that they were staying as a group whether she liked it or not. The lady in question told her that she would do as she was told, as she would not be putting up with any petulant children, *Thank you very much!*

Catherine was incensed. She grabbed Phillip and Georgia and marched away from the chaperone, but found her way blocked as still more children arrived to join the group, and blocked their escape route.

Despite several more protestations, the three were finally herded into the larger group, where Catherine stood, still busily complaining, looking for allies. The chaperone dealing with her particular case, checked something else on her list and ignoring her current outburst, diverted her attention elsewhere. Georgia grabbed Phillip,

51

who had become worried at Catherine's antics, and gave him a hug, and told him not to worry, assuring him that everything was sure to work itself out, in time.

20

Tommy had been on the bus for some time, content in putting good space between he and his most recent crimes. Though he had paid for only a short journey, he had managed to stay on until now, and intended to stay there until he was forced off. As he relaxed, convinced he had seen off his latest foe, he started to think about what to do next. He had jumped on the bus with no initial care or knowledge as to its eventual terminus, and now, looking out of the window, as the scenery became less and less familiar, he started to worry about his next move. He fingered what was left of the money in front of him, counting and re-counting it. He felt uncomfortable as a lady sat across the aisle of the bus from him, looked down at the purse, and he realised the excuse of it being his mum's would probably not sound quite so believable now. He carefully slid it into a pocket, and smiled back, hoping this might satisfy her curiosity. The lady frowned, and looked away.

The bus had stopped several times already, and Tommy had looked up each time to see who got on and off. He had started to feel a little more relaxed the further the bus had travelled, but wasn't yet ready to abandon ship. He decided it would be better to sit tight for the time being, and see what turned up.

The bus pulled up sharply, and a daydreaming Tommy looked out at the station. He weighed his options up in a flash. A train was as good an option as walking the streets, and considering his situation, he decided he really had nothing left in London to keep him there, and....

He jumped up, and fighting his way through the crowded corridor on the bus, just managed to jump off as the bus was beginning to pull away from the kerb. He caught the tail end of a rebuke from someone he had pushed past in his attempt to do so, but ignored it and stood back as the bus drew away, and looked around at his new surroundings. He looked up and down, trying to see across and through busy traffic between him and the station. Despite living on the outskirts of London, the whole scene in front of him was busy and exciting. He felt safe for the moment, and for what seemed the first time in a long while, he didn't feel the need to have to look over his shoulder. He checked inside his coat to see what he had with him. To all intense and purposes, all he had in the world was in his coat pockets. He had a smattering of money, a penknife, a goodly supply of cigarettes, and a lighter. Everything else he had in his coat had been taken randomly from the shop. A smattering of food and several items he would never need. He pulled out a flannel, and laughed at the irony of it. He couldn't remember the last time he had had a wash, and looking down at his state, realised that had been some long time ago.

He walked across the road and onto the station concourse, and after a few moments of familiarising himself with his surroundings, walked inside the station itself.

He looked around him at the various platforms. Nothing meant anything to him. His father had never taken him on a train journey of any kind, and everything was new. He was jostled by a passer-by as he stood beneath a large clock, and despite the excitement of the situation, he suddenly realised he did not have a clue what to do next, or where he should go.

He found himself clutching at the flannel in his pocket, and looking up saw a sign for 'Toilets.' He imagined he was probably not the dirtiest person in the station – there must be stokers in there somewhere - but he hoped a quick wash and brush up would maybe help his case just that little bit more.

The main toilets did not offer any better hope for his future, but having wet the flannel thoroughly, and removed his coat, and despite the odd looks he received from a handful of the others there, he gave himself a fairly thorough going over. He had even scrunched it through his hair, which with the use of the dirty mirror - which had seen more time at the station than most of the trains - he managed to cajole into some reasonable shape.

He stood back and looked at himself. He winked at his reflection, satisfied. He would not pass muster in any of the forces, but it would certainly do for now.

Once he had exited the toilets, and realising that he was settled on a train journey of some sort, he took the purse out of his pocket, and sick of the looks he had attracted so far, finally emptied the contents out into his hand. He looked around, and seeing a large bin nearby, walked over and dropped the now empty container into its depths. He checked on the money he had left in his hand, and quickly realised that, though it had been sufficient for a bus ride, he was certain it would not take him too far on a train, if indeed during the current climate, one could simply walk up and buy a ticket to anywhere.

He was counting the money once more, to ensure his maths was not wrong, as his arm was nudged, and some of the coins fell to the ground. He muttered something unsavoury, and turned to see the perpetrator. It was a young boy, no different to himself. Tommy aggressively squared up to him, but the boy simply apologised politely, and that seemed to be that. Tommy, the matter dealt with, suddenly noticed that there were a multitude of children here. *Why?*

Tommy listened to the hubbub surrounding the children, trying to figure out their purpose here, but the noise seemed excessive, and he was struggling to hear what was going on, or even to be able to concentrate on one conversation at a time.

'Now get in line, my group.'

'Group 'A', are you all together?'

'Stop bunching, and get together, girls.'

'Miss Price! If you cannot get control of your group, I shall be forced to have you replaced. Now, please!'

Tommy looked left and right, trying to catch the owner of each of the voices, and finally, through the exasperation on her face, found the character, Miss Price. She wore the same light tan, tailored uniform the other adults appeared to be wearing. In spite of her age – a hundred years younger, Tommy thought – she appeared to be dressed identically to the other women there. That was with the exception of her hat. All of the chaperones seemed to be sporting a green velvet hat with a dark green ribbon wrapped around the brim. Miss Price sported a red ribbon. She was currently in all sorts of trouble, and Tommy watched as one of her group, a boy, similar in height to himself, and of pretty much the same stature, peeled off, and made his way across the station concourse. He turned to signal his intentions, but unable to attract her attention, as she wildly grabbed at tags, ensuring all the names of the children really were supposed to be in her group, made his way off towards the toilets. In the state Miss Price appeared to be in, Tommy was sure she had neither seen, nor heard him go. Beneath a knee length coat, he was dressed in a smart uniform, with a red blazer, long grey trousers, and smart black shoes, carrying a small haversack, crammed to bursting, and seemed to be the only one in this particular uniform. Many of the others were in everyday clothes, and although not the only one in a uniform, he did stand out a little.

However! No one knows him, Tommy thought.

Miss Price continued to shout out names, and there continued to be little or no response to her calls. But in the midst of her group, having heard their names called, Catherine, Phillip and Georgia stood in a small group of their own.

The door to the toilet was shut fast, but Tommy had been hot on the boy's heels the second he had watched his departure. And, he had noted the cubicle into which he had gone. He stood outside the door, and checked around to ensure that no one was paying him any undue attention. Satisfied, he clenched his fist and hammered on the outside of the cubicle door. There was no answer. He hammered once more.

'Hello,' a polite, slightly weak voice, answered.

'You've got to put this on,' Tommy, yelled. 'I was given it to bring to you.'

'What?' the voice answered, and opened the door slightly.

Tommy forced his way into the cubicle, and shut the door fast, locking it behind him. They were both locked in.

Miss Price had finally managed to get some semblance of order to proceedings, but whichever way she looked at it, she still appeared to be one person short. The other children had been marched off along a platform, and stood, pending orders to climb aboard the waiting train. Miss Price called out once more. 'Edward Burrows! Edward Burrows!'

The smart red blazer hung nicely, and its bright colour immediately caught the eye. The trousers looked a little long, but it was not unusual for clothing not to fit properly during these turbulent times.

'Edward Burrows! This is your last chance before…'

'Sorry! Here, miss!' Tommy, answered, raising his arm, the bright red sleeve of the blazer catching her eye. She grabbed at the tag on the coat to ensure the names matched up, and pushed him into line.

Tommy quickly put his hand down the back of the trousers, and checked the rolled-up canvas was where it should be, and looking back to ensure the chaperone did not have her eyes glued to him, readily joined onto the back of the line by the platform.

Miss Price, exasperated, ticked off the last name on her list, and ushered the children towards the waiting train. She smiled shyly and signalled to the other sterner looking chaperones that she was finally ready. They shook their heads in frustration, and the chief chaperone sounded a whistle to get the masses attention.

Inside the cubicle of the stations Gent's toilet, a bemused child sat, hands tied behind him. He was attached to the cistern, with a long school sock dragged through his mouth, and tied fast behind his head. He struggled, and tried hard to give voice, but amongst the comings and goings of the station, his objections were inaudible, and although not watertight, the constrictions were set to hold for a good while yet.

Tommy hung back, quietly. He tried not to catch anyone's eye, in the event that this 'Edward Borrows' had become 'pally' with anyone who might be able to end Tommy's scam at this early stage. He slunk back, pulled up the collar to the blazer, and tucked his head deep into his shoulders.

The lines of children started to move forward amongst more shouting from the various bodies in charge.

Tommy could not have wished for anything better than this had it been handed to him on a silver platter. A blind man might have seen that Miss Price was totally out of place, he thought. It wasn't just her age. The more flustered she became, the better his chances were of getting away with this. She appeared to be quite pretty, and looked rather appealing in, what was, he assumed, to be an army uniform of some sort. A beige great coat and the velvet hat appeared to have covered most of her, although he thought the outfit, like his, appeared a little large for her sleight frame. He looked along the lines to the other chaperones. In comparison, he wondered if perhaps they had not been taken off the front lines for scaring their own troops. They all looked as if they had swallowed something unpleasant.

Edward Borrows, Edward Burrows, Edward Burrows, Tommy repeated the name inside his head. It would save him looking down at the tag hung on his shoulder every time he needed a reminder. This - at least for the time being - was to be his alter ego.

He looked behind him to ensure that the real Mr Burrows was still held captive. At least for a little while longer. Someone would find him for sure, but he just had to hope his rough bindings would hold him tight until he was loaded aboard, and the train was safely under way.

21

Finally, it was time for Miss Price's group to climb aboard and into the carriage. She frantically ticked at the list as she looked through her folder, trying hard to put faces to names.

'Everything alright here, Miss Price?' one of the stern looking chaperones asked, appearing at her shoulder.

'Er – Yes - Thank you, Miss Stevens,' she informed her superior, none too convincingly. Her superior raised her eyebrows, far from convinced. Miss Price straightened herself up to try to substantiate the point, but in doing so, dropped several of the papers from the folder onto the floor.

'I'll leave you to it, then, shall I?'

Miss Price, nodded, embarrassed at her latest faux-pas, as she stooped to pick up the papers.

'Let's not leave it too long, though, eh? The ship isn't going to wait for you, and it would be a shame to let all these children down, don't you think?' She walked away, leaving Miss Price to try to get everything back in order.

Tommy noticed her demise, and not wanting her to spot the fly in the ointment, quickly made to get aboard before she was at full speed again. He heaved at Edward Burrows heavy bag, and barging two other children out of his way making his way along the platform, reached the door of the carriage, and tossed the bag inside.

The bag struck Miss Price just below the knees, and she toppled forward, only stopping herself from collapsing from the carriage onto the platform by bracing herself against the door surround. Her folder leapt from her grip and down onto the platform, where the papers scattered once more. This was not the best time for Miss Stevens to return. She dismounted the carriage, picked up the scattered papers, inserted them into the folder once more, and pointedly handed them back to Miss Price.

'I don't know if it would be sounder to leave the children to the fate of the German's Miss Price, truly I don't. Now get it together. Do you hear me?'

'Sorry, Miss,' Tommy, said quickly, as she tried to make sense of the papers once more, and used the opportunity to both get on board, and out of sight. 'Edward Burrows, Miss!' he yelled, pointing to the papers she had in front of her, and ignoring her dismay, jumped aboard.

'Thank you, Mr Burrows,' she replied edgily as she tried to compose herself. 'I won't forget.'

The name Edward Burrows would most certainly have been marked as present now, so all Tommy had to do was lose himself for a while till things started to settle down. He looked along the corridor of the carriage, and looked at the other children, frantically grabbing various seats, when he himself was nudged from behind. He looked down, as a younger boy tried to edge his way past him, and as Tommy looked down in admonishment, the boy pointed to the sign on the door behind him. *Toilet.*

Perfect! Tommy thought, and having found a solution, if only for now, he held his hand up and said, 'Sorry, mate. My need is a little bit more urgent,' and he grabbed at his stomach, feigning an upset tummy.

The boy frowned as Tommy opened the door to the toilet, and somehow managed to get himself, and Edward Burrows kit inside and shut the door, sliding the bolt behind him.

'Dear God, I'm going to spend the rest of my life in toilets,' Tommy whispered to himself. 'And I'm even talking to myself,' he laughed, but soon realised that he was the only person he could talk to.

He was alone.

Catherine, Phillip and Georgia had found a compartment, and Georgia, having stowed all their bags above their heads in the luggage racks, sat back with them, not for the first time, catching Catherine berating Phillip.

'Do stop moaning,' Catherine said to Phillip. 'We're all in this together.'

'It's nothing. I just wanted to use the toilet, and...'

'You went earlier on when we got to the station. Anyway, you can use the one on here when we get going.'

'I tried to, but...'

'Phillip!' she yelled once more.

Reluctantly Phillip accepted his fate, and sat back.

Catherine poked her head out of the compartment and looked along the carriage. She watched the faces of the other evacuees as they walked past. She wondered how many others were going against their will. None of the three had yet made any attempt at trying to branch out to welcome, or seek welcome from anyone else in their group. *It was too early*, Catherine had decided, and she was still angry at being here. There were two smaller girls sat opposite them, but they were both shy, and in no mood to chat away the hours.

A loud whistle blew, and several children cheered. The train jolted, then started to pull away from the station, before slowly beginning to build up speed.

'Dear God! There are people looking forward to this,' Catherine said, dejectedly. 'Can you believe it?' She looked aside at Phillip and Georgia, who looked equally fed up. 'Well! That's it then. We're off.'

Phillip frowned, and stared ahead of him, and as Catherine looked in Georgia's direction, she caught her whispering, 'Bye-bye, mum.'

Catherine had been so wrapped up in her own worries, she had almost forgotten that Georgia was in the same boat. *Or train,* she thought and reached across a consoling hand, and rubbed her shoulder gently, smiling. Georgia turned, and weakly returned the smile.

Tommy found himself sat on the toilet seat, killing time and planning his next move as the train rocked beneath him. He would have to go and join the others it was clear, but he was nervous about making new acquaintances under his new guise. He had not mixed well as Tommy Adams, and he was sure it would be no easier as Edward Burrows. *Edward*, he thought suddenly. *Or Ted, or Teddy?* What a pickle. His background need be no different to his own he decided, as long as he could either keep Miss Price away from the papers in her file, or better still, see what she actually had written down on this character.

There was a knock on the door, and a voice yelled that whoever was in there, they had been there long enough. He had indeed, he decided, been there far too long, and it was time to go and introduce the new Mr Edward Burrows to the world.

Miss Price had found a seat among several of the children, with a space next to her, and she had safely commandeered this for her briefcase and papers, which she had started to spread out to read through. She had done a head count, and having allowed for the fact that there was one in the toilet - who had answered her knock - she was just about getting her papers into some semblance of order. She walked up and down the corridor every so often, climbing over the scattered bags and gas mask containers that had been abandoned there, unable to fit into the luggage racks above their owners, but wasted no time in rushing back to ensure that her papers were still where she had left them, and still in order. She had not failed to notice that at least one of the other chaperones did not hold her in high esteem, and she did not want to put another nail in her coffin.   She glanced up as a red blazer passed her door in a blur.

'Edward Burr…?'

Tommy gritted his teeth, angrily, his anonymity blown. He stopped, and leant back, winking at her. 'Miss!'

Miss Price gestured to the vacant seat beside her, and Tommy froze.

'There's room here if you want.'

If I want, he thought on his feet.

'I've got someone saving me a seat, Miss. You can stretch out now, look!'

Miss Price started to get up, but it meant moving her case, and leaving the papers, and… 'Go, on. I'll catch up with you later.'

As Tommy walked away, she made a final tick on a piece of paper inside one of the folders, and business concluded, sat back against the chair she was in, and closed her eyes. Besides! The journey was going to be a long one, and what more trouble could they really get into till their arrival.

Tommy walked as far along the corridor as he could manage to put space between he and her, and peered into the last compartment. A space! This would do fine.

'You don't mind do you girls?' Tommy said in his cheekiest cockney, smiling. He looked up at the already jammed luggage racks, and realising there was no room for his recently acquired number, placed it alongside several others nearby in the corridor. He made careful mental note of the peculiarities of the bag, in case he needed to identify it later on.

He entered the carriage, and without waiting for an answer, planted himself next to the two shy girls.

Catherine was mortified. She lowered her eyelids hoping that when she opened them again, everything would be all right, and he would be gone. Alas no.

'Edward Burrows,' Tommy said, and noticing Catherine's offhand manner, offered his hand to the young lad sat next to her. He modulated his accent slightly, realising that the cheeky chappie image might not be the most welcoming.

Phillip, realising that he had already had an encounter with this particular character, looked to Catherine for confirmation that it was okay. She winced, and then nodded, slightly. Almost undetectably.

Tommy shook his hand heartily, and then looked to the girl sat by the window.

'Georgia,' she volunteered, and smiled shyly, then looked at Catherine who was not willing to join in this backslapping introduction. 'And this,' she said, 'is Catherine.'

Tommy looked at Catherine, and held the look that moment too long. He thought she was beautiful. He quickly broke from what must have been an admiring leer and looked to his left at the two shy girls who appeared to be much younger. 'Edward Burrows,' he offered once more with his hand, but they were far too shy to respond, so he wished them all the best and nodded. They sniggered and returned to their silence.

Tommy had introduced himself, and so far no one had questioned his identity.

'So! Where are you all from?' he asked.

'We…' Georgia started.

'Nowhere you need to know about,' Catherine quickly interrupted.

Tommy shrugged, and inwardly digesting the way she wanted to play things, sighed, and settled back, closing his eyes.

Catherine threw Georgia a look that would have cut paper. Georgia hunching her shoulders, smiled back cheekily, and mouthed the word, 'Sorry!' She then returned to watching the countryside rush past as the train hammered onwards into its journey.

Tommy opened his eyes as the train went across a thunderously noisy set of points, rocking the carriage furiously. He was not sure if he had been asleep, or had simply been sat there with his eyes shut, mulling things over. He looked unconsciously to his wrist, before realising that he no longer had a watch, and in the event that anyone had been watching, waggled his fingers to disguise his stupidity.

Catherine was once more admonishing Phillip. Tommy, although trying not to get involved, and reveal as little of himself or Edward Burrows as possible, could not help but hear the ensuing conversation. Phillip noticed Tommy was awake, and looked at him. Tommy winked back, and Phillip smiled as Catherine continued to reprimand him.

'Phillip!' she ranted. 'Did you hear what I just said to you?'

'I should think half of London heard what you just said,' Tommy said before he realised he was doing so.

Catherine turned and glared at Tommy in a most unladylike manner, and Tommy drew back, slightly. She had not needed to say anything. The look was enough, and he held up his hands in submission. She ignored him totally, and once more started on Phillip.

Tommy pulled a scary face in Phillip's direction, and he smiled again. This, however, only served to infuriate Catherine further.

'You think this is funny?'

Phillip had so far taken the latest admonishment without question, but another look at Tommy, and his attitude changed completely.

'You can go on as much as you want, Catherine,' he shocked her with his retort. 'It's not my fault you're here. It's not my fault any of us are here. Just like you, I don't want to go to Canada, either.'

Every muscle in Tommy's face gave way, and his chin dropped towards the floor. 'Canada?'

22

The train finally pulled into Southampton after a disjointed journey of nearly three hours. The initial excitement of the journey had quickly worn off, and the boredom of confinement inside such small compartments, for such a long span of time, had quickly eroded their spirits. By the time the inhabitants unloaded from their carriages, the whole herding procedure had become that much easier. The chaperones comfortably loaded the children aboard three dusty old charabancs, and as the engines spluttered into life, they finally drove off in the direction of the docks.

The noise was excruciating. Hammering, sawing, whistles and horns, noisily cutting through the silence of the day. Men turned bolts. Welded metal onto metal. Workers busily filed in and out of a multitude of buildings like ants in a nest. Office personnel fought incoming traffic, furiously ticking off both deliveries, and exports. Employees swept and shovelled at debris strewn across pathways and roads. Lorries, cars and cranes further added to the crescendo, wagons hauling away supplies freshly arrived from abroad. Ships under repair, ships sat at anchor, loading and unloading. Others sat motionless, awaiting departure to their next port of call. Men in the forces, in reserved occupation, and civilians too old to enlist, all set about their jobs in earnest.

The children strained their necks as the three vehicles drew up at the gates of the docks. They disembarked to stretch their legs for a spell, while the official papers were checked and signed. The chaperones struggled slightly more to retain order, as the sights of the ships coming in and out distracted their charges' attention. They all pointed excitedly, from ship to ship, trying hard to guess which one was theirs.

Behind the docks, and almost impervious to the war hardened Londoners, lay the bombed out city of Southampton. The dockland city on the south coast of England had also suffered severely from large-scale air raids, another strategic target for the German air force. Even the huge barrage balloons, swaying high over the docks, seemed to hold no wonderment any more, now an accepted addition to the everyday horizon.

Catherine held Phillip close, with Georgia close by her side, and much to her discomfort, Edward Burrows, who for some strange reason, she imagined, Phillip had now taken a shine to.

Miss Price was trying really hard to finally impress the other chaperones, and with the ever-changing emotions of the children, her small group were indeed no worse than any of the others. The atmosphere was a mix of excitement and resignation. Many children stood quietly, wondering if this were to be the last time they would maybe ever see England again.

The chief chaperone, a Miss Baxter by name, already a legend in her own lifetime, had been kept waiting for some time outside the office door. She had been getting angrier and angrier, and her face had already turned a dozen shades of red. Eventually she had had enough. She marched up to the door and hammered and hammered on it until finally a timid face finally appeared.

'Mr Herbert will see you as soon as he's through,' a very unconvincing underling told her. She leaned forward and muttered something inaudible to all but the recipient, and he took a step back, shocked to hear anything quite like what he had just heard from a lady. 'I'd better see if I can hurry him along then.'

A far from concerned Mr Herbert eventually invited the chaperone inside, and was thrust back against the door as she pushed him to one side with a powerful, broad, sweeping arm. Miss Baxter, a Miss for reasons that were becoming more and more obvious by the moment, threw the papers onto his desk, and stood, arms folded resolutely in front of him.

'I have a large number of small children outside, who you seem to think will stay settled while we dilly-dally here all day,' she barked. 'It will not be for much longer, I can assure you.'

'These are my docks, and I run a tight ship. When I am ready, and when I am convinced *all* the papers and names match up, I will see to moving them on. Until then, why don't you just stand over there and wait?'

Miss Baxter looked across to one of the office juniors, whose face suggested it might be both safer, and quicker if she did as he suggested. She looked at her watch, and huffing, to ensure her point had been made, reluctantly stepped back.

Mr Herbert, in his own good time, took a preliminary glance over the various sheets, and checked the names and numbers against a list he had already procured, earlier in the day. He put down the sheets she had brought in, and went across to pick up some other papers on a clip-board, before further examining those she had brought with her again. His work was clearly more than a job to him. Several times the phone rang, and he answered it putting the job at hand on hold. He treated men, children and cargo in the same laborious, arduous attitude. No matter how long it took.

He continued looking through the papers, and several times looked up as Miss Baxter stepped forward and tried to help speed things along.

'Mrs – er…'

'Baxter. And it's Miss!'

'Why don't you wait outside? I'm sure things will precede a lot quicker if you don't keep interrupting. What do you think?'

Miss Baxter's reply was lost in a muffled chain of expletives, which shook even the apparently unshakable Mr Herbert, as she was shown the door. They were clearly a perfect match.

The children standing outside, as she had already pointed out, were now beginning to become restless, and despite various threats from the slightly less fierce members amongst the chaperones, had started wandering. Orders were wildly barked out in their direction but the children had developed selective hearing, and now defiantly continued to stray.

Tommy and his three new companions, despite Catherine's attempts at ushering him away to join the others, had stayed close to the charabanc. Tommy was still not sure whether he was going to get away with this. What Miss Baxter was up to inside the office he had no idea, and he had once again to assume that at a moment's notice, he might be forced to take flight again. He had been knocked for six when he had heard the word *Canada*, and had spent the rest of the train journey contemplating his future. He had wrestled with the idea of escaping from the others as soon as the train arrived at the station, but had also weighed up the options therein. He had nothing in London any more, and knew nothing about where they were now. And someone, somewhere, had arranged for Edward Burrow's evacuation to Canada. On top of all that, and despite her outward animosity to him, Tommy had taken an unexpected shine to Catherine. He decided to soldier on. It was the only real option open to him. Besides, it would not have taken the real Edward Burrows this long to have got out of the toilet at the station. *Would it?* Every time the door to the office opened, Tommy jumped, expecting to have to make a run for it. But as yet...?

The mass evacuation of children had been under way for some time now, and the transportation to safer countries had been undertaken aboard a selection of converted cruise liners. The standards aboard the ships were now much different to what might have been expected. Ships, under wartime requirements, had been carefully stripped of pleasantries, and converted to the bare essentials to suit their purpose. The word cruise was not what it had once meant.

Mr Herbert, in the mentioning of their vessel, *The Maid of Orleans*, may well have mentioned the term, Old Bucket, in his summation, but Miss Baxter had long ago forgotten any pleasantries she might have had with him. He may have run the office as a business, and was undoubtedly a stickler to detail, but everything that left his office, did so under the understanding that he had given it his own official seal of approval, and there would most certainly be no comebacks due to a slip-up on his part.

'Well ...' he addressed the pugnacious chaperone, as he walked outside his office.

'...Miss Baxter!' she reminded him, in her broad Scottish accent.

'Well, *Miss*,' he emphasized the word, making no effort at adding a surname to it. 'This little lot looks to be in order, so let's get you lot over to where you need to be.' He nodded his head in the direction of the dockyard. 'That's your bay over there.'

Miss Baxter looked over her shoulder, and turning back to finish business with him, was infuriated to find that he had already turned his back on her, dealing with fresh business. She was about to complain, rarely dealing with anyone she could not browbeat, but Mr Herbert's assistant quickly stepped in to stop matters boiling over.

'I'll take you all down, then, shall I?' he offered, and quickly led her away to better hurry things along. She muttering something in his ear that Mr Herbert could neither hear, nor would ever care about, even if his junior was ever brave enough to pass on the message.

Having at last reassembled, and now excited about discovering which ship was to be theirs, the children had once more boarded the charabancs for what they hoped would be the short journey to the *Holding Point* Mr Herbert had designated. The drivers had shouted back for a little quiet, but King Canute may have had more luck commanding the sea than they had over these particular children. The driver on Tommy's bus shook his head, and muttered something unsavoury under his breath, which was totally unnecessary, as it would never have been heard above the din if he had shouted it.

They shortly pulled up alongside a rusty warehouse, beside which sat *The Maid of Orleans*.

She was an imposing old lady, and though the children stood, staring up at her in awe, *old bucket* may not have been an over-exaggeration. But as most of the children had never seen a boat before, much less had one to compare it to, she appeared to be beautiful. Her history might once have boasted cruise liner amongst her previous lives, but she was far from that now. She had been thoroughly stripped of any comforts whatsoever, and currently acted as a taxi, ferrying goods to and fro across the Atlantic. Amongst the goods on this particular run, were: Children – Evacuees   Number - 85. Having just returned laden with invaluable imports, she was now fuelled and set to run the gauntlet of the North Atlantic once more.

Members of the boat crew, and a general mixture of stevedores stood aboard, smoking, looking down at the motley crew of children beneath them in a short break from their duties. Any ship sat in dock for too long was sure to be a sitting target during bombing raids, and although open to attack from U-Boats, it was often considered safer for the ship to be at sea.

The crew chatted amongst themselves, occasionally laughing at the new cargo, between cigarettes. One of the sea hardened faces smiled down, and waved in return to a kindly gesture offered from one of the children.

After a short while, a walkway was lowered, and one of the more senior members of the crew ushered Miss Baxter forward, and in due course, the children were slowly ushered on, the chaperones painstakingly checking a face against a name on a list once more.

Tommy, for safety's sakes, had thought it best to continue to hang out with Catherine's group - much to her dismay - and before too long, they too started to load. She had made no secret of trying to distance themselves from the adoptee, to the point of being rude. Something Georgia was quick to point out in a quieter moment. But if his repugnance appalled Catherine, it was having the totally opposite effect on Phillip. And whatever she tried, Catherine could do nothing about that.

The police sergeant looked up from his desk at the unfortunate waif stood in front of him. The boy was dressed in a pair of shorts that were slightly too small for him, and a shirt with sleeves that did not quite reach down to his hands. He looked most upset. The sergeant looked once more at the notes in front of him, then again to the boy.

'Well, well, well!' Mr Burrows!' he began, still unsure about the story the boy had just told. 'What are we going to do with you then?'

The children stood along the side of the ship looking down at the docks as the smoke steadily built up and blew out through the funnel in the centre of the ship. They waved what was now certain to be their last farewell to England for some good time, and more likely the duration of the war. For Tommy however, now resigned to his decision, he could not wait for the ship to set sail. He looked back across the docks to check that he had really got away with it.

The telephone rang for the umpteenth time inside the office of Mr Herbert. He was sat at his desk checking through some figures to which he was using mental arithmetic to solve, and irritated at being interrupted in the middle of a particularly awkward sum, he snatched up the phone.

'Hello!'

A voice at the other end of the phone mumbled something.

'What?' he yelled, standing to kick the door to shut out the noise. 'He did what? No! Stay there, and don't go anywhere,' he bellowed, and throwing the phone onto the desk, ran to the door, opened it, and frantically called to someone across the yard.

23

The Maid of Orleans had slipped its hold onto the harbour wall, and was now under its own steam. It slowly started to draw away from the jetty, and Tommy smiled contentedly. But as he looked down, the smile quickly faded, and was instantly replaced by a look of horror. In the distance, though still clearly visible, a tiny figure rushed from a door to the building they had initially checked in at, and heatedly pointed in their general direction.

Tommy strained his eyes, watching as the angry figure gesticulated with someone nearby, and as he watched the drama unfold in front of his eyes, a truck was dispatched, and rapidly hurtled its way across the dockyard. He stood, anxiously, judging the distance *The Maid of Orleans* was putting between it and the harbour wall, and the distance the small truck was making across the dockyards. He hoped he was the only one on board who could fathom out what was going on.

The truck drew up sharply, and an angry figure jumped out, gesturing furiously in the direction of the ship.

Tommy was just about to take off, but as he turned into another crowd of children, any escape route was quickly cut off. Imprisoned, he hurriedly searched for another option, but penned in as he was, there did not appear to be one.

'Look!' one of the children said, looking down at the dock.

Tommy turned in horror, to see the young girl pointing down at Mr Herbert.

Think!

'Look!' the wretched child continued.

An idea sprang to mind. As he looked down - and despite all the other children around him - he was almost certain that Mr Herbert had picked him out. He looked Herbert as squarely in the eyes as was possible from this distance, and started to wave.

If Mr Herbert had failed to pick him out, the wave might just have done the trick.

'Wave then!' Tommy told those around him, mulling over the stupidity of having drawn his attention. 'Wave!'

Tommy increased the velocity of his waving, and not needing an excuse to do so, the others around him excitedly joined in.

Mr Herbert was now engaged in a furious conversation with one of the workers there, so Tommy whooped, excitedly, to further urge the children on. Though unlikely to come about, the ship was certainly not too far from land for some sort of signal to be delivered. And although unlikely that a thirteen thousand ton vessel would be returned to shore just for him, he might well be put under arrest until the return leg of the voyage.

As his entourage continued with their farewell, he decided he needed to lose himself, and lose himself quickly.

The quarters into which the children and the chaperones were to be sequestered were far from plush. The few smaller cabins that remained, though squalid, were quickly swallowed up by the older of the evacuees. Far from a question of being carefully placed in a preordained routine, order had given way to a battle of first come - first served. For all the efforts of the chaperones on board, the excitement of the new surroundings quickly overtook any authority they may have managed to instil in their charges, and chaos once more appeared to reign.

Some small time later, and authority - of some sort - reinstalled, it appeared nearly everyone was accounted for, and had somewhere to call home. Many of the children had been placed inside temporary dormitories. Holds on board that had been hollowed out and filled with bunks, though far from comfortable, seemed to comfortably fit the bill.

The cabins now occupied, the best of the bunks had been quickly been snatched up. But for the odd cases, where it was thought better to keep certain parties and sexes apart, the chaperones busily scuttled round to tick off names against bunks, and ensure that their luggage had been safely stored.

Catherine, totally disillusioned with the whole thing, had been in no hurry to find accommodation. Not that she had wanted second best, but Phillip had rushed off as soon as they had boarded, and would most certainly not have settled for second class if he could find something better. She would catch up with him in her own time. There was going to be plenty of that. Georgia was with her for company, and although she had also wanted to check out the quarters, she had, out of duty, felt the need to stay with Catherine.

Phillip had taken the first two sets of bunks in the foremost of the quarters they had been shown, and quickly laid claim to this section of the ship. When Miss Price had finally caught up with him, she had decided that there was no reason not to lay siege here herself. She chose a bunk of her own slightly further along the billet, then hastily set about ensuring she had the right number of bunks to occupy the children in her charge.

Catherine, against a slightly more urgent Georgia's insistence, arrived at a much more leisurely pace. Georgia had to try her hardest not to laugh at Catherine's face as she confronted her accommodation for the foreseeable future. She firstly looked to the bunks, upon which Phillip had already made home, and then at the number of other bunks inside the available space. Georgia looked up, carefully, realising exactly what was going through Catherine's mind, and bit down hard on her bottom lip in anticipation. Catherine caught her look, and stared into her face.

'What the…'

Tommy had taken off the second he had suspected he was in trouble. As all the other children had hurried below decks, he had taken the opportunity during the chaos to quietly slip away, on his own. Whereas London had been easy in which to hide himself away, he was now onboard a ship, restricted, and having to think on the hoof. He knew neither where he was, nor the layout of the rest of the decks. He was absolutely certain however that word had somehow got to the ship about the absence of the real Edward

Burrows, that an impostor was present in his place, and certainly that a search party was very likely be out looking for him. He needed to lie low, at least for the next couple of... days? He may have been *Jack the Lad* in his own surroundings, but just at the moment, he was totally out of his depth.

Tommy, still alone, slunk away further along the deck, looking out for any possible cover. He figured he was fine for now, as no one aboard ship really knew what he looked like, and the chaperone, vaguely at that. But as soon as the others were settled and Edward Burrows was once more absent, then things would certainly start to hot up again. He almost felt sorry for Miss Price. He had already seen the state she could get into, although he had happily used it to his advantage. But she wasn't on the run. He was.

Miss Price had checked three times amongst the '*Dorms*,' as they had now been christened, and once more checked the numbers against the list. She was still one charge short, and she knew the name as if it were tattooed across her forehead. She was convinced he had been sent to plague her. Was a bright red blazer really so difficult to spot? She walked for the last time through the different cabins, and finally sat defeated on her bunk with a sigh. Catherine, one of the older children in the cabin looked at her, realised her discomfort, and walked across to sit by her.

'What?' Miss Price blurted a little too abruptly.

'Nothing! I just...' Catherine answered defensively, and getting up, startled, began to make her way back to her bunk.

'I'm sorry. That was rude,' Miss Price quickly apologised. 'It's just I have looked three times for this Edward Burrows, and I can't find him anywhere.'

'Edward Burrows!' Catherine mused.

'Oh, I'm so sorry,' she continued, now breathing at a more regular rate, 'I shouldn't be lumbering you with my problems. It's just he's gone missing again.'

Catherine heart leapt. She was elated. She hadn't liked the boy when they had first met, and was sure she never would, so news that he was in trouble cheered her up considerably.

'You probably don't even know who I'm...'

'Oh, I know!' Catherine said. 'Don't worry. I think I know just the person who can track him down for you.' She looked across to Phillip, who looked up, and defensively, moved backwards. He had seen this look before.

Tommy was walking along the deck, careful to stay out of sight, and trying to get his bearings when there was a shout behind him. He stood still, his shoulders slumped, now resigned to his arrest. He waited as the owner of the voice approached and tapped him on the shoulder.

'You lost, kid?'

It didn't sound as if his liberty was lost just yet. He turned to see one of the crew, apparently concerned over his welfare.

Play it carefully he thought, and you might just get away with this.

'I've lost the others,' Tommy said shyly.

The crewman punched him playfully in the shoulder.

'A ship's the wrong place to get lost if you haven't been on one before,' the old salt started. 'Why! When I was just a lad, I...'

He turned proudly to engage his audience further, only to find his new charge had gone.

Tommy had taken off the second the crewman had looked away and quickly and quietly wriggled his way out of sight. He ran through an alleyway, and tucked himself in behind a small - funnel. He tucked in tight, expecting discovery at any moment. But as the seconds turned into a minute and then another, he was starting to wonder if he really was as high on anyone's priority list as he thought.

It had now been quiet for so long, Tommy decided it was time to make his next move. Having emerged from his precious hidey-hole, he cautiously started to make his way across the deck of the ship, taking every opportunity to shelter behind any of the strange pipes, funnels, and other strange nautical objects he happened upon. He shivered as the ship listed slightly, and he was caught in an exposed gust of wind. Liberty was one thing, he thought. Keeping himself warm was going to be another thing altogether. And certainly something that he was going to have to start looking into at once.

What he imagined to have been the entire top deck covered - and having come across nothing to suit his purpose - the distant smell of food emerging through one of the portholes was almost enough to convince Tommy to hand himself in.

He froze for on the spot as two fresh voices approached.

'Where's he got to? I'll kill him if I get my hands on him!' one of the voices sounded.

Tommy took shelter in the first available shadows, and flattened himself against what he assumed to be a wall, and waited, trying his hardest to keep his breathing to a bare minimum for fear of discovery.

As the voices drew closer, Tommy breathed in, and as he tried to become a second coat of paint on the wall behind him, it moved.

As the two voices, the rest of their conversation lost in a moment of fear, passed safely by, Tommy finally let out his breath, and turned to find himself nestled up against - a lifeboat.

Amazed, and still not fully recovered, he stood back slightly to get a better look at the wooden craft. It was, he imagined, some fifteen feet in length, with a waterproof tarpaulin tied down on the top of it. It was far from elegant, but far more to the point – he had found his hide away.

Life below decks was now much calmer. After hours of travel and initial excitement, the strain of the day was starting to show on the children. They lay quietly on their bunks, some chatting, others simply lying with their heads down, trying to get some rest.

Miss Price had gone with Catherine to Phillip's side as he sat with Georgia, and questioned him about Tommy's disappearance. Phillip, having been the butt of his sister's fury for most of the day, suddenly felt most important, and although he truthfully said he didn't know where he had gone, he informed them he would happily go and look for him for her. Miss Price was slightly worried about having lost one of her flock, and yet having concealed the fact fairly well so far, did not fancy losing another one. She said that he should stay where he was for now, but she might well come back to him later on. Catherine tutted and pointed out that Tommy would soon come back when it was time for food. Surely they had enough to worry about without having to concern themselves over one mischievous miscreant. She added that they were probably all far better off without him. Miss Price smiled politely, but added that everyone had their own ways, and that they should all be treated the same. Catherine mumbled something, but coughed it away as it was probably not what a sixteen year old lady should have been coming out with.

'Oh, don't worry,' Miss Price said getting up, trying hard to disguise her worries. 'He'll probably turn up. Good lord, I don't even know where he is going to bed down anyway.'

'Here!' Phillip said abruptly, pointing to the bunk below his. 'Look! I've saved it for him.'

Catherine looked across, noticing that her bunk would be directly opposite his. She had already suspected Phillip may have had this planned, and despite several offers to more suitable passengers, they had all already settled in with friends of their own. She turned pleadingly to Miss Price. 'He can't. I mean, what about privacy and all that,' she asked, desperately.

'I wish we all had private cabins, Miss Price said, 'but I'm afraid we will all have to make the best of it. I can't separate brothers and sisters,' and looking at Phillip, added, 'especially if they are only wee things.'

Catherine looked directly at Phillip and said, 'You call off your search now. He can find his own way back. And his own quarters.'

Tommy had somehow, and against all odds, managed to loosen the bindings on one side of the lifeboat, and successfully draw back the cover. He had then, carefully - and weighing up the dangers of doing so in the changeable weather - managed to slip inside under the tarpaulin. The luggage of Edward Burrows safely inserted with him, Tommy sat back, fairly chuffed with his efforts. He sat back, leaving the tarpaulin drawn back slightly for light, and what had appeared to be somewhat spacious from the outside, on entry, had now become very cramped.

Several voices approached the vicinity of his lifeboat, so Tommy quickly settled himself into a position that he might be able to hold until the intruders had passed by. Now here, he didn't want any sudden movements on his part to give away his presence.

The voices now history, Tommy lay down on the hard floor of the boat. With time on his hands, he wondered exactly what he should do next. Home comforts were sure to be at a premium, so he carefully undid the haversack he had managed to drag inside with him, and after a very fleet examination of the clothing within, threw it onto the floor.

71

He scattered the contents around him trying to make what Mrs Burrows had best packed for her son, into slightly more comfortable bedding. Sighing, and wishing that Edward Burrows had better packed, if not in quality, certainly in quantity, he bunched up a handful of clothing, and laid his head back against it, slowly starting to gather his thoughts together.

Catherine was sat on the edge of her bunk as Georgia drew a brush through her shoulder-length hair, counting as the brush completed each stroke. They seemed settled and chatted casually.

Phillip, having been scolded by his sister for the umpteenth time, this time for befriending Tommy, sat on his bunk, drumming his fingers, hoping this wouldn't lead to further rebuke. The more she had beaten into him that he should stay away from Tommy, the more resolute he had become to do the opposite. He liked him anyway. And currently, the more it infuriated her, the better. He watched as Catherine was fussed over, and realised that during her preening, neither she nor Georgia were paying him any undue attention whatsoever. The other children were settled in, and having made friends of their own - without including him - he was bored. He looked up at Miss Price, who had returned, after a preliminary search for his new comrade, and she sat nervously, further along the line of bunks, frantically checking through papers once more. He looked across at his sister and Georgia, and nothing else for it, he quietly slipped down from his bunk and away from the dormitory.

24

The *Maid of Orleans*, having steamed into the gathering gloom had joined a collection of other ships of many varying shapes and sizes. She had attached herself to a convoy, under the protection of escort vessels of the Royal Navy for much of the return journey to North America. The flotilla was some thirty ships strong, and would indeed be sitting ducks for the German U-Boats packs, hunting in the North Atlantic, was it not for the armed presence of both the Royal Navy and the Royal Canadian Navy destroyers and frigates accompanying it. For though an arable land, Britain was still an island, and many millions of tons of food and goods were imported into the nation each year, and Hitler's Navy was currently doing its very best to starve the British nation into eventual surrender with the decimation of as many of its convoys as it could manage.

For the moment, however, the weather was good, the sea like a millpond, and the convoy proceeded valiantly on it voyage, undeterred.

For all his bravado, Tommy was now all alone, and had no possessions other than those the kindly Mr and Mrs Burrows had decided to pack for their beloved son, and the few items he had managed to retain from the pockets of his discarded coat from his visits to the shops prior to his arrival at the train station. Tommy smiled, imagining the beating his father would have given him had he found out what he had been through to acquire the goods. But the smile faded as his thoughts shifted back to the last he had seen of his father. He momentarily overlooked the beatings he had received, and spared the man a quiet moment.

The ship shifted violently, hitting a large wave, and he quickly returned to business inside the lifeboat. His stomach grumbled, and his mind turned to food. He was hungry. Despite rationing, he had somehow always been able to scrounge something to eat, and had normally got by. That had been on land, however. His current predicament was a different kettle of fish altogether. It was early days yet though, he realised, and something was sure to turn up.

His body starting to knot up, he moved over towards the edge of the lifeboat, and carefully peered out of the gap he had left himself in the tarpaulin. He looked as far along deck as he could without revealing too much of himself, and noticed that there seemed to be no one patrolling the decks. He assumed that a night watch would be out on patrol at some stage, but hoped that would be reduced a substantially reduced crew.

He quickly drew his head back inside as he heard a cough to his right. He held himself tight up against the side of the lifeboat, and waited out any signs of discovery.

There were none, so after a short while, and convinced of his solitude, he once more opened the gap in the tarpaulin, and stuck his head out a little further, realising that the fast developing darkness would rapidly be closing up a lot of what anyone could see. He included.

Tommy stretched his neck for a better look around, and then abruptly tucked it back inside. A member of the crew was stood quietly along the deck, smoking a cigarette, the lit end kept out of sight with a cupped hand. He had looked almost as shifty as Tommy felt. Tommy fingered the cigarettes he still had with him, and would happily have jumped out to join him for one.

'Oi!' Tommy stopped dead. 'Put that thing out, you idiot!' a voice shouted down the deck. 'Any U-Boat Captain out there gets more than one sight of that thing burning and we might as well start swimming for home, now.'

The seaman stubbed out the cigarette and turned in Tommy's direction.

If he had seen Tommy's jolt to get back under cover, he didn't show any reaction to it. He was probably more worried about the reprimand of his own.

Tommy held his breath, and waited for him to pass. That was far too close, and at the mention of a U-Boat, his need for a cigarette only grew stronger. Just for the moment, though, his smoke would have to wait.

Phillip, at large, was pleased to be free of the dominance of his sister, and was enjoying the independence. He had so far only walked below deck as far as the toilet, where he had unceremoniously been informed that it was nautically referred to as the *Hold*. He decided he would continue to do so, if only to annoy his sister, who was resolutely avoiding anything nautical, or becoming a part of anything that appeared to be co-operative.

He had quickly come across the galley where the food was prepared, and continuing his travels, even walked in on some of the crew in their quarters. He apologised, and wandered off, feigning being lost. He quietly whispered 'Edward!' every time he felt he was out of earshot of anything official, but there was no response, so he ventured on.

He eventually walked out onto the upper deck and started to walk along, as much in boredom now as in any hope of finding *Edward*. His youthful age did not allow anything to sustain his interest overly long, and had this been a fruitless walk, would usually have long since worn off. But knowing how much his discovering *Edward* would incense Catherine, he decided to soldier on.

The immense size of the ship, along with the growing dark, limited exactly how much of it he could physically search without getting lost himself, and unsuccessful to date, he had started to lose heart. He now walked deflated, hands dug deep into his pockets, kicking moodily at the deck as he did so.

Tommy heard a noise, and alerted, stopped moving any more than to peek through the opening he had left himself as a porthole. He was sure that would not be noticed from outside. He strained his eyes, and could see nothing at first, but visibility was indeed slightly better outside the lifeboat than in, due to the light from a moon that had now arrived on the horizon. His heart leapt as he saw Phillip, and he was just about to call out, when he heard another, deeper voice.

'Where do you think you are going, young man? Home?'

74

Tommy watched as another member of the crew, and owner of the voice, marched up and gently accosted Phillip. He quickly overcame any shock at the crewman's appearance, and casually told him he was bored. And life below deck, he further elucidated, was even worse because his sister was there. The crewman laughed, but assured him that it was going to be much safer for him below decks. Sister or not.

Tommy, unable to believe his luck, was desperate to make contact, and even better, Phillip was looking in his direction. For hunger as much as company, he realised he desperately had to somehow gain his attention. Waiting until the crewman was fully facing the other way, Tommy slightly, and quietly opened up the gap he had left for himself, and carefully pushed his head into the opening, quietly waving a hand. He was worried Phillip might start, and give him away on seeing him, but there was also the chance that he may never get the chance to see him again.

Phillip's eyes momentarily looked away from the seaman, who seemed to be quite enjoying the meeting with a young lad. Tommy waved frantically trying to get him to return to his attention to his captor.

'I must go,' Phillip said rather too loudly, and staccato. 'I'm starving. I must go and get some food. Shall I bring you some back?'

'Not me, my old mate,' the seaman said cheerily. 'I've 'ad mine already.'

Tommy, realising to whom the question had been levied, nodded furiously, and catching too much of Phillip's attention, quickly submerged inside the lifeboat.

The crewman, seeming puzzled at the young lad's sudden lack of attention, turned to see exactly what it was that was distracting him.

'Can you show me then?' Phillip quickly blurted out, realising Tommy's dilemma.

'Follow me then, young man,' the crewman said, his attention regained. He patted Phillip on the head, and humming a merry tune, led him away.

Tommy lay back, elated that he had finally made contact with an ally, and his spirits renewed, he settled back, and waited.

'Where have you been?' Catherine demanded on his Phillip's return. 'You nearly missed supper, altogether,' she said, pulling a face at the slop on the plate in front of her. 'If indeed you can call it that.'

'Mmmm! Food!' he said, trying to allay her interest, and avoid answering the question. He looked at his bunk and the plate with something that only just passed as stew, sat on it.

'Well!' Catherine carried on, relentlessly.

'I've been to – the Head, if you must know,' he tried out his newly acquired vocabulary. He looked at Georgia, and shyly hid his face.

'For this long? My goodness, I…' and the rest of it was lost as he shut her out of his head. He had other things to worry about. How was he going to get some food to Tommy?

'I need a word with you,' a voice drew Phillip away from spooning through the mess on his plate.

Miss Price stood beside his bunk with Catherine by her side. Beside the pair of them, the fierce face of the chief chaperone Miss Baxter glared down at him. Her face was like a beacon, and he could almost feel the heat from it from where he was sat. Georgia stood to one side, with a regretful face, trying to pervade that she had had nothing to do with this.

'I have precious little time to waste Master… ?' Miss Baxter snapped.

'Belvoir,' Catherine confirmed.

'…Belvoir. Now! Where is he?'

'Why would I know?' he answered, not over politely, if not, a little short.

'Because you've been out looking for him, that's why,' his sister interjected, smiling ebulliently.

'Thank you for your help Catherine,' Miss Price jumped in, 'but I think I'd better handle this from now on, don't you?'

'Actually, I think I'd better,' the much sterner voice of Miss Baxter said, brushing her out of the way with a broad sweep of her arm. 'I think your inadequacies are all too clear for everyone to see, thank you.'

All the authority Miss Price had built up since their boarding the ship disappeared in an instant, and she almost wilted under the verbal assault. Georgia quickly grabbed her arm and gave her a hug, whispering consoling things into her ear.

'I think you had better come with me young man, don't you?' the battle-axed voice, commanded. 'And you, Miss Price, had better come along and see how the job should really be done.'

'I don't know anything,' Phillip bleated, his last attempt at innocence.   But with Miss Baxter and Catherine, looming over the top of him, he was defenceless, and left with no choice but to climb out of his bunk, and follow them.

Catherine stepped back slightly to allow Miss Baxter's huge frame space, then made to go with along with them. However, a stern look from the matriarch guardian told her she was to stay exactly where she was, and she reluctantly sat back on her bunk.

'Poor Phillip,' Georgia said as the two chaperones and Phillip, disappeared.

'He should know better,' Catherine said firmly, and then relenting slightly. 'I do hope he doesn't get into too much trouble. Mother would be furious.'

Tommy sat frustrated, turning a packet of cigarettes over and over in his hands. He was much hungrier since Phillip's mention of food, and boredom only added to his worries. As darkness took over, he was becoming much more nervous inside his tomb. He wanted to know what was going on, and was worried that he had left his well being to a boy so much younger than himself. He debated getting out of the boat, and checking for himself. It was night, and he hoped everyone would be at rest. After all the good work he had put in with Phillip, he felt he had better not risk it just yet. He would just have to trust his newfound ally. After all, he had been gone some good time, now, and there had been no sound of alarm just yet. He relaxed slightly, but sat back dismayed, nonetheless.

25

Phillip stood in front of a ship's officer whom he could only assume to be the captain. Another officer stood slightly behind and to the right of him. They both looked at him sternly. He wondered if they could have appeared any more severe if he had stolen the crown jewels themselves.

'Now... Phillip...?' the assumed Captain looked across to the Miss Baxter for confirmation.

She nodded.

'No one here is angry in the slightest,' he continued, hoping his patronising manner might cut through his defences. 'Your friend, Edward - er – Burrows?' Miss Baxter nodded again. 'Where is he?'

Phillip shrugged his shoulders without saying a word.

'Look! We need to know where he is young fellow. He might be – No! He *is* in terrible danger if he is wandering around the ship without anyone to look after him. Ships can be dangerous beasts, and we all need to look after him. Now why don't you just tell us where he is?'

Phillip breathed out, noncommittally, and shrugged his shoulders once more.

Miss Baxter grabbed him by the shoulders, turned him to face her, and shook him angrily. 'Just tell us where he is you little...'

Miss Price jumped in between them, and taking Phillip to one side, keeping Miss Baxter at bay, allowed him settle.

'I don't think that is going to do the trick, is it?' she said, smiling at Phillip.

The look she received from her superior would have melted many people, but on this occasion, Miss Price held her ground. She turned to face Phillip, and gently rubbed his shoulders, and crouching down till they were at the same height, asked kindly, 'Where is he, Phillip?'

Phillip shrugged his shoulders. 'The last time I saw him he was on the dockside. I haven't seen him since. Really!'

'This is all very well,' the ship's officer said, but I really have more important things to be worried over than a boy playing hide and seek, and I'm afraid I am going to have to leave the matter in your hands. I will ensure the night watch are told to keep an eye open, and let's all hope ...' he looked at Miss Baxter who was regaining her composure, '...that he's just playing games, shall we?'

'Just playing games?' Miss Baxter started to lose what small self-control she had regained.

'Look!' he stopped her, exasperated. 'This is Lieutenant Nelson,' he indicated behind him, in a dismissive manner who smiled shyly at Miss Price. 'Please deal with him. All of you'

'Shouldn't that be - Admiral?' Miss Price couldn't resist the temptation, receiving a stern frown from her superior.

The officer ignored the remark. This was evidently not the first time he had heard it, and he simply gestured to the door, and the quartet left the room.

'You go back to your sister for now,' Miss Price told Phillip, and playfully patted him on the backside as he went on his way. 'I know it's been a busy day, what with all the excitement and everything, but try and get some sleep.'

'Yes! Make sure you get a good night's sleep,' Miss Baxter echoed, failing to hide the sarcasm in her voice at all.

Phillip looked back, just short of poking out his tongue at her.

'Run along,' Miss Price resolved the stand-off.

'I can't stand around here all night,' Miss Baxter growled. 'I've got my own job to do. And just you listen, Miss Price! You keep a close eye on that one.' Miss Price heaved a quiet sigh of relief, but just as she thought she was out of torpedo range, Miss Baxter added, 'Oh! And believe me! You've not heard the last of this yet.'

Phillip had come back and walked in to face both his sister and Georgia who were sitting up waiting for him. Catherine glared at him, and Georgia who stood slightly astern of her, smiled, enjoying the excitement, but far too scared to admit it to his sister.

'Well?' Catherine scoffed at him.

'Well what?' he answered. 'Look! You can put me up in front of the King, and it won't make any difference. I don't know where he is, all right?'

Georgia pulled a slightly sceptical face, but Catherine failed to see it. Phillip smiled slightly.

'Something funny?' Catherine spat.

'Look! You've still got a bit of your supper to eat,' Georgia interrupted, rescuing the situation. 'You must still be starving?'

Catherine scowled at Georgia's interruption, but let it rest for the moment.

Phillip sat on the bunk, and spooned the last of the mess off his plate, and when he was convinced he had lost his sister's interest in him, carefully placed a lump of bread to one side.

His plate clean, he looked across to see Catherine more settled, and when he was satisfied she was relaxed, he stood, and stretched.

'Where do you think you are going now?' she said, without even looking up.

'The head.'

'The what?' Catherine growled.

He smiled, as Georgia whispered in her ears, reminding her.

'Oh no!' Phillip looked back, openly shocked. 'Not on your own you don't. Georgia, you go with him.'

Georgia looked equally shocked. It had been a while since she had had to take an order from either of them, but realising the situation, she thought it best that she did as she was told. She raised her eyebrows, and followed Phillip, waving farewell to Catherine for the time being.

'Look, Georgia! Can I trust you?' Phillip asked her once they were out of his sister's earshot.

'Well! I – er - guess I should...' Georgia looked at him, and weighing up her loyalties, hesitated for a moment, and then smiled and nodded.

'Can you give me just five minutes?' He opened his hand, revealing the bread that had come with his meal. Georgia reached into her pocket and taking it out, revealed another piece of similar size.

'Look! He's...'

Georgia held a hand up. 'If I don't know where he is, they can't get it out of me,' she said. 'Five minutes. Be quick.'

Phillip kissed her on the cheek, leaving Georgia flushed, and hurriedly took off.

Tommy sat motionless. As a defence against the cold, was wearing most of the clothing Edward Burrows had packed. He was leant against the rolled up bag he was using as a cushion, as he heard footsteps approaching at pace. *Phillip*! He stiffened, awaiting discovery.

'Edward,' a voice called out. 'Quickly!'

'Here!' Tommy whispered, reminding him exactly where he was, and slid back the tarpaulin. Phillip almost without stopping, threw in the bread, and turned around. 'Can't stop! They're hot on my heels!' he said, and swiftly scurried off in the direction from which he had come.

Tommy sat back and forced the bread down greedily. *Who knew*? he thought. Just maybe things were going to work out okay after all.

Catherine sat waiting on her bunk, too wrapped up in her own concerns to join the others in the rest of the quarter's affairs. She watched the second hand on the watch on her wrist, noting exactly how long they had been away, and as it approached five minutes, she started to get restless. She was still furious with her brother, and was not now sure whether it had been such a good idea to let him go off with Georgia. She had started to suspect that Georgia was beginning to be enjoy the disappearance and all that went with it, far too much for her liking. She drummed her fingers, and became more and more agitated. She stood up, sat down, stood up again, and then unable to settle, decided to take off to find them.

Georgia stood anxiously awaiting Phillip's return, worried at exactly how Catherine would react if she had now mislaid her brother along with this other miscreant, Edward Burrows.

'Where have you been?' a voice called behind her. Georgia started to turn. 'And where is Phillip?'

Georgia slowed her turn slightly, trying to think up a quick explanation.

'He's here,' Phillip answered, appearing from around a corner, happily saving Georgia the problem.

'Well! Where have you been? You've been ages,' she continued, glaring at her timepiece once more. Phillip adjusted his clothing slightly, as if not having completed his ablutions properly in the head, and Catherine blushed slightly. 'It's just, I was worried about you both, that's all!'

Phillip smiled, and nodding his head in the direction from which Catherine had come, said, 'Come on! Let's go.'

Catherine shrugged her shoulders defiantly, and led off.

Georgia nudged Phillip, and said, 'You'd better not need to go any more tonight. You've just used up your last chance.'

'I'm fine,' Phillip smirked, and winked. 'Oh! And thanks.'

26

Miss Price was stood in front of Lieutenant Nelson. She had managed to relieve herself of the company of the head chaperone, Miss Baxter for a little while now, and was once more feeling herself.

'I thought I'd better show *you* this, first. We've just had this through,' he said, handing across a small slip of paper. She took it, suspiciously, and read through the information written on it. 'Your Mr Burrows is sat at home in London. *Our* Mr Burrows is …'

'A castaway!' she said almost excitedly.

'That's a little dramatic, but yes, I suppose you could call him that.'

'I'll tell the…'

'Having seen your - boss,' he indicated his opinion of the chief chaperone in his tone of voice, 'I shouldn't tell anyone anything just for the time being.'

'Then…?'

'I suggest you look after the others. It's dark now. I'm sure he'll surface on his own. Hunger tends to be a great magnet, and the lack of hiding places on a ship quite this small…'

'Small!' Miss Price's eyes bulged, looking around her. 'I would hardly call this small.'

'After a day or two, this will seem as cramped as a rowing boat. This old tub was not built for comfort. Once upon a time, yes, but now, it's just a means of getting goods from point A to point B. Look, I'll get the night watch to keep an eye open, and as motherly as you feel, a - stowaway - is no longer your responsibility.'

'I shouldn't think Miss Baxter…'

'Go and get a good night's sleep. Who knows? You'll probably find him tucked up in his bunk - first thing in the morning.'

'I think maybe I'd better just…'

'Go and get some rest. If your boss comes around, I'll fob her off with a story to satisfy her, for you.' Miss Price smiled, shyly, almost embarrassed at the attention being paid to her. 'Go on.'

'Thank you - Admiral,' she teased him, and blushing slightly, headed back in the direction of her charges.

The main bulk of the children had now settled down for the night, and many were already fast asleep in their bunks. Phillip had his head down, and appeared to be one of them. Catherine was sat in front of Georgia who was running a brush through her hair once more, counting aloud, as she did so.

'… Forty-five, forty-six.'

'Why on earth has he taken such an affinity to this - ruffian?' she asked. 'I really don't understand, I'm sure.'

Georgia stopped brushing Catherine's hair as she turned around seeking an answer.

'I think everything is different now, and Phillip just seems to be attracted to something - new to him.' She looked across and noticing his eyes slightly ajar, smiled and winked. Phillip winked back.

'Well! If I find him, you don't want to know what I'll do. My! I'd...' Catherine was not sure what she wanted to do about it, but turned back so Georgia could continue with her hair.

'Where was I?' Georgia smiled behind her.

'Forty-Six.'

Night was truly in, and Tommy slept in fits and starts. Even when he found a reasonably comfortable position, he would start at the slightest noise, and sit upright, awaiting arrest. He now regretted the fact that he hadn't simply turned himself in, in the first place. He realised the convoy would have been most unlikely to turn round on his account, and a night in the *cells* had surely got to be better than his position at the moment. But he still wasn't sure. He turned over and rubbed at a point on his back where the lifeboat had been rubbing against him, and had almost convinced himself that he was ready to confess to his crimes, when he heard quiet voices in the distance. He struggled onto one side to hear the content.

'...like we don't have enough to do without searching for little boy lost? My God, I'd...'

Tommy did not wait to listen to the rest of the conversation. His mind was churning. He sat motionless, waiting for the voices to either pass by, or hopefully disappear to the far end of the ship. Any thoughts that Edward Burrows may not have been missed were instantly dispelled, and thoughts of handing himself in, treated in the same manner.

Eventually the voices receded sufficiently, and Tommy relaxed, slightly, and settled back. His mind spun, as suddenly another voice brought him back to his senses

'Edward?' it whispered.

He sat still and listened, trying to make sense of it. Edward? Edward? Edward Burrows! It was for him.

'Edward?'

Tommy finally recognised the voice. Phillip. He had not expected any more company that night, but was relieved that it was only him. He hurriedly pushed aside the tarpaulin, and looked down. Phillip looked up proudly. Tommy put a finger to his lips, and shushed him to silence before he attracted the attention of everyone on board.

Phillip was taken aback at his offhandedness, and disappointedly stood back a pace.

Tommy, realising he had perhaps been a little too brusque with the young lad, quietly reconciled the situation with a swift apology.

'Let me in,' Phillip whispered.

Tommy recoiled slightly. He had not expected anyone else inside with him.

82

'But you've got a…'

A loud noise down the side of the ship, sounded dangerously like it might attract attention, so he carefully leant out of the lifeboat, and leaning down, heaved Phillip up and inside the lifeboat beside him.

The tarpaulin pulled across tight once more, Phillip sat in the dark beside him.

Tommy sighed, a little too loudly, and sounding ungrateful, and hoping that the young lad didn't take it to heart, he quickly turned it into a yawn.

'Sit down!' Tommy whispered. 'And don't move.'

Phillip sat back, awkwardly, and sitting upon something that did not seem as if it were meant to be there, carefully removed it, and held it out, in the event he might discover its identity in the dark.

'What's this?'

Tommy reached out blindly, and eventually got a hold on Phillip's offering, and realised at once that he had the package containing the canvas in his hands.

'It's - er -' he struggled to explain the canvas, before realising that it was dark, and as far as Phillip was concerned, it could be anything he chose it to be. 'It's something my dad gave me to bring with me,' and placing it to one side, quickly changed the subject. 'How did you manage to get away again?'

'I couldn't sleep. And I wanted to check you were okay.'

Tommy was genuinely touched. No one had said that to him for almost as long as he could remember.

'Thanks.'

Phillip was quiet for a moment, and Tommy was momentarily gagged.

'Why are you hiding in here?' Phillip said eventually.

'What?' Tommy had thought through a lot in the relatively short space of time he had been confined to the lifeboat. But he had not considered that he would ever be in the situation of explaining himself to an ally, much less someone much younger than himself.

'Why are you hiding?'

Tommy's mind was spinning. He was glad it was dark and that Phillip was unable to see the confusion that must have been written across his face. *Keep it simple.*

'I lost my papers at the station, and having lost half my family in a bombing raid,' he started - and suddenly it fell out of his mouth. 'I was settled on the journey to Canada, and it was so much easier for what was left of my family that I go. It would enable them to survive, and the loss of the papers would have jeopardised all that, and I didn't want to…'

'Wow!'

'Uh?'

'I said, Wow!' Phillip echoed his exclamation. 'You must have been really scared. Why didn't you tell anyone?'

'I couldn't… I mean, can't,' Tommy continued, unable to believe his alibi had been bought quite so easily. 'And I can't tell them, even now. I will be sent back on the first ship home otherwise. I just can't.'

'It'll be our secret then,' he offered. 'Just the two of us,' Phillip started, enjoying the scenario. 'Don't worry. I'll help you.'

'Fine! But please know, I am going to trust you with my life,' Tommy further emphasised their confidence. 'Can I trust you?'

'I won't let anyone know. I promise.'

Their eyes had slowly started to adjust to the dark, and they were now able to make out the other through the darkness. Phillip leant forward, and Tommy, keen to seal the deal and buy the boys friendship, spat into his palm, and offered it back. Phillip had never seen a deal sealed this way, but wrapped up in the moment, did likewise. They clasped hands, and the deal was done.

Catherine stirred in her bunk, and uncomfortable in her new surroundings, in the midst of all the other coughing and snoring bodies, turned and looked across to see if Phillip was still where he was supposed to be. She was still angry with him, but seeing him snuggled up, and now sorry for how she had behaved to him, thought she would check that he was tucked in properly for the night. She turned in her bunk and dropped her feet to the floor, shivering in her nightdress as the cold night air fought her bed-warm body. She considered jumping back into bed, and maybe apologising the next morning, but having gone this far. 'Well.'

She climbed up from the bunk, and in the semidarkness, crept her way across towards him. She crouched down, and taking hold of the loose cover, drew it across his body, snugly. She noticed the ease with which his body gave way, and puzzled, prodded him. Infuriated, she snatched back the bedclothes to reveal a scrunched up pillow.

'Right!'

She turned on a sixpence and within seconds was shaking Georgia violently from her slumber. Georgia opened her eyes, bewildered.

'Come with me,' she said in far more of an order than a request.

Georgia didn't have enough time to object as Catherine took off, and only just coming to her senses, thought it wiser to quickly follow her. Better that than leave her to her own devices, quite so far from home.

Georgia quickly caught up with Catherine at the exit to the dorm. She was stood alone, looking like a lost sheep, and jumped as Georgia tapped her on the shoulder.

'Just you wait till I get...'

'Sssh!' Georgia put a finger to her lips, begging her silence. 'And – er - why exactly are we stood out here?'

'Phillip has gone again. Oh!!! So help me, when I get hold of him this time, I am going to have him handcuffed to his bunk until we get to Canada.'

Georgia rubbed her shoulder, kindly. 'Follow me.'

Catherine grabbed at her hand - as much to show her appreciation as to calm her nerves - and nervously followed her off into the dark corridors ahead of them.

Georgia quietly led the way quietly through the dim alleyways outside their quarters.

She felt guilty that she might be letting Phillip down, but had also to placate Catherine. She didn't really know where she was going. Just the general direction.

'Dear Lord!' Catherine whispered. 'It's not enough we are on a boat, halfway across the Atlantic, do we really need all this trouble?'

Georgia was not sure whether she should point out that they probably weren't half way across the Atlantic, and indeed far from it, but decided discretion might be the better part of valour.

The two girls turned a corner, and stared into darkness.

A little more scared than they would ever admit to each other, they stopped.

'Lost, are we ladies?' a gentle voice asked from behind them.

They both screamed, and jumping into each other's arms, hugged, terrified, as a huge figure confronted them.

The two girls relaxed slightly as they realised it was just a member of the crew. They quickly explained to him, one talking over the top of the other, not wanting to get Phillip into trouble, that they were lost, and after a comforting word or two from their saviour, they were both safely escorted back to their quarters.

Catherine thanked the man as they entered the safety of their dormitory, and only then did she relax her grip on Georgia's hand. They both breathed a little easier, and made their way back to their bunks.

'When he gets back, so help me...!'

'Look!' Georgia pointed across at Phillip's bunk.

Catherine, exasperated, looked across, and...

'You little...' Catherine jumped.

It took all Georgia's energy and efforts to stop her throttling her brother, right there, and then.

Phillip lay in his bunk, scrunched up in a bundle of blankets. Fast asleep.

'We'll deal with the whole thing in the morning,' Georgia whispered, and only after blood had finally returned to Catherine's face, did she release her.

Tommy was now more relaxed, having seemingly cleared the air with Phillip. At least to the young lad's satisfaction, and through another series of lies, he had further added to the credentials of Edward Burrows. He now had a story that he was convinced would stand the test of time. Or at least for that of a ten year old boy.

For all that had gone well with Phillip, and despite his encouragement, Tommy was still no closer to handing himself in. He lay back stubbornly; sure he was settled for the night, when once more voices sounded nearby.

'Dear God!' he quietly spoke his thoughts . 'Air raids weren't this disturbing.'

He sat quietly and listened. One voice. *Phillip*? Surely not so soon? Then another. No! Neither voice belonged to Phillip. Of that, he was sure. He slowly crept to the edge of the lifeboat and pushed the tarpaulin back slightly and peered through the gap. He could see nothing, so his ears adjusted to compensate. Frighteningly, the only thing he could hear was the beating of his heart, hammering away inside his chest.

Suddenly the voices started to register.

From what he had heard, it was fairly clear that the search had not been called off after all. And worse than that, another one was currently under way. He tucked himself under the tarpaulin once more, and waited. If they were going to find him, they were going to have to search each and every lifeboat to do so.

As the voices faded slightly, Tommy figured he now had a little time on his side. Despite his bravado, if the search party did decide to search every lifeboat, one by one, then he had better make it that much harder for them. He hurriedly gathered together all the possessions he had accumulated at the open end of the lifeboat, and as quietly as possible, transferred them to the far end, hoping the darkness of the night, and the cover of the tarpaulin would help hide it all away.

'Check inside that!' one of the voices sounded.

Inside what? Tommy thought.

His mind was made up. Quickly.

The tarpaulin drew back relatively quietly, and Tommy slipped silently over the side. Landing on the deck below him, with what he thought was the sound of a cannon, he quickly tucked himself away until he could plan his next move.

The voices of the search party seemed to be some way off. He was sure there was only the one. Or at least, hoped there was. Tommy decided it best to set about repairing any damage or giveaway signs he might have made to the tarpaulin. Satisfied, he scampered across the deck and sheltered behind a nearby bulwark. He crouched down and clutched his knees to his chest, assuming that if he could not see out from behind his shelter, then by the same assumption, nobody would be able to see in.

It took what seemed to be a lifetime before the search party finally approached the area in which he was hidden away. Tommy had now been able to hear the two members of the search party clearly, and they had not stopped moaning about the extra duty weighed on top of the night watch for one moment. It was not clear exactly how long this particular pair had been searching, but as they strolled along Tommy's portion of the ship, their attention to detail was not especially astute. Their conversation was now more atoned to girls they had left behind, than exactly where he might be. He was pleased with this, but held his breath all the same as they approached.

Tommy watched, breathless, as they approached the lifeboat he now called home. They both had their backs to him, but seeing them no more than ten feet away, he pressed himself that little bit tighter into his confinement, and waited.

The older, and slightly stockier member of the search party walked over to the lifeboat and tugged at some of the fastenings on the tarpaulin, and Tommy held his breath as he found a slightly loosened rope. He seemed to concern himself with it for what seemed to Tommy to be about a week, but was in fact little more than a second or so, and he re-tied it without casting the irregularity anything more than a moment's thought. He had not even pulled back the cover, Tommy noticed, as he had done on some of the boats further down the deck. Either the boredom of the search, or the interest in his colleague's lady friend of the moment seemed to better suit his attention for the time being. And for Tommy, that was just fine.

They finally moved away from the lifeboat, and having searched as much of this portion of the ship as they thought it demanded, they started to walk away.

'So! What colour hair's she got then?'

Tommy never found out, and any more of her details were lost in their departure.

Tommy waited a long time before he even dared thinking of moving from where he was. The cold seemed to be the final deciding factor. As uncomfortable as it may have been inside the lifeboat, it was certainly sure to be warmer. If only - just.

Having reattached the rope on top of the tarpaulin, Tommy would now have to spend more time in the open than he ultimately wanted trying to unfasten the bindings again. He hoped the crewmember hadn't secured it too tightly as a punishment for it having come undone in the first place.

Tommy had struggled in the full light of day with the tarpaulin, and now it was pitch black. The thought of the ship listing on an errant wave was an added factor to take into account. If he were to fall overboard during the day, there was the possibility that he might just be seen, but at this time of night, it was sure to take his life. So, carefully struggling with the ropes on the tarpaulin from slightly safer position, he once more weighed up the options of handing himself in. Had it not been for the rope coming loose in his hand quite so easily, he just might have done so, but with the success he had just achieved, he thought he might stick around just a little bit longer.

After a few moments more dilly-dallying, Tommy finally managed to undo the binding, and with much relief, finally climbed back inside the lifeboat. He closed up the gap to the best of his ability and yawning, sat back quietly. He had not considered the amount of time that had passed during firstly the day - and now his midnight escapades - and he was now exhausted. He hoped he didn't fall into a deep sleep. He had to stay alert enough to be able to react to any untoward noise that might affect his safety, but the way he felt now, he wasn't sure if he would even be able to stay awake long enough to…

27

As dawn broke, and daylight spread across the horizon, the convoy had successfully steered its way through the stressful night, unscathed. The weather pattern had suddenly however taken a turn for the worse, and what had been a comfortable night, did not promise to continue for that much longer. The size of the waves had picked up considerably, and the shipping now fought its way through the angry sea. All hands had been brought to order.

Phillip raised his head and looked around the dormitory. The weather was taking its toll on the occupants by the second. The sound of moans filled the air. Various bodies moved in and out of the dorm, the deportees at pace, the returnees at a much slower, plodding rate, holding heavy heads in their hands. Miss Price was stood at the exit trying to offer support to the returning bodies, but she looked no better herself. She offered encouraging words, but as the ship rolled from side to side the enthusiasm in her support dwindled, until even she did not believe what she was saying.

Phillip observing the plague that had hit the ship, tried to drop his feet to the floor when the true reality of his own *mal de mer* hit home.

'Yes. That's right! You stay exactly where you are,' Catherine's voice surpassed any other noise in the ship. 'You are going nowhere, *mister*.'

The condition he was in, and a head that weighed about a ton, the thought of straying too far was far from advisable. He was upset though that his sister might think it was because she had said so. He turned to remonstrate, but as he looked across to Catherine, her face was a finer shade of green than he had ever seen, and he decided just for the moment he would spare her a remonstration. It could wait.

Georgia sat on the bunk beside Catherine, comforting her. She seemed fine, and looked almost as if she had spent her entire life on board a ship. Seeing Phillip's demise, she hopped down from the bunk, and walked across to see to him. Looking down at his demeanour, she put a hand across his forehead, checking his temperature.

'Hi Georgia,' he offered weakly.

'You'll be fine,' she assured him. 'If you need anything, I'll be over with ...' She did not need to complete the sentence, as Phillip's head had already sunk back into its pillow, and he was waving a very weary thumbs-up as a thank you.

Tommy was also awake. Though he felt like death warmed up, there was little he could do about it. Even if he had wanted to hand himself in, he would not have risked a journey across the deck in the current conditions. Rain fell heavily on top of the tarpaulin, and even if he had been able to make himself comfortable, the constant pitter-patter would not have allowed him any rest. His head ached, and as the ship continually rose and fell, he thought he would happily have swapped his place for a night back inside the bomb-shelter in his garden - during a blanket bombing raid. After the past night's antics, he was comfortable that any daylight search would be postponed until the weather took a turn for the better. The way the rain was throwing itself down, it did not look to be any time soon. Besides, Tommy was convinced by the time the weather brightened up, he was sure to be old news.

The only real downside to the conditions was that Phillip, his newly acquired friend and go-between, would be bedded-in below decks for the foreseeable future. It wasn't the food that he would miss. He had been dry retching most of the night, and even if he had managed to get anything inside him, he thought it far from likely that he would be able to keep it there. It was just that, with Phillip, he had a contact with the outside world. He wasn't alone.

Tommy wedged himself into a corner of the lifeboat, and piled every item Edward Burrows had had in his luggage on top of him, and decide to once more contemplate his future. He realised it was something that happened a lot, but the pros and cons of his future changed second by second, and it wasn't as if he had anything else to take it off his mind. There was ample room inside the lifeboat for his limited requirements, and the sacrifice of comfort was a penalty he had to bear for his liberty. He smiled through his sore head, thinking that in the event of any evacuation from the ship, were it to go down, he was in prime position.

His humour was momentary as the ship lurched once more, rocking the lifeboat viciously, and throwing Tommy to one side, smashed his shoulder into one of the wooden struts.

He winced, and cussed at the unexpected pain. He bit on his lip to stop him shouting out – as if his voice might not be swallowed up by the wind and rain – and fighting back tears, huddled up in a heap, and waited for the weather to abate.

28

Captain Browning stood at the bridge of H.M.S. Jackal. She was a 1,800-ton J-Class Destroyer and Matron of the Fleet. She was equipped with 6 main guns, and was fitted with 10 torpedo tubes for employment in anti-submarine work, and seemed perfectly at home in her role in convoy duty.

Browning, a tall lean, dark haired, man in his mid-forties, looked through his binoculars over the port side of the ship checking the state of the convoy in the inclement weather. Satisfied, he took them from his eyes and handed them across to his number one, Commander Robinson.

'Tell me, Number One? Any news on that runaway?'

'No, sir. He's either given everyone the slip, or he never got on board.'

'The real – er - chappie? He's safely at home, yes?'

'Yes, sir. We got confirmation yesterday.'

'Well whoever this other poor blighter is, we'll just have to hope he wasn't washed overboard. We can't turn back for him now. None of us.'

'Yes, sir.'

'Keep an eye out for me, John. I'm going to my cabin. I'd figure this weather should keep us safe for a while. Take over.'

'Yes, sir.'

'You have the bridge.'

Catherine, still sporting a grey face, had finally gathered enough energy to confront Phillip once more. She walked over to him and drew his attention away from a book he had absorbed himself in.

'Right! I want to know exactly where you went last night, *and* where you have hidden this runaway character.'

'Edward,' he corrected, looking over his reading glasses. 'You mean, Edward.'

'So!' Catherine jumped at her victory. 'You know his name. Where is he?'

'He told us all his name on the train. We have had his name rammed down our throats every ten minutes since we've been on board. Surely your memory hasn't gone completely. You've only been seasick you know.'

'Where were you last night?' she demanded.

'You saw me come back with Georgia,' he managed without any hesitation.

'Not then! Later!'

'I might have got up, I can't remember. Maybe I was sleepwalking.'

'I can't understand you. Why are you protecting him? I'm your sister. Why won't you tell me?'

Phillip didn't even do her the courtesy of looking up from his reading matter, but aware she wasn't in a hurry to go away, said, 'You're the colour of mother's emerald dress. Why don't you go and get something to eat? It might make you feel better.'

'Ohhhh!' she exhaled loudly, and stormed back to her bunk.

Georgia looked away, avoiding catching her eye, and feigned tidying up the bedclothes around her.

Catherine sat down angrily on her bunk, and turning her head up, looked to Georgia.

'And if I find out you are involved in any way whatsoever, I swear I shall never speak to you again.'

Georgia slunk back slightly, and as she looked across to Phillip, he crossed his eyes, pulling a face, and Georgia had to be very careful to avoid laughing out loud.

Tommy shifted. The pain in his shoulder, though not having disappeared completely, was a little better, and now having endured the worst of the weather, food was his main concern. He realised that his self-imposed captivity not only hindered his lifestyle, but also loaded a great deal more responsibility onto Phillip's shoulders. He would have the responsibility of fighting off all the chaperones and authorities on board, and battle against the elements, which appeared to change by the second.

Having survived this long, sea-sickness had both come, and gone. Boredom was his current dilemma. During daylight hours, an array of shouted orders passed to and fro, and still resigned not to spend the rest of the trip in a cell – *brig* – he had to content himself with varied peeks out of the top of the tarpaulin, if only for a change of scenery.

He had now thoroughly searched his way thoroughly through the errant Edward Burrows bag - and clothes within – and the best he had been able to come up with was a crumpled packet of cigarettes. And those were his anyway. He currently toyed with one of the contents.

Georgia smiled at Catherine's figure, curled up in her bunk as she passed her. She carefully tip-toed across to Phillip's bunk, and arriving at his side, quickly couched down. She took a peek back in Catherine's direction to ensure she had not awoken, and looked eagerly into Phillip's eyes.

'Well! What happened?' she asked him.

Phillip explained as much as he dared, excitedly, remembering his promise to Tommy, and apologised for getting her into trouble with Catherine. Georgia chuckled, enjoying the challenge.

'What are we going to do about feeding him?' Georgia asked.

'If he feels anything like I do, food will be the last thing on his mind.'

'I'll see if I can get some more bits put away for him.'

'Don't, Georgia!' Phillip scolded. 'You'll only end up feeling Catherine's wrath. Let me do it. She can beat me as much as she likes.' He beckoned her closer. 'She's not actually that strong.' They both giggled together.

'What are you two laughing at?' Catherine's voice boomed over their jollity.

'We were just discussing whether or not we should bother doing anything about getting some food.' Georgia hung on his words, wondering where he was going with this. 'We wondered if it was worth eating anything, if all we were going to do was bring it all up again later.'

Catherine, far from cured, held her hand up, begging him to cease his discussion.

'You both ought to eat something,' Georgia advised. 'You'll have nothing to fight any illness with otherwise.'

'I wasn't planning to contract anything,' Catherine informed her.

'Nonetheless. We all ought to eat something. Why don't we go and get some, if only for later. Do you want us to bring you something back?'

'No.'

Phillip and Georgia could not believe their luck. Given the green card to explore, they had to steady themselves to avoid it looking too obvious.

'No! We *should* eat,' Catherine said, instantly putting a damper on things. She stared at Phillip suspiciously, and her intent registered, looked across to Georgia. 'And don't think I'm not keeping an eye open on you, either, Georgia.'

The energy seemed to almost visibly drain from the pair, but as Phillip slumped, Georgia whispered, 'Don't worry. At least we can get some provisions.'

The food was no improvement over the previous night's meal. It was billed as scrambled egg, but it neither looked nor tasted like it had been any closer to a chicken than the stew from the previous evening had. The children however took what was on offer, along with a piece of bread.

'Just one,' a voice called, and a wooden spoon smacked the back of Phillip's hand as he grabbed at two pieces of bread, forcing him to drop both. He regained his composure, and looking to Georgia, winked, and then started to complain. As all attention was drawn to him, Georgia slipped two more portions of bread onto her platter, and leaving the battle behind her, quickly scampered away. Phillip, having watched Georgia's departure, now took his allocated piece of bread, and leaving Catherine behind apologising for him, quietly followed her.

Miss Price stood uneasily outside the washroom. A number of smaller children were about their ablutions, washing faces, combing hair and cleaning teeth. She ignored most of them as they walked past her wishing her the best, until she finally managed to catch the attention of one of the older children.

'I am looking for Catherine Belvoir,' she asked the bemused child.

'Never heard of her!' the youngster answered carelessly, and walked past her without so much as a moment's more consideration to the question.

It would have been much easier to have spoken to her inside the dorm, but she did not want to bother the younger pair. She stood looking blindly into the mass of children when she was knocked clean to one side by a couple of the children coming out, playfully fighting. Frustrated, and her propensity at forcing a smile even when she did not feel up to it, gone, she forcefully separated the two children, and pushed along them on their way.

As she looked up, she just happened to catch Catherine walking past. She had almost missed her entirely.

'Catherine,' she whispered, suspiciously, and as she looked up at her beckoning, indicated that she wanted a quiet word with her.

Catherine, despite her heavy head, obediently walked across.

Miss Price hurriedly checked to ensure Phillip and Georgia were not glued to her side, but in the melee around her, it appeared they had given her the slip. Or vice-versa. She gently took Catherine's hand, and led her to one side.

'I thought I had better have a word with you,' she said quietly. 'I didn't want Phillip to hear it from me.'

Catherine, intrigued, drew her away into a corner. The thought of an adult chat was most appealing, especially with many of those in their dormitory being so much younger than herself. She looked slightly concerned though at Phillip's mention, and also that Miss Price appeared worried.

'Edward Burrows.'

Catherine raised her eyebrows, biting on her tongue. 'Him.'

'I thought you ought to know exactly what was going on.'

'Miss Price, I have met this ruffian for about five minutes in my entire life, and it would appear to everyone else that he has become the most important person within it. If I never – ever - see him again, I promise you I will not lose one second of sleep over it. Please! Why would I want to know?'

'I just thought that young Phillip and he had some sort of affinity,' Miss Price suggested, apologetically, 'and that you being his sister…'

'I only hope that he hasn't caught nits off the rotten creature. I shall have Phillip disinfected as soon as I get the chance, don't worry.'

'He has completely disappeared.'

'And?'

'And he may have been washed overboard.'

Catherine was about to cast aside what Miss Price had said, but was suddenly stuck for words. With the ship tossing and turning, it was not a nice thought that anyone should be lost in the sea in any weather, let alone the current turbulence.

'Look! I'm sorry, but there is nothing I can do,' she said, finally finding her tongue. 'I haven't seen him since the train, and Phillip swears he hasn't seen him either.'

'They say he might not even have boarded,' she continued.

'Is there a problem there, Miss Price?' a voice boomed from the far end of the corridor.

'No!' she answered, hurriedly, and then turned her attention back to Catherine. 'Look! I just thought I'd keep you up to date, and that maybe you could stop your brother from overly fretting. I don't need another of our number going missing.'

'I will tell Phillip,' she said, but noting the upset on Miss Price's face, added, 'Look! You're right. He probably never even boarded.'

Catherine finally caught up with Phillip and Georgia at their bunks, no small amount of time having passed since they had been separated at the washhouse. Catherine, though full of Miss Price's news, was still angry with Phillip, and she was gradually becoming more and more suspicious about Georgia.

'Yes?' Phillip asked.

'What are you two up to,' she demanded. 'You're as thick as thieves.'

Georgia looked to Phillip helplessly, but he valiantly saved the moment. 'Nothing at all. We just don't want to get under your feet.'

'Under my feet,' she said, gesticulating to the cramped conditions of the dormitory. 'You could be on another deck and still be under my feet. Anyway! Don't change the subject. I want to know what the pair of you are up to?'

'Nothing. We're just worried about Edward,' Georgia said. 'We know you two didn't get along, but …'

'Yeah! You didn't even give him a chance.'

'Whether I liked him or not is neither of your concerns,' Catherine snapped back. 'Anyway! That is what I wanted to talk to you both about. Miss Price thinks he may have been washed overboard.' Phillip and Georgia stared at each other, awestruck. 'Or maybe he didn't even get on board,' she added quickly, noting how abrupt she may have been.

Phillip let out a sigh, which Georgia caught. It was clear that nobody knew anything about Edward Burrows. It was all assumption.

'Well then, there's nothing to worry about,' Phillip said, perhaps a little too lightly.

'But we'll keep an eye out, just in case,' Georgia added.

'Yeah! Right!'

Catherine did not miss the teamwork between the two, but unable to pin anything of substance to it, opted to leave it for the time being. She decided it best to keep an eye on the pair of them from a distance, and still smarting slightly, she walked away.

'Phew!' Phillip sighed.

'What was that?' Catherine.

'Nothing. Just… Phew!'

Catherine was ready to launch into the pair of them, but suddenly a thought of something her mother used to say leapt into her head. *Softly, softly - catchy monkey.*

'Fine!' she said confidently, and smiling, smugly, walked away.

29

The weather had cleared slightly, and as the rocking of the boat changed from a port to starboard swell to a stem to stern motion, Tommy's equilibrium was suddenly all about face. He had no horizon on which to set his eyes, and the sea-sickness that had seemed to disappear, was ready to pay another visit. Tommy scrunched himself up inside the blanket Phillip had managed to bring him the night before, and looked first through one opening in the tarpaulin towards the deck of the ship, and then to the other, out towards the open sea. The only change in the seascape was the occasional change of positions in the convoy of ships alongside. He had thought this might help entertain his longer periods of boredom, but after his initial observations at the new ships, their shapes and sizes, and counting their numbers, it too had become boring. He needed company. He needed Phillip.

Tommy yawned, and still bored, thought getting his head down in the slightly less violent conditions might better suit him after all this time.

All this time! he laughed, sadly. He had been aboard ship for barely more than a day.

Phillip was frantic, trying to get away to check on his new friend, and partner in crime. His frequent looks across to Georgia were little assisted by her casual, careless looks away, so as not to attract Catherine's attention. He could only guess at what she was thinking.

Georgia felt guilty enough as it was. Though she had been a maid in the Belvoir household, she and Catherine had always been that much closer. It wasn't that she didn't worship Phillip. She did. It was just a girl thing. Hiding a secret from her was not only a moral dilemma, it was difficult. Catherine had the knack of reading her like a book. She was going to have to be most careful. She shifted in her bunk, and turning slightly, leant against an uncomfortable lump in her cot. It was the bread she had managed to conceal for Phillip's new friend. She looked over in Phillip's direction, and as he winked back at her, her affinity shifted back in his direction once more. Dealing with Catherine, if she found out, would be an ordeal she would not look forward to at all. But that could wait for now. So! Down to business.

In the background, a small group of children were singing quietly. Georgia suddenly found herself humming along with them as Catherine jumped off her bunk and stood beside her.

'I'm bored,' she said.

'Do you want me to brush your hair?'

'No. I'm even more bored than that.'

'Oh! I'm sorry then.'

'Oh Georgia! I'm so sorry. I didn't mean that. It's just I'm homesick. I miss mother and our chats.'

'I do too.'

'Your mother! Of course! I'm so sorry Georgia. I forget that we're all in this together. I love you, you know I do. It's just I miss talking with someone... my own age.'

'It's okay. Why don't you go and chat to some of the other older children?'

'I can't bear being away from home and my friends there. I don't want to get to know - any of these. We'll all be split up again in Canada again and I shall only miss them as well.'

Georgia watched as her gaze wandered over to Miss Price. She had noticed how well they had appeared to be getting on. Miss Price was only young in comparison to the other chaperones, and must have felt as out of place as they did. She was sat her own on her bunk, writing what appeared to be a letter.

'Go on,' Georgia said. 'Go and have a chat with her.'

'What?'

Georgia explained the plight she had imagined Miss Price must be going through, and Catherine agreed that she should go and comfort her.

Georgia watched her walk across and allowed her to settle down next to Miss Price. She resisted the temptation to do anything too soon, - so as not to attract Catherine's attention from afar – and to ensure she didn't double back – and waited until she finally observed the pair, thoroughly engrossed in conversation.

'Now!' she thought. She nearly charged across, and hurriedly handed her package across. 'Be very careful, and go. Now!'

Phillip jumped at the chance, and was gone without so much as a backwards glance.

Tommy had been totally astounded that Phillip had made the pilgrimage to his dwelling in the current conditions, and gratefully accepted the parcel. Though it seemed ungrateful, and knowing that he wouldn't realise he meant it was only for his safety, he demanded Phillip go straight back inside. Phillip looked back despondently, but Tommy quickly indicated it was far too dangerous for him, *and* being daylight, they might both get caught.

As the ship shifted violently, Phillip comprehended what he was trying to tell him, and turned to go. As he did so, he stepped backwards into a large pool of water that had gathered, and losing his grip on the deck, slipped. Losing his footing, he fell clumsily into a heap.

Tommy leaped towards the side of the lifeboat, and on instinct, was about to jump down to help him. But he had no need. Phillip was nimble, and barely acknowledging the fall, quickly regained his feet. He fully regained his balance and, adjusting to the sway of the ship, offered his trademark 'thumbs up', and once more, took off.

Tommy's unnecessary efforts at an attempt to rescue Phillip had not come without a price. As he had leapt across the boat, he had smashed into another of its struts, and collapsing backwards, he had struck his head. He lay back, mildly concussed, and did all he could to stop himself passing out. It was some minutes before he was able to fully recover his senses, but after a swift examination, no lasting damage appeared to have been done. He shook his head to try to fully clear it, and convinced he was over the worst of it, he lay back and looked down at the prize in his hands. He had a food parcel.

Phillip turned the corner and walked straight into Georgia who had a blanket ready to wrap around him. She quickly rubbed the effects of the sea spray off him. He shivered and gave a nod at her enquiring face, confirming that the job was done. They smiled at the other inquisitive faces passing them, but as they approached the entrance to the dormitory, their smiles dropped, leaving them deadpan. Catherine stood with her arms folded; her head leant on the doorframe, smirking at finally having caught them in the act.

Phillip and Georgia slumped on a bunk and Catherine stood threateningly in front of them. Despite their predicament, neither of the two appeared to be overly remorseful.

'Where is he?' Catherine demanded.

Phillip shrugged.

'Come on. Where is he? You're both in this up to your necks.'

'He isn't anywhere,' Phillip replied. 'I just wanted to make sure he wasn't on board.'

'We just want to make sure,' Georgia helped him out. 'You wouldn't want to think he was stuck anywhere. We just thought we'd take a look.'

'If he was anywhere onboard the ship in this weather, he would be back down here by now. Only an idiot would be out there in this weather. So talk!'

'It's your fault,' Phillip bleated. 'You told us he might have been washed overboard.'

'And unlike anyone else on board, we just wanted to make sure,' Georgia added.

'That he had been?'

'That he hadn't.'

'Whatever!'

'If he was on board and had anything about him, he would have been down here by now. So pack it in the pair of you. One way or the other, he's gone. So get used to it. And *whatever* you do now, I will be watching you.'

Phillip pulled a face, but was careful to ensure his sister did not catch it.

'And you!' Catherine aimed at Georgia. 'I am so disappointed.'

Georgia hung her head slightly.

Phillip was so furious that Catherine might use her spurious friendship with Georgia to bully her into some form of submission, that he was about to jump up and tell her so. Luckily, Georgia had predicted his actions, and as he leant forward, she firmly grabbed his lose shirt, keeping him pinned where he was.

Phillip sat back, resigned to having to allow Catherine her moment.

As darkness drew in, Tommy, aching all over, both mentally and physically, had finally had enough. The weather had not got any worse, and though he ultimately risked discovery, he decided it was time to get out of the lifeboat. If only to stretch his legs, and get some fresh air. The air inside the lifeboat seemed now to have become somewhat stagnant, and he needed to do something about it. He fiddled with the bindings holding the tarpaulin in place, and only half-concerned, checking to ensure there was no one around, carefully squeezed up through the gap created. He jumped down to the deck, and landed awkwardly in a heap as his muscles tried to rid themselves of some of the knots they had accrued. He carefully looked around in the gloom, but nobody seemed to have noticed his presence. If they had, they did not seem to have raised any unnecessary alarm. His entire body ached from having been scrunched up for so long, and he inadvertently stretched his body, trying to get at least some feeling back into his limbs.

Just as he was beginning to feel himself once more, there was the sound of an unusual noise nearby. He quickly tucked himself back in the darkness beneath the lifeboat.

The noise turned out to be harmless, and Tommy, standing up once more, felt like a man at liberty. Electing to remain a free man, however, the deck was to be his only paradise. He looked along the deck in the direction in which Phillip had disappeared earlier on, and considered the benefits of turning himself in. But liberty was liberty. He was currently his own boss, and as long as Phillip could keep him supplied with food, and he could find something to drink, he was going to be fine.

Phillip was so perplexed that Catherine seemed to have won and was now keeping both he and Georgia under her watchful eye that he was unable to sleep. The moans, the groans, the coughs and snuffles in the dormitory did nothing to aid his attempts at slumber. He hung slightly from his bunk, and looked across at Catherine. She appeared to be fast asleep - as he would have been - under normal circumstances. *She wasn't an owl*, he thought. He watched her for some time however to check she was not feigning, and then moved, making as if to get out of bed. She still did not appear to stir. He swung his body round, and vigilantly dropped his legs to the floor. Still mindful of his sister, and her propensity to wake on the dropping of a pin, he slipped silently into his shoes. He waited a moment, and then started to walk towards the exit. He glanced over his shoulder, looking back at her, but still nothing.

He reached the hatch which served as a door, and slunk through, and waited. Still nothing.

Finally convinced he had outwitted her, Phillip paused. *No!* He was still not convinced. His sister was ruthless, and he wasn't sure she did not possess special powers, so, and if only just for the sake of it, he decided to take one final look. He turned his head around the corner, and instantly leaped back. Georgia was stood directly in front of him. She managed to put a hand to Phillip's mouth to stop him shouting out, and putting a finger to her lips, begged him not to give them both away.

Phillip somehow recovered his breath, without shouting out, and surely waking the rest of the ship.

'What are you doing?' he whispered.

'The same as you.'

'But what about…'

'She's away with the fairies. Even Catherine can't live without any sleep.'

Phillip pulled a disbelieving face, and they both had to hold in a laugh. They stopped, and ensuring that she really wasn't an owl, they curled the necks back inside the dorm to check she really wasn't immortal.

'Okay! Let's go,' Phillip said, and grabbing Georgia's hand, led her away.

Catherine's eyes opened wide, and she immediately leapt from her bunk. Now she had them. Both!

Despite the change for the better in the weather, as they made their way up to the deck, Georgia and Phillip hugged together for warmth against the general chill of the night. Or was it just the thrill of breaking the rules together? Either way, they remained huddled together as they ventured onwards. They constantly checked behind them from fear of discovery. Miss Price wouldn't take too long to put two and two together and work out exactly what was going on. And then of course, and far worse an adversary, there was Catherine.

Catherine did not consider herself the world's greatest sleuth, but this 'cloak and dagger' stuff, pursuing her brother and Georgia, was a lot easier than she had thought it was going to be. She wondered if they really thought she could have been so stupid as to think they weren't up to something. She kept a fair distance behind the two, and the more space she gave them, the more confident they became, and the clumsier and noisier they had seemed to become. She finally reached the deck, and drawing her nightclothes around her, followed them outside into the cold.

Phillip led Georgia along the deck, vigilantly tucking into every nook and cranny to avoid detection from the presumed, if scanty, night-watch. Any unexpected noise - and not frequent sea goers, there were plenty - they quickly scurried back into shelter, or at worse, turned round until they found somewhere safe, and waited out the offender. To all but Catherine - and the chaperones - they were only children, and at worst, could comfortably claim to be lost. But it didn't hurt to be cautious.

Tommy was not expecting any visitors till well into the next day at the earliest, and had settled down to sleep. The sway of the lifeboat did little to wake him, having survived the swell of the sea during the earlier bad weather. He simply cuddled up that little bit more.

'Edward! Edward!' he could hear in his dreams. Or was it? Once more, the name, *Edward*! The name meant nothing to him and his mind churned.

'Edward!' Once more. *Edward who*?

Edward Burrows. Tommy opened his eyes, as if reacting to a nightmare, and there was a tapping on the side of the boat. He juddered, suddenly wide-awake. He recognised Phillip's voice, and reached across to answer him, with a sharp, 'Ssshh!'

Phillip was worried as Tommy pulled back the tarpaulin and stared, angrily, at seeing Georgia stood there with him. Tommy quickly ducked back inside the lifeboat. Phillip looked apologetically at Georgia, trying to excuse Tommy's reaction to her.

Tommy was furious. He had no ill feeling towards Georgia, and had indeed found her fun, but his problem was that now, someone else knew. How long before his sister found out? He liked her a great deal, but from any initial contact he had had with her, he was certain that she would turn him in, and in an instant.

He shook his head angrily, not wanting it to be true, but purely for safety's sake, he could not allow Phillip to continue calling his name. He pulled back at the tarpaulin to silence him.

They seemed to have disappeared, but were in fact only crouched down beside the boat to keep out of sight. As he dipped back inside, he suddenly heard a girl's voice. Georgia started quietly apologising for Phillip.

'It's not his fault,' she pleaded, then realising quite how sad she sounded, decided to stick up for herself. 'And just for the heck of it, where exactly do you think your extra rations come from?'

'All right,' Tommy said sharply. 'Just keep it down. The pair of you.'

From her restricted viewpoint, Catherine could still see both Phillip, and Georgia. She had not seen Tommy, but it did not take Sherlock Holmes to work out what was going on. Despite being outraged at their deception, the urge to rush to inform a member of the crew was stemmed simply by the fact that she wanted them to know she had caught them, and ultimately, would not be allowed to be there at the climax. And much more, she wanted to see the guilty look on their faces. It could wait until morning, but catching them in the act was far too good a chance to miss.

She watched them both crouched down beside the boat, and decided their faces looking up at her would be a picture. She crept down to avoid giving her presence away too soon, and finally, judging her moment to perfection, stood just behind them and coughed.

The moon lent ample light to capture the look on their faces. Catherine gloated as she glared down at them.

'Gotcha!'

30

Tommy, having slunk back inside the boat had not seen any of this. The first he knew of anything was when he heard Phillip, apologising profusely. He raised his eyebrows, already having forgiven him, but the talking didn't stop.

'Ssshh!!!' he hissed, quietly.

It must have been too quiet, as just as he was about to repeat the admonishment, he heard the name, Catherine!

'Ssshh!!!' he repeated, opening the vent once more.

'Ssshh, yourself!' Catherine snapped back, angrily.

'I'm sorry,' Phillip pleaded.

'Sorry, nothing!' Catherine gloated.

'Not you! Edward!'

'Ah ha! Not washed overboard, then?'

'Just tell her to shut the hell up!' Tommy said, as quietly as he could without raising any undue alarm.

Catherine froze. She had never been spoken to in such a manner for as long as she could remember. Phillip could barely stop laughing out loud at the sight of his sister's face. She was about to yell something back as Georgia grabbed her roughly, and pulled her to the floor beside them.

'Please don't!'

Tommy poked his head out through the tarpaulin, and tried to make out the trio in the darkness. They stood slowly, and it was probably best that the look on Catherine's face was disguised by the dark. She was just about to say something when there was a sharp noise behind them. Phillip and Georgia shot to the ground, and much to her disbelief, Catherine found herself following them. Tommy had instinctively taken shelter inside his cavern once more.

After a few moments it was clear that the noise appeared to have had no substance, and slowly they rose again.

'It's okay,' Phillip whispered.

Tommy reappeared and looked down, catching Catherine rising. He smiled, but it was missed.

'Look at the danger you're putting us through,' Catherine whispered angrily, indicating the three of them, cowering, trying to stay out of sight.

'Then why are you whispering,' Tommy taunted her.

'Because…'

'Because you're angry that you didn't know anything about it,' he said. 'Your brother is way more caring than you could ever be.'

Georgia, sensing a head-on collision, urged them to calm down and to be quiet.

'Ohhhh!' Catherine growled, and was about to rush off.

'No, don't. I'm sorry!' Tommy quickly apologised, stopping her. She turned and looked back in the direction of his voice.

'I don't know why I'm not stood in front of the Captain of this ship right now,' she said. 'You have caused us all nothing but trouble since you came aboard this ship. Just give me one good reason why shouldn't I turn you in?'

'Because…' Tommy started.

All of a sudden an alarm sounded. It was like nothing they had heard before, and ear-splitting in its velocity. And whereas they had imagined themselves to be alone, numerous naval bodies seemed suddenly to appear out of nowhere. Naval personnel of all ranks quickly rushed across the decks. One in particular, without any thought as to why they might be there, collected the three visible bodies in a wide swipe, and hurriedly ushered them below-decks. A large metal door slammed behind them, leaving a distressed Tommy, sheltering helplessly inside the lifeboat.

In the sky, above the convoy, an aircraft circled overhead.

The shipping in the convoy woke as if from a deep sleep and the crews, caught unawares, quickly came to battle stations.

Tommy watched bewildered from his hiding place as the Destroyers sprang into life, ferrying into a preordained, flanking manoeuvre. He was more in awe of what was happening than scared for his life as he perhaps should have been. He had long ago given up hope of getting below decks as all the doors on the ship had audibly slammed shut. He realised he would now never be heard anyway.

Guns on the Destroyers started to open up, united with guns from the other armed vessels in the convoy, and the sky was suddenly alight.

Tommy could not see what they were firing at, and he held his hands over his ears as the noise of the guns filled the air. He suddenly realised how defenceless he had become, and exactly how close to the elements he was. He curled up into the bottom of the boat, and cried.

Inside the dormitories, children both screamed and cheered at the noise at the ensuing hunt for the aircraft. The chaperones, attempting to hide their own fear, tried their best to keep order, and chivvy the children, ensuring them that everything was going to be alright. Their task was not an envious one. Many of the children were charging around trying to get a view through an available porthole, while others huddled together, terrified.

Catherine, Georgia and Phillip had been thrown back into their quarters, and a door had slammed behind them. Catherine and Georgia were looking around frantically, wondering what they should be doing. Phillip was stood at the door trying to open it and get out again. Catherine realised what he was trying to do, and rushing across, grabbed him and started to drag him away. He yelled '*Edward,*' time and time again and tried to break from her hold, but somehow she managed to haul him back to her bunk, where finally, the three of them huddled together in fear.

Finally breaking from his sister and Georgia, Phillip rushed across to a porthole where one of the other evacuees peered through, excitedly. He unceremoniously hurled the child out of the way, and yelled out Tommy's name repeatedly, in the event that he might be heard amongst the noise of the guns and the screaming children around him. Suddenly, aware that his actions were senseless, he turned and walked slowly across, and sat down on his bunk. He sat there, white as a sheet. Catherine walked over, and drew him to her, gently rubbing his back.

'He's going to be killed,' Phillip yelled in her ear.

'He'll be fine,' she assured him, somewhat uncertainly. 'He'll be fine.'

The noise of the guns slowly subsided as the aircraft flew off. The alarms slowly died, and the hysteria eventually started to die down. Miss Price had eventually grabbed hold of Catherine and begged her assistance in trying to help with the little ones. She patted Phillip on the head, and taking a quick look into his face, and noticing that he was more or less settled, hurriedly moved on to her next cause.

Phillip, watching Catherine, now otherwise engaged, decided to try to get away again. This time it was Georgia, who, stepping in front of him, tried to keep him in place. She was not that much bigger than Phillip, but one look into her soulful and engaging eyes was easily strong enough to quell him for a while. She was his ally.

'We won't be let out again, tonight,' Georgia insisted. 'But it's all over now. Don't worry.'

'But what if he's trying to get back in?'

'There are enough people out there now. If he wants to be found, he will be. If he has managed to avoid discovery through all this, then he'll be fine.'

Tommy was all cried out. He lay in a heap in the bottom of the boat, his energy drained. He breathed deeply, his chest heaving in and out. The noise of the guns had ceased, and apparent quiet had been restored. He listened to various shouted orders outside the lifeboat, but even if he had wanted to hand himself in, he couldn't. He was exhausted.

Order had been restored amongst most of the children below decks, and as the melee had slowly been sorted out, groups were quietly ushered back to their bunks. Catherine had enjoyed the enforced responsibility, and finally, though somewhat exhausted from her efforts, made her way back to her bunk.

Georgia was waiting for her, alone. Catherine looked quickly to the doorway but saw it was still barred. Georgia indicated Phillip's bunk. He lay sprawled out crudely covered in bedclothes. She looked back to Georgia.

'Is he asleep, or is this another one of your ruses?' she asked.

'He's asleep,' Georgia confirmed, and just the look on her face guaranteed her words.

Catherine slumped onto her bunk, swept her feet up, and before she could think of anything else, was asleep.

Georgia, a little shaky herself, looked to her charges. Seeing them both asleep, she sniffed, bravely, lonely, and covering herself up, decided it best to follow suit.

31

Able Seaman George Willis lowered his binoculars, and flicking ash from the cigarette he had secluded in a cupped hand, exhaled the smoke from his mouth.

'Brrrr!' he shivered against the cold night air. Drawing once more on his cigarette, he shook his head. 'We're sitting targets. Sitting targets I tell you.'

'Cheer up, George! It could be much worse.'

'Sat out here on a destroyer, deep into the night, waiting for a wolf-pack to descend upon us? You tell me what could possibly be worse?'

'You could have your missus here with you.'

'Worse?' he mumbled. 'There's not a U-Boat Commander anywhere on this planet that is brave enough to take on my missus.'

'So why all the gloom?'

'Because they're out there somewhere,' he answered. He stubbed out what was left of his smoke, and placing the glasses to his eyes, looked out once more.

Tommy was now awake, and sat up. He rocked to and fro with the movement of the boat and waited. There had already been plenty of action about deck that morning. He was waiting, half dreading, half hoping, in a strange way, imminent discovery. Had Phillip panicked overnight and revealed his whereabouts. Would anyone really have listened to him in all the excitement, anyway? He shut his eyes, rocking back and forth once more.

The dormitories were awake, though unlike Tommy, the excitement of the previous night had not died down, and animated groups had formed, each with their own version of what they imagined had happened. Boys careered up and down the aisles, in and out of the various cabins, mimicking diving planes while others lay back emulating the ships guns. The chaperones had lost any form of rational control for the moment, and shouted desperately, trying their hardest to restore some form of order.

Phillip sat on Catherine's bunk with an enthusiastic Georgia by his side, and for what had seemed like the hundredth time that morning, retold Tommy's story. Catherine, thoroughly sick of the whole thing, had risen on several occasions to put an end to the matter and report his whereabouts. But both Phillip, and a much frowned upon Georgia, had begged her to listen to their protestations.

Catherine sat, turning the whole thing over in her mind.

'Please, sis!' Phillip pleaded. 'What has he done to you?'

'Please!' Georgia echoed his petition for clemency.

'Georgia!' Catherine snapped lightly. 'I've not finished with you yet as it is! Do not push it.'

'Sorry!' Georgia said, dipping her head, guiltily.

'And don't do that. You can't win back my friendship with your puppy dog look.'

'I can't?' she whimpered.

'All right! You can. But I am still very angry with you.'

Georgia smiled triumphantly.

'And Edward?' Phillip asked, trying to gain from the light-hearted reprise.

'Don't even go there,' she rebuked.

'But...'

Catherine fell silent, the jocularity gone. She was silent for a moment, and then nodded slowly. Phillip and Georgia looked at her wide-eyed.

'Okay!' she said.

'Yes!' Phillip and Georgia hugged each other.

'Oh no! Not just yes. There are conditions.'

'Conditions?'

'Yes! Conditions.'

Phillip and Georgia looked at each other, suddenly worried.

'He can stay where he is, and I won't give him away, but...'

'But?'

'But the second we get to Canada, he's on his own, and we never knew anything about him. Agreed?'

More exchanged glances.

'Agreed?' Once more.

'Agreed!' Phillip confirmed for them both.

'And you, Georgia. You can do what you please, but I can't say I'm not disappointed.'

'I'm so sorry.'

'Not that you knew, but that you didn't think for one second that I would want to know about it.'

'But...' Phillip started to protest.

'Butts are for Billy Goats,' Catherine said. 'Anyway! You are both free to do what you want, but if you get caught, I want it known that I never wanted anything to do with it in the first place. You hear me?'

Phillip smirked.

'Do you hear?'

'Yes.'

'Yes, what?'

'Yes, *Miss,*' Phillip emphasised, and moved just in time to avoid a clip round the ear.

Tommy was still sat gloomily, when he heard Phillip's voice trying to attract his attention.

'Is he still in there?' Georgia asked, worried.

The general commotion that had been prevalent earlier on had died down, and having sat in silence for a while he realised he was safe. He came out of his self-imposed gloom, and answered them, gloomily. 'I'm still here.'

'You're okay,' Phillip said, excitedly. 'And guess what? Catherine! She's not going to turn you in.'

Tommy was silent for a moment, not sure if he was relieved, or still harbouring a suspicion of her talking to the authorities now that Phillip and Georgia were out of the way.

'And I'm going to help, too,' Georgia said, excitedly.

Tommy had not turned somersaults at the news either mentally or physically, even if his confines restricted his ability to do so. He pondered the news.

'Well?' Phillip asked, somewhat disappointed at his reaction.

'Fine,' Tommy replied eventually.

'Fine?' Georgia exclaimed, quickly circling to ensure no one could make out that she was rebuking a lifeboat. She immediately dropped her voice. 'We've just sold our souls to keep your existence a secret, and all you can say is fine?'

There was another silence, and then Tommy said, 'Is - *she* - in any way related to Catherine by any chance?'

Phillip laughed, and Georgia scowled.

'What are you two up to?' a voice boomed from further down the deck.

Phillip and Georgia were frozen to the spot, like mice caught stealing the cheese. Georgia was the first to react, and nudged Phillip.

'Follow me,' she said, and as Phillip followed her blindly, she walked to the balustrade, and leaning over the top, started to heave energetically, coughing and spewing.

Whether she could have made a better job of it if she really had been suffering from sea-sickness, was arguable. Phillip caught on quickly, and rushed to her side, feigning interest in her welfare.

Tommy sat back, listening to the charade playing itself out, not sure whether or not to be worried. He listened as the owner of the booming voice arrived.

'What are you two up to?' he asked in a totally different tone of voice, as he saw Georgia's predicament.

'She needed some air, sir,' Phillip piped up.

'And you were going to go out in one of our lifeboats to get it, were you?' he laughed.

Tommy, unable to see any of the proceedings, stopped breathing again, wondering how the pair of them were planning to get out of this. He wondered if he was ever going to be able to breathe freely again.

'Yes!' Georgia joined his laugh, majestically wiping at her mouth, and nudged Phillip, who had been struck dumb at the mention of the lifeboat. He eventually caught on, and laughed.

'Well, I think you'd better get below decks, don't you?'

'I do now,' Georgia shook her head, playing her part out in full.

'Yes!' Phillip agreed. 'Why don't we do that?'

The crewmember, started to lead them away.

106

Phillip straggled slightly behind the two, and managed to say, 'We'll come back when we can,' just before Georgia awkwardly ushered him to catch them up.

'What's that?' the crewman asked, seeing Phillip's mouth moving.

'I... I said, wait for me,' he said, and rushed to join them.

Tommy had sat motionless listening to what was happening outside the lifeboat. Though sure his luck was due to run out soon, he had rather wanted it to be at his doing. But it hadn't happened, thanks mainly to Phillip, and from what he could make out, the quick thinking of Georgia. He had at this moment expected to be stood in front of the Captain, explaining himself. He smiled. Having survived the previous night – Catherine especially – and along with the latest incident, he wasn't so sure someone might just not be looking down at him in a favourable light.

'Or even up at him,' he thought. He would currently take his luck from either of the firmaments. He knew however that he would be on his own again for a while. He was sure Phillip and Georgia had been seen off, and wouldn't be back for a while.

The canteen was full and children pushed and shoved each other, keen to get their share of the food first, hoping that whatever it was, was sure to be better hot.

Phillip, Catherine and Georgia hustled for their places in line. Miss Price stood behind them, timidly. As the voices of the older chaperones barked orders amongst the hoard, her own approach at calmly asking them all to stay in line were quickly swallowed up. She raised her eyebrows and sighed.

'Put that down,' a younger voice bellowed from beside her. It was Catherine. She smiled across at Miss Price, and somehow, between the two of them, a certain amount of order was restored.

Phillip and Georgia took any food they could get hold of, thinking hard as how best to obtain an extra supply for Tommy.

'It's not stealing!' Phillip said, as much for his own sake as Georgia's. 'Edward's food has been catered for. If he was here now, food would be provided for him.'

He wasn't sure Georgia was totally convinced, but she didn't say anything, and helped him hide away the rations they had managed to acquire.

They hastily shielded their antics as Catherine walked past with Miss Price. They looked up guiltily as they caught Catherine's eye. Miss Price ignored them and walked past, closely followed by Catherine. But as she reached them, and looked down in an apparently pious manner, she hurriedly pulled out a lump of bread, and threw it in their direction. They looked up, amazed, as she smiled and winked before walking away.

Phillip's smile should have lit up the entire dorm. He and Georgia reshuffled the bread and a mug containing a portion of the stodgy stew mix, and wrapped them up in yet another blanket they had managed to purloin.

Catherine sat next to Miss Price at a table surveying the rest of the children's quarters.

'Thank you for that, back there,' Miss Price said.

'What?'

'The misbehaving children and all. You seemed quite natural.'

'Not at all. I've got a younger brother, and that kind of prepares you, you know!'

'Oh! Yes!' She stopped and was quiet, contemplating saying anything further.

'What is it?'

'Oh, nothing!'

'Is this your - real job?' Catherine asked her, gently. 'I mean - you don't seem to be... I mean...'

'No. You're right. I was signed up to work for the Air Ministry, and I sort of fell out with my superiors.'

Catherine did not think it wise to mention her father's position, and smiled, waiting for her to continue.

'A sort of clash of personalities,' she continued. 'And they wouldn't listen to me, so I was sequestered into this branch of work as some sort of punishment.'

'I did wonder,' Catherine laughed. 'The other - ladies - look to be about two hundred years old, and you, well... You're hardly older that much older than me. And you're so pretty'

'Thank you.' Miss Price smiled, shyly, letting out a huge sigh. 'Oh!!! What a day!'

As Miss Price removed the rigid backbone the other chaperones seemed to have been born with, she and Catherine started to talk. Forgetting her official duties for the moment, she chatted the time away, letting all her worries wash over her. They looked like sisters who had met up after years apart. It was a good break for Catherine too. She felt grown up, and they both quickly forgot their worries, and it was indeed only when a cry from one of the children brought them out of their revelries, that Miss Price once more donned her authoritative hat. With a pat on Catherine's shoulder, she quickly excused herself, and set out to put the problem right.

It was well into dusk before Phillip and Georgia finally felt it safe to venture upstairs once more. The decks had been unusually busy all day, due mainly to the slightly better weather conditions. They thought they had better get on with it, as after the events of the previous night, they imagined security was going to be much stricter. Certainly, tonight.

Catherine, watching what they were up to from her bunk, sternly mouthed the words, '*Be careful,*' as they set off.

They had somehow managed to gather together a good quantity of bedding and other items to transport to the lifeboat. Any chances of having got it aboard in daylight would have been fruitless, and would certainly have brought about Tommy's fate. Indeed, for all the clutter they had gathered together, they were lucky only to be questioned once as to their intentions. Georgia had answered that they were the dirty bedclothes that belonged to a particularly seasick boy from their dormitory, and, hedging her bets, was just about to open the clothes to reveal the proof, when she was assured she was probably the best one to deal with it, and ushered along.

They managed safely to get to the deck, and happy with the excuse they had tried and tested, decided they would stick with it if questioned again.

They dodged their way along the deck, and after a series of careful manoeuvres and much to luck as anything else, managed to transfer their goods aboard the lifeboat. They stood back nonchalantly, in case they had been spotted, assuming nonchalant would best be acceptable if stumbled upon.   Tommy edged his way to the edge of the lifeboat ready to strap up the tarpaulin having virtually uncovered a good portion of the lifeboat to get the produce on board, and looking down in horror, saw Phillip climbing up the arm of one of the davits attempting to join him. He wanted to shout '*No*,' but it would have been ungrateful for one, and more than that, any attempt to stop his precarious approach may well have ended up with Phillip falling overboard.

He hastily threw the gratefully received goods further down the lifeboat, making room for his uninvited guest, and before he knew it, Phillip was inside, and sat beside him.

Georgia had watched, dazed. Without shouting, she had tried her hardest to vocally encourage him back beside her, but it had been pointless. She looked around nervously, and finally looking back to the lifeboat once more, incredibly saw Phillip offering his arms out for her to join them.

'Come on,' he beckoned.

Georgia breathed deeply, drummed her fingers on her side throwing around the thousand reasons why she shouldn't join them, and suddenly, without a single reason to suggest she should, took his arms and precariously climbed inside with them.

Tommy could not believe it. He strangely, felt invaded, but having granted them entry, and as if by rote, hurriedly fastened the bindings on the tarpaulin behind them.

Suddenly, where there had been one, there were now, three.

Catherine, despite the knowledge of their destination, was still worried. They had now been gone far too long, and like Phillip, she was sure they would all be shut in later on. She didn't want either he or Georgia in danger, in spite of the fact that she had almost condoned the idea of them petting this stowaway. She fidgeted, trying to straighten both her own, and Georgia's bunks, but she was unable to take her mind off them. She eventually stood up and walked off towards the doorway. She looked behind her at the relative safety of the dormitory, knowing that leaving it was sure to lead to trouble. But not to be defeated by Phillip's new associate, and now angry at their prolonged absence, she took off after them.

The huge figure of Miss Baxter appeared to be the size of a mountain, and standing in front of Catherine demanding exactly where she thought she was going, was almost unsurpassable. Catherine thought of several excuses inside about a second, but all involved Miss Price, and would undoubtedly have meant her getting into yet more trouble. *The truth*, she thought. Worth a bash.

'I'm going to find my brother. I've stupidly let him wander off. I'm so sorry. I should have known better.'

Easy! A little self sacrifice and both she and Miss Price were safe. She stared the older woman squarely in the face, quickly plotting her next move.

'Well get on. And be quick about it.'

Catherine swiftly scampered past her without a backward glance, and only once she was out of sight, did she relax.

Now where are you? she thought.

She had not had the experience at navigating the ship as many times as her brother and Georgia, *blast her*, and had simply followed along in their wake on the previous occasions.

She looked around quickly. *Now! Which way did I go? Right, or Left?* Left!

They may have fallen for this runaway, she thought, irritated at being lost, but she had other ideas, and she was only minutes away from sorting the problem out, one way or the other. And, furthermore, doing it in person.

'Please!' Phillip begged.

'It'll be fine. What can they do to you?' Georgia urged him further.

Tommy shook his head vigorously. 'No way! They'll lock me away and send me back.' He looked to Phillip. 'And you promised not to give me away.'

'But…'

'But nothing,' Georgia intervened. 'You'd be a lot worse off but for Phillip. If it hadn't been for him, Catherine would have turned you in the second she found out. It's still only a question of time. You'd better do something, because if we are here much longer, she will call in the cavalry. Believe me!'

Tommy was furious at any intimation that Catherine decide his future. 'She… I…' he struggled to find words. 'Aaargh!' was the best he could manage.

Phillip shrunk back slightly, and was embraced by Georgia's comforting arms. She in turn glared at Tommy in a '*Look what you've done!*' manner.

'Phillip. I'm sorry. I was wrong. You've done great,' he managed, challenging Georgia's charge. 'I mean it.'

'All right then. But just don't shout at me.'

'I mean it. I'm really sorry.'

'Better?' Georgia soothed him. He nodded, sniffing once, to clear his nose, and warily looked back at Tommy.

32

George Willis blew into his hands to attempt to warm them against the cold night air. He cracked his fingers, and drew his collar up around his neck. It was time to start the Middle-Watch. Midnight to four in the morning.

'Keep warm, won't you?' his shipmate said, as he walked off. 'I'll toast you with a nice hot mug of tea shall I?'

The rate at which the departing rating made for warmer climates probably prevented him from ascertaining the clarity of the departing words that were offered him, but had he looked back, the rigid two fingered salute would not have been.

He settled - as comfortably as his station would allow - and taking the glasses from his neck, raised them to his eyes, and started a stem to stern scan of the sea.

'Time to make my way to the nearest lifeboat then, George?' a nearby crewman asked comically.

'If you see my back and I'm running, then yes!' Willis raised his eyebrows.

'Less of the clap trap, and get to your jobs,' a senior midshipman ordered.

Willis shrugged, swallowing a laugh, and raised the glasses. Nothing! He coughed into a clenched fist, and as a strong gust of wind blew across him, he rubbed his hands once more.

The heavy clouds that had shrouded the convoy all night broke momentarily, and as the moon broke through, it was as if the whole seascape had opened up in front of them. Willis looked out without the aid of the glasses, and about to pass caustic comment to his shipmate, looked back.

By the time he raised the glasses again, the clouds had closed in once more, and whatever he – might – have seen, had disappeared.

'Once more, Georgie,' Willis spoke to himself. 'Just in case!' He raised the glasses, and scanned the spot where he might have…

'Rogers!' he called. 'Get over here. What do you make of this?'

Rogers walked over and took the glasses. Willis pointed out to sea, offering the rough logistics, and exactly what he thought he had seen.

'Call it in.'

Catherine had eventually reached what she ascertained to be the lifeboat, but was unable to see either Phillip, or Georgia.

'Pah!' she spat, certain that she had lost her bearings. 'So help me, I give that boy far too much…' and was on the point of turning back when she heard Phillip's voice from nearby. She waited until she could fully hone in on him, and in no time at all, had traced it to…

'My goodness! He's inside with…'

Before the news of Phillip's precise location had fully sunk in, she then heard Georgia. Also...

Quite unbelievably, and against everything that came naturally to her, she crouched down beside the lifeboat, and listened. She tucked herself in and listened as footsteps approached nearby. She held her breath, and waited as the footsteps receded.

What am I doing? she thought. *Why am I hiding here?* The full realisation of the situation suddenly dawned on her. She did not need to take cover. Whatever Phillip and Georgia thought of him, she did not need to protect this - urchin. They had all been warned. Her brother and her maid had promised to be good, and under no circumstances should they be in a lifeboat with someone they had known for about five minutes. She hammered on the side of the boat, and then waited, quietly.

Quietly! Why quietly? She was about to yell so loudly it was likely to bring down the captain of the ship himself, when after a certain amount of kerfuffle, the tarpaulin on top of the boat drew back, and Phillip's head popped out.

In the murky gloom, she could just make out his face. He took off his glasses to clean the drops of water that had formed on them and looked down at her.

'Hi, sis!'

Catherine was not sure why she didn't yell, but the words came out in a sort of worrying whisper. 'What do you think you are up to?'

Georgia's head popped up beside Phillip's and she smiled an awkward smile. But just managing to make out the expression on Catherine's face, words didn't seem necessary.

'Et tu, Brute?'

Neither of the two had any idea what she had just said, but the tone of her voice, along with her manner, seemed to speak volumes.

'We haven't done anything,' Phillip managed, after what had seemed like a gap of a week.

'That's it!' Catherine said. 'All deals are off. I want you both downstairs...'

'...below decks,' Phillip added glibly.

'Don't push it. Below de... Downstairs, dammit. Now!'

The sound of the sirens across the convoy, instantly broke the tension. Catherine's concern in Tommy's predicament, suddenly became secondary. The memory of the previous evening's events vanished, and it was as if it was the first time she had heard them. She stood, awestruck, looking up to Phillip and Georgia. On this occasion, there was no Sir Galahad to sweep her away, *below decks*, and now she did not have Phillip and Georgia beside her. She looked up to Phillip, who far from seeking assistance, held out his arms in an attempt to help her up.

'What's happening?' she spluttered, as commotion broke out all around her. As the noise increased, her head span. Doors slammed noisily, and caught between Phillip and the relative safety of the dorms, she was now totally confused.

'Catherine! Quickly!' Phillip called down. 'Quickly!'

Just how Phillip and Georgia, and an amazed Tommy, managed to manhandle the

112

larger bulk of Catherine inside the lifeboat was a thing of legend. Any attention to a ladylike entrance disappeared as quickly as the crew. Catherine quickly found herself slumped face down on the floor of the lifeboat, and as the tarpaulin was pulled over the top of them, any facial indication to her discomfort was lost in the dark. She stared around frantically, trying to get her bearings, and as Phillip and Georgia's hands groped at her, trying to help her settle, she blindly lashed out at them, before finally coming to terms with exactly where she was, and why.

'We're locked out,' Georgia announced as the slamming of the doors ceased, and as the alarms died down, an eerie silence enveloped the lifeboat.

'You'll be all right,' Tommy assured them, shakily, feeling strangely guilty at their being there.

'But we're locked out,' Phillip cried.

'You'll be all right! I saw it through last night, didn't I? You'll be fine. I promise.'

'Don't you understand?' Catherine shouted, her voice commanding attention. 'We're...'

'... locked out! That's right! They've already told me twice,' Tommy shouted back. 'And I wouldn't have had it this way. Believe me. Just sit still for a minute.'

'You...' She could not find appropriate words, but suddenly pushed past Phillip or Georgia - it was impossible to see whom - and lurched in the direction of Tommy's voice.

Tommy felt the lifeboat sway violently long before he heard her approach, and thrust himself towards the back of the boat. Phillip had somehow caught hold of her dress, and Georgia had managed to deflect her charge, and between the two of them they were just managing to hold her at bay.

'Look at the danger you've put us all in!' she spat.

'Calm down! Just calm down! We're all scared.' Tommy yelled. And for good measure, added, 'I didn't ask you in here.'

Catherine, considering his words, relaxed slightly and was eventually released from their grip.

'What's happening?' Phillip asked.

'I don't know,' Tommy answered.

Catherine was shaking. Georgia noticed her discomfort and put an arm around her, rubbing her shoulder roughly.

'This is all your fault,' Catherine said quietly, and quite controlled. 'All of this. Your fault.'

'I started the war did I?' Tommy replied in his defence. 'We're here because we're here. It's nobody's fault.'

'I can't believe we're in the middle of the sea, in a lifeboat, and *still* aboard a ship, waiting to be...' She managed to resist the urge to complete the sentence for Phillip's sake, but she was still angry. 'For God's sake, we're totally up the creek, and all because of you, you... you... urchin.'

'Catherine!' Georgia uttered, shocked.

113

'Well he is.'

'Well, forgive me if I don't speak all *la di da,*' he exaggerated, 'like yourself. But trust me, I don't hold that against you.'

'Catherine, apologise,' Phillip, urged.

'I will not.'

'I wouldn't accept it.'

Once more Catherine lurched across the lifeboat, and this time there was little anyone could do to stop her. She lunged at Tommy, who by good judgement, and probably a little more experienced in the art of fighting, just managed to avoid the full force of her attack.

'Get her off me. She's mad!' he shouted. 'She's a mad woman.'

'I am going to make sure you walk the plank for this,' she yelled, and pushed herself off him.

'Walk the plank? We'll be lucky if we don't get a torpedo up our...'

'Why don't we all try to calm down?' Georgia tried desperately to interrupt.

Catherine sat back. Her chest heaved as she tried to control her breathing.

'Just sit still, for God's sake,' Tommy implored. 'We're going to be here for a while. Now just sit back and relax.'

Georgia clenched Catherine's shoulder to try to persuade her to relax, and ever so slowly she felt the tension ease out of her rigid body.

Tommy quickly scrambled on the floor, and started to gather together his possessions. He groped around blindly until he managed to get his hands on the parcel containing the canvas. He tried not to make too much of a point of it as he collected all the other belongings. He found the bag Edward Burrows possessions had come in, and placed the canvas deep inside it.

'What are you doing?' Catherine demanded as he scrambled around inside the cramped conditions.

'Just making space,' he answered, quickly and calmly. 'I wasn't expecting guests.'

'What's happening?' Georgia asked, ignoring their conflict. 'We heard the alarms ages ago, and now, nothing.'

'Same as last night,' Tommy said.

'What was it like out here last night?' Phillip asked. 'Weren't you scared?'

Catherine huffed, expecting a story of bravado beyond the call of human expectation.

'I was scared to death. I didn't know what to do, or where to go, and then, suddenly it was today.'

'You are very brave,' Georgia commended him.

Catherine huffed.

33

The convoy sailed cautiously into the night. Whatever had brought about the general alarm, it had mercifully not been a U-Boat. Affairs aboard *The Maid of Orleans* finally returned to a more manageable state. All but for Miss Price. Where she had been one short, she was now missing four.

Inside the lifeboat, the excitement had eventually played itself out into a reluctant stalemate. Catherine, Phillip and Georgia were cuddled together under a blanket and several of the other items they had previously brought Tommy. They had positioned themselves at the foot of the lifeboat – at Catherine's insistence – and were snuggled up together. Tommy, for all his insistence that he had not invited company aboard, was scrunched up uncomfortably at the head of the boat. Covered in what was left of Edward Burrows possessions, and the remainder of the items Phillip and Georgia had smuggled aboard, he had somehow managed to get to sleep.

Catherine Belvoir had only just started to come around to accepting life on board - and under strong protest at that - spending unbearable hours in a bunk, in the company of hundreds of other screaming, smelly bodies. Life, scrunched up in the bottom of a lifeboat, beside her brother and maid, however, quickly superseded that. It was only slightly more bearable than the alternative. And that was to be anywhere closer to the loathsome figure at the far end of the lifeboat.

After fitful attempts at slumber and having managed only sporadic snatches, Catherine sat up, shivering in the cold. She looked disdainfully either side of her, at the apparently, comfortably slumbered pair of Phillip and Georgia, who just might have been treating the whole episode as an adventure. Then she screwed up her eyes to better look across at the loathsome figure, Edward Burrows, who even dared to emit a loud snore, amongst other such unwelcomed sounds coming from his direction. Either way, she appeared to be the only one awake. She was so cold. Phillip looked positively comfortable and she poked a finger at his slumbered state, simply for appearing so. He mumbled something in his sleep but refused to wake, further infuriating her.

The breaking dawn outside the lifeboat afforded dim lighting inside the canopy over them, and short of shutting her eyes, she was forced to stare up the boat at Tommy's sleeping figure. She sneered at the recumbent form, but got nothing back from it, so decided she might save it for later, when it might be better appreciated. She turned firstly to one side, and then the other, trying her hardest to relax, but the body on either side of her seemed to have transformed into the space that had been available that much better, and left her nothing. She lay back, staring up at the tarpaulin, hopelessly planning her next move.

Tommy rolled over, and mumbled something in his sleep, and she looked across, hoping he might have woken up, and that she might be able to vent some of her stored up anger at him. But much to her annoyance, he just rolled over, and remained asleep. She watched as the blanket shifted from his body, revealing the bag, containing the remainder of his possessions that he had not handed out. The top to the bag seemed to have fallen open slightly.

Maybe, just maybe, there might be something inside that was just the thing she needed to ease her discomfort. She stared at it that little bit harder.

Her mind made up, Catherine slowly moved across, trying not to wake her bedfellows. But as she did so, it appeared that Tommy's hand unconsciously reached for the bag, and drew it closer to him.

'Aha! Hiding something, are we?' Catherine thought.

Tommy had honestly handed round anything that might have kept the quartet warm the previous night, but there appeared to be something deeper inside, and Catherine was cold enough to wear it, even if it were only a finger stool. She loosed her contact with the bedding and once more edged her way across the boat, and not wanting to wake him, she stretched out a bony arm and reached inside the bag.

She paused for a second, ensuring that everyone was still asleep, and then, slowly reaching down into the depths, closed her hand around a parcel of some sort. She released it immediately, as if it were something repulsive, but after some seconds, and still the only one awake, intrigue took over. She curled her hand round the small parcel, and the owner apparently undisturbed by her presence, slowly started to draw it out. She stopped several times, expecting him to pounce, but he stayed asleep, and finally, she revealed the treasure.

She held it out in front of her for examination, but the apparent lack of light revealed nothing. So, slowly, and carefully, she made her way back to the other end of the boat, and scrunched up next to Georgia, displayed the parcel.

Like a pirate having discovered a treasure chest, she was just about to reveal the contents, when Tommy voice yelled out, 'Don't you dare!'

Georgia and Phillip woke and blinked sleepily.

'Give it back,' Tommy demanded. 'That's mine.'

Catherine in her sleepless state was in no mood to take orders. Tommy scrambled across the boat, but she turned away from him and held it away from him at arm's length.

'Give it back.'

Phillip and Georgia looked on, unable to fully grasp what was going on.

'Catherine!' Phillip called, assuming she may well have instigated whatever was under way. 'Stop it!'

'Give it back!' Tommy repeated his demand.

'Why? What is it? Something you've stolen. Is that it? Is that what you are? A thief?' She held it out tempting him. Tommy in turn, snatched out in the direction of the covered canvas, but once more Catherine drew it away from him, and this time, backed still further away.

'Give it back, Catherine,' Phillip yawned. 'Please!'

'Yeah. Give it back.' Tommy confirmed.

'Or what?' Catherine demanded, defiantly.   Tommy looked frantically round the lifeboat, but nothing immediately came to mind. 'Well?'

Tommy turned, and drew back the tarpaulin, and stared back down the lifeboat.

'And?' Catherine goaded him further.

Regardless to anyone's presence outside, Tommy climbed from the boat, and stood on the balustrade. He grasped at the release mechanism attached to the lifeboat and stared back in her direction.

'I'll drop her,' he snapped. 'Don't tempt me.'

Catherine led the rush towards the front of the lifeboat to see exactly what he was talking about. Tommy stood defiantly, one of his hands on a stabilising rope attached to the ship, the other on the release hook, taunting her.

Catherine crawled through the gap in the tarpaulin, and unfazed, held the parcel out proudly, threatening to jettison it. Tommy and she locked eyes, defiantly.

Catherine, not to be beaten, smiled, almost spitefully, and held out the parcel further, mocking his threat.

Tommy returned the smile, and as Phillip and Georgia arrived at Catherine's side, he released the restraints holding the boat to the side of the ship, and as two horrified faces glared back, the lifeboat swung free of its mooring. Phillip and Georgia cried out, but nothing could break the spell between the bull and the matador.

'You're mad!' Catherine snapped, regaining her balance.

'Give – it - back,' he nodded angrily, in the direction of her hand.

'You wouldn't dare. You don't know how,' she told him, though she was more than a little worried at the ease in which he had freed the lifeboat in the first place. But still furious, and refusing to relent, she continued, 'Just give yourself up.'

'I've spent enough time in here to work out this old thing,' he indicated the lifeboat. 'And give up? Never! Just give it back.'

Catherine, despite desperate pleas from Phillip and Georgia, not to be outdone, once more threatened to throw out the parcel. 'Give up, or else.'

Tommy, though free from the confines of the boat, was still not steady on his feet. His muscles were slowly adjusting to the freedom from the lifeboat, and he stood shakily on the banister. His hand was held firmly on the release hook, his eyes locked on Catherine's.

It was now early morning and a shrouding mist clouded the sea. It was cold, and Tommy shivered. The morning dew, and a fine spray off the sea seemed to have clung to everything on the ship. As Tommy tried to stand up slightly taller, he slipped slightly on the railing, and just to keep his balance, had to retain a firmer hold the release hook.

'Catherine. Just give it back,' Phillip cried, seeing Tommy's slip.

'Never!'

'Fine!' Tommy, regaining his balance, resolutely pulled at the restraints, and the lifeboat slipped from its hold, and plummeted in a heavy drop, down into the sea below.

'Help!' Georgia screamed, grasping at Phillip's hand as they were both thrown around the boat. Catherine too fell back and grabbed wildly at anything she could to avoid being thrown from it.

Tommy awoke, as if from a spell, totally bemused, and as the realisation of what he had done sunk in, he leant over the side of the ship to discover the full extent of what he had done.

'What on earth have I ...?' he garbled, looking down, and wobbled once more.

He had heard the collected, desperate shouts of the three inside the lifeboat as it crashed into the sea below, and the look of Phillip's trusting face was now etched inside his head. The senselessness of his decision to even loose the lifeboat in the first place suddenly hit home, and as the immensity of what he had then done settled in, he rapidly lost control of every muscle in his body. His grip on the restraining rope attached to the davits lost all adhesion, and he slipped, staggering forwards. His knees buckled, and as his feet failed to maintain any grip, he screamed and toppled forward into the depths below.

The lifeboat had thrown the three children around the lifeboat unmercifully, though by God's good grace, they were all somehow still aboard. Georgia had landed on top of Catherine, who had bumped her head hard, and currently lay there, dazed. Phillip had come to rest closer to the stern of the boat, and for this reason only - and as dazed as he was – did he see Tommy's body falling from the ship at all. Instinct took over, and ignoring any grazes or injuries he may have sustained, he threw his head forwards through the tarpaulin and with both hands firmly grasping the point, called out to him.

The fall from the ship had taken no more than a second or so, but had seemed like an hour. Tommy had seen his relatively short span of life flash before his eyes as he fell, and he had all but said goodbye to the world when his body hit the icy water. He had involuntarily curled up as he fell, more by chance than design, and he had entered the water in the shape of a ball, breaking the surface without any apparent damage to his body. The effect of the freezing water struck him instantly. Though far from damaging him, it had indeed concentrated his jumbled thoughts to the fact that he was still alive. He had survived the fall. He surfaced, spluttering, and without any attempt at swimming, he threw his arms up, gasping for breath - more from the effects of the cold than having been underwater for any length of time. He splashed frantically, and kicked with his legs against the cold. He could see nothing in the mist, but shouted out, regardless.

Phillip looked out desperately into the mist, and shouted Tommy's name. He waited a second, then called again. He listened hard, with his hands clenched onto the boat in anticipation. Once more he called, and then waited.

'Over here!'

He almost jumped with excitement hearing a voice. 'Call again!' he shouted.

Though he had been in the freezing water barely seconds, Tommy was fast losing feeling in his arms and legs. He heard Phillip's voice. *So near*, he thought, and the mere fact that rescue was so close seemed to summon energy into his failing body. He called back, flapping his frozen arms in a swimming motion, and despite his condition, set off in the direction of Phillip's cries.

Phillip looked hard into the blinding mist, and called again, then waited. On hearing Tommy's weakened voice, he called across to him once more.

Tommy's arms had all but given out when suddenly his hands smashed into something hard. He had somehow reached the lifeboat. He grabbed at the boat, and feebly edged his way around the point, calling weakly to Phillip. He reached out unsighted and as if from nowhere, something grabbed his arm. He looked up into Phillip's eyes.

Georgia, now having gathered what had happened, had joined Phillip, and together they somehow managed to drag Tommy's flaccid body into the boat, where they dumped, him, unceremoniously, onto the floor, and hurriedly threw whatever warmth they could find around them, on top of him.

As they looked down at him, frantically trying to chivvy some kind of life back into his frozen body, the stern of the *Maid of Orleans* passed by them, totally oblivious to there being there at all. The wake from the rear of the vessel violently shook the lifeboat, and for a short while, all four passengers aboard the lifeboat lay flat, awaiting the worst.

After some moments, the effects of the large vessel passing them, relented, and ever so slowly, the lifeboat steadied, and rocked, now only from the effects of the sea.

Tommy lay, motionless, and Catherine, lay spark out only feet away from him. The bump on her head had originally left her dizzy, but the full effect of her collision with the lifeboat had finally kicked in, and she too had lost consciousness. She lay in the rear of the boat, her head lolling to one side.

'Oh my goodness,' Georgia said to Phillip, shaking her head. 'What are we going to do?'

Phillip, momentarily ignoring the plight of the injured twosome, crawled to the front of the boat, and steadying himself against the swell, yelled, 'Ahoy!' several times, as loud as he could. But it was hopeless. He finally sat back dejectedly, and stared into another blanket of fog, as it enveloped their craft. He could not even hear the sounds of the engines of any of the ships in the convoy any more.

'It's no good. They've gone,' Georgia informed him needlessly. Phillip stared back at her crestfallen.

Tommy now lay shivering uncontrollably on the floor of the boat. His teeth chattered, and he was curled up with his knees clutched to his chest, his arms clamped fast around them, as Phillip looked on mesmerized.

'Help me get his wet clothes off him' Georgia told him. 'Quickly!'

Phillip looked aghast.

119

'Don't worry. I'll do it. Go over there, then. Look after your sister,' she said, and pushed him to one side. She hurriedly grabbed hold of Tommy and started to remove his saturated clothing. The process seemed to take forever as the sodden clothing seemed to have formed an extra layer of skin. But patience and perseverance finally won over, and job done, she finally managed to wrap a blanket around him, and rubbed it vigorously all over his body trying to get the blood rushing through his veins again, trying her very hardest to put some kind of warmth back into his body.

Tommy shifted, and looked up frightened.

'Move your limbs,' Georgia said, ruffling his hair. 'You've got to help yourself.'

Catherine finally opened her eyes to see another blow raining in from Phillip, who was slapping her face, trying to bring her round a little too vigorously. She shook her head, trying her best to come round, just in time to grab hold of Phillip's hand, and avoid the next bombardment. It took her a few more moments to finally work out exactly where she was, and recall what had happened before she passed out. Phillip watched as she blinked, twice, looked at him, non-committally, and slowly the realisation of their situation dawned on her. She slowly sat herself up, and somewhat settled, focussed her attention on Georgia, who was fussing over a shape in the centre of the boat. She looked back to her brother once more, and his apprehensive face changed from a caring concern, to worry. A frown developed across her face, and Phillip shrank back slightly.

'It's – er - Edward,' he said tentatively. 'He fell in the sea, and I got him out.'

'He should have drowned,' she said bitterly, looking round confirming her surroundings.

'Catherine!' Georgia scolded, half relieved to see her alert again. She looked totally bedraggled, and was now exhausted, having rubbed at Tommy's frozen body so vigorously.

Catherine made her way along the boat, and carefully by-passed Georgia. She looked down at Tommy's sagging body, covered in bedding. She glared back at Georgia, almost disappointedly, but never having seen Georgia quite so dishevelled and worn out, relented slightly. She rubbed Georgia gently on the shoulder, then pushed her out of the way, and without any thought to her loathing for the figure in front of her, started where Georgia had left off.

Tommy's drained face looked up at her, and somehow he managed a thankful grin.

'We're far from finished yet,' she whispered, then turned his head away and continued massaging the cold from his body. She didn't want to see his face, and most certainly did not want him to see the tears streaming down hers.

Catherine finally stopped for a moment, sniffed loudly, and looked across to Phillip, who was now crouched at the point of the lifeboat, waving frantically into the fog. Georgia looked across to her, and as Catherine nodded, she crawled over to Phillip. Reaching him, she carefully put her arms on his shoulders, and firmly coaxed him back inside under the tarpaulin, and sat him down. Catherine looked at them both, and said, 'Well!'

34

Tommy had been placed in the stern of the boat, and covered up as best possible. He had been placed under every conceivable piece of bedding that they had managed to transfer from the ship to the lifeboat, and whether he slept or simply did not have the energy to raise his head, he rested where he was.

Catherine crouched in the middle of the boat, shaking her head, inanely. Georgia and Phillip had both tried to talk to her, but she would not answer, and they were not quite sure what to do, so they started to set about tidying up what little else there was inside the boat. Phillip picked up the parcel that had been the cause of their misfortune, and was about to show it to Catherine, when Georgia, crouched behind her, shook her head. *Best not, eh!* Phillip took the parcel and pushed it back inside the bag from which it had originally been taken, and sent a tentative thumbs-up to Georgia.

'Do you think they will even miss us?' Catherine suddenly said, to no one in particular. 'Do you think they will come back and find us?'

'Of course they will!' Georgia said, as much for her own sakes as anyone else's. 'Just as soon as the fog lifts, eh? Eh, Master Phillip?'

Catherine glared at her, then to Tommy. If he had noticed the title, it was unclear. But in truth, he did not seem able to take in anything in the state he was in, so the reproachful look was unnecessary. Georgia took on board the message, and looked away.

'As soon as the fog lifts,' Phillip echoed. He worked his way over to his sister, and forced himself into her arms.

Catherine relaxed slightly, in her enforced, matriarchal role, and stared blankly into space.

Georgia watched quietly as Catherine held Phillip close, and then across to Tommy, lost in a world of his own, and she suddenly felt very much alone. She slumped to the floor, her shoulders sagged, and she wiped a tear from her eye before anyone noticed.

It was mid-morning. On top of the erroneous Edward Burrows, Miss Price had now lost Catherine - to whom she had recently become very close - Phillip and Georgia, and was now stood in front of the head chaperone. She shook her head in total disbelief, tutting, without even bothering to look up. She thumbed her way through the papers in front of her, and sighed.

Miss Price, in a state of total panic, had tried to confide her loss to one of the friendlier officers aboard, without having to do so officially below decks. But it had been hopeless. As nice as the officer might have been, the information had soon been relayed to Miss Baxter, and she had duly been called in front of her. A standard role call had revealed the loss, and a further search of the ship ordered immediately.

The discovery of the missing lifeboat had further added to the confusion, if not offered a possible solution to the mystery. How they had escaped Miss Price's clutches was not clear - and would be dealt with as soon as the children's absence was agreed. A meeting with the Captain of the ship had no effect however. He was powerless to turn the boat around, and away from the convoy, in what had now become a dense fog, and after many raised voices had been heard, he had to inform them that the children were in his opinion, *'In a lifeboat,'* and sadly, there was nothing he could do. They were on their own.

'I'm hungry,' Phillip said.

'I know you are. We all are,' Catherine confirmed.

'We'll have to ration what we've got,' Georgia told them.

'What have we got,' Catherine bemoaned. 'Nothing! That's what we've got.'

Phillip held up the provisions they had managed to bring to Tommy, and handed them across to his sister. She cupped her hands to receive the meagre bounty. She drew back the cloth they were wrapped in, and looked inside.

'A handful of stale bread and a cup full of - stew? This is it?'

'We hadn't planned on a cruise,' Georgia observed. 'We're lucky to have this.'

'And water? My God! What are we going to do for water?'

'Just hang your head out in the open when it's raining, don't stop moaning, and there is every possibility you'll drown,' a voice mumbled.

'Oh, ha ha!' Catherine groaned, without observing the donor of the comment.

'Edward!' Phillip chirped, looking across the boat.

Tommy was sat up under the pile of clothes that had been thrown on top of him, looking a hundred times better than he had. Phillip scrambled across, knocking Georgia and Catherine clean out of the way, and leapt on top of him.

'Steady. We'll capsize' Tommy said, and moving some of the linen on top of him, hugged him back.

'I should keep those on top of you until your clothing dries out a bit,' Georgia suggested.

'Who did this to me?' Tommy asked, a little shyly, regarding his state beneath the blanket, and then, with a slight grin on his face, looked across at Catherine.

'In your dreams,' she retorted.

Catherine sat away from the otherwise elated group reunion, and said nothing. Phillip and Georgia sat beside Tommy, nursing his needs with the precious little they had available to them. Catherine laid her head back and sighed. She could not believe that the perpetrator of all this was now being pampered.

'Just wrap him in vinegar and brown paper, and put him in front of the fire,' Catherine boomed, exasperated.

'Catherine!' Phillip reprimanded.

'I'll just get up. Don't worry,' Tommy said looking at her, and made to draw the blanket back to reveal his naked body.

'No!' Catherine screamed. 'Stay there. This whole thing is frightening enough without that, thank you very much.'

'What then?'

'Oh Georgia! For goodness sakes, dry his clothes or… just do something with him.'

'I'm cold' Tommy feigned a whine. 'Give me a cuddle.'

'I would sooner throw myself overboard,' Catherine puffed, shaking her head, and turned away again.

The full thirty foot length of the lifeboat rocketed up violently into the air, and smashed back down into the turbulent sea. It had been designed to carry well in excess of the four inhabitants now there, and was therefore sufficiently spacious, but the luxury of such expansive dimensions would happily have been swapped for the cramped bunks, on the safety of their errant transport to Canada.

How the four residents had set about best putting the space to use, and to the best advantage, was arguable. Currently, Catherine had elected to occupy the stern of the boat. Tommy and Georgia were currently further to the bow, holding firmly onto the legs of Phillip, who had suddenly become aware of the true reality of seasickness and all it endured. The tarpaulin had been drawn back and he retched fiercely over the side of the boat, and spent large periods of time commuting between the midsection of the boat and there.

'I didn't miss too much in the food department on the ship then?' Tommy asked him. Phillip smiled through a jaded green face, held his look for seconds, and then made for the bow of the boat once again, hotly pursued by his safety team.

Georgia suggested they all sit down, and look at what was left of the rations, and how best to distribute them.

'They won't be any more startling if I don't journey down, will they?' Catherine asked from her throne at the stern.

'Maybe not,' Tommy said. 'But no one is going to bring your share down to you.'

Catherine, reluctantly made the pilgrimage over towards the others, and they all looked into the larder.

'A feast,' Catherine declared. 'A positive feast, and well worth the exercise.'

'Do we eat what there is now, or leave it till… whenever?' Georgia asked practically.

'Whenever? How long is whenever?' Catherine asked. 'It's bread, and it's not going to get any fresher by leaving it, is it?'

Tommy nodded. 'She's got a point. And it's not going to last us forever, even if we ration it out.'

'I'm fine,' Phillip added to the conversation, and took off once more, about his ague.

'Bon appetite,' Catherine said.

They each ate the last of the food they had, and sat back. Tommy belched, and rubbed his stomach richly. 'A feast fit for a king.'

'We've got to get some water,' Georgia said.

'Wait for it to rain again,' Tommy started, avoiding looking at Catherine, for fear of the need to reiterate his earlier observation. 'And we will have to gather it in any containers we've got. I'm no Quartermaster, but we're fairly restricted on that front, so we'll have to improvise.'

'Oh my goodness! You make it sound so practicable,' Catherine whined.

'Practi… what?' Tommy asked.

'You make it sound easy.'

'We'll have to work together then,' Georgia advised, saving any unnecessary conflict.

'And if we are here too long, we can always eat Catherine,' Tommy said. She glared at him. 'She's by far the biggest. We could easily make it to Canada with plenty to spare.'

Georgia grimaced, but grinned shyly at Catherine, who raised her eyebrows, in a *Pathetic!* gesture, before relenting, and smiling back. Phillip was laid out. His colour was best described as the colour of a ripe lime, but even he managed a slight smirk.

Tommy had still not fully recovered from his encounter with the sea. Georgia looked curiously bedraggled, and Catherine's hair, usually free flowing and enviable, was everywhere other than where it should have been. But, that was currently low on her list of priorities.

'Don't worry,' Tommy said, as the boat surged up onto a violent wave, and they all lurched forward violently. 'Things could always be worse.'

'How on earth could things be worse?' Catherine questioned, angrily.

35

The sea appeared to be alight. Oil and fuel, spread across the sea, burned freely. Sirens sounded, and the noise of one explosion after another filled the black, smoke filled air.

The first torpedo had struck just before dusk, and the convoy was forced apart. The anti-submarine vessels had launched depth charges, one after the other into the sea. The U-Boat, or boats, had gone to ground, and there was now a standoff between the aggressor and the oppressed, awaiting the outcome of the depth charge assault.

A full account of exactly how many lifeboats had actually been launched, or bodies salvaged, was one for statisticians at a later date, but it had taken no time at all from the initial strike to her final disappearance. As the stern of the ship forced its way down to the bottom of the ocean, the last that could be seen of her was her name, emblazoned on the bow. *The Maid of Orleans* was now an official war statistic.

As the survivors of the raid took flight, the sea started to settle behind them, leaving only flotsam and jetsam to reveal that the ship had ever been there at all. Amongst the carnage, and deserving no more than a second glance, a green velvet hat, with a red band wrapped around it, surfaced for a second, before finally disappearing into the depths along with both the ship, and its owner.

What had registered as bad weather on board the ship, was just a taste of what it was like inside a thirty-foot lifeboat. A lifeboat, under the control and expertise of four inexperienced children. The heavy swell that had brought about another bout of sickness in Phillip had subsided for a short spell, but just as they had thought the worst of it was over, another came along to replace it.

Despite the lack of fresh water, and an eventual decision on how best to trap it, the severity of the weather had quickly put pay to any plans they had decided upon. The boat was lifted higher and higher on waves, and it was well the occupants were unable to see their surroundings, the tarpaulin having been strapped on as tightly as possible. The law of physics and gravity ensured that what went up...

As the lifeboat crashed down off a twenty-foot swell, it was only to be picked up by the next. That the boat had not capsized was a credit to both the designer of the lifeboat, and Neptune, for not wishing their company just yet.

Words inside the lifeboat were few, and when muttered, unintelligible. The four children observed a truce, as much thrust upon them as agreed upon, and they huddled together in a clutch in the centre of the shell as best possible. They clutched to anything that seemed likely to hold them in place until once more the strength of the sea further dictated its next turn. Cries were uttered and left unanswered as fear replaced anything that could be expressed in words. They were thrown from stem to stern and all points in-between, and only the thought that they were not alone, stopped them cracking up altogether. Any injury that was sustained had little or no time to settle in before the beneficiary was thrust off into another part of the boat, and another wound appeared to replace it. Any water that managed to seep it way through the temporary roof was miraculously minimal. The battle between the need to procure water for consumption, and the need to stop it sinking them was a paradox. Vague attempts, in the most ludicrous of conditions, were made to stem the flow, and somehow they seemed to be managing.

The storm finally abated after two days. The lifeboat, valiantly living up to its name, sat, rocking gently in the now balmy sea. What had seemed an eternity, had finally come to an end. That the inhabitants of the boat were aware of the change in conditions was arguable. They sat, gloomily in the boat, occupying all four major compass points, silent and motionless, and stared into an apparently invisible void. The tarpaulin was still taut, and if it was a bright sunny day outside the confines, it appeared no one was in a state to do anything about it. They sat, and they sat, in their hunched states, one or the other drifting off into a spell of involuntary slumber, only to be jolted back into consciousness as the boat rocked awkwardly as it hit an errant wave.

A small pool of dirty water had settled into a small puddle in the centre of the boat, but it was both dirty, and sitting in between slats in the flooring, and as thirsty as they might have been, virtually unattainable.

Georgia was the first to break from the trance. She moved her body, agonisingly sensing each ache and pain. Limb by limb, muscle-by-muscle, bone-by-bone. Her head ached, and even moving her eyes caused her pain, but the sight of the others brought about a surge of energy that usurped the sensitivity. She slowly edged her way to water that had settled in the centre of the boat, and dipping her fingers into the slight pool, scooped what she could into her hands, and tentatively sipped at the dirty liquid within. She grimaced and quickly spat out the contents of her mouth, choking on the salty residue. Even the moisture did nothing to relieve her parched, dry lips. She looked hopefully around the interior of the boat, but her three compatriots were still useless. She sighed, wearily, and carefully edged her way to the front of the boat. She looked at the complicated knot they had applied to the tarpaulin to save themselves from flooding, and slowly, ever so slowly started to pick at it, trying to let in some fresh air.

She finally dragged back the front of the tarpaulin, and suddenly her head popped out into daylight. She breathed deeply at the fresh air, slightly rejuvenated at the effort. As she looked along the cover of the tarpaulin, she noticed small pockets of water that had formed n small dips in the material. She hurried back inside, tentatively picking up the cup, and returning, as carefully as her tortured body allowed, scooped at one of the pools of water. She hesitated before finally testing the product.

It was rainwater. Well as close to drinkable as it was likely to be, but drinkable at that. She tugged at the contents before once more filling the mug, and delicately disappearing inside.

Georgia moved across to Catherine, the closest to her, and having nudged her and got no response, placed the mug to her lips and slowly tipped it until water seeped inside her mouth. She spluttered as the water entered her throat, and finally woke. She looked at

126

Georgia, and seeing the cup, drank greedily. She did not speak, and any contact was made through her silent eyes. Georgia muttered something and turned first to tend to Phillip, and finally Tommy.

The tarpaulin had been dragged back from most of the boat. It had not been fully detached and was able to be reattached at a moment or so's notice, in event of a sudden change in the weather. No one on board was qualified to foretell the next squally spell, and they would have to be ready to react fast when it happened. For the moment however, the calm sea and tranquil air was a welcomed relief. The water they had gathered so far, had far from fully satisfied their thirst, but it had at least relieved it till the next rainfall.

The tarpaulin was kept back during the next gentle downpour, and they all lay back. They opened their mouths wide, allowing the spots of rain to enter their parched mouths. Georgia had carefully arranged the waterproof cover in a devious manner to collect the rainfall, and somehow store it for transfer into the mug, which was then passed around sparingly. They would not die of thirst tonight.

The water problem solved, to some small degree, they now sat in the boat in a silence that could have been cut with a knife. Words seemed hard to find, and futile at that, and any animosity from days gone by, had been left there. There was not enough energy amongst the four of them to raise a quarrel, much less a confrontation of any substance. Any energy they had had, days before, had been sapped from their bodies. They were hungry, and peculiarly, almost welcomed the next downfall of rain, and blow the consequences that came with it.

The ever-changing weather brought them a fresh, strong, downpour late into the evening, and despite Georgia's new process at retaining the fresh rainwater, they still sat with their mouths pointed skyward until it was their turn to drink more substantially from the mug. The rain soon started to increase in its intensity, and with it the strength of the sea. The waves increased in size, and before long, the tarpaulin was once more returned to its original purpose. Between Georgia and Tommy, they had somehow fudged a method in which they could channel some of the heavier rainfall, without flooding the inside of the boat, and before long, they had all had plenty to drink, and eventually divert their minds to other worries.

The next morning was calm once more. Though they were now more refreshed, they were now much the hungrier for it. Phillip seemed the least able to conceal it, and it soon became a game to see when he would start up next. When he wasn't complaining, he insisted on thrusting his head through the cover to see if there was any rescue in sight. If that wasn't enough, he also seemed to have his sister constantly on edge. She angrily threatening to throw him overboard on several occasions, but his bleating and lookout duties were not to be doused that easily. He was eventually threatened with physical restraints, but on the occasions even those held no fear, he would return to his perch, and eventually return with the news. A shaken head, however, saved many words, and slowly the boat returned to a reluctant silence.

With the uncertainty, and inability to be able to do anything about their situation, a spite and retribution had returned to the boat. The two oars that were wedged inside the boat were a constant source of argument. Catherine had suggested that Tommy get them out and utilise them. He had pointed out that none of them knew where they were, and asked in which particular direction she suggested they row. Only the ever-resilient Georgia, and their sheer lack of physical energy, managed to stop outright open warfare. Even the overly keen lookout, Phillip, grew less and less amiable, and despite trying to keep a cheerful face, his lack of age, and aversion to boredom was growing more and more for all to see.

Boredom had forced Tommy to mention how much he would have loved one of his cigarettes, which he had long since smoked his way through on the ship, and Catherine, having already used up most of her animosity on her brother, had then launched another unnecessary attack against him. The comment about the cigarette appeared only to have been a catalyst. The camaraderie during the danger and torment of the storm had long since evaporated, and the misplaced animosity between the pair, re-ignited.

Phillip, who had now tired of his self-imposed lookout duties, had resigned himself to staying put in the boat for at least a couple of hours at a time. He had been reserved for some time now, but was now restless again. He edged his way to the bow of the boat, and rubbing his chin, considered a resumption of the lookout vacancy, when a, *Don't you dare* glare from Catherine stopped him. He sat back resigned, and nudged Tommy playfully who jostled him back, causing the boat to sway from side to side.

'Enough!' Catherine yelled, shocking Georgia, who was sat quietly by her side. 'Just behave. We've got enough to worry about without you two - rocking the boat.' Georgia smirked. 'What are you laughing at?' she asked. Georgia was about to explain when the lifeboat jolted sharply.

The children froze.

'We've been hit,' Phillip yelled.

'Not been hit,' Tommy yelled. 'We've hit something.'

'Land!' Georgia exclaimed brightly.

'Land!' they all yelled together.

36

The excitement to exit the boat and be first to set foot on dry land was never in doubt. Phillip had ripped back the tarpaulin before anyone else could move, and was closely followed by Tommy, who may have made a better race of it, had he not delayed himself slightly, grabbing his bag. Catherine and Georgia looked at each other in wonderment, and then hugged jubilantly.

Phillip leapt from the boat, which had edged ever so slightly away from where they had struck land, and with a shriek, found himself up to his waist in water. His feet slipped on the ground beneath him, and as he scrambled to get ashore, he was no longer sure he would ever regain his footing.

Tommy, in an equally desperate effort to hit land, also stumbled, but recovered the better. Now standing on a slightly better footing, he reached down and grabbed at Phillip, and heaving at the scrawny shirt on his back, just managed to draw him to his feet.

Any words of thanks that Phillip may have offered, were missed as Tommy leapt past him, planting both feet firmly on *terra firma*. He looked back at Phillip, and as they both shouted in joy, only a sharp rebuke from the lifeboat, reminded them about the girls, who, a little more reticent about leaping ashore, urgently demanded their attention.

The elation still rife, they quickly turned and helped Georgia to scramble ashore, and then spent a lot longer, landing the much more refined Catherine, who despite the discomfort of the previous days, was intending to avoid getting her feet wet until the last possible moment. She landed in soft sand, which encircled her feet, and seawater soon seeped inside her footwear. Phillip was so amused that he bent down, and cupping his hands, splashed water all over her, and burst out laughing, joined quickly by Tommy, and more belatedly by a reticent Georgia. Catherine looked back at them, furiously.

'It's land, Catherine,' Phillip said. 'Land! And you! You'll dry.'

She looked down at her feet, and stamped twice testing the ground.

'Yes. Yes it is,' she exclaimed. 'We're safe.' She dipped down and threw water back at Phillip, and after a short think about the consequences, scooped up several more handfuls, and threw them in Tommy's direction.

Georgia laughed, and laughed, until Tommy turned his attention to her. He slowly started towards her, and as his intent slowly sank in, he rushed across and scooped her up in his arms. Struggle as she might, she could not break his hold, and slowly he started to walk her back to the water's edge.

'Don't you dare,' Georgia screamed.

He dared.

The water fight lasted until all four were soaked, from head to foot, and finally, with all scores settled, sanity finally settled in.

In their urgency to get ashore, the lifeboat had nestled gently into shore in a small rocky inlet, and as they decided to concentrate on getting further inland, it was left to settle where it was, all gratitude forgotten.

The simplicity with which they had landed was turned on its head as they encountered the rocks they would have to surmount in getting up onto drier land. A wet green slime covered most of the rocks in front of them, and getting a firm hold or footing was made that bit more difficult, by their water covered bodies. Phillip slipped and crashed down onto his knee as he headed up a slight incline leading up the rocky face. Catherine went to comfort him, but Tommy beat her to it. He looked down at the knee, and noticing it had not drawn blood, rubbed vigorously at the point which appeared to be causing him pain. Phillip winced, but refused to cry.

'You'll live,' Tommy said, and not allowing him time to think about it, pushed him up past the troublesome rocks, and safely onto dry ground.

Catherine, who had baulked at being pushed aside, was strangely taken aback by the way Tommy had quickly dealt with the potentially tearful situation, and far from making a fuss over it, had simply carried on. She looked across at Georgia, who, equally impressed, nodded her approval.

Phillip had quickly forgotten any injury incurred in his fall, and he, and Tommy, the slippery rocks conquered, looked around them excitedly at the new terrain.

Georgia, having waited for a show of chivalry from the two boys - and receiving none - had now managed to scramble up the rock face all on her own. She brushed herself down, looking reprovingly across at the two boys, but any acceptance of guilt on their part was sadly missing. They were excited and ready to push on when Tommy turned to watch Catherine standing desolately once more.

'Come on,' he said.

'Don't shout at me.'

'I'm not. Come on.'

'I can't.' She looked down at her dress, which due to its contact with the sea water, along with a design that had not been wholly intended for seafaring, was now wrapped firmly around her legs, and had left little room in which to stretch out her legs at all.

Tommy smiled at her disposition, which only made matters worse. She was about to turn round and walk off, before realising her only option was back out to sea. She turned back and scowled at him, furiously.

'Just roll it up a bit, and take my hand,' Tommy said kindly. 'Come on! We'll do it together.'

Catherine looked indignant that Tommy should even think of suggesting what a lady should do with her dress.

'Georgia!' he called.

Georgia poked her head over the bank and looked down. She quickly realised the predicament, and ably went back to assist her.

As she was finally sorted out, Tommy held out his hand to aid her in the last leg of her journey ashore. She hesitated and stared at Tommy, who had managed to maintain a straight face, before reluctantly accepting his gracious gesture, and he gallantly helped her up.

Catherine, somewhat far from grateful, released his hand the second she was stood firmly ashore. She stood, proudly, and brushed her dress down. Finding her footing, she composed herself, and looking to the three onlookers, said, 'Now then!'

Phillip rushed and hugged her, knocking any deportment out of her, swinging her round. 'We're home.'

Besides Phillip, the idea of being home had been something they had not even considered. It was just the relief of being safe. Finally hitting land. Exactly where it was, no one had registered.

'Home,' Catherine echoed. She looked excitedly to Georgia. 'Home?'

Georgia was slightly more reticent. 'Let's wait and see shall we.'

'I'm off,' Phillip shouted and started to rush off. 'I'll see you all later.'

'No!' Catherine yelled. 'Wait for us.'

Phillip rushed off regardless, leaving the three others to their own devices.

'Phillip!' Georgia cried.

'Don't run into any snakes,' Tommy called as he passed him.

Phillip stopped. Catherine was once more astounded at Tommy's grounded effect on Phillip.

'Don't say anything,' Georgia whispered into her ears. 'Don't spoil a good thing.'

'Don't worry. Not a word. Promise!'

They all caught up with him, and he slumped, sulkily to the ground.

'One step at a time, mate,' Tommy said. 'We don't know where we are. Let's just be a bit clever. There's no hurry.'

'But I'm hungry.'

Tommy looked at the girls. 'He's not wrong.'

A strong gust of wind suddenly blew up, sweeping Catherine's hair across her face. She shook. 'And it's cold.'

'Let's all work out what we're going to do,' Georgia said. 'Together!'

Tommy started to walk away quietly.

'Hello! Together! That means we all do it,' Catherine said noticing his quiet exit.

'I've gotta go,' he advised her.

'What? And leave us here?' Catherine growled angrily.

'No! I've got to - go!' he tried to elucidate.

'Of course you have,' Catherine said, as if she had understood all along.

'I need to go too' Phillip confirmed the point.

'Back here in five minutes then' Catherine said firmly. 'Five minutes. You hear?'

The two girls sat where they were while the boys walked back towards the shore.

'Whatever we decide, they always want to do something else,' Catherine, complained.

'It's early days. We'll get there, in the end.'

The boys stood looking out to sea, their ablutions complete, adjusting their clothing, as Tommy cried out, 'No!' and not waiting for Phillip, turned and rushed back to the spot where they had come aground.

'What?' Phillip spluttered, arriving at his side.

Catherine and Georgia, hearing the dismay in Tommy's voice, arrived in seconds, and shuffling for position, both joined him looking out to sea.

The lifeboat had been drawn out to sea and was now a good distance from the shore. The sudden swell in the sea and the change in the wind was drawing it farther and farther out by the second.

'Do something,' Catherine cried.

Phillip did not need asking twice. He slipped from the group, jumped down onto the shore, and clumsily making his way across the rocks and shingle, started to swim out.

'Phillip! No!' Tommy cried out, rushing from the girls, chasing after him. He slipped slightly, but managed to regain his footing, but then slipped once more. He stopped, looking for safer footing.

'Don't stop!' Catherine ordered him. 'Go on! Go and get him!'

Tommy rushed down to the edge of the sea, leapt into the water and swam out quickly. Fortunately, he was a much stronger swimmer, and got to Phillip, just before he swam too far out his ground. He managed to grab hold of his shirt, and drawing him back, just managed to put a stop to his heroics.

Phillip, not to be outdone, struggled, and it was all Tommy could do to hold onto him. In the ensuing struggle, Tommy managed to utilise his larger frame, and slowly dragged him back to shore.

Phillip rose, spluttering and looked angrily at Tommy. 'But the boat...'

He fought to get free of his grip, but Tommy held him firmly. 'Look. It's gone too far.'

Phillip broke from his hold and reluctantly looked out towards the lifeboat ,which was rapidly receding into the distance.

'It's gone,' Tommy told him, breathing heavily. 'It's gone.'

They sat down together on a large rock and looked out as the girls came down to join them.

'But...' Catherine started.

They all slumped on the floor and watched, as the lifeboat, almost waving them a fond farewell, finally started to disappear.

'I could have got to it,' Phillip protested. 'I know I could.'

'And like the boat, you may have washed up on shore again. One day!' Tommy said to him.

Phillip furiously wiped his glasses on his clothing, to no avail. Georgia took them from him, and wiped them on her dress before handing them back.

'Humph!' Phillip muttered.

'I'm sorry?'

'Thank you, Georgia.'

The children regrouped on slightly higher ground, and sat dejectedly. Catherine glared at Tommy, but he ignored her.

'Wait a minute!' Georgia piped up. 'What are we upset about? We're fine, aren't we? It's served its purpose. Ten minutes ago we would have swapped it for land in a trice. We're safe.'

'But we've lost all our...' Catherine started to say, and looking at Tommy, who was sat with his bag, stopped.

'We've only lost a few blankets. That's all.'

'But what if there are cannibals here?' Phillip interrupted.

The three elder children looked at each other, and after a moment or two, burst out laughing.

'What?' Phillip grizzled.

'Don't be silly. There are no cannibals here,' Catherine said. But there was a little more worry on three other faces now than there had been seconds before. 'There can't be.'

'What time is it?' Georgia asked.

Phillip looked to his wrist at his watch. 'It's ten o'clock.' He hesitated. 'Or was!'

'Was?'

'It's stopped working.'

Phillip took it from his wrist and handed it across. Catherine looked closely at it, shook it, put it to her ear, and then tapped it gently on the floor.

'He's had it in the water' Georgia reminded her.

'But my watch!'

'The best you can do is hope it dries out. Don't worry.'

Everyone looked to their own timepieces.

'Anyone got better than ten o'clock?' Georgia asked.

All the watches had met the same fate.

'So, ten o'clock it is, then,' Tommy said in answer to the original question. 'If it's good enough for Phillip, it's good enough for me.'

'But it's broken,' Catherine said.

'Out of order' Georgia said, trying to comfort Phillip. 'Out of order! It can be fixed, I'm sure. The first watch menders we come to.'

'So it's ten o'clock. What of it?' Catherine snapped.

'Well! We'll have plenty of daylight to search. To find out where we are,' Georgia said.

'I'm going to go with Edward,' Phillip said at once. 'You two can go off together.'

By now, Tommy had had a lot of time getting used to his new name, but it never failed to catch him by surprise, when caught off guard. He had had an age to reveal his true identity, but Edward Burrows had stuck, and he didn't see any reason why anyone should know differently. No matter where they had ended up!

'Do you think we ought to split up?' Catherine asked. 'Shouldn't we just settle here for a while?'

'It would be stupid to stay here if there is anyone else here already,' Tommy said. 'We need help.'

'And if we do split up, we would cover twice as much ground. And we are all hungry,' Georgia reminded everyone. 'We can separate and come back here in half an hour'.

'Half an hour on broken watches,' Catherine said.

'Or just sit here for the rest of our lives,' Tommy said. 'I'm all for teamwork, but can we at least get going?'

'Fine!' Catherine.

'Fine!' Tommy.

'Stick to the coast, and come back here as soon as you find something', Georgia broke the deadlock, again.

'Let's go,' Phillip said, not needing a second chance, and quickly took off.

37

Georgia was all set to encourage Catherine, and turning to do so, was shocked to find her gone.

'Come on,' Catherine demanded, already on her way. 'We'll show them who can find what. Come on. Hurry up, Georgia!'

Georgia obediently did as she was told, and followed on behind.

Phillip had taken no time in rushing away, and Tommy had to run quickly to catch up with him, and call for him to slow down. 'We need to take bearings for our return journey,' he yelled.

'You heard Georgia. Just stick to the coast. There's only one.'

Tommy shrugged, and with nothing to add, allowed him to lead on, and now concentrated on catching up with him.

Catherine came to a halt fairly soon. Her long dress, drying out by the second, had caught in every possible branch, bush, snatch of bracken, or any living things that had hooks or barbs on it.

'Oh!' She yelled. 'Help me Georgia. I'm sure I'm not meant to be a castaway.'

Georgia rushed to her side, laughing.

'Don't laugh. If I'd been meant to live on an island, I would have been blessed with suitable clothing. Look! There aren't even any paths. Make it stop, now!'

'Persevere. You'll be fine.'

'We're on an island. I know we are. And what's more, no one has ever been here before. We've had it!' Her shoulders sank, but she held her hands up, awkwardly, carefully avoiding contact with anything green, just in case. 'And I'll tell you something else for sure. If I get stung once more, I'm giving up and the boys can do everything.'

Besides the plant life, there were no paths or tracks, giving strength to Catherine's theory that they had indeed landed on a deserted island. And furthermore, the ground was uneven, and made progress even more difficult.

'Look!' Georgia stopped, bringing Catherine to a welcomed halt. She closed in, and glared down into the grass where Georgia was pointing.

'What?'

'Can't you see? There are animal droppings.'

Catherine, if she took on board the importance of Georgia's statement at all, did not register it in her face.

'There's wildlife here. If there's wildlife, there's food!'

'I can't go on. Let the boys get it,' Catherine yelled, fighting off a green plant that refused to release her dress.

'Do you really want the boys to take all the credit?'

'Just at the moment, happily'.

'Really?'

'Of course not, really, but…'

'Come on,' Georgia urged, grabbing her arm, pulling her along.

Catherine in turn, turned, cursed, and took a fierce kick at something that she had just managed to free herself from. 'We've found nothing. I bet the boys have found a pavement, a town, and are already sitting down to a hot meal.'

'Come on'.

Phillip and Tommy were far from comfortable in their search, and neither had they happened upon civilisation. They too had struggled in the conditions, and the earlier elation of finding land, was quickly starting to flag. Especially in Phillip. The ragged vegetation was fast taking its toll on him. Not only physically, but mentally. He lagged, some good way behind now, and when Tommy chivvied him along, the smile he offered was forced, and any dedication to the task was no longer there. He tripped over on one occasion, and Tommy had to all but drag him to his feet, or he would simply have stayed where he was.

Catherine walked with her arm linked through Georgia's, supporting herself. Georgia looked across oddly. Catherine caught the look and stopped. 'What is it?'

'Nothing,' Georgia said.

'No. Come on. What is it?'

Georgia sighed, reluctant to say anything.

'Georgia!'

'It's nothing, Miss Catherine,' Georgia said.

'Miss Catherine? What on earth is that all about?'

Georgia released her arm, and turned away, sniffing. Catherine was totally confounded. She turned Georgia towards her, and looked her straight in the eyes. 'What is it?'

Georgia pushed herself away, sighed again, and then said, 'I am your maid. I shouldn't be…'

'Shouldn't be what?'

'I am your *maid*.'

'Georgia. Things have changed ever so slightly over the last couple of days. I thought you might have noticed. And what are you on about anyway? We were always friends. Now stop it.'

'It's just… Edward - and everything!'

'What about him? He doesn't need to know anything. And what he doesn't know, won't hurt him. Georgia, you're my friend, now smile.' Georgia managed a weak effort. 'Smile!' Georgia smiled and Catherine grabbed her around the shoulder and hugged her. 'We've all had troubles of our own, and forgotten all about you. Now come on.' Georgia linked arms once more. 'I'll look after you. Silly!'

The boys had started to edge inland and away from the coast. Tommy had once more

136

had to return to a reluctant and dejected Phillip. He was not ready to be pulled along this time.

'Come on.'

'I can't'.

'Look, if that's how you're going to be, you stay where you are, and I'll go off and have a look.' Phillip was suddenly scared and found the energy to raise his body, but Tommy pushed him back. 'Stay there. I won't go far, and I promise I won't be out of shouting distance.'

'Promise?'

'Promise.'

Phillip settled back and sulked.

Tommy checked Phillip was settled satisfactorily, and then set off. He rambled slightly farther than just out of sight and finally pulled up. Checking to see that Phillip wasn't anywhere in sight, he reached to his back, and untucked his shirt. Looking around carefully to check that the girls hadn't given up and followed them, he drew out the parcel containing the canvas, which he had carefully concealed once they had landed. His fingers tapped the parcel, anxiously, as his eyes searched the immediate vicinity. He checked and double checked the surrounding ground until his eyes settled on a small pile of rocks that appeared to have fallen in front of a small hillock. He rushed over and hurriedly pulled at the individual boulders to see what lay behind.

He continued to drag them out of the way, one-by-one, until a small hole appeared. Excitedly he laid the parcel to one side, and with both hands, pulled at the rubble in front of the gap, slowly revealing a much larger opening.

Before going any further he stood and called out Phillip's name. Nothing. He called again, slightly louder, and was rewarded with a response. He called once more to see he was okay, and told him he wouldn't be long.

'Okay,' an only half-interested voice called back.

Tommy returned to his excavating and in minutes had revealed an entrance to a tiny hollow. A small cave.

Georgia stopped and looked around, and held up a hand in order that Catherine do the same.

They had travelled a fair way, with little concern as to what they were leaving behind them.

'What's the matter?'

'Nothing,' Georgia lied. 'I just don't think we should go too far. On our own, I mean.'

'You're right.' Catherine nodded strongly. The thought had not been Georgia's alone. 'I know we are safe now... I mean – safer - but if we are shipwrecked, I don't think we should be off on our own.'

'I mean,' Georgia tried to shore up their worries, 'that maybe we ought to make sure that that brother of yours isn't up to any mischief.'

'Definitely.'

'Let's go back then. We'll check on the pair of them. They won't last five minutes without us to keep them in order. '

They turned and looked back in the direction from which they had come. It all appeared new to them.

'Should we have left a trail or anything?' Catherine asked. 'We've come well in from the coastline, haven't we?'

The general landscape, along with the wild, thick foliage, had restricted their best efforts to hug the coastline too carefully, and just at the moment, they may well have been anywhere.

'Let's go back then,' Georgia held out a hand which Catherine happily clasped hold of, and not sure who was leading who, they started to tramp their way back across the ground they had just covered. Hopefully.

Tommy had cleared away an entrance to the small cave that was just big enough for a small body to crawl through.

He checked over his shoulder several times, to ensure that he was still alone, and even called across again. Tapping around the entrance, he checked exactly how sturdy it was. Though no architect or structural engineer, it appeared to be sound, and from where he stood, looked to be fairly watertight. There did not appear to be any water residue inside. *Perfect!*

Tommy took a final look at his one treasure in the world, and momentarily considered the benefits of leaving it, when suddenly the memory of Catherine holding the canvas over the side of the ship returned to him, and his mind was quickly made up. He knelt on the ground, and trying not to dirty himself too much, to give away the reason for his extended absence, started to edge his way inside.

The girls had continued on their return, and currently, any recognition of anything they had passed on the outward journey had not exactly leapt into view. They looked to each other a number of times, as much for reassurance as anything else. The conversation had died, and anything that was said, seemed pointless and trite.

Catherine was by far the more nervous of the two, and Georgia, despite having lost the responsibility of being Catherine's maid, still felt an honour to look after her.

'I'll bet this is the first time you'll be glad to see Edward's face,' Georgia said.

'Him! Pleased to see him? I'm not sure if I wouldn't rather just keep my eyes shut. Phillip will do.'

'Come on!'

'He is the least of my worries. Now lead on, Hiawatha.'

Georgia laughed. 'Okay, Minnehaha.'

The pair giggled nervously.

The interior of the cave was to all intents and purposes, just a small grotto. It was small, tight, and closely confined, and much less a cave than a dugout. It was clear it had not been used before, which although positive for secrecy, also showed that there appeared to be no other life here beyond themselves. It was however now claimed, and currently belonged to Tommy.

He had needed to stoop to get inside the cave. He had only just managed to crawl inside the small entrance without taking off the top of his head. He examined the hole quickly, wishing he had not left Phillip quite so close to his new hide out. He was going to have to be quick to do what he wanted before Phillip, bored with being alone, came in search of him.

As time passed, Tommy urgently scampered around the interior of the small cavern. He scratched around on the ground, trying to find any signs of damp he may have missed in his excitement, but it seemed perfect. The interior had nothing more than a few fallen rocks inside, and little else. *No lost treasure then!* Tommy realised. *Time to leave one, then*!

He laid the small parcel under a natural ledge that had formed over time, and covered it carefully with some of the twigs and leaves he had gathered, and edging out, heard a distant cry.

Phillip!

He yelled a positive response, and hastily set about disguising the exterior, to return the cave to its natural façade once more.

His work done, he stood back proudly, brushing the dirt from his clothes. Even he would not have suspected an opening behind what he now looked at. He had to check his bearings carefully to ensure that even he could find it again when he needed to.

Though satisfied with his work, the sound of a branch cracking nearby caught Tommy by surprise. He jumped, and realising how guilty he must have looked, started an exaggerated search through the surrounding undergrowth.

'Anything?' Phillip appeared, looking eagerly in his direction.

'Oh, there you are. I was just coming back.'

Catherine and Georgia had finally returned to the spot where they had last seen the two boys, and sat down.

'You see,' Catherine said. 'I told you they would have had better luck than us.'

'Says who? They're just not back yet. That's all. They would soon have rushed back to tell us if they had found anything, believe me.'

'You're right I suppose.' Catherine shivered, and rubbed her arms and legs. 'Oh dear!'

'What?'

'We really are alone, aren't we?'

'We've only been here five minutes. It's probably a bit too soon to assume that, don't you think?'

'Maybe. But I don't think we've washed up on the Serpentine, do you?'

'No.'

'Oh, I'm sorry, Georgia. It's just that everything is going wrong.'

'Wrong? We were lost at sea an hour ago. We're on land now, and I'm afraid we are just going have to make the best of it.'

Phillip was now looking a lot keener. It may only have been from being sat alone for such a long time, but whatever it had been, the rest seemed to have done him good. He rushed over to Tommy, who outwardly, looked pleased to see him. Tommy took a last fleeting look over his shoulder, and was satisfied his hideout would at least pass the Phillip test. For sure, in the short time that he had been there, he had not noticed anything out of place.

'Have you found anything yet?' he asked, hopefully.

'No. Not yet.' Tommy realised he had been gone for far longer than he would have wished, and would need a good alibi. 'I'm afraid when you weren't here, I didn't want to go too far.'

Phillip's shoulder's sagged. 'So we're not better than the girls then?'

'Course we are. We're a team, aren't we? We've just been unlucky.'

'So, we've got nothing, then?'

'Not yet. Something'll come up.'

'Do you think we ought to go back and check on Sis and Georgia?' Phillip asked. 'Just in case?'.

'D'you think they might need us?'

'Well... '

Tommy did not want Phillip familiarising himself with this particular spot, but at the same time had to get his own bearings on the area. If he walked away now, and couldn't find it again, the whole charade would have been for nothing.

'Well, come on then. They're girls. Of course they're going to need us.'

As Phillip set off, Tommy turned round, checking every little thing that might serve as a guide to where they had been, and as Phillip called again, quickly hurried after him in the girl's direction.

38

The sun was out, albeit rather weakly, but it was still very cold. Catherine and Georgia had gathered together all the loose sticks and twigs they could assemble, and amassed them into a pile. They stood back and looked at it, satisfied.

'Looks good,' Georgia said.

'It's only a pile of wood!'

'We are going to have to put in some hard work on your enthusiasm,' Georgia said, and they slumped down, waiting, and craned their necks looking expectantly for the boys.

'Hey!' Phillip called out, somewhat relieved as they finally caught sight of the two girls. They too had become slightly lost on the return journey. He had suggested that they shout out long before now, but Tommy did not want the girls to have the satisfaction of knowing that they may have got lost, and to date, they had kept quiet.

'Hello girls. Scared without us?' Tommy shouted, in case Phillip was in a mood for a spell of soul searching. He needn't have bothered, as Phillip had already bounded past him, proudly.

'Oh look, Georgia! The Knights of the Round Table!'

'Fresh back from the Crusades, ready to defend us against all enemies!'

'Something like that,' Tommy answered, not quite as chirpy.

'I take it by your tardy return, you don't come bearing good news?' Catherine asked.

Tommy sneered back. 'And seeing how long you have obviously been here, I take it you didn't get too far either?'

'We didn't find anything,' Georgia admitted, gloomily.

'Nothing!' Tommy almost gloated. Phillip sagged.

'But we didn't go that far. We didn't want to go too far from you,' she continued, rubbing the top of his head.

Phillip pulled sharply away from her consoling hand.

'Don't patronise me, any of you! We've had it.' He walked off, slightly, and leaning against the trunk of a tree, slid down to the floor, wrapping his arms around his knees, and rocked, moodily.

Tommy looked to Catherine to see if she had anything that might brighten him up.

'Leave him,' she mouthed, almost as if she came across this daily. She turned her back on him and returned her attention to Tommy.

There was a sudden lull, in what had moments before, been a joyful reunion, so Catherine coughed into her hand, pointedly, and walked across to the would-be fire, hoping for some recognition of their labours.

Georgia looked up at Tommy, holding her hands together, prayer-like, begging him not to say anything controversial.

Tommy raised his eyebrows, weighing up placating Georgia, or getting the better of his arch-nemesis.

'Well!' Georgia mouthed, and waited as he looked across.

The pause was longer than she would have liked, so she briskly walked over and stood beside Catherine, and patted her gently on the shoulder.

'Nice fire,' Tommy said. Georgia smiled, and nodded gratefully. Catherine looked up satisfied. 'How are you going to light it?' he added.

Georgia scowled at him.

'At least we've done something,' Catherine bit back instantly. 'What have you done? Nothing!'

'Oh! Maybe we should have collected some water to make sure the flames didn't get out of control.'

'You!'

'Shall I go and get you two sticks to rub together?'

Catherine trembled furiously, and searched for something on which to take out her anger.

Tommy walked away smugly, offering Georgia a conciliatory shrug. Georgia scowled at him.

Catherine suddenly jumped to her feet, and defiantly started to look around for a solution. Her eyes settled on Phillip, still sat petulantly, indignantly daring her to do something. She smiled contentedly, and rushed across to him. He shielded himself, putting his arms around his head, unsure as to her intentions.

'Leave me alone,' he said, as she reached for him.

'Sure. Take it out on your brother,' Tommy said.

'Shut up!' she snapped, in a most unladylike manner, and grabbed Phillip by the shoulders and raised her hand.

'Don't hit me,' he flinched, expecting a blow.

'Don't be stupid. When have I ever hit you? Just hold still.'

'No!' Phillip baulked as Catherine reached to his face, and holding his head straight, took the glasses off the end of his nose.

Tommy having made to defend his new ally, stood back at the lack of violence, and looked on baffled. She defiantly held the glasses up in front of him, and walked smugly back towards the fire. 'You want a fire, you'll get a fire.'

Catherine crouched by the edge of the sticks they had put together, and held up the glasses out once more in the direction of the audience. She then held them up towards the sky. Her spectators looked on, transfixed. She carefully adjusted the distance between the fire and the lenses on the glasses, trying her best to create a focal point on the wood. Georgia and Phillip started to crowd her, trying to see exactly what she was doing, blocking what little sunlight there was. Catherine shooed them out of the way, as Tommy burst out laughing.

'What?'

'Phillip would need to be virtually blind,' he apologised to him with a non-verbal gesture, 'and need specs like magnifying glasses to do what you are trying to do. And

142

that!' he indicated the weak sun, 'couldn't light a candle if it came through a telescope.'

Catherine's face fell, the wind taken straight out of her sails.

'But a jolly good idea, anyway,' Georgia interrupted hastily, and rushed forward to take Phillip's glasses from Catherine for safety's sake, before she got the chance to hurl them in Tommy's direction.

Catherine stood angrily. 'Fine! You're so clever. You do something.'

'I would do if you'd let me smoke.'

'You don't even have any cigarettes.'

'No. That's right. I haven't. But what I have got...' He looked around for the big bag he had managed to get off the lifeboat before it disappeared. He rushed across to it, and dug through what was left inside.

'What are you doing?' Catherine demanded.

Tommy dug deep, and finally clutched what he was after. *You were here all the time. I thought I'd lost you*, he thought to himself. He threw the bag to one side, and stood triumphantly.

'Well?'

Tommy, triumphantly held out the lighter he had had onboard ship.

'Golly!' Phillip exclaimed as he saw the trophy displayed.

'You've had that all the time, and not told us. Just so you could get one over me?' Catherine yelled. 'Are you mad?' She looked at his victorious face, and rushed off and slumped down, alone.

Phillip remained transfixed on the lighter, and Georgia was torn between Catherine's discomfort and the thought of the possibility of some warmth.

A cold wind blew across, and Phillip looked up. 'It's just as well, Catherine! The sun's gone in.'

Catherine glared back at him, then looked away.

Tommy was jubilant at the outcome, although he had actually forgotten all about the lighter, and fate had seemed to play out on his side on this occasion. He crouched down by the wood for the fire, and looked at the impressive way it had been built.

Georgia, looked across at Catherine, hoping she would swallow her pride and come over, but she was ignored, so she pointed Tommy to the smaller twigs, sticks and dry leaves that they had laid carefully for the larger wood to draw on, once it was lit.

Tommy looked across at Catherine, who finally looked back. Refusing to show him any interest whatsoever, she turned away again.

Tommy struck at the lighter.

Nothing.

He struck again.

'It's not working,' Phillip called out with enough volume for Catherine to become interested.

Tommy struck at the lighter once more. Sparks flickered, but there was no flame.

'Let me,' Georgia said, and without waiting to be offered, she took the lighter, gently pushed Tommy out of the way, and crouching down, continued to strike at the lighter.

Three and a half faces watched as the sparks sputtered, and she blew gently on the kindling. Tommy and Phillip's heads bobbed either side of Georgia's, watching for some reaction, obscuring Catherine's milder interest.

Georgia blew, gently, but regularly, and ever so suddenly, a small flame appeared. She placed one dry leaf on top of the next on top of the tiny flame, and ever so slowly, a small amount of smoke drifted past her shoulder.

'It's a fire. It's a fire!' Phillip yelled, and ran round and round in circles.

Catherine looked up with a little more interest, but resigned to Tommy's success, stayed where she was.

Tommy had desperately wanted to take over, once he had seen the first wisp of smoke, but Georgia held him back.

'Wait!' She continued to blow gently on the now established, though as yet, small fire. It was becoming clear she had done this before.

The fire was burning up brightly, and Georgia was loading some larger sticks and branches on top. Phillip had twice been rebuked for wanting to throw huge sticks on top, nearly spoiling all her good work. He now resigned himself to watching the fire grow, from beside it, gleefully holding his hands out to the gathering warmth.

Tommy remained by Georgia's side. He looked across at Catherine, who eventually looked back at him, forcing herself to hold his look, and raised her eyebrows in a half impressed gesture. Phillip walked over to her and took her hand and tried his best to drag her towards the fire. She resisted, slightly.

'Come on. Georgia's got it going.'

Catherine did not move at first, but slowly took on board exactly what he had said. That was it. Georgia had started the fire. Georgia. Not Tommy. She stood up, trying to do something with her dress, and suddenly more impressed, started across.

'Well done, Georgia,' Catherine blurted, just in case Tommy had missed the real reason she was here.

Georgia could feel the heavy tension between the two, and to save taking sides, just nodded, in acceptance of the congratulations.

'All better now?' Phillip asked.

Deciding not to labour the conflict, she smiled, and feeling slightly warmer, said, 'My way would have worked. It might just have taken a little bit longer.'

'We needed it before the end of the war though,' Tommy muttered.

'What?' Catherine barked.

'He said 'We *needed it before the end of the war though*',' Phillip repeated, verbatim.

Catherine glared angrily at her audience, but it had tickled Georgia, and unable to keep it in any longer, she laughed out loud. She giggled and giggled, and the laughter became infectious, and pretty soon, everyone was laughing.

The fire had now grown to a good size, and established, they all sat around it, warming themselves. The frosty atmosphere had melted with the heat it threw out, and by chance, rather than design, Tommy and Catherine were sat apart. Phillip sat between them, putting on more and more wood until they had to move back slightly as the heat grew in intensity. Georgia however, was now quiet, and unusually, sat to one side, pensively.

'What's the matter, Georgia?' Phillip asked, never one to leave one to their thoughts for long.

'I've got what you've got,' she said, lightly. Phillip looked puzzled. 'I'm hungry,' she said. 'We're warm now, but we haven't got a thing to eat. We're surrounded by trees and foliage, and we can't find a thing to eat. Or drink, come to that.'

'The fire...' Catherine started to say.

'... is lit,' Georgia continued. 'Now we've got to move on.'

'But the fire,' Phillip repeated. Although hungry, he was warm now, and he didn't feel that he was going to be of any use to anyone - cold.

Catherine informed them all, rather than suggested, that whatever they did, they must now all stick together. *For Phillip's sake.* Phillip tried to protest, but it was not the strongest objection, as he was now curled up contentedly beside the fire, and was currently next to useless.

'Look!' Georgia said, standing up, demanding their attention. 'The fire is built and burning. Short of a monsoon...' she looked up into the sky and though not burning hot, rain did not appear to be imminent, '...it is going to be here when we get back.'

'And what if we find somewhere else?' Phillip questioned.

'If we find somewhere else and its better, then ultimately we won't need the fire.'

'Unless we're cold.'

'The fire will be here. It is not going anywhere,' Georgia emphasised. 'We however, have to find food and water.'

'She's right.' Tommy said, standing beside her. 'Let's get it together.'

Catherine rose to her feet, but much as she hated it, had to wait to be told what she should do. Shipwrecks were clearly not her thing.

'I can stay and look after the fire,' Phillip said, yawning.

'Fine. Good luck!' Tommy wished him. The two girls looked to him, puzzled at his acceptance of Phillip's idleness. 'As long as you are here, you can look after the fire, and we can be gone for a good couple of days.'

'Right!' Georgia agreed, and prodded Catherine who was weeks behind the logic in Tommy's thinking.

'Yeah! Right!' she said, not totally convincingly, and still not one hundred percent with the sting.

Phillip quickly ran the options available to him through his head, and slowly starting to shake it, said, 'No. You won't be able to do anything with two girls. You're bound to need me.'

'Okay,' Tommy said, 'But only if you want to?'

'Come on,' he answered, climbing to his feet. 'What are we waiting for?'

In spite of the fact that the girls too had come back with nothing, the lack of success on their part still gnawed at Tommy. His chance to assert himself had been wasted, and the furore over the fire had gained him nothing either. He decided that they should all go on the same route the girls had originally searched, as he was sure they must have missed something. He couldn't wait to come across something that Catherine might have walked by without noticing and point it out.

There was also the welfare of his canvas to consider. He may well have bluffed his way past Phillip, and Catherine did not appear to be a sleuth in the making, but Georgia seemed to be on top of everything. He wasn't really that worried if she found out, but he had noticed her affinity to Catherine, and if the pair of them ganged up on him, the canvas was sure to be discovered. Much better they search in another direction, and allow them all to forget about it.

'Fine by me.' Georgia grabbed Phillip by the arm and took off. 'Whichever way you want. Just as long as we get going.'

Tommy cheekily looked across at Catherine, and nodding at the manner in which Phillip and Georgia had led off, held out his hand, as if to do the same. Catherine pulled a face and snorted. It wasn't happening. She gathered herself together, and ever the lady, dusting herself down, brushed past him and rushed off to catch up with the others.

Tommy laughed, and followed on, maybe a little less energetically.

Progress, as before, was slow, and nothing seemed either familiar, or any more useful than it had last time the girls had come this way. Catherine quickly caught up with Georgia, worried that she may have to spend the search with Tommy. She looked around, gloomily, and tutted. Georgia urged her on encouragingly, but it was an uphill battle.

'There's nothing here,' Phillip said dejectedly, after a short while, and a even less enthusiastic Catherine seemed to agree.

Georgia needed to react quickly to stop the positive momentum fading. She searched desperately, digging through the various plant life around them.

'There's nothing there, Georgia,' Catherine informed her. 'We're all going to starve.'

'Starve!' Phillip bleated.

'She doesn't mean it, Phil,' Tommy interrupted.

'Oh yes she does,' Catherine confirmed. 'And it's Phillip!'

Tommy pulled a face at Georgia, and continued the search.

'Look!' Georgia said excitedly. 'Here! These are definitely animal tracks.'

Everyone gathered excitedly around her to see what she was talking about. But as she studiously pointed out the way the grass around them had parted in certain directions, and further displayed various animal droppings, the lack of an immediate solution to their food worries quickly drained their optimism. Even Tommy, a normally reliable supporter of her talents was unimpressed.

'It just goes to show what food there is available here,' she continued her enthusiastic

146

drive.

'And?' Phillip asked, far from impressed.

'And we won't starve.

'And Phillip and I will find it for you,' Tommy said, trying to save a flagging Georgia.

'My hero!' Catherine sneered.

Tommy hoped he had not been hoisted by his own petard. He was no more at home with wildlife than he had been as a sailor. He just had to hope Georgia knew what she was talking about. Wildlife? The only thing he knew about food was that it came from shops. He dug his hands deep into his pockets and looked to Georgia, when… Tommy's hand circled the penknife he had found, what now seemed like a lifetime ago. He thought of offering it to Georgia, but things being what they were, decided to keep it to himself for the time being. He realised there was no point in giving away all his treasures too soon. He would play it by ear for now. There was no immediate advantage to revealing it, just yet.

'Here!' Catherine announced as she and Georgia drew to a halt. 'This is as far as we got.'

'Then it's time for us to take over,' Tommy bustled his way through, grabbing Phillip by the shoulder and dragging him with him.

Georgia looked to Catherine, expecting a string of objections, but she barely shook her head, and hooked her arm through Georgia's.

Tommy suddenly pulled up sharply, and pushed Phillip behind him.

'What is it?' Catherine demanded. 'A bear?'

He held out his hand, begging silence.

His three followers drew up, worried, and looked on, nervously.

Tommy's face was puzzled. He turned his head, listening carefully. Georgia made to join him, but Catherine gripped her arm so tightly she yelped, and stayed where she was.

Tommy slowly started to edge his way forward.

Tommy wasn't really sure about anything, exactly, and he knew he ran the risk of humiliation if he was wrong, but there was something new in the air. Up to now, he had not been looking or listening out for anything in particular, assuming the girls- and especially Georgia - would not have missed it earlier, and it was only when he had caught up and walked forward of the group that he had chanced to notice anything at all.

Phillip, convinced it might be something positive wanted to go with Tommy, but Georgia held him back.

Tommy crouched, and edged his way deeper into the undergrowth, fighting his way through trees, bushes, rocks and boulders and whatever the sound was, it was quickly becoming much clearer. He increased his pace the louder the noise became, and finally his eyes confirmed his thoughts.

147

39

Tommy's eyes lit up like lanterns. A stream of fresh, clear water flowed down over a raised layer of stones, creating a small waterfall. It dropped down into a small shiny pool and spread out in front of him. The thought that it might have been a salt water stream never entered his head, so he rushed down towards the edge of the stream. He came to a halt, sliding down onto his knees, and leaning forward, scooped up a handful of the precious water and placed it to his lips. He closed his eyes as he tasted it, and elated, splashed the remainder over his face.

Georgia saw the excited look on Tommy's face long before he managed to convey anything else. Expectantly, she grabbed Catherine and Phillip's hands and pulled them along with her in his direction. Tommy saw them coming, and seeing no point in stopping them to explain, turned and rushed back.

Catherine, Phillip and Georgia stood looking at the water in wonderment, as if they had not spent days at sea with nothing to drink.

'Look!' Catherine sighed. 'It's beautiful.'

'Then let's go!' Phillip shouted excitedly, and snatching his hand from Georgia's, rushed down to the water's edge. Spotting Tommy crouched down by the water's edge, he jumped clean over the top of him, and scrunching his knees to his chest, landed in the middle in a giant splash, scattering water all around him.

Tommy smiled at Phillip as droplets of the water splashed over him, and about to join him, he suddenly had to duck his head as first Georgia, and then the larger framed figure of Catherine leapt over his head and landed beside Phillip in the middle of the pool. Georgia took no longer than a second to surface, and turning, smiled, cupped her hands, and splashed water back in Tommy's direction.

Tommy ran into the pool, and an amazed Georgia hastily took flight as he charged in her direction.

'No. Mercy!' she begged, slipping on the hidden stones beneath her feet.

'No mercy,' Tommy said, and as she scrambled to find her feet, he picked her up and dropped her flat into the water again.

The second water of the day fight erupted, and the inevitable outcome left four soaked bodies lying horizontal on the riverbank, giggling and screaming with laughter.

'That's the water problem dealt with,' Georgia said, lying back, looking up into the treetops around the pool.

'Yes! After all the bad luck we've had, we deserved a little bit of the good,' Catherine sighed, turning over, chewing on a piece of grass.

'A little praise this way, please,' Tommy demanded.

'Hip hip hooray!' Phillip cheered.

'Yes. Well done you.' Georgia echoed the praise.

'I don't wish to throw a spanner in the works,' Catherine said, 'but I do believe that this is the girl's route. Had we gone off on your route, we would have been thirsty for a month. So a cheer this way, I believe.'

'Hip hip hooray, again!' Phillip cried shrilly, hedging his bets.

'Well!' Catherine stared at Tommy, defiantly.

'Do it!' Georgia demanded. 'I dare you.'

'You what?'

'I dare you.'

Three faces stared straight into Tommy's. He eyed all three.

'Hooray for the girls!' he whispered, almost inaudibly.

'Again!' Georgia insisted.

'And louder,' Catherine added.

Tommy strained a look at Phillip, who chuckled, and turning away, said, 'Hooray for the girls,' and grabbing dramatically at his throat, fell backwards. 'Oh! It's choking me!'

Phillip leapt on him. 'He said it! He said it!'

Catherine and Georgia cheered, and rolled in the grass until their breath ran out.

'We will cheer you,' Catherine declared, 'When you prepare a feast, fit for a King.'

'I'd settle for a carrot at the moment, but indeed a feast it must be,' Georgia kept it light. 'Go from my kingdom and return when you have slain the mighty dragon.'

Hearing 'Dragon', Tommy looked across at Catherine.

'Don't you dare,' Georgia warned him to hold his tongue.

'What?' Tommy exclaimed, and they all broke out in fits of giggles once more.

Phillip lay on the floor absentmindedly gathering together small pieces of twig. He started to build them up into a small stack. Catherine rolled over and asked what he was doing.

'I want to stay here, but our fire is way over there,' he indicated with a huge sweep of his arm.

The thought had not gone unnoticed in the others heads, and as they looked at each other, Catherine, judging the mood, said, 'Well?'

In the shelter of the trees where they were resting, there was an abundance of loose branches, dried leaves, twigs and just about anything a fire connoisseur might demand. It did not take long for the four children to compile another fire, and they stood back proudly.

Tommy reached into his pocket and drew out the lighter. He handed it across to Georgia, but she passed the task back in his direction. He smiled, gratefully and flipped back the lid. They all watched as he pulled back sharply on the striker.

Water and petrol had never been a great chemical blend, and a damp flint had not added to the process. The despondent faces looked down as strike after strike produced not so much as a flicker, and it mattered not who grabbed at the lighter to see if their particular method might be the right one, there was no flame to be had.

'Well! Not so clever now, are we?' Catherine berated Tommy.

149

'It's not my fault,' he defended himself after all the good he thought he had done.

'Our saviour! One lighter. That was all you had to keep safe, and you couldn't even do that.'

'It will dry,' Georgia said. 'Once it's dry, we won't have a problem.'

'It won't dry. It's useless, he's useless…'

'We've got a fire,' Phillip interrupted. 'We don't need the stupid lighter. What is the matter with all of you? Stop fighting, just for the sake of it.'

'That is not the point,' Catherine said.

'Then what is?' Tommy begged. 'What is?'

'Everything was perfect,' she blurted, 'and now you've gone and spoilt it all, again.'

'Yes. We've got a fire, but, we haven't got any food, and we're lost. Explain to me what part of perfect I appear to have missed?'

Catherine slumped down in tears. Georgia walked over to her, and was about to console her, when Catherine struck out, her arms flailing.

Georgia jumped back, more from shock than hurt, and shied away from the blow. She stood back, her eyes starting to fill with tears. Phillip looked on, torn between running to his sister, or Georgia.

'Oh no you don't,' Tommy snapped.

'What?'

'You can yell at me, and Phillip is your brother, but you don't fly off the handle at Georgia. She's the only sane one amongst us, and you want to stop that.'

'I don't.'

'Look. Just look!'

Catherine looked across at Georgia, and fell speechless.

Georgia looked up, shyly as everyone looked at her, and she suddenly felt like a circus act. As a further tear made its way down her cheek, she stood up, turned, and ran off.

Catherine sat guiltily.

'Nice one,' Tommy said, and not waiting for anything from Catherine, rushed off to catch up with Georgia.

When he finally caught up with her, Georgia was flopped down by the burning embers of the fire they had lit, seemingly hours ago. She was breathing heavily, and busily picking at small pieces of wood, placing them on the remains of the fire.

'Hey!'

'I'm fine,' Georgia said bravely, wiping away another tear that had dared to escape.

'No, Georgia. I'm sorry. She was horrible.' He walked across and placed a comforting arm around her shoulder. 'Why do you put up with her? I wish we'd left her on the ship.'

'No you don't,' she laughed.

'Well!'

Georgia laughed again.

150

'There you go. That's better, isn't it?'

'Thank you.'

Tommy sat down beside her, and together, and with no need for words, they continued to feed the fire.

As the atmosphere became more relaxed, Tommy eventually looked at Georgia and cast her a smile which she returned.

'So what's the story with you guys?' he asked. 'How did you get mixed up with these two? You're not a relative?' Georgia shook her head. 'What's going on?'

'Oh! You know!' Georgia blushed, and turned away shyly not wanting to feed Tommy any ammunition for him to use against Catherine at a later date.

'No. That's just it. I don't.'

Georgia thought for a second. 'Look. If I tell you... No. I can't.'

'Hey! You want to keep it to yourself, fine. I just wondered. That's all.'

'It's not that. It's just... Well...' Georgia sat back and stared deeply into the fire.

Once she had started, the words simply fell out of her. There was no turning back.

Tommy sat back and listened, glued to her words.

'Oh my! I've said far too much,' Georgia finally stopped. 'Catherine will kill me. Listen, Edward...'

'You're fine,' Tommy held up a consoling hand. 'I won't say a word.'

'Promise? Promise me.'

'I promise.'

Georgia relaxed, slightly.

'So you were a maid?' he exclaimed as the news sank in.

'Yes.'

'To - both of them?'

'Yes. But till we get rescued, we're all in this together, and that's that.'

Tommy lay back and laughed. 'Ha, ha, ha! It explains so much.'

'Please don't mention anything. You promised.'

'I'll do my best, but...'

'Edward!'

'All right! All right! Anyway. We have way more important things to worry about.'

'Like?'

'Like, how we get this fire across to the pool. I guess that's where we all want to be isn't it?' Georgia nodded. 'Okay. Let's get our thinking hats on, then.'

'When do you think they'll be back?' Phillip asked, lying back in the grass, fidgeting.

'When they're ready. Really! I can't see why Georgia, and you especially, seem to take his side all the time.'

'We don't take his side. It's just, sometimes you're impossible.'

'What?' Catherine said, lightening up.

'You heard me,' Phillip said, laughing as she approached him. He stood up with his back to the water. Catherine had him cornered. He looked left and right for any hope of

151

escape, but Catherine had her arms out, and he was stuck. He turned towards the water, weighing up the option of jumping in. His clothing was still damp and he didn't really fancy getting any wetter. But neither did not want to give in to his sister. He stared into the water.

'Right, mister. Impossible, am I?'

'Wait!'

'I'll give you wait, young man.'

'No really. Wait!' he whispered seriously. Catherine's stared over his shoulder, looked into the water.

'Well I never!'

40

Tommy had gathered together a collection of longer, thicker sticks and laid them into the fire, hoping for them to catch and stay alight long enough for the journey back to the pool. His sacrificial efforts lay smouldering in the ashes, untried as yet, as a slightly less hopeful Georgia looked on.

'Maybe we should build a camp here, and let Catherine stay by the pond,' Tommy joked. 'We can trade her water for heat. What do you think?'

'I think we should all stay together. We are lost, and haven't even set about finding exactly where we are yet.'

'We're on an island. I don't know why, but I just know.'

'I think we are too, but I just don't want it to be true. Till we've done something about finding out, I'm just going to go on hoping. Now! What are we going to do about this fire?'

Tommy, having discarded Edward Burrows blazer at the stream, took off the jumper, and picked up a large stick.

'What are you doing?' Georgia asked.

'I'm going to wrap it round the end of the stick, and hope it makes a torch. Like in the films at the...'

'No!'

'What?'

'Not that. Not the jumper.' She looked around frantically, before looking down at her dress. Just turn around.'

'What?'

'Turn around.'

Tommy turned, curiously.

'Promise not to look.'

'What?'

'I said, don't look! Just stay there.'

'Sure. But I don't know what you are doing.'

'Just stay turned around.'

Georgia walked behind a large bush, and carefully removed the petticoat from beneath her dress. She pulled down the cotton slip, and making sure she was still presentable, said, 'Alright! You can turn around now.'

Tommy turned and looked at the underskirt she held out for him. He took it and compared the two garments, feeling the quality.

'But this is too good to burn.'

'And that,' she pointed to his jumper, 'is all you have to keep you warm.'

'And you?'

Georgia took the petticoat back, and to save any further dispute, sat down and struggled to tear at the bottom of the skirt. 'I'll use some of it.'

Tommy watched for a moment, and then putting his pullover back on, asked if he could help. Georgia told him she was fine, but was unable to make any progress in the tearing of the material. So Tommy took it from her, and producing the penknife, nicked at the cloth, creating a tear, and handed it back to her to finish what she had started.

'A penknife!'

'I thought it might come in handy.'

Two strips of cloth had been taken from the petticoat, and Georgia held up a slightly shorter article of clothing than she had had before for his approval.

'Just the job,' he said. It was shorter, but it still had its form and would still serve its purpose. 'You'll just have to pull your socks up.'

Georgia frowned.

The same rules applied in the redressing of the petticoat. Tommy turned his back and allowed Georgia space to make herself up.

'Don't you think we ought to be getting back?' Georgia asked, presenting herself once more for approval.

'What's the worst that could happen?' Tommy said.

The look between the two spoke volumes.

'Quick as we can, then!' Tommy said, and taking the material from Georgia, started to bind it firmly around the end of a large stick.

'Wait! Try this,' she said. She took several small twigs, and various pieces of dried out plant and interwove these with the strips of cloth, until finally they had what looked to be a substantial torch. It was never going to start the Great Fire of London, but it might just do the trick for now. They stood back and looked dubiously at their finished product, and then to each other..

'We'd better build up the fire here just in case this goes all ends up,' Georgia said, and set off to collect some more wood.

'You stay there, girl. I'll do that. You don't have to look after me, you know?'

Georgia looked at him sternly, reminding him of their promise.

'We make a pretty good team, don't we?' Tommy said, prodding her in the arm.

Georgia scrunched her nose. 'Yeah! We do.'

The newly bound torch lay beside the freshly stoked fire. They had built it up until it was almost too strong to approach.

'This should last,' Tommy said. 'Last chance. Sure you don't want to leave Catherine where she is?'

Georgia frowned, playfully.

'Oh well! Just thought I'd ask.'

Georgia picked up the torch, and approached the fire. She stopped.

'What is it?'

'You do it,' Georgia handed the torch across. 'Oh! And just in case this burns through in seconds, we are going to have to run.'

154

Tommy took the torch, checked the bindings for the last time, and then looked excitedly at Georgia. 'Ready?'

'Ready.'

Catherine was sat with her legs hanging over the bank by the pool, studying Phillip. He was stood bent double with his hands dangling in the water in front of him, transfixed.

'Anything?' she asked.

'Sssh!' Phillip chided her.

'We're back!' Georgia called proudly from the distance, and seconds later, heralded Tommy and the mercifully still flaming torch. They smiled jubilantly, holding out their prize.

Catherine looked over, relatively unconcerned, and raised her eyebrows. Tommy and Georgia looked at each other, confused.

'I give up,' Tommy said.

'Just light it,' Georgia said, totally brought down to ground.

Tommy raised himself up on tiptoe to try to catch a look at Phillip's face to see if he might be able to shed some light on things, but he was equally as non-committal as his sister.

'Well!' Catherine said.

Tommy handed the torch across to Georgia, and stormed over towards Catherine, who looked away.

'I *give* up. Just light it, Georgia, and be done with it,' Tommy said, and walked back to stand beside a disappointed Georgia. She took the torch and inserted it into the middle of the fire, and stood back as it slowly started to catch.

Phillip climbed from the water, and came across and stood beside his sister. His face was strangely contorted, his demeanour bursting to reveal something, and only just managing to conceal it.

'Well! Did you bring us back a feast then?' Catherine asked.

'I have never met anyone so ungrateful,' Tommy said, and returned his attention to the fire, where Georgia was tending it carefully. 'We really can't do anything right, can we?'

'No. But we can,' Catherine said, raising her voice to make a point, attempting to grab their attention.

Tommy didn't even turn to acknowledge her, and sulkily stood beside Georgia, looking forlornly into the burgeoning flames. Neither of them moved until slowly over their shoulders, a stick appeared.

'We've *got* the wood,' Tommy started, but stopped suddenly as he looked to the tip of the stick. 'Where did you...?'

'I caught it,' Phillip screamed pointing to the fish punctured on the point of the stick.

'We've been waiting ages to tell you,' Catherine said excitedly, 'and couldn't do anything with it till you both got back.'

'We nearly ate it,' Phillip said, 'But raw fish? I don't think so!'

Georgia had said nothing, but had quietly taken the stick from Phillip, and now held the catch over the burgeoning flames.

'It's not very big,' Phillip confessed.

'It is a positive feast,' Georgia exclaimed.

'One more to us,' Catherine said.

'Me, actually,' Phillip stood his ground.

'Well... Yes... I mean...'

'Well done Phillip. Georgia is right. A...' Tommy paused.

'...Positive,' Georgia prompted.

'...Positive Feast,' he concluded.

Catherine looked slightly less proud, so Georgia assured them all that with Tommy's lighter, the Girl's pool, and Phillip's fish, everyone should feel very proud.

'A draw then,' Tommy bravely offered Catherine under the circumstances.

'Very well. A draw it is.' It was the best either of them was likely to receive, and it was amiably accepted.

Phillip ignored the combat and watched dreamily as the fish started to change colour as it was turned over the flames.

Tommy's knife, its appearance better left between he and Georgia, ensured equal portions of fish for all, and the children had picked dry the very last flesh that the bones had tried to hold on to.

'I normally only like my fish covered in batter,' Tommy said, 'but as this fish goes, it is certainly the best I have ever tasted.' Everyone laughed.

'And had we a drink, I would offer a toast,' Catherine said. 'But instead, a hearty round of applause for all involved.'

The applause was heartening, and briefly chivvied their flagging spirits. But as the applause died, and the barely satisfied tummies welcomed the effort, they looked to each other realising exactly how hungry they really were.

Phillip jumped up and smiled to his audience, and rushed off back towards the stream. 'What are you doing?' Georgia asked.

'Getting pudding.'

By the time evening arrived and the light was starting to disappear, Phillip had successfully managed to tickle a few more fish. The meat it had provided had done little more than to quell the hunger pangs, but it had not gone unappreciated. His afternoon had been put to good use. Georgia had helped Tommy gather some more wood for the fire and pile it up beside it, for use throughout the night, and Catherine had assisted as best she could, and in a way in which only she could do. But as useless as it may have been, it was appreciated, if only for the sake of a spell of peace and quiet.

Exhausted, and drying out from the substantial time he had spent in the water, Phillip sat close to the fire. He had been excused duties for the rest of the day.

156

The three elder children sat together. Phillip looked up into the sky and flinched as a drop of water hit him in the centre of his forehead.

'Rain!' he shouted.

After the conditions they had experienced aboard the lifeboat, nobody reacted more than to acknowledge his comment.

'Rain,' he repeated, now getting to his feet.

'We're by the fire,' Catherine tried to pacify him.

'But it will put the fire out.'

So settled were they, the second warning met with as little attention than the first. Only after the intensity of the rain increased to such a state that it started to penetrate the cover of the trees high above their heads, did they pay it any attention at all.

Georgia, the first to break, pushed her head out and looked up.

'Are we okay?' Tommy asked her.

'We'll have to wait and see.'

The rain that continued as a light shower soon turned into something slightly more substantial. The overhead branches did everything they could to keep it off the fire, but still it managed to work its way through. It splashed and hissed, and despite the extra wood they had added to the fire to ward off the attack, the three elder children looked to each other nervously.

'Well?' Georgia asked.

'Keep your fingers crossed,' Tommy advised, and slowly, and hoping it was unobserved, three sets of fingers quietly crossed.

'We are going to need better shelter' Phillip griped, sleepily, as a large drop of rain that had amassed on an overhead branch fell and caught him square on the chin, waking him up. He shook himself, and was now fully awake.

'It's dark,' Catherine told him. 'Stay where you are. We don't know what's out there, or what dangers there are. Just stay here with me.'

'If this goes out, we've had it,' he continued, relentlessly.

'Just lie still.'

'He's right,' Georgia said to Tommy. 'We've got to keep this alight at all costs. The original fire wasn't half as covered as this one is. It probably went out ages ago.'

'We are under cover,' Tommy said, and shook his head, shaking water all over her.

'Hey!'

'Okay. Maybe you're right.'

'If we're going to do something, we'd better do it now.'

'I'll go,' Tommy volunteered.

'You won't be able to see anything,' Phillip, the instigator of the problem said.

'You'll need another torch,' Georgia said.

'You won't have any petticoat left at all at this rate,' Tommy pointed out. Catherine looked across, confused. Tommy looked at Georgia, and they both giggled. 'Don't worry. I'll just go for a scout round here. We only need to keep the rain off the fire. I'll

157

be back before you know it.'

Phillip stirred slightly more, and making to get up, offered to help, but his sister needed only to apply a little restraint to keep him where he was.

'You've done your bit today,' Tommy winked at him, and he smiled back.

'Where are you going to go?' Catherine asked. 'You'll have to be careful.'

'Steady on. You almost sound like you care.'

'I just want to stay warm. I will care for whoever finds somewhere for me - I mean - us, to keep warm. Even you.'

'Take it as a compliment,' Georgia whispered.

Tommy nodded, and got up to go. He looked forlornly at the fire, shivered, rubbed his hands over the flames and without waiting for a fanfare, disappeared into the darkness.

Georgia moved closer to Catherine and Phillip now that Tommy had gone. An animal cry cut through the dark silence, and Catherine drew Georgia closer still.

'It's just a bird,' Georgia assured her, trying to comfort herself.

'Right. Just a bird.'

Phillip was asleep, and the two girls felt alone.

'I wish he'd hurry up and get back,' Catherine confessed after no time at all. 'Maybe it's dry enough here as it is.'

'He'll be back. Don't worry.'

'I'm not worried.'

Silence.

Once away from the light of the fire, vision was that much more difficult. It did not help that he kept looking back, taking a bearing, and walking straight into overhanging branches, or stumbling over roots and rocks set into the ground.

As he progressed, the rain increased its intensity, and looking back, he wasn't sure whether he had walked out of distance of the fire, or if the rain had in fact put it out. He considered walking back, but did not want to go back empty-handed. He thought about revealing the cave where he had stored his canvas, but quickly threw away the idea. The space inside had barely been big enough for him to crawl inside. Besides, he would have trouble finding the spot again in daylight. He had no chance of finding it again in this light.

The sound of a – bird - stopped him in his tracks.

'Hello!' he offered nervously in response. He should turn back. There would be no shame in it. He stood breathing heavily, and shivering from the effect of the rain and the growing cold, shoved his hands deep into his pockets. He clutched at the penknife in one, the extinct lighter in the other.

He drew the lighter from his pocket and looked down towards his hand. He shook his head, opened the cover on the lighter, and just for the sake of it, pulled back against the striker.

The sparks that discharged from the lighter caught Tommy totally by surprise. He was so shocked in fact, that he threw the lighter away from him. Georgia had been right. It had dried out - to some extent at least. The worst of it was, he had dropped it.

The darkness grew around him again.

'What are we going to do now?' Catherine asked.

'We can't do anything till he gets back,' Georgia said.

'No. Not now. I mean, later. Tomorrow. What are we going to do?'

'I don't know. We will have to keep searching I suppose. Who knows? We might even...'

'We're on an island. I don't know how big it is, but there is no sign of anyone here. No tracks, no paths. Not even one sign of anyone having been here before.'

'Sssh!' Georgia indicated Phillip, not wanting to worry him unnecessarily should he wake.

'He's fine,' Catherine indicated the sleeping form.

'Anyway! We haven't been anywhere yet. It's not like we've spent the day exploring extensively.'

'I love your optimism, Georgia, but don't think for one minute I am as stupid as I look...' She stopped. 'I mean...'

'I don't think anything,' Georgia laughed. 'Come on. We really don't know anything yet. Let's face it. We've spent all day getting warm and fed. Tomorrow is another day, and things are sure to look better in the morning.'

Another shriek in the distance as one more inhabitant announced its presence, and they huddled closer together.

'Tomorrow cannot come too soon.'

Tommy had spent a fruitless age searching for the lighter, and only the excitement of having discovered the ability to make fire again, encouraged him to sustain the search at all. He had scrabbled through the mud in front of him and had almost given up when he finally nudged at something with his fingertips. He stopped and groped blindly until he finally established where it was. He carefully picked it up, and having wiped it on the few square inches of dry cloth he could find amongst his clothing, he held his breath, and tried to strike it once more to check it had not been a fluke.

Catherine screamed as Tommy's dark figure loomed up in front of them.

'Why didn't you tell us you were there?' she scolded him.

Georgia looked up. 'Did you find anywhere better?'

'I didn't get that far,' Tommy confessed. 'But look.' He took the lighter from his pocket and struck at it. The sparks it created looked all the better in the dark of the night, and an audible sigh erupted.

The excitement at Tommy's revelation, and a suddenly energetic Catherine, woke Phillip from his sleep, and he looked up wearily. He rubbed his eyes and smiled at seeing Tommy back with them.

159

'Hey, partner!' Tommy said in his direction.

'Is it morning yet?' he asked in a daze.

'Not yet,' Catherine said, now realising they had woken him, and she gently stroked his head. She was ready to explain to him when the influence of the sandman overpowered him once more and he rolled over and returned to sleep. 'It will wait,' she whispered.

The high spirits having died slightly, Tommy pocketed the lighter, and went across to join them round the fire.

'You can rain all you want,' Catherine said. 'We're not bothered.'

'It's not,' Georgia said.

'It's not what?'

'It's not raining.'

They all looked up into the night sky, and the rain that had started the panic in the first place, had stopped. The only occasional trickles of water that fell at all were from the tree tops where they had caught up in the leaves and branches. The fire continued to burn brightly. The damage the rain had done to the ground around the fire was minimal, and here seemed as good a place to remain for the night as any other, and despite lack of bedclothes of any description, they curled up with just the warmth of fire for company, and one by one, they joined Phillip in dreamland.

41

Daylight came about, and a weak sunlight broke through the same gaps in the trees that had allowed rain through the previous evening. The fire was now charred wood and ashes, but smoke still rose amongst the remaining embers. Catherine was cuddled up next to Phillip, with Georgia curled up on the other side. Her skirt having dried by the fire had spread out around her like a fan. She opened her eyes, and blinked at the light. She shook her head, and took a few seconds to remind herself of where she was. She checked that Phillip was still asleep, and noticed Georgia, likewise. She smiled at the thought that Georgia used to be up hours before she and Phillip, but the smile faded as she remembered how far away those days were.

She finally managed to break from Phillip, and turned to get up. She started to rise when she felt something dragging at her skirt. She looked down to discover Tommy's head lying on her billowed skirt as if it were a pillow. She baulked slightly at what she saw as an unwelcome intimacy, and thought about how best to free herself from this dilemma. Tommy, like the others, was still asleep, and as much as she wanted to be free of him, she did not really want to deliberately disturb him. Looking around her, her eyes settled on a large stick that had been brought back for fuel the night before, and stretching slightly, managed to bring it down until she had it under her control. She reached down slightly, and gently rubbing the stick at Tommy's back, he stirred, slightly. She repeated the manoeuvre, tapping his back slightly harder, and as he unconsciously arched his body against the irritation, she just managed to rescue her dress.

Georgia had opened her eyes on hearing Catherine stir and had watched, amazed at her antics. She was amazed at how she managed to keep her dignity in the most bizarre and unlikely situation in which she had ever found herself. She continued to watch her, guiltily, several times feigning sleep as she looked back in her direction, as she started to gather together some pieces of wood and delicately placed them on top of the fire, at fingertip length.

Georgia waited for an opportune moment, and slowly started to rouse herself as if waking for the first time, and Catherine, welcoming the company, proudly pointed to the fire, displaying her efforts. Georgia quickly realised she was going to need help.

The children sat around the fire, which no real thanks to Catherine, was finally burning brightly once more. The gloomy thoughts of the night before still smouldered, and what the day was likely to bring about was fresh on their minds.

'I wonder what time it is?' Catherine yawned.

'Ten o'clock,' Phillip volunteered positively. 'Spot on.'

'Ten o'clock? What do you mean?'

'Ten o'clock,' Phillip offered his watch for confirmation.

'But your watch is broken. They all are.'

'Like I said then. Ten o'clock. It always is, and always will be.'

Tommy and Georgia laughed, but Catherine found it far less amusing, and seemed in no mood for light banter this morning. No matter what time it actually was.

Phillip had taken to the water to battle his wits against those of the fish once more. The three older children sat sombrely around the fire.

'Well?' Catherine asked. 'What now?'

'We need to build a fire,' Tommy said.

'A fire?' Catherine looked in front of them incredulously. 'What's this then?'

'Not this one,' he sighed. 'This is great, for us. But if the rain didn't fully get through to us last night, then it is unlikely that the smoke from this is going to get through it.'

'And?' Catherine again.

'We have to build a fire that can be seen from the sea. For miles around.'

'A beacon fire,' Georgia exclaimed excitedly.

'But where are we going to build it?' Catherine asked. 'We don't even know where we are or anything.'

'Then it's time to find out.'

'Don't you think it would be better if we looked around first?' Georgia said. 'We won't be able to build one just anywhere. It needs to be along the coast, or at least on top of a piece of high ground, surely.'

'Well?' Catherine asked, rather hopelessly.

'And we're not even sure if we're alone yet,' Georgia continued.

The thought that they might not be alone was greeted somewhat soberly.

'We're alone,' Tommy said. 'I know we've only been her ten minutes, but I know we're on an island, and I just know we're all alone.'

The two girls said nothing. He was only really echoing what they were both thinking deep down.

'Well we've got to do something,' Catherine said. 'We can't just sit here.'

Tommy smirked. They did not seem like words he had expected to hear from her, but he kept his thoughts to himself.

'We've got to have a better look around,' Georgia said.

'Well he'll want to go with you,' Catherine pointed down to the stream where Phillip was still battling it out with the fish. 'You know that, don't you?'

'But what about getting something to eat?' Georgia said. 'He's really rather good at it.'

'Yes. He's taken to it like a fish to water,' Catherine said, and smiled. 'I don't know where he picked it up from. Father must have taught it to him.'

'Well whoever taught it to him, he's better off where he is,' Tommy said, thinking back to yesterday, and how easily Phillip had tired. 'But you'd better tell him the bad news.'

'No problem,' Catherine agreed a little too readily.

'Not yet!' Tommy said. 'Wait till we know exactly where we're going to search.'

Catherine rolled up the sleeves on her blouse, and brushed her hands together.

162

Georgia and Tommy burst out laughing.

'What is it?'

'Why don't you let us do it,' Tommy said. 'Why don't you just stay here with Phillip?'

'Fine!' Catherine snapped, hurt. She turned and started to walk away. 'I'll do just that then, shall I?'

Georgia walked over and comforted her, and helped explain how she just might be better off where she was.

'What do you both want me to do then?' she asked.

Tommy refrained from the easy jokey reply, and relenting, explained to her that if this was the best place for them to be, and if they were to be here for some time, they had better start to make it liveable.

'You can also tell Phillip we need a camp. It will stop him feeling left out,' Georgia suggested. 'And besides, he appears to be happy there. Mind you, if he spends any more time in the water, he will never need to bathe again.'

'Maybe I could search for berries or something,' Catherine suggested, helpfully. 'Making a camp? It's not quite me.'

'Berries are good,' Tommy said. 'Let's all do something that is to our benefit.'

Catherine wasn't sure whether or not this was a rebuke, so stood, and bade them farewell and promised she would see them later. She started to walk off to impart the bad news to Phillip.

'Will she be okay on her own?' Tommy asked Georgia.

'There's only one way to find out.'

Phillip was stood fishing, moodily. Catherine in breaking the news of what was going to happen during the day, had once more managed to irk him, and just as Georgia and Tommy had been preparing to set off, they had had to return and defuse the situation. Catherine was so upset that they thought she couldn't even handle one simple task, she stormed off, and Georgia had been left, the better to pacify him. She had somehow convinced him that the hunter was by far the most important person on an island, and that was him. It seemed to have done the trick.

Appeased, he accepted the responsibility thrust upon him, and just as Georgia was about to journey off with Tommy, there was a loud scream from Catherine, some way off into the distance.

Phillip, all fore-planning gone to waste, quickly jumped out of the stream, and led the way as the three rushed off to see what had happened.

Catherine, angry, and desperate to do something positive, had taken off on a route through the bushes that even an adept squirrel might have thought twice about. Her now dry, flowing dress, had snagged on a collection of thorns on a bush, and currently it was unclear as to who exactly was winning the battle to keep it. The search party arrived and looked on in consternation as she glared back at them angrily. Tommy ventured forward to try to help her, but the glare she offered in return stopped him in his tracks.

163

'I think you had better go off on your own for now,' Georgia whispered, out of Catherine's earshot. 'I think maybe she and I should work this one out together.'

Catherine looked across, suspiciously, to see what they were concocting, and just as she was about to say something about it, another thorn dug into her and she screamed again.

'See you later,' Tommy said, and gratefully left the scene.

Tommy, suddenly finding himself alone, quickly thought about trying to make his way back to find his hideaway. He wanted to find out if the previous night's rain had penetrated it in any way and damaged the canvas, but it was a long way away, and he didn't want to be away for too long, in case they thought about trying to follow him. He decided it wasn't going anywhere for the time being, so boldly set off in search of virgin terrain.

Catherine, now doggedly independent, dismissed Phillip, and then glared across at Georgia, helplessly.

'Get me out of this, now!'

Georgia helped her pick her way out of her predicament, and finally free, she brushed her to one side, and stubbornly walked straight into the next thorny, impenetrable obstacle.

Only when Georgia had dragged her free from her new shackles did she reluctantly agree another route may in fact be preferable. She followed on behind Georgia, mumbling, though quietly grateful for the company.

Georgia carefully selected a route that appeared likely to be more Catherine-proof, and watched as she insisted on taking it on, on her own. She had told her they would cover far more ground if they weren't on top of each other. Georgia agreed, but decided it might be better to keep her within earshot, just in case. She had wanted to explore with Tommy, but though currently excused her duties as a maid, found it difficult to rid herself of the task.

Tommy, having been raised mostly under the stern hand of his father, had taken on the responsibility of the leader and provider of the group by right. The rivalry between he and Catherine was something totally new to him. Maybe it was the age difference, or more perhaps, the chasm between the two in class. Whatever it was, it was on-going, and a solution did not seem imminent. He set off about his task at speed. He imagined the faster he went about his search, the more of the - island he was likely to discover. His surety in the streets of London had been admirable, and he had managed to surmount most of the problems he had come across. His naivety of a country life though was very soon apparent as he was sent sprawling as his foot caught the concealed route of a tree. He cussed angrily, and looked around expecting to need to apologise. No. He was on his own, again. Same old story, different setting.

He picked himself up, carefully examining his body for any new damage, and

164

stunned slightly by the fall, decided to walk on with a little more attention to exactly where he was going. He rubbed his hands roughly together to alleviate the pain, and then brushed any fresh debris from his body.

He looked up for the first time since the fall and stopped. He quickly crouched to the floor and drew himself in behind a large bush, and looked on from there.

Tommy slowly poked his head around the bush, and looked across the clearing in front of him. He stared deeply into the eyes of countless rabbits, scattered in front of him, chewing on a large variety of greenery. They did not rush off immediately as he had expected, and they shared a quiet moment of reflection before he finally moved towards them and they scattered. He had never eaten rabbit before, but he imagined that it was edible, and as good a substitute for the apparent lack of fish this morning as there was likely to be. Catching one however, was going to be something else altogether. For all his streetwise wile and cunning, this was going to be a very different battle of wits.

Tommy, his head spinning, as the rabbits took off in all directions, dropped back and settled down on the ground.

'Right you are! We'll have to try another way. You'll be back. I hope.'

He did not have long to wait, and the rabbits soon appeared again. They spread out into the apparently sumptuous feeding ground, and started to chew on the grass and other vegetation, unconcerned, and if aware of his presence, apparently unconcerned by it. Tommy eyed them from his seclusion, and bandied ideas around his head as exactly how to best to get his hands on even one of them. He imagined what a trophy a rabbit would be, let alone the meat it would provide. But imagination was one thing. Catching one, another altogether.

Determined not to give in too easily, Tommy set his eyes on what appeared to be the largest rabbit he had ever set eyes upon. He did not in fairness have more than its compatriots to compare it to, but this was certainly the one. He turned over several methods of trapping the rabbit, inside his head. He certainly didn't want to jump out on them again. One would spark the other and in seconds he would be on his own again.

Decided on stealth, he started to inch his way forward on his hands and knees. He was not paying much attention to the ground he was covering, his eyes locked on the intended victim, and unbeknownst to him, his knee landed heavily on a branch that snapped under his weight.

The resultant crack immediately woke the seemingly lethargic rabbits. They stopped eating in a second, and looked up, their whiskers twitching.

Tommy stopped where he was. There was an apparent stand-off between he and the entire rabbit population on the island, each waiting for the other to move.

Now! Tommy thought, and leapt forward.

The rabbits scattered and had quickly found the safety of their burrows long before Tommy's body even hit the ground, where he landed with a thump. He looked up in vain as the bright tails disappeared down the entrances to their hidden burrows. Tommy lay winded from the unproductive dive, but smiled. There was more food on the island than just the fish. Catching them was just a new challenge, that was all. So, he climbed to his feet, brushing off the nrw debris hanging off his clothing, and far from despondent, decided to return to regale the others with the exciting news. The discovery of the rabbits suddenly heavily outweighed the need to explore the island. Food was far more important. He would trade ideas with Georgia, who was bound to have something up her substantially logical sleeves.

The longer time wore on, the more Georgia was torn between her instinct to roam, and her loyalty to stay with Catherine. In spite of her admiration at Catherine's sudden urge to become part of a master plan, she was not sure if she actually wished she had not stayed back at the pool with Phillip. It wasn't that she wasn't proud of her newfound spirit, but she knew she would be able to accomplish far more if she was on her own. Or at least by Tommy's side.

She broke from her thoughts as she heard Catherine angrily confronting another species of plant life. She made to help her, and then stopped. Looking after Catherine was going to be a full time job, but if she didn't at least give her a chance to do it on her own, she was never going to make it. So, still feeling guilty, she chose a nearby spot from where she could pounce if the need truly arose.

Catherine searched 'manfully' through the terrain she had been allotted, but it was clear she was never going to have a country named after her. She stumbled across the ground in a pair of shoes that might better have suited a Ball. She slipped and stumbled several times, and though too proud to call out, she dearly wished Georgia were there to lend her a helping hand.

For all the troubles that seemed to have heaped themselves upon her, she was inwardly very proud of herself. She would have been the first to admit she and a deserted island were as far apart as it was possible to be, but she was trying her hardest. She grimaced as her foot suddenly jerked to one side and gave way. She yelped, and fell to the floor, and as she closely examined any damage, she whimpered slightly. Had she had an audience, she was convinced she would have cried, but to her credit, she cussed quietly and struggled back to her feet. She wiped her hands down her skirt, leaving it dirtier still, and looking down at the state of herself, growled angrily, before finally returning to the task in hand.

Georgia sat motionless in her secreted spot, convinced that Catherine had stared straight at her. She had not wanted to appear to be patronising, and proudly convinced that her charge was managing to adapt comfortably, turned away and managed to safely put some space between the two of them. She turned delicately and walked straight into a spiked bush, and found herself barbed. She shouted out disconsolately as the thorn dug into her side.

Catherine hearing her anguish, happily broke from her fruitless search, and rushed to where she had heard the cry. She saw Georgia caught up, as she had been, and coolly walked across.

'So! Who needs whose help now?' she asked.

'Oh, Catherine! It's you,' Georgia said as if she hadn't known where she had been.

'In trouble?'

Georgia struggled to get loose, trying anything she could to free herself unaided, but like Catherine, the more she struggled, the harder the task became, and finally she had to resign herself to wait for Catherine to delicately pick her way round firstly one thorn, then the next, until at last she was free. It was going to be a long job. She just managed to resist the urge to tell Catherine to get on with it, but, in no position to do anything about it, and the strong likelihood that she might take umbrage and leave her to it, she patiently waited out the rescue.

Catherine finally stood back proudly, having released her, and brushed her hands awaiting a little gratitude. Georgia, having waited so long, had momentarily forgotten to do so, but as she saw Catherine's questioning face, finally relented.

But Catherine continued to stare, almost looking through Georgia.

'I said, *Thank you*,' Georgia reiterated, but Catherine simply raised her hand and pointed behind Georgia, who turned, puzzled.

Under closer examination, the bush, of which she had only minutes before been a part of, revealed small black berries hidden within the thorny foliage. Catherine gently pushed Georgia to one side, and cautiously picked at one of them. She looked first to it, and then to Georgia, to whom she handed it across, this seeming more her department. Georgia took the berry and looked at it, trying to give it a name of some sort. It was not something she had come across in all her tender years. She had been a housemaid, and though having spent a lot of time with Cook, the kitchen had not been her department. She held the berry in front of her, racking her brains to try to identify the culprit as Catherine continued to pick, squealing, as she was attacked time and again by the thorns the bush had evolved as defence against violation.

They each held a small handful of berries and looked firstly to them, then to each other. Catherine had clearly never come across these berries before either, at least not in their natural state. The only time she had ever seen berries at all, they had usually been covered with crumble and custard.

Georgia picked up a berry from her hand and studied it carefully. Catherine did the same. Georgia squashed it between her fingers and a red juice ran down her fingers. She smelled her fingers, and looked at Catherine and shrugged.

'Together, then,' Catherine suggested. 'One! Two! Three! Go!'

42

Phillip was lying face down beside the pool, staring into its depths. He had long since left the confines of the pool as the excitement of the previous day had worn off. The pool was now colder and with everyone away, there was no excitement to get the blood flowing. And it appeared that the fish had completely disappeared. Or he had caught them all already. He had not seen even a single fish, and was now bored. He had promised he would not venture away from the pool, and although he was not averse to breaking the odd rule, he was slightly worried about wandering too far without Tommy, or maybe Georgia by his side, so he slumped down and waited.

'Phillip,' Tommy bellowed from some distance.

'Edward!' he snapped out of his mood, and jumped up, a different person altogether.

'Where are the girls?'

'I don't know,' he answered somewhat miffed. 'I've been here on my own all this time. Remember?'

'Yeah! Of course you have. Sorry,' Tommy apologised half-heartedly. 'Now, where are they?'

'They won't have gone far. Well, Catherine won't anyway.'

'Come with me.'

'What?'

'Come with me. No. Wait. Strength in numbers.'

'What on earth are you on about?'

Tommy was so excited that he could not stand still, torn between rushing back to the warren, and waiting for the girls' eventual return.

'Got any fish?' he asked, without really worrying about an answer.

'No.'

'Never mind.'

'But I caught a tiger and a peacock.'

'Great.'

Phillip slumped to the floor and turned his back on Tommy, who had not noticed this, either.

'Shall we go and find them?'

Phillip didn't say anything.

'Phillip. I said, should we go and find them?'

'No. You go. I'll stay here.'

'What is the matter with you?' Tommy asked, none the wiser. 'And where are the girls.'

Phillip turned angrily, and was just about to let him have it with both barrels, when almost with a fanfare, Catherine and Georgia arrived, looking very pleased with themselves.

'We're here,' Georgia said, proudly.

The two girls advanced, holding out the front of their skirts, clearly concealing something in the folds. Tommy looked across and raised his head.

'You so much as look at my petticoats and I shall scream,' Catherine warned him in advance.

Tommy ignored her and rushed across, knocking her aside in his attempt to reach Georgia, forcing her to stumble and drop a fair quantity of her wares.

'Look what you've made me do.'

Tommy looked down at the berries scattered on the ground, and as much in apology as surprise at the offering, crouched down and started to gather them into a fresh pile.

Phillip, the excitement of their arrival stifling his mood, rushed to his side and stared down at the berries.

'Tuck in then,' Georgia advised, and the boys, needing no second invitation, started to stuff their mouths.

After some moments, Tommy looked up guiltily to Georgia, and gestured to the berries.

'We already had some,' Georgia confessed, opening her mouth and poking out a crimson tongue. Tommy looked across at Catherine who poked out her own tongue. But it was in a totally different manner, altogether.

Georgia regaled the boys with tales of their exploits in both the finding, and the gathering of the berries. She held out her hands to reveal the cuts and scars she had endured in their retrieval. Catherine interrupted and studiously pointed out that if it had not been for her, they would not have found them at all. Georgia had to conceive the point, but it did not take anything away from the story.

Phillip, his face covered in juice, had to apologise for the absence of fish. To cover their apparent dearth, he told them that word had obviously got around the fish world that a dynamic hunter had arrived. And further, that tales of his angling techniques were rife, and that they were all now hiding away.

Tommy jolted. The arrival of the berries had completely driven his own revelation out of his head. The rabbits.

'Rabbits!' Georgia said. 'You've found rabbits?'

'Can we eat rabbit?' Tommy asked, nervously.

'It makes a lovely stew,' Catherine said.

'But we are a large pot short of a stew, I'm afraid,' Georgia pointed out.

'And we are sadly twenty carrots short of getting our first rabbit yet,' Tommy professed. 'I should enjoy the fruit for now.'

The girls, hearing the news about both the lack of fish and the assumed difficulty in capturing a rabbit, decided to help the boys finish off the berries, just in case it was a long time before they ate again..

'Eat up,' Tommy told them. 'You'll need it.' Catherine looked up. 'You're all helping me with the rabbit hunt.'

169

Tommy led the hunting party, and his enthusiasm, and the thought of meat, had quickly spread through all of them. Phillip professed that his expertise with the fish would naturally spread into the world of hunting down a few rabbits, and that Tommy shouldn't worry. Catherine, also full of beans, proclaimed that the girls would easily catch a rabbit. It was just a question of using technique, and not brute force.

Tommy reminded them of the cunning of the rabbit as if he had had a life long battle with them. He suggested that for once, they all work together, and share the glory of the haul while Georgia stewed them all for dinner.

'We may have to just roast them,' Georgia smiled. 'But they will be equally as tasty, I'm sure.'

Phillip, who was getting a little too excited in anticipation, had to be physically restrained from charging too far ahead and scaring everything in his path, much less any rabbits.

Despite Tommy's enthusiasm in the upcoming hunt, he quietly sneaked up beside Georgia and asked her about sharing some of her advice about rabbit hunting with him. She informed him that she knew a rabbit was edible, but had not actually been brought up in the woods. Tommy apologised and confirmed novices, they carefully worked out a relatively feasible plan between them.

As they approached the outskirts of Rabbit Wood, as it had now been named, they all split up. It had been agreed to circumnavigate the area, and approach it from all four corners at once. The girls had discretely removed their petticoats, Georgia for what seemed the umpteenth time, and were going to use them as would-be nets. The boys had decided to make the best of it with their pullovers and try to smother anything that came their way.

Several rabbits sat lazily in the open, basking in the weak sunlight. Tommy crouched down, and raised his hand gently into the air, hoping that the three others could see it from the hiding places of their own. He raised his head slightly and noted quite how far away the rabbits actually were. He stuck out three fingers, and taking them away one by one, arrived at zero, and in a sudden blur, they all charged in.

The coordination between the quartet was obviously lacking both in technique and practice. Each child had selected a different rabbit, and it was with the same alacrity and ease that each of the chosen prey had sought and found their chosen burrows, untouched.

The children rose and excitedly examined the clothing they had thrown or collapsed on top of, and the evident disappointment and deflation cut through them all. They looked as one to Tommy.

'It's not my fault,' he said. 'Tell the rabbits.'

'Maybe we should all be a little more subtle the next time,' Georgia said.

'Next time,' Catherine shouted, examining a minor graze on her elbow. 'What next time.' She stood angrily, and threw her petticoat at Tommy, and was about to storm off. Tommy held out the petticoat, innocently, and Catherine charged across and snatched it from him. 'I knew it wouldn't work.' She turned around and stormed off in the direction of the pool, grabbing Phillip by the arm.

170

'But…'

'But nothing. You're going fishing.'

Phillip was hauled away.

'Sorry!' Georgia said. 'It was worth a try.'

Tommy and Georgia returned dejectedly.

Phillip was stood in the water looking less happy in his forced labour than he had when he had chosen to carry out the task of his own free will. Catherine glared at him.

'What?'

'Well do something then.'

'I'm the one who has read Tom Sawyer and Huckleberry Finn,' he said. 'And anyway, it takes time.'

Tommy, always keen to side with Phillip, looked perplexed. Georgia saw his blank look, and shook her head, telling him not to get involved.

'Tom Sawyer would have more fish than he could shake a stick at,' Catherine snapped at Phillip.

Tommy was becoming more and more confused by the second.

'I think we are a long way away from the Mississippi,' Georgia said. Tommy gave up trying to follow the conversation. 'Tom Sawyer he might not be, but he is the only one who has got us anywhere near a decent meal. Why don't we all try and calm down?'

'We could always tuck into your rabbit stew,' Phillip ignored Georgia, and answered Catherine back, who in turn glared at Tommy.

'The rabbits are there,' Tommy told her. 'I come from the city. You…' Georgia's sharp warning glance stopped him in mid-sentence reminding him of his promise not to mention their conversation.

'I what?'

Tommy was tongue-tied.

'I - what?' she repeated.

'We come from different sides of the track, that's all. I didn't know you could even eat rabbits. I just hoped you could. You knew.'

'It's just as well I do, or we'd be chewing tree bark.'

Tommy looked across discretely at Georgia, who shook her head slightly dismissing that idea, mouthing, 'She's kidding.'

'I'm doing my best,' Tommy shouted.

'Well your best just doesn't seem to be good enough.'

'You all stay here. I'll go and put that right.' He turned away from them.

'The berries are that way,' Catherine acerbically aimed at him. Tommy did not turn to receive it. 'Shall we stoke the fire up, and prepare the spit to roast the beast?'

Tommy turned and glared, shocking her. She took a pace backwards.

'If you got up off your arse and did something, instead of pussyfooting around, we might just get somewhere.' He then turned and marched away without so much as a

171

backwards glance.

Catherine looked at both Georgia and Phillip for support, but neither was prepared to hold her eye.

'It's my fault?'

Phillip jumped from the pool and ran off after Tommy.

Catherine sat sulking by the fire. Georgia eventually walked over to her and sat by her side.

'I'm not made for this sort of life, Georgia.'

'None of us are.'

'Then why do I get all the blame? Even Phillip has taken *his* side again.'

'You don't get all the blame. Its just life would be that little bit easier if you and Edward at least tried to get on together. You don't have to be friends forever, but you could both try.'

'It's not my fault.'

'It's both your faults.'

Catherine surrendered and allowed Georgia to placate her anger with calming words.

'If we're going to base ourselves here, why don't we try to make something of a camp out of it?' Georgia suggested.

'Here?'

'Where else do you suggest?' Georgia shrugged.

'You're right,' Catherine took the hint. 'Here it is, then. Let's get going.' Georgia smiled at her encouragement. 'Well come on then.'

Georgia jumped up.

43

Tommy had stormed off. Despite his initial attraction to Catherine, the reality of her character and nature had diminished his feelings for her completely. He was furious.

Phillip, disgusted with his sister's behaviour once again, had rushed off to catch up with Tommy, but he had to run to catch up with him, such was Tommy's anger.

Tommy paused by a tree, catching his breath, trying to control his actions. He looked behind him, and soon caught sight of Phillip, who shied seeing his face.

'I thought it might have been your sister, rushing after me to apologise.'

'No you didn't.'

'No. I suppose I didn't, really.'

'She's not such a bad old stick, really. You just have to get used to her. She's not that bad when you get to know her'.

'Know her?'

'Yes. It's taken me all this time, and I'm sure I still can't work her out all the time.' Tommy laughed, and nodded for Phillip to join him. 'Come on. Let's get some rabbits. We'll show her.'

The rabbits had not seemed to take any umbrage at the children's presence on the island, and appeared relentless in their pursuit of devouring their succulent feeding ground. They seemed content their feeding, almost with renewed vigour, and any lookout they might have placed, was currently otherwise occupied.

Tommy, in a fresh approach to the problem, had armed himself with a large stick. There was a stick with a large knot of gnarled wood on the end of it and seemed ideal, if not utilising a sledgehammer to crack a nut. Phillip had adopted a similar sized weapon, if not slightly larger, and though he looked almost comical with it, Tommy did not think to mention it. He tried to heave the club over his shoulder and almost toppled over backwards with the weight. But managing to right himself at the last moment, he stood tall again and looked across at Tommy.

Now within sight of Rabbit Wood, Tommy put a finger to his mouth for silence, and with a series of gestures with his free hand, managed to convey his plans to Phillip. Phillip nodded excitedly, and scurried away surprisingly quietly - and as peacefully as the bludgeon would allow him - to the far side of the clearing. He adjusted the glasses on the end of his nose, sniffed into his hand to stop the noise, and crouched down awaiting Tommy's signal.

Tommy looked across, trying to judge the moment to perfection, dropped his hand and he and Phillip both charged across the clearing.

The rabbits, still new to the hunting game, scampered for escape. Tommy and Phillip swung wildly with their cudgels, screaming wildly trying to confuse their prey, and suddenly it was a battle of wits.

Georgia and Catherine were working together trying to arrange the area around the pool into some sort of camp, and make it appear slightly more liveable, if nothing else. They cleared sticks and repositioned stones, and tried to create a shelter of some sort around the fire between them. For all the good work Georgia did however, Catherine could not help but get in the way, and continually adjust what she had already done. Having done so for the umpteenth time, Georgia finally snapped.

'For goodness sakes, Catherine, do something useful, or come out of the way and leave me to do it.'

'What?'

'Oh, I don't know. I'm sorry, but just do something useful, can't you. Go and see if there are any fish in the pool or something.'

'Oh!' Catherine stared helplessly into Georgia's eyes. She had rarely been answered back before, and never from Georgia. But now to hear it from her one ally in the world, it hurt even more.

'I'm so sorry,' Georgia said immediately. 'I didn't mean that. You know I didn't.'

Catherine turned and walked away, and finally sat down by the edge of the stream looking deep into the pool.

'Come back. I'm sorry.'

'No. I'll sit here, and - look for fish. Like you said, I might be of some use then.'

'Catherine!'

'I'm fine.'

'Catherine!'

'Catherine! Georgia!' Phillip's voice broke the spat. He rushed into – camp – and straight across to them, loudly heralding Tommy's arrival.

Tommy, following closely behind Phillip's grand serenade, duly walked into camp. He held out his arm rigidly, displaying a dead rabbit. He held it out by its hind legs, and it dangled heavily beneath his arm. It may not have been so much holding out the trophy for display, as not being quite at home with a dead animal in his clutches.

The girls quickly forgetting their personal problems, rushed across to get a closer look. Phillip jumped in front of them both and grabbing the bloody rabbit from Tommy, waved it in front of Catherine's face.

'Don't you dare,' she yelled, and swiped at his mischievousness. Tommy took the back rabbit, as Catherine chased Phillip away.

It was now time for Georgia to come into her own. She took the rabbit from a grateful Tommy, who had had quite enough contact with it for the time being. His job was over as far as he was concerned, so Georgia took the rabbit down to the edge of the stream.

'Good luck, girl,' Tommy bade her, and started back towards the fire.

'I'm going to need your knife.'

Tommy nodded, handing across the knife as requested. A hesitant Catherine poked her head over Tommy's shoulder, but another look at the bloody beast, and she and Tommy both retreated to the fire under the surmise that it probably needed stoking. Phillip, surprisingly less squeamish, excitedly rushed between both points.

174

Two sticks at either end of the fire, formed into an X, provided the basic spit with which Georgia had decided it best to cook the freshly caught rabbit. The rabbit had been cleaned, and Georgia had passed a stick through the length of the body, and it currently lay over the fire, being turned regularly. The fire sizzled as the natural juices of the rabbit dripped into it, and if anything was needed to further heighten the appetite, the smell to do the job admirably. Georgia had even managed to do something with the offal, what little of it there was. Everything except the skin, which had been put to one side for the time being, had been cooked in some way shape or form, and the offal passed around as it changed colour, and appeared ready for consumption. It was quickly gobbled up.

As the rabbit cooked, the story of its capture was told and retold, and so expanded upon by the loquacious Phillip, that by the time it was ready for consumption, its eventual seizure would have taken a troop of soldiers to have captured it.

Georgia praised them both as the rabbit was consumed, and whatever Catherine mumbled whilst chewing at a bone, it was taken to be something similar.

Phillip had now commandeered the pelt of the rabbit, and had it laid across his lap, stroking it.

'You'll either have to shrink, or we will need a few more rabbits before you can start to plan on sleeping under that,' Tommy said as he nodded in its direction.

'I thought you might like it as a handkerchief,' he said to his sister, and threw it across at her.

Catherine screamed, dropped the bone she was sucking on, and at fingertips picked up the pelt and cast it to one side with no care as to where it ended up, and further verbally threatened Phillip.

'Anyone got any use for a pile of old bones?' Georgia asked pointing at the residue of the meal.

'Don't talk about Edward that way,' Catherine laughed. 'We must be able to find *something* for him to do.'

'Ha ha!' Tommy sneered. 'We've just eaten what I'm good at.'

'And delicious it was, too,' Georgia confirmed, if it needed any verification.

'But what's for pudding,' Tommy asked.

'A Summer Pudding,' Catherine said, shutting her eyes, losing herself in thought. 'Covered in thick cream.'

Tommy looked once more to Georgia, pleading for guidance. She shook her head slightly, and it was enough to suggest that he should simply accept it as pudding.

'Summer Pudding would be just fine,' he said, receiving an approving nod.

'And a pot of fresh coffee.'

They lay back laughing, and only as the merriment naturally petered out, and a stale silence took its place, did their thoughts return to their plight.

Georgia suggested that since they were fed and watered, they should start thinking about building the beacon fire, and aimed the task pointedly at the boys.

'But we got the food,' Phillip complained.

175

'And I cooked it,' Georgia said.

Tommy looked across at Catherine, who looked awkward, seemingly unable to join in the bartering. 'And I...' she started.

'Well?' Tommy said, with no threat intended.

Catherine quickly picked up a handful of the bones and threw them over her shoulder into the woods. 'I did the washing up.'

'Seems fair to me,' Tommy agreed, tittering. 'Okay. We'll see to the beacon.'

'We should have kept the original fire burning,' Catherine said. 'It was less sheltered. The smoke would have easily been seen from there.'

'And would have gone out at the first fall of rain,' Tommy pointed out. 'We stoked it up, but it won't be there now.'

'Humph!'

'And let's not forget the fleets of ships, and the squadrons of aircraft that have plagued us so much since we've been here.'

'Well I still think it should have been...'

'No! You're right. We've got to do something.'

'I want to explore,' Phillip demanded.

'Every time we set out to explore, something seems to get in the way,' Catherine pointed out.

'Yes. The last thing that got in the way, we just ate,' Tommy informed her.

'We haven't needed to search,' Georgia said. 'We have somehow always found everything we need.' She pointed to the stream, the rabbit pelt, and the fire.

'Here we go again,' Catherine complained. 'Two seconds ago you were going to build a beacon fire, and now everyone wants to go off exploring.'

'But there may be someone else here,' Phillip protested. 'Just think.'

Catherine looked up, nervously. The thought of someone else on the island still seemed to somehow present itself as a worry rather than a virtue.

'We would know by now,' Georgia assured them, though she did not sound overly reassuring. She gestured down to the fire. 'If anyone had been out there, they would have seen the smoke from this. We only need a bigger fire for emergencies. To be seen from the sea, or above.'

'So there is definitely no one else here?' Phillip demanded absolute confirmation.

'No,' Catherine said.

'Hello!' Phillip bellowed at the top of his voice.

'Stop it, Phillip.'

'Hello!' he yelled even louder, turning round in circles. 'Hello! Hello!'

'Stop it.' Catherine scolded him, as his voice boomed through the silence.

'Why? Who am I going to disturb?'

'We're on our own,' Tommy said, dejectedly. 'Get used to it.'

Phillip stopped and looked at his mentor. 'I know. I just hoped. That's all.' He shrugged his shoulders, and slumped to the ground.

'Then you both have to do something about it,' Georgia said. 'We're relying on

176

you.' Phillip looked up. 'Now get going.'

'I don't want to,' Phillip sat deflated, his confidence blown.

'Then just sit there,' Catherine said. 'I'll go.' She looked at Tommy, but still couldn't find it in herself to become his lone cohort just yet. 'Better still. Georgia. You go with him. Phillip can find out where the fish have disappeared to.' She turned away, the matter sorted.

Georgia smiled, but nodded. 'Fine!'

'Are you coming back tonight?' Phillip asked, slightly recovering from his depression.

'We're not going that far,' Georgia said. 'I really don't think there is much we will find out by tonight. We'll just go and have a look. If we get to London, we'll send you a postcard.'

'How will we know if you get into any trouble?'

'You won't,' she said, tapping him on the nose. 'So we'll just have to be careful.'

She looked across to Tommy for reassurance. He nodded slowly, and then realising it was for Phillip's sake, said, 'Yeah! We'll be really careful. Georgia won't let me out of her sight.'

'But what about Catherine?'

'That's right. I need someone to look after me,' she said, grabbing his hand. 'You'll have to do. I think that's what brothers are for, aren't they?'

He smiled back, weakly.

'Will you hold my hand when it's my turn to look after you?' Tommy asked.

'We could be here for the rest of our lives. That day will never come, believe me.'

Georgia grabbed Tommy by the shoulder and dragged him away.

'Let's go back to where we landed,' she said. 'We can see what's been going on out there.'

'And we'll get this place licked into shape,' Catherine shouted, lightly.

Phillip waved as they left, and turned back to Catherine, who was watching them go. 'It's all right. He'll be back soon,' he said.

'What are you talking about?'

'Tommy. He'll be back soon.'

'Be quiet. And don't be so silly. Oh! And if you are going to be Huckleberry Finn, *you* can start to make this camp a bit more like home.'

'Fine. Roll your dress up to your knees and you can go in there and catch all the fish then.'

44

Tommy and Georgia arrived at the point at which the four of them had originally come ashore. They hurried up to the shore line and excitedly looked out to sea. Georgia sighed miserably.

'What's up?' Tommy asked.

'Nothing.'

'Come on?'

'What do you think? Look out there. We're miles from anywhere. We haven't seen a ship, or even heard a plane…'

'We haven't really been looking. We haven't exactly posted a lookout or anything have we?'

'No, I suppose not,' Georgia sighed, and slumped to the floor.

'Well there you go then. We can't expect miracles.'

'But we don't know where we are, and Catherine is the eldest one amongst us. What chance do we really have?'

'Hey! That's enough, yeah?' Tommy scrunched down and grabbed her by the shoulders. He held her in front of him. 'We have every chance.' He looked straight into her face. 'But not if the sanest person here starts having doubts.' She stared back, and put on another of her brave smiles. 'Now! Are we better?' Georgia nodded. 'I can't hear you.'

'I'm better.'

'We're all gonna get through this. But we need each other's help.'

'Even Catherine?' Georgia said suddenly recuperating.

'Especially Catherine.' Tommy stopped, a puzzled look on his face. 'Yeah! Especially Catherine.'

As the laughter stopped, a strange squawking noise sounded nearby. They stood up and looked at each other, puzzled.

'You're the sane one,' Tommy said, holding Georgia in front of him. He turned her around and gave her a gentle push. 'You find out what it is.'

'And you are the man,' she answered switching positions, pushing Tommy forward.

Tommy laughed again, but neither sure of what exactly the noise might be, he gestured that they should both find out together. They crouched down onto their knees and edged their way forward. They stopped just as they reached the top of the cliff face.

'Well?' Georgia whispered over his shoulder.

Tommy started to peer over the top of the crag, when a huge gull launched itself towards him. He over-balanced, but Georgia, equally shocked, just managed to grab hold of him, and they both watched as the gull hobbled away further along the top of the cliff.

'What on earth!'

'It's damaged its wing,' Georgia said. 'Look! It can't fly.'

'Ouch!' Tommy grimaced, watching its weak efforts. 'The poor bird.'

'Go on,' Georgia pushed him towards it.

Tommy slowly made his way towards the startled bird. Despite its condition, his presence did nothing to calm it, and the bird fluttered desperately in an attempt to fly off.

'Go on!' Georgia urged him further.

The bird squawked nosily, and tried all the harder to get away, but its damaged wing failed to straighten. It became more and more alarmed the closer Tommy got towards it. He stood, cornering the bird, and in its attempt to escape him, it fluttered its way back towards the woods.

Tommy turned to tell Georgia to stay where she was, but in turning to do so, discovered she had gone. He now stood up, more concerned about her whereabouts than the plight of the gull. He looked around him, but she had vanished. He was about to call out her name, when there was a sudden, '*Crack*'.

Tommy stood back, amazed. A bedraggled Georgia emerged from the woods with a lifeless bird slumped in her arms.

'Are you any good at plucking?'

'But...' he mimicked the broken wing.

'It's dinner. It's big. We've got four mouths to feed. Hey! There might even be enough for breakfast.'

Tommy shook his head, startled, and stood back, and clapped his hands in admiration. 'And I thought you were going to look after it.'

'Let's just say I put it out of its misery.'

They started to walk back along the cliff, Georgia proudly, Tommy slightly more guiltily. Just as they were about to head back inland, there was the increased sound of further squawking. A lighter strain, but loud enough to attract their attention. Tommy left Georgia and walking over to the cliff, lay down on his front and peered over the top.

Slightly further down the cliff, and lodged into the rocks, was a nest with four open beaks poking out, crying pitifully for their mother. Tommy looked down in wonderment. It quickly became clear that they were alone. A protective influence quickly took him over, and he started to reach down towards them. After several sharp pecks at his approach, he withdrew slightly, and watched them, trying to find a solution to their predicament.

Georgia, intrigued, walked across, and carefully looked over his shoulder. 'Let me through.'

'No!' Tommy cried, looking amazed. 'You can't.'

Georgia threw the large dead fowl to one side and well away from any eye line the chicks might have had, and pushed at Tommy trying to get him out of the way. 'Let me get to them, or they'll die.'

Tommy was not sure, still amazed at her treatment of the bird with the injured wing, but finally relinquished his place above the chicks, and hesitantly let Georgia through.

'They're even too small to make gravy with,' Tommy said, as a last chance plea for their lives.

'It looks like we've got four more children on the island now.'

179

A carefully constructed circle of stones had been hastily prepared. Various pieces of twigs and wood, as similar to the nest from which they had been abducted had been placed inside, and the chicks now had a new home. Phillip was in his element. He was now no longer the youngest on the island, and he fussed over the four orphans like a mother hen.

Catherine, despite having Phillip out of her hair for the moment, looked down at them warily. She did not appear to have a motherly bone in her body at the moment, and saw them as yet another problem for them all to deal with.

Georgia, for the sake of the chicks, was sat well away, busily plucking handfuls of feathers, throwing them carelessly into the air. She was covered in light down and looked as if she had been caught in a blizzard, and Tommy having been excused the task, laughed.

'We've got to eat,' she said, brushing further fluff from her lap. 'It will taste much better without a mouthful of feathers.'

'What do they eat?' Catherine asked, walking over, gesturing back towards Phillip and the chicks. The three of them exchanged glances.

'Fish?'

Phillip, defiant in his new position as keeper of the chicks, and truly the only angler amongst the group, had been charged with the task of hauling in a fresh catch. He was now split between standing in the middle of the pool, and rushing back to see if the chicks had sprouted wings and were preparing to fly off. His position on the island had been further cemented, and he looked every bit the part.

Georgia, still busy by the pool, had made steady progress with the dead fowl. Tommy was rearranging the spit on top of the fire for its second outing of the day, and Catherine, in her delicate manner, offered verbal advice wherever she saw fit.

'Do you really have no purpose in life?' Tommy asked as she carried a stick across for the fire, catching him on the side as she did so.

'You do it, then,' she said, throwing the stick to the floor. 'I don't seem to be able to do anyth…'

'Shut up.'

'Don't tell me to shut up. How dare you? I…'

'I mean it. Shut up. Shut up and listen. All of you. Listen!'

'I…'

'Catherine! Sssh!' Georgia hushed her, listening.

'Hear it?' Tommy asked urgently.

They all stopped what they were doing, and listened carefully.

'I can't hear anything,' Catherine interrupted the silence. 'But for those wretched chicks. I don't know what you're all going on about.'

'Sssh!'

'There it is,' Tommy said.

Far in the distance, there was the faint whine of an engine, almost imperceptible to the ear, but there none the less. They focussed their attention, and slowly the noise seemed to become louder, and slowly louder.

'It's a plane,' Tommy yelled. 'It's a plane.'

'Run. Get into the open,' Georgia shouted. 'Make yourselves big. Wave like mad.'

Tommy led the way, quickly followed by Georgia, Catherine, and Phillip who hurried to catch up having dragged himself from the pool and his fishing duties.

The young pilot frantically struck at the several dials and clocks on the facia of the cockpit of the aircraft. His eyes stared hard through the goggles, trying his best to make some sort of sense out of the readings. The needles on the majority of the clocks had long since given up, and it was clear no amount of prodding was going to make any difference.

The sound of machine gun fire sounded loudly above the throaty roar of the engine, and he turned desperately to see exactly where the donor might be. He shouted something to the body beside him, but it did not take long to realise that his co-pilot was no more than that. A body.

He thrust the yoke of the aircraft roughly to one side in an attempt to avoid further gunfire, and the twin-engined aircraft turned, slowly. Far too slowly.

The excitement at the sudden contact with another human being, albeit thousands of feet up in the clouds, was almost too much to bear. The children chased madly through the undergrowth in an attempt to return to the original landing point. It was their only other true point of land that they knew, and they rushed from the confines of the woods into it. Tommy, failing to control his speed had to apply the brakes sharply to avoid falling off the top, and having done so, held his arms wide in the air to stop the others doing something similar. They all placed their hands across their eyes, straining to see anything against the rays of the sun, and stared blankly into the sky.

High above their heads, and intermittently flying in and out of the cloud formation therein, two aircraft fought for position. The children caught sight of the display, struggling to make out the markings on the wings, uncertain as to which was which.

'It's one of ours,' Tommy shouted excitedly, turning in circles trying to follow the dogfight.

'Get him!' Phillip called up. 'Get him!' He jostled with the others, and they all joined in the rancour of the cries.

As Tommy looked up and the aircraft shifted position above him, he suddenly stared straight into the sun. Momentarily blinded, his imagination took over. The night sky was filled with German bombers, their payload emptying from their bellies. His attention focussed on one particular bomb and followed it as it plummeted furiously through the air. It grew larger and larger as it approached and crashed through the roof of a house. His attention focussed on a bombed out house, and suddenly a stretcher came into view, sitting on the pavement outside, with his father's body stretched out on it. Dead.

He broke from his thoughts, and stared once more as the two planes continued their fight.

'Get the jerry. Get the jerry.'

The German pilot struggled hard at the controls of the aircraft, trying everything he knew to keep it in the air, and out of the gun-sight of the fighter behind it. He banked the aircraft to the right, and then struggled to straighten it before the engines stalled. He shuddered as another volley of bullets just missed his starboard wing, and he looked around, as if to God, looking for a miracle.

He flew straight into the direction of the sun, momentarily blurring his vision, and veered away into the next bank of clouds and sat, hoping it would hide him forever. All too soon though, he was out into the open once again. He checked over his shoulders once more, both left and right. He saw nothing, and just as he started to relax, the aircraft juddered as the aircraft was struck by a strafe of gunfire. Black smoke suddenly blew back and across the cockpit cover.

The children cheered wildly seeing the black smoke discharging from the plane, having already decided, at that distance, that it was the enemy aircraft that had been hit. They hugged each other, and spun in circles, round and round and round.

Tommy broke and waved wildly as the victorious aircraft started to break from the battle, its job done.

The three other children quickly realised what he was doing, and also started to jump up and down, frantically waving their arms, trying their hardest to make their presence known. They watched as the German aircraft flew away over their heads, its fate decided, and as they watched the allied aircraft fly off into the distance, there was a loud explosion from somewhere behind them. They cheered loudly, but barely cast it a backward glance as they returned to the dot that was fast diminishing into the distance.

The euphoria of the battle died as they finally accepted that they could no longer see their saviour, or indeed he see them. They sat forlornly on the ground, sighing, trying to catch a collective breath from all the excitement.

45

They sat for what seemed like an eternity, staring out to sea, without saying a word. They could no longer see anything, and their hearts sank. They stared reluctantly into the ground on which they sat.

The children after a long reflection on the recent events returned to their camp, dragging their feet dejectedly. The journey back had been wordless, each of the children left to their own thoughts. They all slumped to the floor by the fire.

'Do you think he saw us?' Phillip asked breaking the silence.

'N...' Catherine started to say.

'Yes! Of course he saw us,' Georgia interrupted, throwing Catherine a strong glance of disapproval. 'Of course he did.'

'Yes,' Tommy agreed, catching on fast, though he harboured a thought of his own that they may well have caught the attention of the victorious pilot. 'I'm sure I saw him wave his wings as he flew away.'

Phillip sighed, and was about to descend into a state of gloom, when an excited burst of chirping nearby broke him from his doldrums, reminding him of their needs.

'Go on, Phillip,' Georgia said, encouragingly. 'Get to it.'

The chicks twittered loudly, and hearing the voices, refused to be ignored. Phillip straightened up, and went over to attend to their needs.

Tommy suddenly burst into life with a shattering imitation of the gunfire they had recently heard. Phillip looked back.

'Did you see the way he cut him to pieces?' Tommy exaggerated the execution to perfection to a waiting audience.

He went on to recount the story they had all just seen, giving the version he was sure only he had seen.

Phillip, excited by Tommy's interpretation, returned, offering a version of his own, his arms extended, imitating the actions of the aircraft, and the two of them charged around each other in a like manner until Tommy finally allowed Phillip the kill and fell to a heap on the floor.

Georgia was amused, and she looked across to Catherine, who was also immersed in their antics, and as Phillip finally flagged, she assured him that she too had indeed seen the aircraft waggle its wings as it disappeared. Phillip, thriving from his battle, smiled, and puffing from his exploits, returned to tend to the chicks once more.

Georgia had not said anything since their return, and was now unusually pensive. Tommy noticed this and crouched down beside her.

'What's up?'

She looked up sombrely. 'We should have had a beacon fire lit,' she said. 'Or at least, ready to be lit. We've let a great opportunity slip by.'

Phillip having heard about the fire, and not fully absorbed in his adopted quartet, started back once more. But Catherine, with no intentions at taking over the reins of rearing the chicks, coughed to attract his attention, and pointed back in the direction from which he had come. His shoulders slumped, and releasing a sigh, he returned to his duties.

'We could do it now,' Tommy said.

'It's too late now,' she said. 'That is a job for a full day. I'm just surprised. We have lots to do, plenty of time to do it in, and yet somehow, nothing gets done.'

'Something always gets in the way,' Tommy defended their work ethic. 'But don't forget. We do have a gull for a meal, and four new mouths to feed. Maybe we're just not meant to get stuff done.'

Georgia smiled, but still looked fed up and slumped to the floor once more.

'Go on, girl,' he told her in his finest London brogue. 'You haven't got time to sit there. Go and get my dinner.'

'Yes, dear,' she laughed.

'We've got to get something for these babies to eat,' Phillip called over.

'You're the fisherman,' Catherine said. 'Go to it.'

Tommy laughed at her temerity, and looking at Phillip and Georgia in cahoots, added, 'We should *all* be doing something.'

'You're welcome to finish plucking the dinner,' Georgia said sprightly. 'And who knows, maybe gutting it if you're bored?'

'If you want dinner this side of Christmas, I should get someone else to do it,' Phillip shouted across, then quickly turned away and tended the chicks to avoid any backlash.

'It's alright. I'll do it,' Georgia said reluctantly, walking back to the edge of the pool.

'Oh, okay then!'

'Phillip's looking after the babies,' Tommy said. 'Why don't you have a crack at the fishing?'

Catherine looked back, alarmed, and thinking on her feet, said 'Maybe I should get a few sticks together.'

'But we haven't decided where to build the beacon yet,' Tommy said.

'Not the beacon. I meant...' She looked up and saw Tommy and Georgia exchanging smirks.

'It's not fair. I was not built to work with my hands.'

'What were you built for?'

'I was probably... er ...'

'Everyone has their place,' Georgia leapt to her defence, seeing her waning. 'Maybe Catherine's purpose just hasn't come along yet, eh?'

'Well, you can still gather some wood until you find it then,' Tommy said, and walked over to help Georgia.

It was late afternoon, and Catherine sat by the fire, turning the sizzling bird on the would-be spit over the flames, glaring at anyone who as much as dared to look at her. Phillip sat by the chicks with an unlucky fish that had happened by. Tommy had cut it up into hundreds of tiny pieces, and Phillip tried and tried to get them to take it, but they stubbornly refused. He looked helplessly across to Georgia. She got up, and walking past Catherine who tutted as the fat of the bird spat in her direction, cast a glance at her work.

'I *can* turn a bird,' Catherine snapped at her. Georgia held up her hands, defensively and quickly scurried over to join Phillip.

The chicks were weak, and looked frail.

'They won't stop crying,' Phillip said. 'And they won't eat anything. Don't they like fish? They're gulls. They live at the seaside.'

'Try this,' she said, moving him gently to one side. She took the fish, making sure Phillip was watching, and offered it to their open beaks.

'I told you,' Phillip said, sitting back, looking at both Georgia and the still unimpressed chicks. 'I've been doing that for ages.'

Georgia sat back and tried to compose herself. She tried to make the diet look a little bit more palatable. She mashed the fish slightly more and tried again, to the same, if not inevitable outcome.

Tommy noticed the hubbub, and walked over to try to sort out the problem. He listened to both of their versions on their feeding regimes, and told them both to come out of the way. 'This needs my gentle touch.' The audience looked to each other, and raised their eyebrows.

Tommy parted their bodies and squirmed his way in between them. He offered the pair a knowing glance, and taking a small amount of the fish, placed it on his little finger and offered it up. Georgia and Phillip smiled, and sat back contentedly, with their arms folded. He turned round to look at them reluctantly.

'Well?' Georgia asked.

'Maybe they're not hungry.' Tommy said. The chicks looked up. 'Maybe not.'

'Don't let them die,' Phillip pleaded.

'Alright! We'll have to try something else,' Georgia said, but after a long pause, blew out threw her lips, beaten. 'Ohhhh! I give up!'

'Problems?' Catherine called over. 'Anything I can do?'

'Probably not,' Tommy whispered.

They looked first to the fish, then the chicks, the fish, to each other, and then had to concede.

'We can't get them to feed,' Phillip called the problem across.

Catherine pointedly strolled over as if she was doing them a favour. Tommy did not want to give in, but Phillip's explanation that all three had failed, saved him having to admit any personal defeat.

'Don't babies drink milk?' she asked, and walked down to the side of the pool.

'Saviour! Problem solved,' Tommy said. 'No! Of course they don't. Did you ever see anyone feeding milk to birds in the park?'

'No. Bread. But until you've built the bakery, grown the wheat, and run it through a mill, we'll have to come up with something else. And don't forget, these are seabirds, not pigeons.'

185

'Really!'

'These aren't the only birds on the island, I gather?'

'Really!' Tommy stressed, and cupping his ear, drew attention to the raucous chorus of the gulls in the distance.

'Don't ask then!' Catherine walked back to the fire.

Tommy followed, hot on her heels. 'Well?'

She turned to look at him, and said, 'Go back to where you... found these, and see what the other ones are feeding their young,' and then, point made, turned back to her dinner duties.

'Well, bravo, mummy duck.'

Catherine looked up, condescendingly. 'Well, do something.'

'Fine. I'll go. First thing in the morning,' and quietly under his breath, 'If they last that long.'

'I'll go with you,' Georgia assured him. Tommy pulled a face. 'What?'

'Nothing.'

'No. What?'

Tommy pointed in the direction of the fire.

'What?'

'If you come with me, we will end up with an orphanage of chicks to deal with.'

'Well you can forego your share of tonight's meal in that case.'

'I didn't mean...'

'I'll come with you,' Phillip said. 'But we need to go now.'

'No,' Georgia said. 'It's too late, certainly for you. And if *you* want to go now, fine!' she addressed Tommy. 'But, if you go now, the only thing you'll come back to is a pile of bones.'

The birds chirped.

'Save me a tasty bone.' Tommy said, and set off into the gloom, promising to be back soon.

Tommy scrambled along the cliff face as safely as he could, keeping a safe distance from any angry parents that might have noticed his presence and decided to take evasive action. He sheltered behind a tree and watched as the birds flew in, answering their infant's hungry cries. He focused on one particular bird, and watched it carefully as it flew in. It perched on the edge of the nest, and rocking back and forth seemed to regurgitate its food supply, and the chicks ate greedily at the produce.

Tommy grimaced at how he might possibly be able to replicate this, but was at the same time fascinated, watching nature at work. It was so far from his normal lifestyle, and so spellbound was he, he started to unconsciously edge his way forward to better his view.

Crouching down, his knee settled onto a rough patch of rocky ground, and the pain shot through his leg, and he jumped back with a yelp. He stumbled as he got to his feet, and as he spent the next few moments, rubbing at his knee, he returned to watching the gulls at feed.

Recovered slightly, Tommy once more edged his way forward to see if there was anything else he might glean in the pursuit of aiding the chicks. As he closed in, he suddenly found himself under attack from a large angry gull, and the chorus of other disapproving parents did nothing to hide his presence. He hurriedly took flight under a heavy barrage of attack, and eventually managed to take cover some distance away where he sat quietly, waiting patiently to allow things to settle down.

Enough time having safely elapsed, Tommy finally came out of his refuge, and strangely, despite the last encounter, ventured towards the cliff face once more. He looked up to check he was not in for a repeat onslaught, but it appeared the offended parent had returned to its feeding responsibilities and he was currently of secondary interest. He crouched down, edged slightly further along the cliff face, and finally deciding to lie flat on the ground, peered over the edge once more. He checked carefully through the gathering gloom, to make sure that he hadn't been mistaken.

Besides the various nests, full of squawking youngsters, he examined the cliff carefully. He nodded confidently, self-gratifyingly, examining the other nests. Sitting nestled into the twigs, feathers and rock, Tommy looked longingly at his latest discovery. Eggs.

Phillip was sat beside the chicks, chewing meat from a bone, looking equally pathetic. He was both tired by the day's events, sad that he was unable to help his charges, and disappointed that Tommy had refused to let him go with him on his latest escapade. It was only due to the fact that they had decided to eat prior to Tommy's return that stopped the pangs of hunger further adding to his woes.   Beside him, there sat another fish that he had procured from the pond, and with the gull roasting over the spit, it was decided to save it for the chicks. *If* Tommy had finally found out how to prepare it to meet the taste of the youngsters. It currently sat beside the mashed fish that had been left from the original efforts, and just at the moment, both varieties were useless.

Catherine and Georgia were sat by the fire, happily tucking into healthy portions of the gull. They had put aside a large quantity of the bird, awaiting Tommy's return. Despite this goodly sized portion there was still plenty remaining, and Georgia had been correct. It was more than likely there would be some left for the morning.

'I don't think I will ever confess to roast gull being my favourite meal ever,' Catherine said, 'but just at the moment, it ranks right up there with roast rabbit.'

Georgia laughed, nodding agreement, but out of nothing, the joy seemed to suddenly drain from Catherine. 'What's the matter?'

'Oh I don't know. I am just totally mixed up,' Catherine bemoaned. 'I think you are all right. Everyone here has found a purpose. Every one of you has found something that is useful to all of us. Me! I feel totally useless.'

'Don't be silly. Like I said, you haven't found your – calling - yet, that's all.'

'That's sweet, but I know you're only trying to be nice to me.'

Georgia was spared having to further placate her by Tommy's call from the distance, announcing his return. She jumped up, but was not fast enough to beat the suddenly rejuvenated Phillip from meeting him. Catherine stayed where she was, not quite as excited at his return.

'You're back,' Phillip cried as if greeting a long-lost relative.

Tommy had to carefully avoid Phillip clasping him as he held out his pullover in the same manner the girls had with their dresses on returning with the fruit, and as they greeted him, he gestured to his haul.

'What is it?' Georgia demanded

'I'm the egg man,' he proclaimed, displaying his wares. 'How many do you want, missus?'

Catherine was not quite as excited at the news of the fresh food source, and sat back. She sighed, accepting that her use here had dropped yet one more notch.

Tommy laid the eggs on the ground by the fire, and noticing Catherine walked over. He held out an egg to her. 'Present.'

Catherine smiled sweetly trying to disguise her current feelings. 'Thank you.'

'And look!' Tommy drew back the sleeves on his shirt to reveal the scars he had incurred in the pursuit of the harvest. Catherine was momentarily concerned, and about to get up to tend his wounds, but Phillip and Georgia, far more impressed by his exploits, quickly led him away to the side of the pool, to deal with him there. Tommy, absorbed in the attention, missed Catherine's attempt at clemency, and segregated once more, she walked back to the fireside where she sat down and cuddled her egg.

A restored Tommy, his wounds nursed to the best of Georgia's ability, was led back to the fire, where he was duly feasted. The returning hero. He gratefully ripped at the meat clinging to the bones of the cooked gull, and only once he had stripped the skeleton as far as it would go, did he finally sit back to recount them with tales of his injuries. For Phillip's sake, probably more than Georgia's, he described each attack and wound sustained from the angry birds, in gory detail. Catherine sat slightly to one side and listened, but said nothing.

'And these little chaps?' Catherine asked, pointing across to the chicks, still unimpressed. 'Did you actually find out anything that might...'

'Oh my God! Of course!'

As Phillip rushed across and sat down beside the chicks, Catherine sat back, not half as impressed and waited.

'Oh, you're going to love this!' Tommy aimed his response at her, and went on to graphically describe how the birds went about feeding their young.

As Phillip listened, he started to turn a nasty shade of green, and his excitement visibly diminished by the second.

'Then, what?'

'Wait!' Georgia announced, thinking. As her audience waited, she walked down to the side of the stream, and jumped in.

'Georgia!' Catherine exclaimed, thinking she had gone mad. 'We've got the fish.'

Georgia reached down by her ankles and suddenly emerged with two rounded rocks which she held out for examination.

Even Catherine shared a glance at Tommy, suggesting the girl might finally have gone mad.

Georgia, almost despairing in her team mates, climbed from the pool, taking her recently acquired rocks with her, and settled down beside the chick's enclosure.

'Knife,' she demanded with the precision of a surgeon.

Tommy, holding out his knife, followed closely by Phillip, and a still concerned Catherine walked across beside her and waited.

Georgia took the fresh fish, and with the help of Tommy's knife, cut it up into small pieces, and adding it to the remainder of their previous attempts, placed it between the two rocks and started to grind it into a new concoction altogether.

She looked carefully into the mixture she had created, and then spat into it, and further ground it between the two stones until it was a fine, almost liquid paste. The entire procedure had even drawn Catherine from her doldrums, and she came to watch the proceedings. They all looked down into the sickly mixture.

'I'm not so sure it wouldn't have been easier just to have been sick,' Tommy said.

'Let's try it out, shall we?' Georgia said, and made to offer the new mix to the weak open beaks, their owners barely strong enough to complain. Phillip moved forward, and Georgia, despite her efforts at preparing the meal, conceded to his soulful eyes. 'You're right. You are the nurse Phillip. The job is yours.'

'Maybe Doctor Phillip,' he said shyly, taking the mixture from her.

The three other children surrounded him as he leant forward, and took a small amount of the mixture on his little finger.

A small amount of the gluey substance entered the first of the beaks, and seemed to be swallowed without too much damage or objection. The owner considered the offer and soon, the same beak opened again for more.

189

The children cheered excitedly, but had to be hushed so as not to scare their new babies, and far from a lack of volunteers in wishing to nurse the chicks, each of the children insisted on taking a turn in accomplishing what in their eyes was a remarkable feat.

'Guess I've got my job sorted out. At least for the time being,' Georgia said.

'You keep the fish coming in,' Tommy said to Phillip, 'and if I can keep my arms away from their beaks, I'll deal with the eggs.'

Georgia foresaw the inevitable outcome of this rota. Not in the jobs that had been given out, but what had not.

'We'd better start storing this food away in a larder,' Catherine said, surprising Georgia.

'Larder?' Tommy queried.

'Food store,' Georgia clarified quickly, with no fuss about it. 'You're right. Then we can start to regulate the food we eat.'

'It puts us no closer to getting rescued, but at least we'll have something to eat while we do something about it,' Catherine said.

'I think we should build a raft,' Phillip said out of the blue. Catherine pooh-poohed the idea, and sneered.

'Do you have a better idea?'

'I've told you before. If you want to be Huckleberry Finn, that's fine. But don't forget, he had the resources to build a paddle steamer, had he wanted it. We however, do not.'

'In that case, I shall keep my ideas to myself in future,' he said, and walked away dejectedly.

'A raft is a great idea,' Tommy shouted across as he quickly slunk into the evening gloom, and walked off in his wake.

'Yes!' Catherine shouted. 'Pity really. I'm not so sure, but do remind me. Didn't we have a lifeboat a short while ago?' Tommy was about to respond, when she carried on. 'And if I'm not mistaken, not too long before that, weren't we on an even bigger raft. What did they call it? Oh that's right. A ship. Bound for Canada. Not ideal, but somehow a little more secure than we are at the moment.' She folded her arms, smugly, and looked to him for a comeback.

Georgia, as ever, was ready to jump in to mediate, but Tommy shook his head abruptly, stopping her. She held her hands in a, 'You had your chance,' manner, and left him to it.

'It's so easy to criticize,' he said. 'That's half of your problem. You keep looking back. We've got to look forward, and you keep bringing up the past. The sooner you accept where we are, and how we are going to deal with it, the better it will be for all of us.'

Georgia, almost for the first time, was stuck for words. Her normal raison-d'être deserted her, and she looked across at Catherine, waiting for her to explode.

'We didn't want to go to Canada. It was never our choice. We 'dealt' with that, and

190

as much as we didn't like it, we had to live with it. Then, we met you. We were fine till then. Now? Well, you tell me whose fault it is?'

'You found *me.*'

'Phillip found you. Not me. I would happily have lived the rest of my life without our paths *ever* crossing. You, Edward, or whatever your name really is.' Tommy looked awed, wondering if she was waffling, or maybe knew something she shouldn't. 'We know nothing about you. Everything about you could be a lie. You, and your parcel!'

Tommy had not thought about the canvas for some while, and suddenly found himself on the retreat, having to defend himself. Catherine stood, staring straight at him waiting for a reply, now confident in having got the upper hand for once.

'That was mine. Not yours. And you will undoubtedly be pleased to hear that when the lifeboat - 'went west' - my parcel went with it. And don't fly at me. All I did was bring back the eggs.'

'That's just it. Mr Wonderful! Is there no end to your talents?'

'No. I was born to collect eggs. My life is complete.'

'You!' She looked at Tommy, Georgia, and a startled Phillip, and finally having exhausted her verbal onslaught, screamed out loud, turned, and rushed away from them.

Georgia, breaking from her trance, looked firstly to Tommy, then to Catherine's figure, disappearing into the distance.

'Let her go,' Tommy growled, sulkily. 'It's her fault, not ours. She'll be back. She'll get lost after five minutes or so. *She* won't be able to look after herself.'

Phillip looked across worried.

Catherine flew from the camp along the edge of the pool, and passed the stream. She ran blindly, without a second thought as to her safety. She had finally been pushed too far, and in this instance, her pride would not stop her running. Angry tears streamed down her cheeks as she hurtled onwards.

Georgia was furious. Phillip hugged her, alienating them both from Tommy. As if she didn't have enough on her hands, she was now torn between chasing off after Catherine and staying with him and Phillip.

'She'll be back.'

'She's delicate.'

'She's as tough as old rope.'

Phillip loosed himself from Georgia, and ran off to sit with the chicks.

'I can't believe it,' Georgia said. 'Ten minutes ago, we were all happily feeding the chicks. What is it with you two?'

'Oh! And it's all my fault is it?'

'It's both of your faults. She's not meant to rough it.'

'She's the oldest. Let her get on with it.'

'She is a girl!'

Tommy breathed deeply. 'Look! She'll be fine. Let her walk it off. We're all

191

convinced we're on an island. If she keeps walking, the worst she can do is come back here, and so far, the fiercest animal we have come across is an angry rabbit.'

'What about the gulls?'

'They won't attack her. They wouldn't dare.'

Georgia smirked, despite her onslaught. 'Look! She's gone off that way. None of us have been that way yet.'

'She's always complaining that we haven't searched the damned island. Now we'll know.' Georgia slumped to the floor, deflated. 'We've got the fire, the food, and the shelter, and if you say she can't rough it, how long do you really think she can stay away? She'll be back in no time at all. You can bet your life on it.'

'Just at the moment, it's not my life I'm worried about,' Georgia concluded, and reluctantly went to sit with Phillip, to comfort him for a while.

Catherine eventually stopped running and slowed down into an awkward walk. She kicked angrily at any flora or fauna that happened across her path, and staggered on, her anger far from abated. She sniffed away a tear in a far from ladylike manner, and slowly drew to a halt. She crouched on the floor, breathing hard, coughed away an obstruction in her throat, and gulped to regain her breath properly. She muttered angrily to herself, cursing first Tommy, and then herself for having stupidly decided to leave the safety of the camp. She reluctantly turned and looked behind her, unsure whether she wanted a search party to be there or not. She looked around her, and for the first time realised quite how dark it had become. She had now wandered so far, the likelihood of her return to camp in daylight would be easier by simply following the stream back, but in this murky light, it was becoming close to impossible, and the thought of walking back in to face any ridicule tonight was much more than she could bear.

She got up and wandered over to the side of the stream and sat down to consider her options. What else could go wrong? She looked up into the sky, and blinked off the first drop of rain.

As the rain fell, Tommy looked across guiltily at Georgia and Phillip, who quickly took shelter by the fire, and pessimistically stoked it up against any rain that may penetrate the cover of the trees again. They huddled closer still to the flames against the cold, and looked guiltily from one to the other.

'Go and find her,' Georgia called across. 'She'll be scared.'

'I don't know where she's gone,' he said.

'But she's...'

'... but she's the only one who knows where she is, and therefore, she's the only one who'll know the way back,' Tommy clarified, and after a moment added, 'I'm worried about her too, you know!'

'What are we going to do?' Georgia whispered in Tommy's ear, to keep their shared worry down.

'As long as the fire is lit...'

'She'll be cold too.'

'As long as the fire is lit, she'll have something to guide her back. We could all go out, and we could all get stranded.'

'She'll be back, soon,' Georgia turned her attention to Phillip. 'Don't worry.'

Catherine looked miserably into the air, and realised quite how much cover they had had within their camp area. The rain, though not torrential, was enough to cut through the limited clothing she was wearing, and very soon, wet through, she shivered. Any natural human instinct to return to safety and warmth met an even more resilient pig-headedness that she was unable to detach herself from. The weather only intensified her anger, and as it got darker, she decided to continue to follow the stream, even if only by its sound after dark. She hoped by then she would be able to find somewhere for the night.

For the night? She stopped, and realised that she would now be on her own for the night. Her eyes opened considerably in fear, and as her breathing increased, she stumbled on.

Catherine finally pulled up further along the bank, audibly noting a change in the strength in the way the water was running. Though her eyes had somewhat acclimatised to the darkness, she could now only just make out the shape of the ground around her. She noticed what appeared to be a high bank up ahead of her, and for the lack of anything better to compare it to, she stumbled on towards it.

The ground, as far as she could make out, rose high into the air and forged itself out, creating beneath it, a welcomed shelter. She carefully managed to creep in underneath it and immediately felt the benefit, both from the rain and a distinctly noticable change in temperature. She sat cross-legged on the dusty floor, and looked out. Despite the fact that she was on her own, she now felt safe for the first time since leaving the camp.

The camp, for all its conversion, was dark and gloomy. Outside the light from the fire, one could barely see more than a foot or so in any direction. The rain had not broken through as much as it had promised and the area around the fire, although it had been spruced up slightly, was dry. Georgia sat by the fire with Phillip lying by her side, his head on her lap, fast asleep. Tommy sat the other side of the fire and stared deeply into the red embers.

'Penny for them?'

'What?' Tommy looked up.

'What are you thinking about?'

'What do you think I'm thinking about? I'm surprised Phillip got off to sleep. I don't think I'll be able to.'

'Are you missing her?'

'No. Well - yes - of course I am.'

'She's a little bit independent, I'm afraid.'

'A *little* bit?'

'Well you know what I mean.' Georgia looked up into what little of the treetops she could see, and scratched her head. 'I should have gone with her.'

'I should.'

'Maybe we shouldn't have got into a situation where anyone needed to be alone.'

'It's early days yet. I hope we don't fall apart.'

'We'll be fine, but I guess there's nothing we can do until morning,' she said through a yawn, stretching out her arms.

'I'll go off first thing.'

'I'll come with you. I think…'

'No. It's my fault,' Tommy said, but looking across the fire, realised he was now talking to himself. Georgia, for all her worries about her charge, had succumbed to sleep. He looked across at both she and Phillip, and checked to see if there was anything he could do to make either of them more comfortable. But the way they were snuggled up into each other, he decided they were settled for the night, and he seemed to be the last thing they needed.

He stood, a lonely figure, and walked over towards the chicks, who in the limited light seemed to have settled down for the night, and it was all he could do to force himself not to prod them to wake them up so that he was not the only one awake. He couldn't find it in him to do so, and eventually decided to walk back to the fire. He looked down at Phillip, smiled, and as he looked at Georgia, he noticed a piece of hair lying awkwardly across her face, and he bent down and carefully pulled it out of the way. He turned to the fire, threw on a few more pieces of wood, and settled down for the night.

'Goodnight,' he whispered to them both. 'Sleep tight.'

47

Daylight broke through the trees, and it was evident that the rain had fully stopped at some time during the night. Tommy shifted uncomfortably and opened his eyes. Despite all they had been through, it still took him a few moments to remember where he was, and slowly the reality of his – their – situation returned. He wasn't sure how long he had been asleep, but he vaguely remembered something about – Catherine! He sat up sharply and looked around him to see if she had eventually slunk back into camp last night and was now tucked up - safely – beside the fire.

The fire, through a mixture of the previous night's weather, and exactly how long he had managed to sleep through the night, urgently demanded attention. He looked across at Georgia and Phillip. They too appeared to have slept through the night, but still seemed to be under its sleepy spell.

Catherine! The girl seemed to haunt him. His initial plan of getting up at first light had been scuppered by finding quite such a comfortable spot in which to try to sleep off the previous evening. He had not meant to sleep quite so soundly. He was not as distraught as he might have been. He imagined if Georgia had been slightly more worried, and not having done so herself, she may have ensured that he was up much earlier to set out looking for her.

Tommy, trying not to wake his sleeping companions, slowly climbed to his feet, and made his way down to the water's edge. He stretched out, and crouching down by the water, splashed some of it onto his face to fully introduce him to the day.

The water was cold and certainly did all he hoped it would. *Catherine!* The name leapt into his head once more. He looked back at Georgia, who seemed almost to open her eyes, sleepily, before closing them again and rolling over to return to sleep without fully regaining consciousness.

Some help! He was going to have to do something about it on his own. And he was going to have to do it now.

Georgia may not fully have come round when he rose, but a noisy chattering from the pen holding the chicks, certainly wasn't going to be ignored for long. Catherine was going to have to wait. At least until Phillip was back with the living.

Catherine shivered and woke. She turned uncomfortably and looked around, mystified, as slowly the previous night's events suddenly caught up with her. She scowled angrily, the night's rest, and fractious periods of sleep she had managed, doing nothing to rid her of the animosity she had thought she might have slept off.

She stretched out her body recovering some feeling in her redundant muscles, and started to sit up.

As she started to fully come to her senses, she looked out from the shelter into which she had blindly stumbled the night before, and seeing the sunnier outlook, started to feel slightly better. She had survived the night. *Take that, Edward Burrows!*

She got up and walked out from her shelter to discover exactly where she had ended up. The sanctuary in which she had taken refuge was a recess, tucked away inside a small knoll. The hillock stood but a few feet from a large pool, similar to the one beside which their own camp sat, but looked a good deal deeper, and certainly somewhat prettier, she thought. She heaved a sigh, realising how fortunate she had been not to have stumbled into it the previous evening. The sun shining across the water however gave it a much healthier appeal. She smiled.

Georgia had finally woken, and like Tommy, was alarmed that Catherine still hadn't returned. She got up and walked across to his side.

'Well?' she asked, almost surprised that he was still there.

The chicks were still hungry, and though a good quantity of their food had been left from the previous night, they did not care who fed it to them, and complained angrily at Georgia's intrusion in Tommy's efforts at feeding them.

'These guys seemed a little more desperate for my attention,' he explained. 'Don't worry. She's next on my list of duties.'

Georgia brushed him to one side and looking down at their charges, mellowed slightly. 'I'll take over here. Now, go on!'

Tommy wiped off the chick food clinging to his hands, and looked off in the direction in which Catherine had disappeared.

'She won't have gone far,' he ensured her. 'We'll be back in no time.'

'Go on. Before Phillip wakes up.'

Tommy patted Georgia on the shoulder, and winking, encouragingly, started off along the bank of the stream.

Tommy and Georgia had already decided that it might be best or him to stick to the stream. She had already stressed on him, even though he already suspected it, that Catherine was unlikely to stray too far from something she could recognise. Even if it had been under duress. He had agreed, and the route of his search was decided.

The journey along the course of the stream was far longer than if he had followed a straight line. Tommy wanted to make sure she had not slipped during the night, and sustaining an injury, been unable to get out. He laughed, sure that if Catherine had sustained an injury, there wasn't a spot on the – island – no matter how large it was – that wouldn't have known about it.

He walked on.

As the journey progressed, Tommy started to feel far less worried about Catherine, and started to take in the wildlife around him. He stared at insects and tiny things far too small to be considered foodstuff, and watched as they preyed on something still smaller than themselves, and entranced, could not have been farther from his task.

A loud cry from just up ahead of him broke him from his revelry. He smiled, mostly relieved at the discovery of the only other person it could really be.

He quickly left the side of the stream, and taking advantage of the overgrown bushes and scrub, keeping low, worked his way forward, silently. He was going to jump out on her. He could still hear Catherine in the distance, and though he could not swear to it, he was sure she was either talking to herself, or – singing?

He approached with care, and despite the excitement of surprising her, and an urge not to be heard, he slowed down his pace, placing his feet carefully to avoid making any noise that might reveal his presence.

Catherine's voice was coming from still further along the stream. In trying to keep in cover, his approach was now that much slower, and he was almost at the point of jumping out, and ending the charade altogether. But the closer he came, the clearer her voice. He stopped and listened to her sweet voice, almost entranced.

It's Catherine! His inner self reminded him.

He headed for a small clutch of bushes, and convinced he was as close to her as he might be, without revealing his presence there, he ever so slowly edged his way through. He set his feet carefully for balance, and gingerly, he edged his head around the greenery to see exactly what she was doing.

Catherine was immersed in the pool with her back towards him. The water came up to just above her hips, and waved up and down her body as she washed. Tommy was shocked at finding her naked, and could barely take his eyes away from her.

Suddenly she ducked down fully below the surface of the water, and as Tommy shifted his head slightly to better see where she had gone, she suddenly sprang from the pool, shaking her head from side to side, water cascading from her hair with the motion. The water jettisoned in a thousand droplets, and they scattered in a large circle of beads around her like raindrops.

She let out another sharp cry against the cold water, and Tommy, fearful that he might have been spotted, darted back behind the bushes.

Catherine, though not certain, thought she may have had heard something and startled, turned to look behind her.

Tommy, his bravado disserting him, and now far from wishing his presence revealed, carefully dropped back. He stepped back, awkwardly, and caught between looking where he was going, and taking his eyes off Catherine, landed on a branch that had parted company with its mother tree an age ago. It noisily snapped in two.

Catherine, now certain, on hearing the noise, span around like a spinning top, her arms automatically crossed over her naked chest.

'Who's there?' she spluttered, and lowered herself in the water so that only her head was exposed.

Tommy stayed where he was, hoping against hope that she might just leave it at the one enquiry, and that he might be able to slip away, unseen.

'Who's there?' she repeated more urgently.   Tommy started ever so slowly to edge away.

'Is that you?' Catherine boomed furiously.

There was no disguising to whom she might have been addressing that particular question. He bit his lip hard, threw his head back, slapped his hands down his thighs, guiltily, and said, 'Yes.'

197

The barrage of words Catherine released from her mouth were not words that she would ever be proud to repeat, even in a future re-telling of events, and even Tommy baulked.

'I didn't see anything,' he tried to barter his way out of this particular pickle, trying hard to break through her onslaught.

'You mean you were actually looking?' Catherine stopped her assault as she finally took in the substance of what he had said. 'And what do you mean, *you didn't see anything*? You've been there all the time? Oh my God!'

Catherine began a further salvo of unladylike words, and Tommy, without any rational thought, came out to better defend himself.

Catherine screamed and fully immersed herself again.

Tommy, realising what she must have thought, turned his back immediately, and uncomfortably waited for her to surface.

Catherine spluttered again, coming to the surface having spent longer beneath water than her short breath had allowed, and seeing him stood there still, let loose a further tirade, bellowing at him to go away.

'I didn't see *anything*,' he repeated not realising the mistake of having said this the first time.

'Ooooh!' Catherine growled.

'What?'

'Go away!'

'I… I came to find you.'

'And you've found me. Now go.'

'I'll – er -wait for you over here, shall I?' he said.

'So help me, if you so much as turn round within the next week, it will cost you your life,' she warned him. 'And shut your eyes.'

Tommy, finally getting to grips with her discomfort, closed his eyes.

Catherine, never once taking her eyes off of him, ever so slowly started to make her way across to her pile of clothes. She hesitated before starting to climb out, and angrily warned him once more about his safety should he even think about turning around. He mumbled some form of agreement though what he actually said was lost in a mumble.

Catherine hastily grabbed at her clothing and leapt away from the pool, and dived behind the nearest cover.

Catherine finally appeared, looking somewhat dishevelled in her haste to don all her clothing in such a short space of time. She was still angry, but now felt better able to handle the situation.

'Right. You can turn around now.'

Tommy turned holding his hands in the air, with a face that could not have been more apologetic.

'You look nice,' he tried feebly.

'You are just the limit!'

'I only just got there. Really! I swear.'

'Swear!' She let loose with more heavy artillery.

'I don't know why I even agreed to come to look for you. I wish we'd drawn lots.'

'And if you'd won.'

'I would have cheated.'

'Ha!'

Tommy had had enough. He had tried to explain himself away, and failed, but now he had had enough. He shook his head in disbelief, staring up into the sky.

'Come on,' Catherine told him as she nudged him heavily out of the way.

'Ssshh!'

'What?' she snapped. 'Sssh? Don't you even think of giving me orders!'

Tommy was unmoved, and staring up, said, 'Look!'

Catherine, stopped, sneered, and turned round to berate him again, when she noticed his face fixed on a point, way off into the distance. She followed his look but was unable to focus on anything.

'What is it?' she asked, concerned.

Tommy beckoned her over without moving his head.

'This had better not be another one of your tricks.'

Once more without moving his head, he reached out an arm and grabbed at whatever of Catherine he could put his hand on. Her shoulder. He drew her across, gathered her in his arms, and turning her, pointed. 'Look!'

In the distance, a column of smoke rose into the sky.

'That's ours, right?' Catherine said, edgily.

Tommy gestured to his left along by the stream with his arm. 'No! That's us!'

Catherine backed into his body and stood in his grip as they continued to stare, in silence.

Georgia and Phillip, now awake and in the land of the living, battled with each other in a struggle to feed the chicks, almost for something to keep them busy. They were both a little more nervous now. Catherine having gone had been one thing, but with Tommy now absent, they were nothing if not a little shaky. Neither of them wanted to stray too far in the event that either Tommy or Catherine returned, and that they should be second to the news. So Georgia stayed with the chicks, trying to make their pen a little more secure, and Phillip returned to fishing, sure that if both Tommy and Catherine had left along its banks, it would be their most likely point of return, and he should be first to see them.

Tommy and Catherine broke through the trees and scrub at a rush, and charged into camp. Phillip, climbing from the pool, was pushed slightly to one side in their excitement to impart their news to Georgia.

Georgia, a mixture of excitement at seeing Catherine fit and healthy again, and angry at her stupidity at having rushed off the previous night, was ready to let her have it with both barrels, but the excitement in their faces allayed her rebuke for a later date. They quickly ushered her to sit down. An angry Phillip, slightly confused at their reluctance to involve him, sat down grumpily beside them nonetheless, demanding to know what was going on.

Georgia and Phillip scrunched up next to each other, worried, as both Catherine and Tommy gasped for air attempting to regain their breath before finally endeavouring to reveal the news.

Georgia tried to make them both sit down by the fire, but neither of them wanted to sit still, and eventually Tommy managed to get out the words.

'There is… There is… Someone else on the island.'

Catherine, though not strictly necessary, nodded her affirmation.

48

Phillip clutched at both Georgia, and now Catherine's dress, frightened. Catherine was close to tears, more a mixture of the chase and the excitement, than the shock, and she was still panting.

'Who is it?' Phillip whimpered.

Both messengers slowed their rate of respiration, and Tommy slowly shook his head. 'We don't know.'

'How many?' Georgia asked.

'Where?' Phillip cried.

'We don't know,' Catherine snapped. 'We just came back to let you both know, first.'

'Oh my goodness!' Georgia gasped.

'Oh my goodness, indeed,' Catherine agreed. 'Let's go.'

'What do you mean, *Let's go?*' Georgia asked. 'Wait!'

'What for? It's what we've waited for. We've been rescued.'

'Hold everything,' Tommy said. 'We don't know who that is. We can't just go - charging in.'

'Whoever it is, they will be much better off than we are, and certainly able to help us.'

'Even if they're German?' Georgia asked bluntly.

'Well... I mean... I ... We're not alone. That's all.'

Phillip hearing the mention of Germans, tugged at Catherine's skirt that little bit harder. 'They're not Germans, are they?'

'I don't know,' she snapped.

'We don't know yet,' Georgia tried her best to calm his fears without overly revealing her own.

'When are we going to find out then?' Catherine demanded. 'I for one, am ready to go home.'

'Go on then,' Tommy said. 'Off you go. If they're friendly, come back and tell us. If not, stay with them.'

'Fine!'

'They'll soon give you back.'

'All right. I will go,' and she turned to set off, forcing Georgia to run across to stand in her way. Catherine tried several times to get past Georgia, but on each occasion, Georgia just managed to block her path.

'What is wrong with you all?'

'I think we should sit down and talk it through first,' Georgia tried to reason. 'Just to be safe.'

'Let's do something,' Phillip insisted, caught half way between both camps.

'We mustn't just charge in,' Georgia told them. 'Let's go together. But in case it's dangerous, let's just do it carefully.'

'Let me go, then,' Tommy suggested, apprehensively. 'I'll see what's happening, and come back.'

'Oh, right! You go and get all the glory.'

'You go then,' Tommy said. 'Just like I offered you a minute ago. I'm sick of it.'

'Oh. I so hope it is cannibals,' Catherine glared at him. 'And that they eat you.'

'What will happen if they catch you?' Phillip asked. 'I don't want you to be captured.'

'*I* don't want to be captured, but it might be safer for everyone if I go alone.'

'There's safety in numbers,' Georgia advised them, perpetual mediator.

'And what happens if whilst you're away, he – they - come here?' Catherine demanded.

'We can stand here and argue all day,' Georgia said, 'We – You - spotted the smoke from that fire. What's going to happen if *they* have spotted ours?'

There was a moment's silence as Georgia's thought settled in.

'At least let's make a plan of some description,' Tommy said. 'It can't hurt.'

'Whatever we do, we decide it together,' Georgia advised.

Tommy and Catherine looked across to each other and reluctantly agreed.

Several solutions were aired, thrown into the ring, roughed up and spat out, and still nothing had been positively decided upon. Whatever one person wanted, another either wanted to accompany them, or thought it better another left to do it on their own. In the latter case, mostly Tommy.

'We have to do something,' Georgia said, when first able to get a word in, uninterrupted.

'That's what I've been saying all along,' Catherine confirmed.

Tommy drew the knife from his pocket, and drew the larger blade.

'Are we all going to die?' Phillip asked, shrinking back from Tommy slightly.

'No. We're going to be rescued,' Georgia assured him, and looked across to Tommy for assurance. He in turn winked back at Phillip.

Catherine walked across to the fire and picked up a lit stick, and held it out in front of her.

'What are you going to do with that? Burn them to death?'

She turned to Phillip and told him he was joking.

'If we don't stop squabbling,' Georgia informed them, 'then whoever that is will find us before we find them.'

'Or be rescued and gone before we even get there,' Catherine said.

'We haven't even been that far yet,' Phillip explained. 'We don't know what's out there. He – she – er, they do. And I'm scared.'

'Like he says,' Tommy pointed out. 'Either we go to him, or he comes to us.'

'Okay! We go there.'

The children were lined up ready to depart. Tommy held the knife in his hand, whilst

202

Georgia and Catherine both held sticks that Tommy had sharpened to a point. Phillip had demanded a weapon, but had been talked out of it, and Catherine had promised to stay by his side. It had been decided to head back along the stream to the point where the smoke had first been spotted, ford it at that point, and attack their journey from there.

The precise point at which the smoke had originally been seen was not essential per se, as the second the smoke came into view, they all stopped, drew together, and stared quietly. The smoke continued to rise into the air, unchecked.

'Ready?' Tommy asked, tentatively, looking around. The others hesitated with a slight reluctance. 'Anyone?'

'Let's go then,' Georgia said. She pushed her way past the three ditherers, and started off across the stream. She stumbled slightly, and Tommy hurried across to steady her. She regained her balance, and hesitated. Tommy, spotting the waver, patted her on the shoulder, and took the lead. He turned several times though to ensure Georgia was right by his side.

The stream was a little more treacherous to cross than they had first thought it would be, and Catherine, for all her affiliation, and almost Piscean affinity with water earlier in the day, had now, fully clothed, become somewhat more fragile, and now had to be coerced across. In deference to what was left of her footwear, she had insisted on removing her shoes, and Phillip, on consideration, had decided to do the same.

The journey across the stream, up to their knees in the fast flowing stream across a mixture of weeds, sands, gravel and pebbles, was much longer than they had envisaged, and by the time they all reached the far side, much of the courage seemed to have drained from them. The distance from the rising smoke had seemed so much farther and safer from the other side of the stream, and a shiver ran down Georgia's spine as she mounted the far bank. She hoped it was just a reaction to the cold water of the stream, but she wasn't so sure. She clutched Tommy's hand as he helped her up, and squeezed it for a burst of encouragement. Tommy cast her a confident wink, patted her on the back as she passed him, and stayed and waited to help the others up.

Once they were all back on dry ground, they stopped under the premise of Catherine and Phillip putting on their shoes, and looked to each other again.

'Let's go,' Georgia said, and strode forward, manfully. Tommy caught her up, and turning around, found Catherine and Phillip hard on his shoulder.

Once across the stream and deep inside the trees and plant life, the smoke which they had been following disappeared.

'Which way?' Georgia asked.

'This way,' Tommy answered assuredly, and looking at her puzzled face, said, 'Hey! If we can't see his smoke from here, there is no way he will be able to see the smoke from ours.'

Tommy and Georgia struggled through the trees, twisting and turning, trying to find the easiest way forward. It was perfectly clear that whoever the smoke belonged to, they too had not been here long. The terrain they were traversing was virgin territory. For both them, and whoever else might be there.

Catherine, now struggling with a slightly less confident Phillip glued to her side, struggled uncomfortably with the terrain, and several times Georgia was forced to go back to help her out.

As a multitude of sounds echoed through the wood, the children scampered for hiding places, unsure if they had disturbed a rabbit. Or whatever it was.

'We are far too noisy,' Tommy told Georgia, now some distance clear of Catherine and Phillip. 'I'm sure we can be heard for miles.'

'I know,' she said. 'And I don't think we are going to have the element of surprise for too much longer.'

'We should have left them back at the camp,' Tommy gestured to the stragglers.

'It's not their fault. We all agreed to go together.'

'I know it's not. It's just the numbers!'

'We can't leave them here.' Georgia told him. Tommy raised his eyebrows. 'Besides! We might need the numbers later on. Go on.'

Tommy nodded and closed his eyes in disbelief as Catherine fell, and yelped, stifling the noise when she realised three incredulous sets of eyes stared at her.

'Sorry!' she whispered, looking up.

There was a disrespectful silence a deaf man could not have missed, and Catherine was left to get to her feet on her own.

The sound of the sea washing up against the shore announced their arrival at the fast approaching coast. The journey thus far had thrown up few startling new discoveries. They had come into contact with a few more rabbits, and Tommy had made mental note. Something that sounded a good deal larger had made its presence known at one point, and everyone had frozen, expecting discovery. But whatever it had been, it had sounded as if it had four legs and not two. If it was indeed just a larger rabbit, it would have to wait until a later date. They had other worries.

Tommy crouched down as the trees started to thin, affording them less cover, and motioned for the others to do likewise. He held up his hand, stopping them, and indicated that he was going to go on alone. There were suddenly no objections.

Tommy carefully edged his way forward, constantly looking around him. He looked behind him and three heads poked out from behind a tree. He waved them away and with a deep breath, started forward again.

He clambered up on top of a small stony shelf that looked down and across a small sandy clearing. *A Beach!*

He listened. He could hear a fire burning nearby, but from where he lay, he could not see it. He carefully manoeuvred himself into a slightly better position and looked across.

In the centre of the beach, a small fire burnt fiercely inside a circle of stones. It appeared freshly fuelled, and Tommy ducked down, sure the proprietor of the fire was sure to be close by, but even after something more than a hesitant peek, there did not appear to be anyone there, and if they were there at all, they were not making any noise.

Tommy looked back, expecting to have to reprimand his cohorts, but whether he had moved across too far, or whether they were remaining where they had been instructed at his last reproach was unclear.

Alone, he paused. He considered rushing out onto the beach, and sacrificing himself to whomsoever it might be. But considering himself the leader of the quartet, he realised what a pointless surrender this might be. *No. Gently does it.* He slowly edged himself out of cover, and inch by inch, he crept forward.

Now with a better view of the beach, he wondered just how their erstwhile lifeboat had not chosen this point to wash itself ashore.

I mean just look at all the…

Tommy shrank back into cover, breathing hard. He almost dared another look, but shaking his head, assured himself that he had not been mistaken. He started breathing heavily. It had been… He was sure… No! He crept forward once more, still unable to believe his eyes.

A vast white silky cloth was attached to the upper branches of a nearby tree. It had been further stretched across a section of the beach and safely anchored at various points with small piles of rocks to create a shelter.

'A parachute!' Tommy gasped, quickly ascertaining its former existence.

He drew back and lay flat. His rate of breathing had increased to that of a steam train, and he imagined Georgia and the others could clearly hear his heartbeat from where they had hidden themselves.

He ensured there was no movement on the beach, before quickly making his way back into the midst of the trees, and apparent safety. He waved frantically to the three faces that had appeared once more hearing his approach.

Georgia boldly led the way forward, followed a little more hesitantly by Catherine, and then Phillip, a little further behind. Tommy held his hand up, desperately. Georgia stopped, relaying the instruction down the line.

Tommy quietly and carefully made his way across to Georgia, quickly joined by the others.

'Are we saved?' Phillip asked brightly.

The four children shied back to what appeared to be a much safer distance from the beach, and finally regrouped, Tommy related exactly what he had seen.

'Is it definitely a German?' Georgia asked.

'I didn't stay around too long to find out.'

'Then it could be one of our boys,' Catherine said in the same manner her father might have used.

'Was he there?' Phillip asked, now wracked with fear.

Tommy shook his head.

'Let's go back,' Catherine said. 'To our camp. It'll be much safer there.'

Tommy looked firstly to Phillip, who seemed far the most likely to side with that option, and then to Georgia, who seemed sat firmly on the fence, committed neither one way nor the other.

'You all go back then,' he whispered. 'I want to see what we're up against.'

'Then I'll stay with you,' Georgia finally sided.

'We'll wait here then,' Phillip changed his mind.

'Yes! No use splitting up too much,' Catherine blurted, not wanting to be left alone with her brother at this precise moment. 'You may need our help.'

'Yes. We can't leave them on their own,' Phillip concurred.

'Just stay out of sight,' Tommy said. 'And you,' to Georgia, 'let's go.'

Tommy was far too agitated in the presence of another body on the – island – to overly worry one way or the other about Catherine. He did however fancy having Georgia by his side. Just for support.

Tommy and Georgia crept forward to the top of the shelf overlooking the beach, and satisfied that it was clear, safely dropped down onto the sand below. Tommy gestured for her to follow him, and slowly they edged their way along the beach, keeping close enough to the edge of the woods to be able to rush off into cover if the need arose.

As they finally approached the fire, they spotted a backpack lying nearby. It was opened at the top, the flap lying back, and several of its contents had spilled out and were scattered out across the sand.

Catherine now needed to utilise all her sisterly influence to manage to keep Phillip back with her. She was still unsure if she really wanted to be here at all – especially when she had seen Georgia disappear. Though still a million miles from being at home, she far preferred the somewhat safer surroundings of what had now become their camp beside the pool. She was totally at a loss here with Phillip, neither one place nor the other.

Unable to hear or see anything, an excited Phillip had started to edge forward several times now, and Catherine had had to physically manhandle him and employ a certain amount of brute force just to keep him where he was. She was more concerned about either of the pair of them being discovered on their own than worrying about what might actually be happening on the beach. With no fresh news from the direction of the beach, she was forced to look behind them constantly. So intent had she been in this pursuit that she had missed Phillip's latest break totally, and turning round to check on him, had been reduced to visually following his backside, scurrying off in the direction the others.

'Phillip!' she whispered frantically. But he was out of the range of a whisper – or chose not to hear - and despite the fear she felt being alone now, she still managed to resist the urge to shout. She had to let him go, and after only a moment or two alone, decided it best to take off in his wake.

Tommy and Georgia, having seen as much of the camp the visitor had set up as they needed to, had hurried off to seek shelter again. They sat nervously behind a large rock, desperately trying to work out what to do next.

'Is he German?' Georgia asked.

'I don't know,' Tommy murmured. 'I need to get a better look at what's inside that bag.'

'Is it safe?'

'Dunno!'

They peeked around the corner of the rock and looked along the beach once more, to see if anything had changed. But it still seemed devoid of anyone but themselves. No one that was, except for... Phillip!

'Nice one, Catherine,' Tommy growled.

Phillip arrived at pace. Boredom had quickly killed off any nerves he might have had, and he now desperately sought Tommy's company compared to that of Catherine. Unable to see either of the advance party, he assumed that everything must have been fine, and he walked out onto the beach, taking in the new horizon. He stared, as transfixed as Tommy had been on first seeing it, at the way the parachute had been utilised, and walked towards it as if in a trance. The fire that burnt beside it had not for one second surprised him, but the backpack drew him like a magnet. He knelt down beside it, and without a second thought started to examine the contents.

'Phillip!'

He turned his head slightly, not remotely unfazed by the call.

'Phillip!'

Finally, and thankfully recognising Georgia's voice, he turned and smiled.

'Look!' he said, indicating the array of items he had now spread out on the sand.

'Get over here.'

Selective deafness and tunnel vision had overtaken Phillip, and the side effect of his inquisitive nature had further glued him to the spot.

Georgia broke from the cover of the rock, and hurriedly rushed over to him.

Tommy looked on perplexed, all his carefully thought out plans ruined, and nothing else for it, he hastily made his way over to them and dragged them both to the floor, where they all lay, flat and still.

'Where's Catherine?' he asked Phillip, urgently.

'She's... back there,' he indicated where they had come from with an uncomfortable gesture of his hand.

'If this is a German and he doesn't shoot her,' he informed Georgia, 'I'm sure I'm going to.'

Georgia could not help but smirk at his levity, and slowly they started to get up and look around at their surroundings.

Phillip having received a reprieve for breaking curfew, returned to examine the various items from the bag, physically picking them up and turning them over.

Both Tommy and Georgia, though equally as intrigued at what there might be inside the backpack, were currently more concerned about the return of the owner, and spent

207

the majority of the time walking up and down the beach awaiting any sign of his return. Tommy held out his penknife as if it were going to keep a tiger at bay, but any other weapons they might have been able to utilise had been dropped at Phillip's surprise entrance. Georgia looked back towards Tommy and glancing down at the floor, stopped.

'What is it?' Tommy asked.

'I think we've lost our anonymity.'

'Anno… who?'

'Look.' She pointed at the sand. 'Footprints. He's going to know we've been here.'

'Shi… I mean, damn!'

'You two!' Phillip called warily. 'You might want to see this!'

'Wait a minute.'

'No really!'

Georgia and Tommy carefully worked their way back towards Phillip, trying to erase any telltale signs of their being there with their feet. But at best, they were going to have to hope the tide was on its way back in, or hope it indeed came this far up the beach. It was strange that the fire had been laid on the top of the beach if indeed there was a tide.

'Look!' Phillip held out a black leather belt. Tommy walked across to see the cause off the concern, but Phillip saved him the need, holding it out for all to see. 'Look!'

Tommy picked up the clasp and he and Georgia needed just one look. The metal clasp was inlaid with black enamel. It was a German cross, similar to the insignia emblazoned on the German vehicles and planes Tommy, for one, had seen during the news reels at the cinema, and in the newspapers.

'I think we have our answer, ladies and gentlemen,' Tommy said, looking first to Georgia, then to Phillip who stood in front of them, looking strangely over their heads.

Tommy looked to Georgia for clarification, then watched astonished as Phillip started to raise his hands into the air. He closed his eyes, and his head dropped realising what had happened.

'Put your hands in the air.'

'Turn around very slowly and go and join your friend,' a nervy German accent announced.

Tommy and Georgia raised their arms and joined Phillip in submission.   They slowly looked up, almost pathetically. The astonishment on all four faces was a state of parity.

A German pilot stood in front of them holding out a pistol, which he pointed at them, astonished. He was nearly six foot tall, with close-cropped blond hair, and towered over the three of them. He was in his early twenties, and with a youthful face, did not really appear that much older than they were. He wore regular grey Luftwaffe trousers, and had stripped off his jacket and shirt, now sporting a white vest. His braces were attached to the uniform trousers, and were strapped over his shoulders to keep them up.

Tommy was advised with a wave of the revolver to drop his knife, which he reluctantly obeyed. The pilot crouched to pick it up, and though worried about taking his eyes off them for a second, managed the task without any of the three moving.

Standing tall once more, he carefully repositioned his pistol on the three of them, equally as astonished as they were. He looked them up and down, and eventually asked, 'What are you doing here?'

The three children stood, speechless, staring at the pilot, mouths agape.

'Are you on your own?'

The same silent result.

'How did you get here?'

Nothing.

He looked around as if this might reveal an answer, but was clearly as puzzled about them as they were with him. Perplexed, he indicated that they should sit down on the floor while he thought what he ought to do next, and indicated that Phillip should throw across the belt that they had been examining. It landed at his feet and he kicked it further away from their grasp.

He looked down, examining the penknife, turning it over in his hand, trying to obtain at least some information about them, but eventually shook his head, defeated, and once more asked, 'Where are you from?'

Phillip moved slightly and was about to say something, when Tommy stopped him verbally. 'Stay there. We'll give you nothing but our name, rank and number.'

'What?' he asked, amazed at any reply at all, and offered a slight smile when he took in exactly what Tommy had said.

'Name, rank and number. That's all you'll get from us.'

'I think you have been watching too many films, my friend. I just want to know your names.'

The three captives looked to each other, their attempt at outwitting the pilot shelved for now. Tommy made to get up, but was urged to stay where he was with a further waggling of the gun.

'You are children'.

'Really?' Tommy answered, a sight more assuredly than he felt.

'Where are your parents? You can't be here on your own.'

Phillip was desperate to tell him something, but every time he started to say something, Tommy interrupted him.

'Just let me say something,' he blurted.

'You tell him nothing,' Tommy shouted. He jumped up causing the pilot to step back a pace, surprised. 'Tommy Adams. Private. Chiswick Three Seven,' he blurted, adding his house number for good measure.

Georgia and Phillip looked to each other hearing the name Tommy Adams for the first time.

'Tommy?' Phillip mouthed to Georgia who looked equally puzzled.

Tommy sat down again, his performance complete, suddenly realising exactly what he had revealed.

'Good!' The pilot said. 'So! Tommy, then!'

'Who?' Georgia sniggered.

'I made him up,' he whispered quickly, hoping a short answer, and Georgia's giggle might have saved his true identity for a later date.

'Private?' The pilot laughed, waving the barrel of the revolver up and down again, indicating Tommy's size. 'The British really must be short of soldiers if you are anything to go by.'

'I'm small for my age,' Tommy taunted him.

'And him?' he indicated Phillip. 'And look! Girls too!'

'They're in disguise.' Tommy was running out of answers.

'Do I get their names?'

Phillip was ready to stand up and emulate Tommy's performance, but Georgia held him where he was. She stared through the pilot.

The pilot looked mystified for a moment, and catching Phillip's eyes staring past him, started to turn, when...

Thump!

49

Catherine stood with a large rounded lump of rock in her hands. She looked as dumbfounded as her audience. She looked down at the pilot, lying unconscious at her feet.

'Catherine!' Georgia exclaimed, jumping to her feet. 'You were fantastic!'

'And I was wrong.' Tommy said, full of admiration. 'You really do have a reason to be here.'

Catherine looked up through glazed eyes, and dropped the rock. Georgia had to rush to her side to steady her at the point at which her body decided to lose all feeling, reducing her to jelly.

'I will never criticize her again,' Tommy stated, shaking his head in disbelief, relieving Georgia of her duties of keeping Catherine upright. 'You were fantastic!'

Catherine looked into Tommy's eyes, and coming to slightly, flapped her arms, relinquishing him of any need of his assistance, and stood on her own once more.

'Catherine!' Georgia called across.

Catherine, looked back, and her eyes seemed to grow and stared way past Tommy.

Tommy turned to see whatever it was that was more important than having nearly decapitated a German airman, and quickly caught up.

'Put it down, Phillip,' Catherine used her most authoritative voice. 'Nice and slowly. Put it down.'

Phillip stood holding out the pilot's revolver in front of him, studiously turning it round in his hands.

'Do what she says, Phillip.' Tommy said slowly. 'Put it down. Slowly.'

During the dissolution of the German pilot's reign, and whilst they had been distracted with Catherine's heroics, Phillip had picked up the revolver. He now held it out proudly in front of him, his finger lodged eerily by the trigger.

'Put it down, mate,' Tommy reiterated.

Phillip looked firstly to the revolver, then back to the other's worried faces, and slowly, he bent down and placed it on the sand in front of him. He stepped away from it, nonchalantly, as if nothing had happened, and Georgia stepped smartly forward. Bending down, she picked it up carefully by the handle between her index finger and thumb, and carefully took it off, placing it well away from everyone.

'That's better,' Tommy said, heaving a huge sigh, and turned to look for Catherine, who had finally had enough, and lay in a heap. Like her opponent, she was unconscious.

Tommy and Georgia had hurriedly acquired some of the cord from the parachute and used it to tie up the pilot. He had been left in a heap on the beach with his hands trussed behind his back, and still appeared a good sleep away from waking up just yet. Catherine was also slowly recovering, and Phillip, having shaken off his encounter with the revolver, was now almost uncontrollable with excitement.

The pilot moaned, not as lost to the world as they might have thought, and rocked his head from side to side, trying to regain full consciousness. His eyes cleared slightly and as he looked up, he stared directly into Tommy's face. He held the pilot's pistol in his hand, and had it pointed directly in the pilot's direction.

'Be careful with that,' the pilot mumbled. 'It has a very light trigger.'

'Just like the ones on your plane's bomb releases, eh?'

The pilot sighed.

'Not so brave now are we?'

'Just be careful, that's all.'

'Don't tell me what to do. Nobody tells me what to do.'

'Come over here,' Georgia pleaded. 'Maybe… Well, maybe he's right about the gun.'

Tommy was ready to say something, but patiently controlled his temper. He walked back across to rejoin the others sat a good distance away from their captive, and almost heeding the pilot's words, carefully placed the pistol onto the sand..

'I think Catherine should have the gun,' Georgia said. 'As a reward for her bravery.'

Tommy picked up the gun between finger and thumb as Georgia had earlier, and waved it in front of Catherine's face.

She shied away. 'No thank you.'

Tommy stood up and walked across, tossing the gun up and down, from hand to hand in the style he had seen in many of the Western films at the cinema.

'Please! Be careful!' the pilot strongly advised him.

'Shut up,' Tommy taunted him, catching the revolver and pointing it at him once more. The pilot cowered. Tommy laughed and threw it up into the air again. As if performing in front of a variety show, he offered a cocky grin to Georgia who looked back worried. As he looked back and reached for the gun, he stubbed his finger on the handle and it fell away and out of his control.

As the handle of the gun stabbed into the beach, a piercing shot rang out.

Everyone dived off in different directions at once, and settled, waited for the echo of the shot to die down. Slowly, and one by one, they started to move their limbs, checking their bodies to see if anyone had been caught by the discharge.

'Is everyone okay?' Georgia yelled, the first to fully recover her wits, and started a role call. 'Catherine…?'

'You idiot,' Catherine said finally. 'You idiot!'

Tommy stood, shakily, his eyes wide in shock. He quickly looked around to check any injuries not clarified by the roll call. He slowly turned his head and disconsolately looked across at Georgia. She could not hold his look and shook her head disappointedly. She turned away, and so doing, missed Catherine's lunge in his direction.

The lunge caught Tommy deep in his midriff and sent him sprawling. She leapt on top of him, and started beating at him frantically. She had to be physically dragged off him by a combination of both Georgia and Phillip, and as they did their best to hold her back, he shakily crawled away and sat alone.

212

'You're mad,' he yelled at her, rubbing at his various aches and pains.

'I'm mad?' she yelled back. 'I'm mad!' Once more she lunged at him, and once more was tackled by the restraining committee. 'I'm mad? You haven't even seen me mad yet.'

'I'm sorry!' he yelled, for everyone's benefit. 'I'm sorry!'

Georgia, leaving Catherine to her brother's tender mercy, climbed to her feet and walked across to check on the pilot, who having thrown himself to one side, and still trussed, was having trouble sitting upright again.

'Are… Are you okay?' she asked.

'Just a little shocked. I might need a hand sitting up, though.'

Georgia was hesitant about setting him upright again. She stood off slightly, carefully deliberating over what she should do.

Tommy, in an attempt at avoiding further assault from Catherine, stumbled to his feet and walked across to try to regain a little of Georgia's respect. Catching the tail end of their conversation, he spared her the responsibility. He walked straight past her, grabbed the pilot by the shoulder of his shirt, and with no attention to finesse or detail, dragged him upright until he was seated in a more comfortable position, and then walked away.

'Thank you,' the pilot offered.

'Humph!'

Unbeknownst to everyone else on the beach, and lost in the chaos therein, Catherine calmly walked across the beach and stooping down, picked up the revolver and held it out in front of her. She breathed heavily, staring hard at the offending weapon. She turned the pistol until the barrel of the weapon lay in her hand. She clasped the barrel so tightly it was doubtful she would ever let it go, when Georgia arrived at her side.

'We've already had one accident. Let's be careful, shall we?' She put her arm around Catherine, and whispering a few more soothing words in her ear, finally relieved her of the pistol.

Catherine sniffed heroically, but was not brave enough to stop tears flooding down her cheeks, and she turned away to walk off along the beach.

'Do you think I might stand up?' the pilot asked Georgia, who was the closest, and whom he had assumed to be the most affable of his gaolers.

'I'm – er - not sure,' Georgia answered.

'You have the advantage of the pistol,' he nodded towards her hand, 'and if that is not enough, you will notice you have me trussed up. There is not really much I can do.'

'I'll go and check.'

She stood up and walked over towards Tommy, and latterly Catherine, for advice. Phillip who had watched everything from a distance, walked across and sat himself down, realising that anything he had to say was likely to have little sway.

'Why do you hate us?' he asked the pilot, who was sat just in front of him.

'I don't hate you,' the pilot answered chuckling. 'Why should I hate you?'

'You're a German.'

'And you are…'

'English. Why do you hate us?'

'I don't hate you,' he insisted.

'Get away from him,' Tommy bellowed, catching sight of the interplay between the two. He snatched the pistol from Georgia's grasp and started across.

'Why? I just…'

'Just get away from him, Phillip. Don't let him poison your mind.'

Phillip raised his eyebrows, folded his arms irritably as the pilot said, 'Go on. Don't worry. I'm not going anywhere.'

Tommy brushed past Phillip with the revolver, and once more walked up to threaten the pilot.

'Put it down,' Catherine yelled from a distance. 'Why won't you ever learn?'

'Here!' Tommy stopped Phillip, and after a moment's consideration, turned and handed the gun across to him. 'Give this to your sister.'

'Be careful!' the pilot warned.

'Don't you even think of getting anyone on your side,' Tommy turned again. 'You don't say anything unless we say, do you hear?'

The pilot nodded.

Tommy glared at him, and was all set to let loose another torrent when another shot rang out. Tommy dived down landing at the pilot's feet, who likewise, had once again curled up to avoid being struck.

'Not again. Dear God!' Catherine snapped angrily, and looked up from where she and Georgia had been sorting through the pilot's things. She was far less concerned now than she had been at the original report from the pistol, imagining that Tommy had been showing off once more. She looked up into Phillip's stern face as he held the gun out in front of him.

'Phillip!' Georgia yelled.

'You! But I thought…' Catherine looked around for Tommy. 'Put it down,' she shouted.

Phillip's hand started to shake, and Catherine climbed to her feet and carefully took the gun from him, alarmed at his shaking, and now, two bullets to the wise, carefully lay it to one side.

Phillip's face had turned white, and he reached down and rubbed at the top his leg, and slowly held up his hand. He held it palm upwards and looked at it, and held it out towards his sister. It was covered in blood.

'PHILLIP!'

50

Once the initial shock had finally registered, Phillip cried out and fell to the floor. Catherine looked up at Tommy, who was just getting to his feet. He started to walk across inquisitively, unable to see exactly what had happened. He had not seen anything directly, but as he saw Phillip fall to the ground, he guessed, and rushed across.

'Go away!' Catherine screamed, reaching for the pistol. 'Go away, or so help me I will shoot you myself!'

Georgia, a witness to what was unfolding in front of her was slightly faster to the weapon, and just managed to push it out of her reach.

'Is he all right?' the pilot called over, anxiously.

'Shut up!' Tommy cried out, trying to look over Georgia's shoulder. She was crouching over Phillip, having pushed Catherine to one side to allow her to see the extent of the damage. Catherine cradled Phillip's head in her shoulder as he started to shake as shock set in.

'If he dies, so help me, I swear I will kill you myself,' Catherine spat at Tommy.

'It's not my fault,' he barked back at her.

'Why don't we all calm down?' Georgia interrupted, sternly. 'We need to work on this together. I'm going to need the knife.'

'Don't cut him,' Catherine pleaded.

'I need to cut away the material,' Georgia explained.

'I'm sorry.'

'If you are both going to crack up on me, maybe you should both go away for a minute or two.'

'Is he all right?' the pilot yelled across, again.

'Shut up… Jerry. This is all your fault,' Tommy bawled back, trying to apportion the blame.

'I've told you once,' Georgia said angrily. 'Give me the knife and calm down, or go away.'

Tommy reluctantly handed over the knife, and stood back to let Georgia do her stuff.

Phillip, apparently unconscious, continued to shake in Catherine's arms, and she quietly whispered kind words into his ear.

'Hold him tight,' Georgia said. 'I don't want to slip.' This did not seem to be a problem as Catherine had him held so tightly, no one could have taken him away from her if they had tried.

Georgia slid the knife into the material hiding the wound on Phillip's leg, and angrily rebuked Catherine as he jumped at her touch.

'Keep him still!'

She cut further into the fabric increasing the size of the gap to enable her to better see the damage. Phillip jerked violently in Catherine's arms, and coming to, she kissed his forehead.

Georgia baulked slightly at the sight of the wound, but after the initial shock,

215

returned to her work. Cutting up a rabbit was one thing. A ten year old boy was a different thing altogether.

'Tell me what he has done,' the pilot shouted.

Tommy and Catherine both turned to reproach him as Georgia interrupted.

'Shut up! Both of you! Listen to what he has to say.'

'Let *me* have a look,' he shouted.

'If you don't shut up, you're gonna get what he's got,' Tommy barked across.

'Let him have a look,' Georgia said. 'I don't really know what to do. I can only keep it clean.' Catherine looked to her sternly, but Georgia nodded, confirming her request. 'It makes sense, I promise.'

'Get him over here,' Catherine demanded.

'You're mad!'

'Just do it.'

The pilot was helped to his feet and hopped over as quickly as his restraints allowed.

'Untie him,' Georgia said.

'Are you mad?'

'At least his hands.'

'No way!'

'He's no use trussed up like a chicken,' Georgia tried to hurry things along.

'Fine. But don't say I didn't warn you.' Tommy picked up the pistol and stood back, pointing the gun in the pilot's direction. 'Just in case, eh?'

'Hasn't that caused enough problems already?' Georgia asked.

'You can let him have his hands back, but he's not going anywhere.'

Georgia picked up the knife and cut through the bindings on his hands as the pilot held them out to her.

'Let me have a better look,' he said, gently pushing Georgia to one side, and pointing to a small package that had been taken from his backpack said, 'Pass me that.'

'What is it?' Tommy demanded an answer, placing a foot on top of the package.

'It's for him,' the pilot said without further explanation.

Georgia scrambled over and threw Tommy's foot to one side.

'Can you help him?' she asked, bringing back the package.

'I need some water. I have a bottle over there somewhere,' he indicated with his head. 'Or wherever you have put it.'

'Seawater any good?' Georgia asked, unable to immediately locate the container.

'No. Fresh water.'

'The stream,' Catherine said. 'We can get some from there.'

'It's too far,' Tommy said. 'Go and look for his.'

'Got it,' Georgia said, returning, holding up a flask. She handed it across.

'Hold him tight,' the pilot told Catherine. She looked worried. 'It's going to…' he searched for just the right word in his broken English '…sting a bit,' he told Phillip, who looked back at him, nodding through the pain. 'Ready?'

216

Phillip nodded.

The pilot poured a small amount of the water over the wound clearing the blood away from the flesh. Phillip cried out pitifully in pain and had to be held even tighter to avoid his pulling free. Tommy took a pace forward, but Georgia held up a hand, urging him to stay back, indicating that things were fine.

The bullet had fortunately not entered the leg, but it had badly grazed it. It had taken away a good deal of the skin with it, and though, to the children the wound appeared terminal, it was not life threatening. The wound had bled profusely, and had had to be cleaned as thoroughly as possible, but the news that the package Georgia had brought back was a Red Cross box was a revelation.

Georgia, elevated to the role of Nurse, unwrapped several of the bandages and dressings and handed them across as directed.

They all stood back and watched as the pilot cleaned up and finally dressed Phillip's leg to the best of his ability.

'All done,' he said finally, and lowered his hands slowly, holding them out to be coupled once more.

'Do we have to?' Catherine asked, looking from Tommy to Georgia.

'No,' Tommy said. 'Just put your own hands out and let him do it to you. Of course we have to.'

'But he just saved Phillip's...'

'And if we are rescued by a German ship, we will all be his prisoners. Just do it.'

'Do it,' the pilot said. Catherine looked at him confused. 'He's right. I don't mind.'

'I've told you once. Don't try to soft talk us, mister,' Tommy said threateningly. 'You're our prisoner. We're grateful for what you've done, but that's where it ends.'

The fire that had been built on the beach had grown substantially. It was now at least twice the size, and burnt brightly. The German pilot had been positioned on the side of the fire closest to the sea, and remained adequately trussed. Phillip lay curled up by his sister, and was finally sleeping after much fuss. He stirred intermittently, as the dressing smarted against the wound each time he moved. Catherine patted his head each time he looked up, and assured him that everything was going to be fine.

Georgia and Tommy had separated themselves from the others. They had sorted through what few possessions the pilot had managed to salvage. But for the revolver and another knife, which was slightly studier than Tommy's, he appeared to be about as badly off as they were. They were almost back to square one.

'What are we going to do now?' Georgia asked him.

'We've got to keep him under guard.'

'With what?'

'The gu...'

'The gun! Don't you think we've had enough trouble with that thing already? Besides, Phillip is ill, and I don't see Catherine wanting to stand guard duty. And certainly not with a gun. What about during the night?'

217

'He'll have to stay tied up. It's not my fault where he was born. I'm sorry.'

'He probably saved Phillip's life.'

'He…'

'He did what we couldn't. We couldn't treat the bleeding.'

'What do you want to do?' Tommy asked unbelievably. 'Let him go?'

Georgia shook her head. 'Of course not,' though she was not convincing in her response.

Tommy jumped up, angrily, looked at her shaking head, and far from satisfied with her sincerity, stormed off to the far end of the beach. He dumped himself down with his back towards both she and the others, and stared out to sea.

Georgia walked over to the fire, and sat down. She looked across at Phillip to check he was settled, and nodded at Catherine, whose face was now a mixture of care for her brother, and anger at Tommy.

'It's not his fault,' the pilot assured them from the far side of the fire. Georgia looked up, confused. 'The gun. The injury. It's not his fault.'

'And how do you work that out?' Catherine asked, irritably.

'We were not all meant to be brought together. And the gun is just a - result - that came with it.'

'He's a fool.'

'Catherine!' Georgia reproached her.

Catherine realised just how easily she had sided with the pilot, and looked awkwardly back at Georgia, who frowned.

'He *is* a fool. Why did he give the gun to Phillip in the first place? He couldn't look after it himself. We should take the bullets out and throw them all away.'

'Hmmm!'

51

Georgia decided after a short time that envoy should be added to her growing list of duties. She walked across to Tommy and without saying anything, sat down beside him.

'Have you crowned him King yet?' Tommy asked, after a while.

'Don't be silly.'

'We're nothing to do with him. We didn't invite him here.'

'None of us are meant to be here,' she pointed out. 'Things are different now.'

Tommy got to his feet, still irked at the others' reaction to the pilot. He walked away from Georgia and back towards the fire that was starting to die away.

'We're going to need some more wood for this,' Catherine told him, without acknowledging his return.

'Why? Are we staying here?'

'Just get some wood. We've got to keep Phillip warm. He won't be going anywhere for a while.'

'Untie me. Let me help you,' the pilot said.

'What is it with you?' Tommy snapped. 'Can't you get it into your head?'

'If we are the only ones on this island, then where am I going to go?'

'Island? The only one's here? How do you know we're the only one's here? And what do you mean - Island?'

The pilot's eyes drifted to Catherine, but he realised Tommy had noticed.

'You've told him all about us, haven't you?' Tommy snapped incredulously. He was about to march off, but far from done, turned to confront her again. 'Well you were hard to crack, weren't you? Remind me not to tell you anything personal.'

'He told me how he got here. He parachuted down, and...' She saw Tommy looking up to the parachute hanging above the beach, and realised how easily it appeared she had been duped. 'We're on an island. We're all alone. We're all casualties of war.'

'Maybe he's right. He can't go anywhere.' Georgia joined the latest debate.

'He bombed my house. He killed my dad,' Tommy blurted. 'We are never going to be friends. And while he's here, he stays tied up.'

Tommy's revelation silenced everyone.

Catherine's brow wrinkled and as her head sank into her chest, she whispered, 'I'm sorry.'

'I'm sorry, too. For your father,' the pilot added quickly.

'Don't you even think of being sorry,' Tommy glared at him, stabbing a finger in his direction. 'Don't you even dare!'

The conversation died and there was an uncomfortable silence.

'What are we going to do?' Georgia asked him eventually, trying to redirect his pain.

Tommy shrugged.

Phillip moaned and reminded them all that there were other concerns. Tommy looked down to him, then to Catherine. 'How is he?'

'I don't know. I'm not a nurse. I'm just trying to comfort him.'

'I'm sorry,' he pointed down at Phillip. 'It might have been my fault.'

Catherine looked up. A strange mixture of emotions were flying about, and the mood was confused. 'We have to do something with the gun. It has to be put somewhere safe. Maybe we should get rid of the bullets,' she reiterated, trying to use the lull in tension to advantage.

'A gun is about as useful as a stick, without bullets.'

'Can't we just put them to one side?' Georgia said. 'We'll still have them. It's just we've had nothing but trouble with the thing so far, and we've only had it for about ten minutes.' She looked down to Phillip once more to emphasize the point.

Tommy sat alone, turning the revolver over and over in his hands. He handled it more in deliberation of what to do next, than studying its design. He carefully laid it to one side on the sand, and stared at it. Georgia coughed, attracting his attention. He looked up, and she gestured to Phillip, lying asleep, trying her best to help him decide.

'If you want to remove the magazine holding the bullets...' the pilot interrupted.

'I don't. Besides, who knows? The second we take out the bullets, five more of your mates may just come out of hiding.'

'Please! Come here,' the pilot called Georgia across.

Georgia looked to Tommy, who glared back at her for even considering it. She bit her lip, and as Tommy and Catherine watched, almost reluctantly walked across to the pilot and sat herself down. The pilot whispered something to Georgia that neither of them could register, and slowly she reached down to his trouser leg, and started to roll it up.

'What's going on?' Tommy demanded, jumping to his feet.

Georgia ignored him and continued with her task.

Just above the pilot's ankle, was a black leather sheath strapped to his calf. Inside the sheath was a large dagger.

Georgia carefully drew the dagger from its scabbard, and held it out for examination.

'Would I have given you that if I wanted to - kill - you all?' the pilot raised his voice.

The knife had a five-inch blade and dwarfed both Tommy's smaller knife and the other they had recently discovered in his pack. The handle was made of a hard leather-like compound, and the bright silver blade appeared pristine, and did not appear to have been used before. Georgia tested the keen side of the blade, and smarted as it caught on her thumb. She bit her lip, and sucked on her thumb. She shyly undid the sheath from the pilot's leg, and carefully placed the razor sharp knife back inside, and held it out to Tommy.

'Well?'

'And the bullets?' the pilot asked.

'What about them?' Tommy snapped, still unconvinced. Despite the relative easing of hostility between the pilot and the two girls, Tommy was still vehemently opposed to any bonding with him.

The pilot, refusing to allow Tommy an opportunity to stop the positive momentum, continued relentlessly. 'Listen! Just in case!'

The pilot carefully talked Tommy through the removal of the remaining bullets, watched by an intrigued Georgia until he finally held out the magazine in his hand.

'Put them somewhere safe - and dry,' the pilot said. 'They may be valuable at some time in the future.'

'They'll be safe,' he insisted, and whispering, solely for his own benefit, said, 'and the next time we take a prisoner, I'll do the search.'

'So?' Georgia punched him in the shoulder.

Tommy shrugged, and looking down at the magazine, realised he had no idea. He stuffed it inside his waistband, and sat back.

Tommy sat with the weapons displayed in a circle in the sand in front of him. He raised his head and looked across to the pilot.

'Why do you speak such good English?' he asked. 'I don't know one word of German.' He looked across to Catherine to see if she had already covered this ground and simply decided not to pass on the information to the rest of them. Either way, she said nothing.

'Of course.' the pilot laughed. 'Why would you know? My father was a professor of languages in Germany before the war, and I lived in England for one year, studying at one of your universities. There is your answer. Or should I give you only my, name, rank, and number as you so carefully pointed out earlier?'

'You lived in England?'

'For one year before the war broke out. Yes.'

'You lived in England, and now you fight against us?'

'It is a little more complicated than that.'

'You could have killed people you knew. Friends!' The pilot lowered his head and turned away slightly, realising what Tommy was making reference to and did not answer. 'Well?'

'It is a little more difficult than,' he defended himself. 'You may understand when you get a little bit older.'

'Older?'

The pilot breathed in, looking for a better explanation. 'Not older. Wiser! I did not declare war on you. People I have never even met decided that for me. I am just an airman.'

'So?'

'I am just...'

'Following orders?'

'Yes! Following orders.'

Tommy shook his head strongly, far from convinced.

Phillip moaned, and winced as the pain in his leg awoke him. He opened his eyes, and momentarily confused as to his whereabouts, stared straight into the eyes of the pilot. He shrank back into his sister's legs, and slowly came to his senses. She mopped his brow with a dirty sleeve, and comforted him to the best of her ability.

221

Phillip absentmindedly reached down to the dressing that had been applied to his leg, and yelped.

'Sssh!' she assured him. 'You'll be fine. Just relax.' He gulped down the frightened breath, and lay his head back down again. 'He will be fine, won't he?'

Georgia moved across and checked the dressing and ensured that the bleeding had been controlled, and looked nervously across at the pilot.

'Keep the wound clean. It could do with stitching, but…' the pilot hesitated. 'Well, just keep it clean.'

'How did you know how to treat his wound?' Catherine asked.

'I don't really know much more than the lady there,' he indicated Georgia with a nod. 'I was probably just a little less shaky than she was at the time.' Georgia smiled. 'I just treated it the best way I could. It will be much better clean, and we will have to wait and see what happens.'

'So you didn't study to be a doctor then?' Tommy queried.

'No. I studied engineering.'

'Well, thank you anyway,' Catherine said, shyly.

'So! Georgia said, as Phillip settled down again. 'Are you the one that was shot down the other day?'

The pilot nodded, almost embarrassed.

'Yes. I was unlucky. Instrument failure and I ran into… Well, anyway,' he pointed up to the parachute hanging from its housings.

'Did you land in the sea?' Catherine asked.

'What's the matter with you all? Do you want to know his life story?' Tommy shouted. 'Why would you want to know if he landed in the sea?' He glared at her.

'Well?' she asked him again.

'Yes. I did.'

'Why do you want to know?' Tommy tried to exact an answer.

'How did you get ashore?' Tommy looked down at himself to check he had not developed the ability to turn invisible. 'Did you have a lifeboat?'

Tommy clicked.

'No. I swam.'

'Have you built a raft yet?' A weak voice piped up. Phillip had come to, and appeared a little stronger.

Everyone looked across in his direction. Catherine offered her dirty sleeve once more, but Phillip weakly brushed it aside.

'No. Not yet,' the pilot answered, and his question answered, Phillip almost instantly drifted back to sleep.

'He's sweating,' Catherine explained, primarily to the pilot.

'He has a fever,' the pilot informed her.

'Should he be sleeping this much?' Catherine asked. 'He is so hot.'

'He's an engineer!' Tommy blurted. 'An engineer, not a nurse.'

There was an awkward silence, and Catherine switched her attention back to Phillip

222

to avoid further confrontation with Tommy.

There was an uneasy silence, and for a while, all that could be heard was the sound of the fire crackling.

'Why are you here?' the pilot asked, breaking the silence. 'Where are your parents?'

'We were…' Catherine started.

'We were nothing,' Tommy barked. 'What more do you need to tell him? We do not owe him anything.'

'No?' Catherine pointed to Phillip.

'That's done. We're grateful. Now what? Give ourselves up? Is that what you want?'

Georgia had had enough, and could no longer understand the inconsistencies in Tommy's temper.

'Shut up and give it a rest,' she told him. 'We're being silly.' She picked up the smaller knife and walked over towards the pilot. 'We can't just leave him tied up, and that's that!'

The blood suddenly rushed to Tommy's head, and desperately he snatched up the revolver and drew the magazine from his side. He slapped it back inside the revolver, and with no care, or attention to safety, raised it and pointed it straight at Georgia.

'No!' the pilot yelled.

Tommy was unmoved and followed Georgia with the barrel of the gun. 'Leave him as he is.'

'Don't you dare!' Catherine shouted. 'What on earth do you think you are doing? Are you mad? Don't be so stupid. For God's sake put it down.'

'You heard,' Tommy confirmed. 'Put down the knife and come away.' Georgia delicately did as she was told, and walked away, muttering words of disbelief. 'I've already lost one person to the Germans,' he explained, 'and I don't want to lose anyone else.'

'Is that supposed to be some sort of back-handed compliment?' Catherine asked furiously.

'It is what it is.'

A traumatised Georgia walked away, shaking her head, and as her shoulders started to shake, she slumped to the sand in a heap, almost as Tommy had earlier, and stared away, sobbing.

Catherine was so upset, she carefully laid Phillip to one side, and swearing at Tommy, stormed off up the beach.

Tommy glanced in the Pilot's direction, before finally glaring down into the sand by his feet. 'I don't need your compassion. Any of you,' he spat.

The pilot said nothing.

Tommy jumped up and looked around him furiously. Catherine and Georgia were currently the better for each other's company. Phillip, after a quick glance in his direction, was lost to the world again, and then there was the pilot. He was on his own.

The morning slowly passed into afternoon with no noticeable change in circumstances, and clearly no new bridges had been built. The girls had now returned to the fire to care for Phillip, completely ignoring Tommy. They had gone about their business without acknowledging him at all. He had tried to say something to them, and although Georgia had made to answer him, Catherine had raised her voice above hers, and quickly changed the subject.

The fire had died down and the pilot shook slightly, and sneezed.

'Bless you,' Georgia said, and looked to the fire. 'We will have to build that up.'

'We're staying here, then?' Tommy asked them.

'We will do what we want,' Catherine said. 'We don't need your permission. Besides, I've been thinking…'

'Praise the Lord!'

'…if we could see the smoke from this fire, then maybe someone else might see it.'

'We saw it because we were here. On the *island*. You think this is the beacon we need? Anyway! I didn't think you were talking to me.'

'We're not.'

'Fine!'

'Fine!'

Georgia snatched at a number of pieces of wood that was lying nearby for the fire, and ignoring them both, built up the fire, staring into it as the wood started to catch.

'Could we build it here?' she asked the pilot.

'Perhaps!'

'But…?'

'It should be built on a piece of higher ground, but I haven't explored yet.'

'Neither have we,' Georgia confessed, but turning around and looking up, said, 'I don't think there are too many mountains to worry about.'

'Don't talk to me, but you talk to him? Is that it?' Tommy interrupted. 'Would you rather be rescued by the Germans?'

'Don't be so stupid,' Georgia spat at him. 'And if you can't say anything nice, why say anything at all?'

'For goodness sakes! Don't you want to be rescued? We are four children,' Catherine pointed out. 'What do you really think they will want to do with four children?'

'Oh! Forgive me for being so stupid.' Tommy interrupted, making the best of being acknowledged again, as Catherine eyed him spitefully. 'They'll probably want to go back via England and drop us off, I expect. Don't you think so?'

'We were going to build a beacon of our own,' Georgia said. 'Did you really think for one second it would only be spotted by our side? Or should we have sent up a special coloured smoke, just in case? And anyway! Why not here?'

'Why not back at our camp?'

'Because our fire is under the trees.'

'And this is on the beach. Unless that is waterproof,' he pointed to the parachute nearby, 'The next fall of rain will put this out.'

A paradox had presented itself.

'You are just making excuses,' Georgia said to him. 'Do you want to be here for the rest of your life? I don't. We're lucky to have lasted this long already.'

'So we declare a truce? The only reason we are still alive is because of me.' He stared resiliently at Georgia, ignoring Catherine, who might have stood her ground a little more soundly.

'You are not going to make me cry again,' Georgia said. 'Do what you want. But don't involve me in it.'

'Fine!'

'Fine!'

Tommy had once more trapped himself in a corner. But for Phillip, he had no one on his side, and that only really because Phillip was asleep. He looked deep into Georgia's eyes, hoping she may relent, but it was unlikely. A half-glance at Catherine was no more promising. Finally he looked across at the pilot, but all he could see was a huge German swastika stuck in the ground, and not the man. His anger re-ignited. He either had to back down, or…

'Fine! Have it your way then,' he said. 'You can stay here. I'll take my knife - and the revolver. You…' he gestured to the others. 'You can do what you want with the rest. Oh! And good luck!'

He started to leave.

'What about Phillip?' Catherine looked at him dourly, and subconsciously shook him slightly in an effort at waking him, that he might somehow add further weight to her cause.

Tommy looked down at Phillip's prone, weak body, and fought with his conscience, but it was no good. His mind was made up. He shook his head, disappointedly, and pointing across to the pilot, said, 'You've got Florence Nightingale over there. You don't need me now.'

Phillip looked up helplessly to Catherine who quickly filled him in on what he had missed, albeit her side of the story. Phillip looked up to Tommy weakly, and cried, 'Please don't go!'

'That's not fair!' Tommy told her. He looked once more to Phillip, and shook his head again. 'Using your brother against me. Haven't you got any morals?'

'Morals! Hah! No. You want to go? Go!'

Tommy looked to each of them in turn and once more at the German pilot. He picked up the revolver, stripped the magazine holding the bullets, threw the gun to the floor, and clutching at his few other possessions, turned and ran off.

'Where are you going?' Georgia shouted, but her voice did not travel quite as far as Tommy had run. Or if it had, he ignored her.

52

As Tommy flew through the forest, he clattered his way past trees, branches, and knee high bushes and shrubs as if they weren't there at all. He clasped his scant possessions so tightly to his chest, that if he had happened to have fallen, there was little he would have been able to do to protect his face.

Breaking from the woodier area of the trees, he ran straight into further obstacles. He stumbled and slowed as he tried to overcome several larger rocks and stones, but still nothing stopped his flight from the beach. His mind was overflowing with anger.

He quickly reached the point at which they had crossed the stream earlier that day, and now, far less delicately made his way across it. He bounded through the running water, with barely a thought as to getting wet, and though the water tried its hardest, it barely slowed his pace. He quickly broke from its hold and reaching the far side, ran on desperately.

He rushed into what just a few short hours ago had been their camp. Despite its starkness, and cramped conditions, he could not believe they had all left it so easily, for…. He rushed across to the fire and stared down at the dwindling ashes, suddenly desperate for warmth. He snatched at a small stick and dug deep into the ashes searching frantically to see if he could find any dwindling life.

'There!' he struggled, puffing hard on a glowing ember. He offered it several small twigs he had gathered together, and blew hard once more. Slowly, a small flame appeared and Tommy stopped blowing in the event that he might put it out. Gradually the twigs started to catch, and slowly he added slightly larger pieces of wood, until at last, something that passed for a fire started to take shape in front of him.

The crackling from the larger pieces of wood as they finally caught soon filled the empty air. He sat, a lonely figure, lost in thought. A thousand pros and cons pecking away at him.

Pecking away at him! The chicks!

Suddenly the air seemed to clear, and as the sound of the chicks clearly broke through, his own worries seemed, if not to disappear, then certainly to ease slightly.

Phillip fought his body's affinity with sleep in his fight to recovery, and tried his hardest to stay awake. Drifting in and out of sleep though, he vaguely remembered Tommy's departure, although his memory as to the reasoning behind it was vague. Though still drowsy and weak, he badgered both Catherine and Georgia about Tommy's disappearance. Georgia had tried hard to pacify him, but his sister, in her inevitable way, had found it necessary to tell it as it was, helping no one. Even though her main agitator was now out of the way, she still seemed to retain the ability to find fault and put people on edge at a moment's notice.

Tommy sat beside the noisy offspring and set about scraping together the meagre food that had been left behind. He stared into their noisy imploring faces and ensured them that he would look after them, even if the others had forgotten all about them.

'How short their memories,' he told them, as if they could hear his every word.

Over the next couple of hours, Tommy split his time between tending first the chicks, then the fire. Finding what was left of a fish Phillip had left behind, he fought his way through the somewhat cumbersome process of preparing the chicks' food to what he imagined the correct consistency to be. Both tasks kept him busy, but it was never long before his attention was drawn back to Phillip and the two girls on the beach with… The thoughts angered him, and he returned to his work with a lot more vigour.

The chicks had happily and readily swallowed every scrap of the food Tommy had prepared for them, and for all the excitement of his return, they were now tired, and had settled back quietly for the while. Tommy realised the silence was only temporary and that it would not be long before the angry children would wake hungrily again. He looked around, and realised a fresh supply of foodstuff would needed before too much longer. Both for he and the youngsters. It had always been a job that Phillip had excelled in, and as he thought back to the last time he had seen Phillip's face looking up to him, his last words, *'Please don't go,'* stabbed at him. He looked to the chicks for some sort of reprieve, but it had appeared that even they had lost interest in him for anything more than their next course.

'Traitors,' he condemned them, and then looking at their weak helpless figures, confided in them, 'They're on their own from now on. Now it's just you and me guys.'

Despite Phillip's constant griping, Catherine had insisted that Tommy's disappearance was nobody's fault but his own. Though Catherine had admirably assisted in any nursing Phillip had required, Georgia had sat by her side and babysat the pair of them.

'He'll be back,' the pilot's voice cut through a moment's silence.

'He can stay away,' Catherine jumped in. 'Even if we are rescued, I might just forget to tell them he's here at all.' Georgia dug her in the ribs. 'Well!'

Georgia had finally had enough. She jumped up, and picked up the sharp dagger and walked across to the pilot. She expected a reaction from Catherine, but she too seemed to have had enough, and watched, intrigued. She knelt by the pilot, and picked up his tethered hands.

'I hope I'm doing the right thing?' Georgia said quietly, looking into his face. The pilot nodded. She breathed hard before carefully drawing the blade across the bindings, and suddenly his hands came free.

'Thank you,' the pilot said quietly, and having removed all his restraints, slowly stood and stretched.

Catherine and Phillip flinched slightly and watched in sudden trepidation, unsure about exactly what Georgia had just done.

Tommy sat himself down by the fitful fire which spat and hissed angrily. Now he and the chicks had had time to calm down, time passed, and both the fire and the feeding regime dealt with, there was little to occupy his mind besides Phillip's condition,

Georgia's trust, and though he hated to admit it, Catherine.

Tommy's warning about the tide turned out to be unnecessary. As the sea started its journey up the beach, though it held Catherine's eye, it stopped comfortably short of the spot that the pilot had set up his camp. The positioning of the parachute had been set out to perfection, and the fire remained unhindered. The two girls were both struck by the amount of the desirable fabric on display, and both had ideas of their own as to the use to which it could be put in the ideal world, along with the right conditions. It was however, currently, ideally employed. If they were missing Tommy, it was not obvious. They were now absorbed in the company of the newly liberated pilot.

The chick's stomachs seemed to be bottomless pits. Tommy had fed them every last vestige of the food he could manage, but after what seemed to be a very short break, they shouted a reprise. He had eventually warmed himself up by the fire, which now burned with some fervour, and now, their diet established, was left with the task of standing in the cold water of the pond to somehow restock their food supply.

He wearily mulled the task over, wondering just how long he could put off the inevitable. The impatient chicks were not so forgiving however, and the noise they created could in no way be ignored for too long.

So it was, he removed his shoes and socks and left them beside the fire to dry, not yet having done so fully from his recent crossing of the stream on his return journey, and climbed to his feet.

He looked to the depths of the pond unfavourably and shouted to the persistent chicks to be quiet and informed them that he was doing the best he could. He walked to the side of the pond and lowered the toes of one foot into the water to test it, and shivered at the result. But, he decided that having come this far, there was no going back, and slowly he lowered himself in. He shivered uncontrollably the further the water rose up his legs.

Finally acclimatised, Tommy stood and barked one final rebuke back at the chicks before glaring down into the water. His thoughts wandered back to Phillip, and he smiled as he remembered how he had spent countless hours in pursuit of the catch he had somehow procured. Tommy wished he had spent a little more time watching exactly how he had managed such a task. He had just taken it as read that Phillip would always be there. He set his feet and lowered his hands into the clear fresh water, now adding to the cold of the afternoon. He shook his head irritably. He could see absolutely nothing. What *had* Phillip seen? Had it been his glasses? He imagined that he must have had the constitution of an owl to stay concentrated on something for quite as long as he had. He had so far only looked into the water for less than a minute and already he was bored. He curled his lip and stared across at the noisy chicks, then guiltily resumed his concentration.

Catherine and Georgia sat watch over Phillip beside a much larger fire as it grew in intensity from the wood that had been freshly, and collectively gathered. The pilot sat on the far side of the fire, allowing both the children space, and the chance to tend Phillip. He had offered to fetch wood for them, but although they had little more than a knife with which to protect themselves - or keep him there - it was clear they were not yet ready to let him out of their sight just yet. Georgia and Catherine had shared the task instead.

'I am sorry about your friend,' the pilot apologised for Tommy's disappearance.

'Harrumph!' Catherine chortled, warming to the pilot's calm, friendly nature, and soon they all chatted like old friends, hostility the farthest thing from their minds. 'Edward can look after himself,' she assured them all, although she had felt a little guilty, remembering her own solitude the night before.

'Edward?' the pilot asked.

'Yes. Edward.'

'He introduced himself as Tommy… something.'

'You don't really want to listen to too much that comes out of that mouth,' she said. 'Tommy indeed!'

'What's your name,' Phillip asked groggily. They all looked down at him as he joined in the conversation, experiencing another spell away from his ailing slumber. 'We don't know it.'

'Walter,' he said. 'Walter Muller. Do you want the rank and number?' he continued, laughing.

'Walter!' Phillip confirmed, impressing the name into his memory.

A short spell of pointless introductions were undertaken, the children never having hidden their names in conversation, but it seemed to make the conversation flow a little easier, and soon it stretched to far more than just names.

It was soon extracted from the pilot, Walter, that he had not explored much more of the island than they had. He confessed that in the short time he had spent in the air during his descent from the damaged aircraft, he was only really able to confirm that they were on an island.

'An island!' Georgia exclaimed, as if she hadn't heard his earlier references to it. 'It is still disappointing to have it confirmed.'

Walter went on to explain that in his opinion, if there were anyone else on the island, they would all more than likely have known by now.

'We didn't know you were here,' Phillip confessed, but the seeds had been sown in their minds, and any thoughts of early rescue seemed to disappear there and then, and almost involuntarily, they all slumped into silence.

Tommy had stood for what had seemed like a lifetime staring down into the water. Things had looked slightly more positive as a number of fish ventured along the stream to heed his efforts, swimming perilously close to his statuesque figure, but it was almost as if they were teasing him. He smiled, lunging forward, but they were gone almost as quickly as the rabbits had on his first contact with them,

Three or four more fruitless swipes at the occupants, and he realised exactly how easy Phillip had made the whole escapade seem. Not one to be easily beaten though, it now became a challenge. The boredom of the task had now evaporated as he wilfully pitted his wits against those of the fish, who he was now sure he could see smiling at his pathetic efforts. The fact that Phillip had succeeded, and reportedly Catherine had tried, he was sure he was going to stay there until a winner was declared one way or the other.

Time seemed to ebb away, and several more fruitless attempts finally turned the challenge from intrigue to frustration. He had called the fish a number of unsavoury names, and was about to give in when a prime sized fish swam between his hands, and cupping them beneath its belly, he pulled back hopefully.

The startled fish flew through the air, and landed on the bank. It flapped around helplessly.

Once the surprise had settled in, and the astonished look upon Tommy's face had had time to settle, he waded as fast as he was able to cut off any escape route the startled fish might have planned for a return to its watery home.

The pair met face to face, exchanging startled looks. Tommy had imagined the difficult part of catching the fish had been successfully completed. The task of actually getting his hands on it as it struggled to get back into the pond was another challenge altogether. It had nearly succeeded more than once, but somehow or other, Tommy managed to finally block its passage, and ensure it was going nowhere.

Having finally cornered it, and the inevitable outcome almost registered on the face of the fish, Tommy now faced the chore of putting an end to the poor creature's life. He suddenly realised that he did not have the ability that Georgia and Phillip had to end life face to face, circa the gull and the fish, whose careers they had both ended. His own battle with the rabbits had certainly been far less hands on.

The fish, now much less vigorous, was laid a safe distance away from the pond. Tommy was sure that if it could now find its way back to the water, he would accept defeat and let it go. It was true it wasn't going to happen, and Tommy, unable to find it in him to put a swift end to its life, quietly walked away and let nature take its course.

Walter and the three remaining children had quickly consumed what little food he had, and the problem over their ultimate survival soon came to a head. Georgia had furtively mentioned that one of the main suppliers of their food had disappeared when Tommy had gone.

'Rubbish!' Catherine said. 'Phillip supplied the fish.'

Georgia motioned down to Phillip's body and the state it was in, and she yielded slightly.

'Where *is* Edward?' Phillip demanded, for what seemed like the five hundredth time.

'He'll be back,' Georgia assured him, and nudged Catherine for support.

'Yes,' she smiled through gritted teeth. 'He'll miss you far too much,' she said tousling his hair.

As the weather turned, closing in for the night, Walter gathered his clothes together, and started to put them back on. He stood over the fire warming his hands, once more the Luftwaffe pilot, in front of the children. The three children stared back at him, speechless.

Walter suddenly realised the cause of their concern, and held his hands up in defence of his actions.

'I'm sorry! I didn't think. Look! It's still me. Just a different outfit.'

'It's just a bit of a shock,' Georgia confessed.

'My uniform is all I have to wear, and I have to keep it,' he told them. 'If I am captured out of uniform, I can be shot as a spy.'

'What? Even if you are here?' Phillip demanded.

'Well, technically, yes.'

'Spy!' Catherine shrieked. 'What on earth is there anything to spy upon?' She fell silent as her mind drifted, and she thought back to herself bathing in the pool, and pictured Tommy hidden in the bushes looking down at her. She closed her eyes, and shivered at the thought.

'Anyway. I forgot to bring a change of clothes with me,' Walter elucidated, lightly.

Catherine was still a little wary of Walter dressed in his uniform. She wasn't the only one. Even Phillip flinched slightly. She thought for a second of her father in his uniform, and contemplated the irony of his position in the forces, and she now sharing light-hearted banter with a pilot in the Luftwaffe.

'What is it, Catherine?' Georgia asked. 'You're all pensive.'

'I'm fine!' she declared, changing her expression to a milder one, giving nothing away. 'So! Where were we?'

'We are going to have to find some food,' Walter informed them. 'I have not been here long, but you have already found some food. I need to know how much of the island you have explored. Where have you set up your camp?'

The questioning and the appearance of the uniform were having a mixed effect on all three of the children, and they huddled together.

'I promise not to pass on the information to the German High Command,' he told them, laughing lightly.

The mention of the war, albeit lightly, did not have the same effect on the children. Georgia and Catherine looked from one to the other, neither wishing to be the first to reveal anything about their camp. Tommy's face was engrained in their minds, and neither of them dared think about the consequences of giving away his – their camp's location. And to Walter at that!

Georgia said, 'We've got too many heads to feed now without some cooperation. What are we going to do?'

'I don't know,' Catherine griped. 'Whatever I say is going to be wrong in the end. Especially when... if...'

'If we are going to be rescued soon, then I don't know. But if we are going to be here a long time, then we are all going to have to work together,' Georgia gave it her

231

best. 'What about Edward?'

'Yes! And what about your friend?' Walter joined the conversation, the girls not realising he had been listening to their discussion.

'Him!' Catherine jumped, the mention of Tommy dropping any frailty from her voice. 'He is big, and most certainly ugly enough to look after himself.'

'Do you think you ought to see if he is all right? He is on his own don't forget.'

'You've already said it once. We're on an island, and he can't have gone far.' Catherine told him. Walter shrugged, slightly thrown by her lack of concern for her colleague. 'He can only be in one place.'

Phillip was a little more concerned regarding his colleague's welfare, and scolded his sister for her lack of care. Catherine, not worried on her own account, was about to launch into another battle with her brother about loyalty, but he shifted, and winced at the effect his wound was having on him. It was not clear whether it was actually pain, or if he had managed to use the injury to his advantage, but his sister backed down slightly, either way. Phillip laid his head back in Catherine's lap, and she was unable to see if there was a grimace or a smile on his face. But she was in no position to judge, so she accepted her reproach, and said nothing more on the matter. She would have plenty of time to get him back once he was fully healed, she thought.

'Don't worry,' Georgia said. 'He knows where we are, and how to get back. He got us here in the first place, didn't he?'

Phillip grunted.

'If you keep going on like that, I shall start to think you are his twin,' Catherine told him. 'I shall tell father when we get back to check your records.' She fell silent, casting her mind back to her parents again. She breathed in deeply, composing herself.

'Are we going to stay here?' Phillip asked from his prostrate position.

'Why?' Georgia questioned.

'Are we going to stay here, or are we going to go back to *our* camp?'

Tommy sat next to the strangely silent chicks, beside which the remains of a freshly made mush had been carefully prepared and left ready for their next feed. He had nursed them through their latest feed and they had returned to a welcomed slumber, ungratefully leaving him to his own devices.

Sitting back, he picked and ate at the remainder of the fish that had proved big enough to meet all their needs. He had skewered the fish onto the end of a stick, as he had seen the girls do, to the best of his limited cooking ability, and had turned it over the flames of the fire. He was convinced he was never going to cook for a living, but having tasted it, he was more than satisfied with his efforts. Though picking a multitude of bones out of his mouth, he now added cooking to his newly discovered abilities.

Both parties satisfied, as far as the food front was concerned, Tommy looked down at the sleeping chicks. He stroked at one of their bodies, and started to talk to it as if it really cared one way or the other, and before long, found himself regaling it with the majority of his worries. He stopped, finally realising that neither it, nor any of the others

232

chicks were paying him any attention, and starved for conversation, he started picking at what little of the fish was left on the bones in front of him. He had caught it, cooked it and eaten it. Even if the others finally decided to swallow their pride and come to their senses, if they returned hungry, they would have to find something for themselves.

The light faded as the evening drew in, and the question of returning to their camp was all but decided by nature. They would soon be unable to find their way away from the fire, much less through the woods and across an uncomfortable stream. Phillip, still tending to drift in and out of consciousness, though now awake, sat sulking. He had badgered them for so long, and been fobbed off so many times, that by now he was convinced that they had fallen out with Tommy for good. He was certain he would be most unlikely to see him again until he was fit enough to do something about it himself.

'I had better have another look at your wound before night,' Walter drew Phillip back from his brooding.

Despite a gratitude for all the good Walter was managing to do for him, Phillip could not help pulling a defiant face, silently displaying his allegiance to Tommy.   Walter, though young himself, read through this, and thought it best just to treat the outer wound and let his sister deal with the psychological ones.

Phillip winced at the discomfort as the dressing was removed, and cussed angrily, a mixture of pain and a missing friend. Catherine scolded him for his rudeness, and he reluctantly accepted that it was only being done for his own good, and perhaps he should at least appear to be a little more grateful.

Walter made good the dressing, and as Phillip settled down, shrank back from him to rejoin his sister and Georgia for company, on the far side of the fire.

'What are you going to do about your friend?' Walter asked, looking at the heavy sky beyond the shelter of the canopy.

'Nothing!' Catherine said, vehemently. 'At least, not for now. He'll soon come back in the morning. He'll miss having me to moan at.'

Walter smiled.

'I thought he might have been back by now,' Georgia confessed, gloomily, slightly withdrawn.

'No. No way,' Catherine said defiantly, shaking her head. 'He'll be back at his camp now, moaning his head off. But be grateful. At least we're not there to hear it.'

'His camp?' Phillip piped up. 'What do you mean, *his* camp?'

Even Georgia looked across at her.

'Oh! What I mean is - our camp. You know!'

'You don't even miss him,' Phillip goaded her. 'You don't even miss him.'

'Of course I do. I mean, we do. Oh Phillip, just be quiet and go to sleep.'

'Catherine!' Georgia said.

'Well! He's only been gone five minutes. It's not my fault.'

'It's *all* your fault,' Phillip shouted, and winced as he shifted awkwardly, forcing Georgia to get up and go and tend to him.

'It was up to him whether he stayed or went,' Catherine continued. 'I'm sure he'll survive the night.'

'No thanks to you.'

'Besides. Someone has to be there to look after your chicks,' she checked herself quickly.

'The chicks!' Phillip yelled, wincing again. Georgia had to hold him down. 'We've left the chicks alone.'

'Yes we have,' Georgia confessed, feeling slightly guilty. But she rallied quickly, and assured him that they would all be fine. Especially if Tommy was now there with them.

'I want to go back,' he yelled, struggling against Georgia's hold.

'Phillip!' Georgia had to physically hold him in place, and scolding him, demanded, for his own sake, that he remain still.

'Anyway! He didn't exactly give two tuppenny-ha'penny damns about you when he ran off, did he?' Catherine continued spitefully, on a roll.

Phillip simmered, digesting what she had said, but just as Georgia started to relax, he shouted, 'If I was fit, I'd have run away too.'

'I don't know what you see in him. Georgia has done far more for all of us than that creature. Why can't you see that?'

'And that's more than you have done. You're the oldest.' He caught sight of Walter. 'Were the oldest. Enjoy getting the food then. We'll get fat on berries, won't we?'

Catherine was flustered and unprepared for the latest onslaught from her ungrateful brother. She was tired, and sick of having to defend herself against Tommy and all the good he had apparently done for them. She looked across to Georgia for help, but she was equally as tired as Catherine and had truly done all the mediating she could do for one day. All she could offer was a reassuring smile.

'Tell him, Georgia,' Catherine demanded, not remotely aware of anyone else's feelings.

'Catherine is your sister, and there is nothing she wouldn't do for you,' Georgia tried, wearily.

'And Edward isn't! And he has put himself out far more than she has.'

'I give up. Say what you want. I can't believe you are so ungrateful,' she concluded. 'You should listen to me instead of shouting down everything I say. Shouldn't he, Walter?'

Phillip was not so much amazed that his sister had felt the need to turn the decision to a third party - he recognised this as the norm if she were ever on a slippery slope - but he was shocked that she had so easily by-passed Georgia, her usual aide de comp. He looked firstly to her, then Georgia, and finally across to Walter.

'Well?' he asked.

'I think perhaps the decision is yours,' Walter wisely deferred any leading answer.

Catherine paused, and looked across to Walter.

'Don't look to him – mother. Decide something for yourself.'

The mention of their mother quietened the pair of them, and as a hollow silence developed, Catherine, disappointed with herself, looked away disappointedly.

'I will go and see if he's alright in the morning,' Georgia ensured both parties. 'Now stop fighting and for goodness sakes, call a truce.'

Catherine and Phillip looked across at each other through the limited light provided by the fire, but neither side seemed willing to give ground, and as silence descended, only a nervous amnesty remained.

53

Tommy stood proudly beside a fresh catch of fish, and with a ragged stack of wood already gathered, considered the bulk of his work for the day, done. He had woken early, and having stoked the fire, had scouted the immediate area around the camp to ensure he was still alone. He had mixed feelings. He was not sure if he had really wanted to wake up to find the others back with him or not, but finding himself alone, he was no angry. No one had bothered to come to check on him.

An otherwise cloudy day had brought the fish out in increased numbers, and what could have been another long boring task had been set about swiftly and successfully. He had even prepared an excess supply of chick-feed to save him the task later on.

Now with so much time on his hands, Tommy's options were endless. The worse thing about it was that he had no one to share them with. He desperately missed Georgia's organisational skills, the company of Phillip, and even if he had to admit it, the challenge of Catherine. But the second his mind drifted towards the pilot on the beach, and the ease with which they had formed an allegiance with him, all feelings for the three of them diminished immediately. However he looked at it though, he was on his own. Well, nearly.

The chicks had been fed to a point of almost being stuffed. They were tired, and any interest they may have in him could wait until they woke later in the day. Tommy ensured they were still penned in sufficiently, and then turned his attention back to the fire. That done, he did not intend to wait any longer for any visitors. He was off.

Phillip had badgered Georgia constantly since first light about Tommy's whereabouts, and her promise to find out if he was still safe. Her initial reluctance to do anything about it caused him to try to get to his feet and set off on his own. Sadly, it did not take more than a few delicate movements for him to realise that he was still days away from doing so unaided. Any healing the wound may have benefitted from was not helped with his constant shifting, and despite regular harrying from his three nurses, it was hard to convince him to stay still. The benefit of lying still for a sustained period of time could not be stressed strongly enough. That it came from Catherine was probably not the most practicable. The wedge that Tommy had driven between the two was widening, and currently showed no signs of mending.

Georgia, taking all things into account, though still unable to forgive him for his antics the previous night, especially the pointing of the gun in her direction, agreed it might be better for everyone involved, if it was she that set out to look to Tommy's welfare. The decision to leave Catherine to look after Phillip was greeted as probably the wisest move, and she had promised to keep her hands away from his throat, under the proviso that she wasn't away for too long. The only hiccup was what they were going to do with Walter. Catherine was nervous about being left alone with him, and any thoughts about his disappearing with Georgia to explore the island without Phillip, were currently under debate.

'But I want to go,' Phillip demanded.

'Off you go then,' Catherine said. 'See you when you get back.'

Phillip defiantly tried his best to get to his feet, but his efforts were futile. He collapsed, and Georgia scolded Catherine with a glare that could not be missed. All the good that had been done since his last attempt at getting to his feet, seemed once more to have been put to waste.

'Just go. The pair of you,' Catherine said. 'I'll keep everything under control here.'

The decision made, and leaving the pair quarrelling furiously, Georgia and Walter gently slipped away.

Free from the restraints of Catherine and Phillip. Tommy decided it was a good time to check on the condition of his canvas. Firstly that it had not by chance been discovered, and secondly that it was still safe. The task of finding the exact spot in which he had left his treasure was that much more difficult approaching it from the camp by the pool. Several times he had had to work his way back towards the coast to remind him of any waypoints he may have missed, until finally he stood in front of the entrance to his cave.

Once there, and at no stage on the extensive journey having suspected that he may have been followed, he became suspicious, at the same time becoming guarded about being caught. He moved away some considerable distance, and crouching down, waited. Listening.

After some time, undisturbed, Tommy finally felt confident enough to clear the entrance to his lair. He dragged away at the camouflaged entrance to the cave, and was impressed at how thorough he had been in his work at disguising the entrance.

The inside of the cave was still dry. Any rain that had fallen had comfortably dispelled itself long before becoming a problem, and his choice of this spot to stash away his ill-gotten goods had been first rate. Content with his decision, he did not bother to examine the canvas, leaving it where it was, and hurriedly set about disguising the entrance once more. Despite the fact that he was sure a thousand eyes burned through the woods around him, by the time he had finished, he was convinced a rabbit may well have been unable to detect any recess behind it.

He stood back and brushed his hands against his clothing, thoroughly satisfied. He would have to do something to his clothes to avoid unnecessary questions into their filthy state. *A wash, maybe*, he thought, but realised he had spent most of the morning fishing. He didn't really want to get used to being clean, did he?

Georgia led the way as best she could remember, and Walter, virgin to the new territory, tagged along like a faithful dog. Georgia was still nervous having known Walter for so little time, and in her mind she was worried about the trust they had all put in the man in such a very short space of time.

Walter stumbled on a patch of rough ground, and attempting to gain his footing, grabbed at Georgia's shoulder. Georgia screamed, and turned into a block of stone. She shut her eyes, clasped at her face with her hands, petrified, and waited for...

Walter apologised, immediately. He realised what must have been going through her mind. He pulled back, well away from her, and held his hands high in the air for the umpteenth time, trying to gain some trust from her. He, like Tommy, realised that Georgia was by far the best adjusted person on the island, and it was she whose trust he most had to gain.

Georgia opened her eyes, slowly, and saw Walter's face looking almost as scared as she felt. She melted slightly, and after a shared, worried moment between the two, they opted to carry on their trek.

Despite a renewed reliance, and an unspoken agreement, Georgia had decided it might be best if she walked on just a few paces ahead of him.

Tommy, after a further journey to the cliff, happily made his way back towards his camp, as he had now decided to call it. He was not too far from completing his journey when he heard a voice, way off into the distance. He stopped and listened, to check which of the party it might be.

He smiled as he recognised Georgia's voice, gently calling his name, and he happily realised it was just a courtesy visit, and not one of urgency. Phillip must have survived the night. He was both anxious to see her, and nervous because of the way he had reacted towards her the previous night. It hadn't been Catherine. It had been Georgia. There was no way he should have any cross to bear with her. He looked down at the state of his clothing, and quickly realised that most of the mud on his clothes had come from his visit to his cave. Was there any likelihood Georgia might notice? From what they had all been through, cleanliness was not something of major importance, but he certainly did not want to have to answer any uncomfortable questions. His trip to the cliffs would have to suffice until pressed.

He looked down at the two eggs he had gathered earlier, and realised he had only catered for himself. He did not mind Georgia sharing, but for the time being, Catherine would have to either beg, or go without.

Georgia's voice was fast becoming clearer, and guilty, he decided to make his way back to the cliff, where he could try and see if just maybe he could rob the angry mothers of perhaps one or two more of their tasty eggs. He would make Catherine beg though.

Walter had led the way across the stream as Georgia stopped and gathered her dress together, and though the tension had eased, she refused the hand he held out to aid her journey across. Her anxiety eased moment by moment, the closer she believed she was to coming face to face with Tommy. She called his name more and more frequently, more for her own satisfaction, and further to set into Walter's mind that help was not that far away, if she needed it.

Tommy had quickly and safely managed to make his way back to the cliff face, just a stone's throw away from their original landing spot. Carefully placing the eggs he had already pillaged to one side, he slipped his body over the edge of the cliff, and sat with his feet dangling loosely over the face. He looked out to sea for the umpteenth time, trying to focus as far into the distance as was possible. But still there was nothing there. There never was.

Right! Back to his real purpose for his being here. Food. He was almost grateful there were no more birds with damaged wings. He was prepared to eat anything, but in his mind, Georgia would forever be the butcher. Eggs was much more his forte.

Seconds later, and under attack once more for his presence there, he started a new search. The angry birds rained in. It was almost as if it was revenge for the two eggs he had taken earlier, but he was sure they didn't really remember.

Thinking of Georgia arriving at the camp and finding him elsewhere, he thought she might extend her search and eventually find him here, he decided he had perhaps better get down to work. It didn't matter as such, but he wanted to meet her on his terms, and that involved at least two more eggs. He carefully slid his backside further along the top of the cliff, pulled down his sleeves once more to prevent too much damage from the parents, and spotting a prospective egg, looked at all the possible pitfalls between he and the prize. He poked out his neck, and peered over. There appeared to be a small pile of jagged rocks, protruding slightly further out to sea below him, but from where he perched, this appeared to be his best approach. Time was not too imperative. Georgia, despite an urge to find him, would not have been able to bypass the chicks on arrival at the camp. She wasn't just a guardian to Catherine and Phillip.

Tommy should perhaps have paid a little more attention to what he was doing, than in what was going on elsewhere. He baulked, as another angry gull flew past him. He slipped slightly in his task, and a rock upon which his hand had been resting, came loose from its hold on the cliff, and plummeting towards the sea below, it crashed into the very egg he had had his eye on.

Tommy cursed himself, and now distracted from his task, decided to take a break for a moment. If Georgia arrived, she arrived. He would wait at the top and try his hardest to keep his distance from any other irritated mother that might have designs on him.

Georgia had hesitated as they had approached the outskirts of the camp under the preamble of finding out if Tommy was still alive. She had been unusually quiet for some time, and Walter, falling in behind her lead, had respectfully kept his silence. She was shrouded in guilt at revealing the location of the camp to Walter quite so soon, and had now had to prepare herself for the expected onslaught from Tommy.

She hesitated, nervously, wondering just how fiercely Tommy might react. She too had been unable to forget the incident with the revolver, and she realised she no longer really knew him as well as she thought she did, even in such a short space of time. But they were here now, and if he had spotted them already, it would be pointless in turning back.

Walter had already been warned not to expect Tommy to have mellowed too much. His revelation about the death of his father the previous evening had answered a multitude of questions. She had gone on to explain that it would have been much better for her to have come alone, but it was far too to late for that now, and he would just have to be prepared.

Georgia had been impressed at the way Tommy had prepared the camp for the day. The chicks, which she had almost unforgivably forgotten about, so fixed was she on her reunion with Tommy until she had stumbled across them, were still sleepy, but raised their heads in recognition. She looked down at the prepared food, and thought about feeding them once more, in case they should be left for a slightly longer spell when she finally encountered Tommy again. She wasn't sure how he was going to react, but was sure, on his seeing Walter, that it wasn't going to be smooth. The chicks, however, unaffected by anything happening around them, had been excited by her arrival, and opened their greedy beaks, offering her a chorus lest she forget them again. Her decision was made for her.

'In a minute,' she promised them.

A quick look to the fire, and she realised that Tommy had not been away for too long. Could it be an hour old? She wasn't sure. She did not feel though that she was being spied upon. What to do?

She turned to see where Walter had gone, and discovered him crouched over the chicks, engrossed in their antics.

'These are our orphans,' she proclaimed, loudly.

Walter was fascinated by them, and smiled at their angry greeting.

'Can I feed them?' he asked, as if being too intrusive into their affairs. 'If they are hungry?'

'They are always hungry,' she told him, and 'Yes,' of course he could.

He bent down and engrossed himself in their welfare. Georgia smiled, and seeing him settled, decided it might be a good time to go and find Tommy, alone. Perhaps prepare him slightly. She enlightened Walter of her intentions, and he nodded, half-interested, immersed in the task of his own, and barely acknowledged a soft farewell as she departed.

Tommy, having returned to his work, had now gathered together a healthy supply of eggs, and had placed them in a pile on the top of the cliff face. He checked both his arms and the sleeves of his shirt to see if there was any further damage he may have incurred from the recent onslaught the birds had rained down upon him. It was clear he had been in a fresh battle, and still awaiting Georgia's arrival, he considered entering the ring for another round with his combatants. The birds seemed as keen on the encounter as he did, so slowly, he edged his way forward. The birds squawked loudly at his approach and he defiantly ducked under another attack.

Tommy was finally distracted from his pursuit by the arrival of Georgia, who had called out his name, loudly. He climbed back up, precariously, and popped his head up to be greeted by a shy smile. He waved, and sat himself on the edge of the cliff face on a small rock, unable to hold her look.

'You're safe then?' she noted. 'Survived the night, did we?'

'Yes. Never in doubt! You okay?' he inquired, the inflection in his voice indicating he only meant her.

'Yes. We're fine.'

'Is Phillip okay?' He lowered his head, almost apologetically.

'He's fine,' she confirmed. 'Walter has patched him up.'

'Walter?' Tommy's mind instantly reacted to his name, and his conduct turned sour.

Georgia walked back from the cliff slightly and bade him join her, but he was not for moving till he had at least heard more.

Georgia tried to explain away the previous night's events delicately. It was all a smokescreen, all the time trying to ease her way round to revealing that they had released Walter from his bindings. She urged him to come to the top of the cliff before she told him more, but he was having none of it. As pleased as he had been to see Georgia, the mention of the pilot had instantly lost her any ground she might have gained.

'We released him,' she said, finally, as much in despair as anything else. 'And he's still there,' she lied.

'Released him?' Tommy stumbled slightly, but as Georgia quickly made her way forward, managed to get a firm footing, and shooed her back.

'Well, you shouldn't have run off,' she goaded him. 'And when you did, you should have come back. We were worried about you.'

'Yeah, right!'

'We were.'

'We?'

'We.'

'So! How is your saviour, then? You released him? You'll soon come to regret it.' He shook his head in a mixture of disbelief, and disappointment at her.

Georgia was so angry at his inability to listen to reason, she swallowed the bullet, and carried on with the morning's events, and finally came round to mentioning his current whereabouts.

'Feeding the chicks', she added quickly, trying to soften the blow.

'At *my* camp?' he reacted furiously, forgetting his precarious situation, and unwisely tried to stand up.

The heel of his weight-bearing foot dug into a loose pile of shingle, and little solid ground beneath that, it gave way. Tommy realised just a moment too late, and his last-minute grasps at the tufts of grass on the lip of the bank were in vain. He took a fleeting look up into Georgia's face, and started to fall.

Georgia leapt forward, but it was far too late.

Georgia rushed across to the edge of the cliff, and taking care not to join him, desperately threw herself to the ground. She carefully leaned over the edge and looked down, horrified.

241

Tommy was mercifully perched precariously on a small ledge. He breathed carefully, though fitfully. He looked down towards the sea beneath him, caught his breath, and faced the cliff once more.

The ledge on which Tommy had come to rest was slight, and did not look like a weight bearing one. He shifted slightly, and further loose shingle beneath his feet toppled down into twenty or thirty feet of emptiness, and down into the jagged, rock strewn sea beneath him. Tommy regained his limited balance, and sent a panicked look up to Georgia's enquiring face.

'Help!' he murmured.

Georgia looked around her desperately having seen the outcome of his fall, and hurriedly searched for something with which to help him. The more she looked, the less she could see.

'Help!' Tommy called once more.

'Wait there,' she called. 'I'm going to get help.' She leapt to her feet and rushed off.

'I'm not going anywhere,' Tommy whispered to himself, and once more hugged the rock face.

54

Phillip and Catherine had managed to co-exist, at least for the time being, but his rancour still bit hard. He had ignored any attempt to engage in light conversation, and having had his wound dressed by Walter before his departure, as long as he sat still, there was little nursing required.

'I still can't understand exactly what you see in him,' Catherine said, fed up with his lack of interest in her company.

'Because he is more fun. He never sits still. He's always up to something.' He turned away from her.

'You've changed. You were never like this. At home you wouldn't even have the time of day for anyone like him. Besides, what sort of excitement could he possibly get up to here?'

Walter was sat admiring the chicks as his attention was caught by Georgia's noisy arrival. He looked up, concerned, as she literally flew into camp. She was breathing so hard it was impossible to make any sense of her garbled words. He tried to grab hold of her, to try to calm her, but she broke free, gesturing frantically that he should follow.

Walter, still at a loss as to what she had mumbled, took a fleeting look at the chicks to ensure they were safe, and purely on instinct, took off after her.

Tommy had not dared to move, and he felt that he had been there an age. He had called out to Georgia every time he heard a noise but it had always turned out to be some other form of wildlife scurrying by, or a bird of some description mimicking her return. He was only grateful the gulls had decided to leave him alone for a while.

He looked up as he finally identified Georgia's voice announcing her return. He breathed slightly easier, but nearly slipped for his efforts. He readjusted his stance, and realised quite how precarious a position he was in.

'You still okay?' she yelled.

'Never better,' he lied, not thinking it necessary to tell her he had been inches away from lying at the bottom of the cliff.

Walter's face appeared over the top of the ridge beside Georgia's, and Tommy, as parlous as his position might already have been, flinched. For all his patience in having found a secure hold, the appearance of the pilot totally threw him. The grip he had on the cliff face seemed to crumble beneath his fingers, and as small pieces of rock came loose from the surface where his hands had moments before held firmly, he quickly had to find another anchor.

'Edward!' Georgia yelled, and had to be physically held back as she tried to climb over the top to lend her assistance.

Tommy looked around frantically, and within a split second, had to look down to find a foothold into which he could quickly thrust his shoe, to avoid becoming fish food at the base of the cliff. He stuffed his foot into a small crevice, and finding a firm base, gratefully forced his body back against the face of the cliff. He waited until he had slowed his breathing considerably before he dared to look up again.

It was all Walter could do to restrain Georgia, and the look on her face mirrored Tommy's. He dragged her back, whispering reassuring words into her ears. He now had two patients.

Tommy glared up the cliff at the pair of them. It was now something more than just fear on his face.

'Just stay calm,' Walter told him. 'And don't do anything stupid.'

'And you brought him to *help*?' Tommy ignored Walter's face, and asked Georgia, lying beside him.

Walter, ignoring Tommy's refusal to accept his presence there, quickly scanned the surrounding area for anything that may be useful, but likewise ended up fruitless. He thought for a second and then told Georgia to hold onto his legs.

She looked back, puzzled.

'Just do it,' he told her, sternly, and started to lean further over the edge of the cliff.

Tommy looked up, frightened.

Georgia realised what Walter must be trying to do, and took as firm a grip on his legs as she could, all things considered.

It's no good,' Walter growled, and scrambled back up, shaking his head. 'We are going to need some rope,' he continued. Georgia looked non-plussed. 'How safe are you there?' he shouted down at Tommy, and ignoring Tommy's petulant answer, asked the question once more, slowly, demanding his full attention.

Tommy wedged his back further into the wall and tried to jam his feet further into the ledge, but as he did so, more fragments of rock dislodged, and his cock-sure attitude dissolved. He shut his eyes and held his breath, and waited for the ledge to crumble away beneath his feet.

It didn't.

Walter shouted down that Tommy was to stay still and do nothing. He waited for another barrage of abuse, but the latest rock and soil erosion beneath his feet had silenced him. He turned to Georgia and told her to run back to the beach and bring back as much of the cord that was attached to the parachute as possible.

'Maybe you should go,' she started to say.

'Just go!' he told her in no mean terms. Georgia, shocked at his abruptness stared back at him. 'Now!'

Georgia, mortified at the speed things were happening, scurried away, and started to run back.

'And you stay still,' Walter shouted down as he leaned over the edge once more, trying his best to keep Tommy company.

Catherine was pacing up and down the beach, tired of waiting for Georgia. Her best efforts having been ignored for so long, she was now bored of Phillip's company. She kicked at several stones and pieces of wood. Phillip called out to her but she ignored

244

him. She had already seen to it that his dressing was safe, and had soon realised that her brother was milking her compassion to its limits.

Georgia called out constantly on her way back, hoping in some obscure way that it might help, or that Catherine might have maybe come half way to meet her. Eventually though it was Phillip that heard her distressed call. He shouted up the beach to his sister once more, but it was clear he had now burnt all his bridges with her, and she was having none of it.

Georgia broke onto the beach at pace, and glared at Phillip for not getting Catherine to answer her calls, until he pointed up the beach to a solitary figure still some way off. She yelled down the beach at her while she hurriedly searched for a knife.

Phillip having noted her distress, badgered her to find out exactly what the problem was, but he was ignored.

Georgia found a knife, and staring up at the parachute, hurriedly attacked the cord with which Walter had attached it to the beach. She quickly cut the cord into a number of lengths, and hurriedly wrapped it into a series of loops, the better to carry it.

Catherine strolled back, not having noticed the concern in her call from where she had been stood further up the beach. When she finally saw the anguish in her face, she ran across and Georgia quickly explained as she went about her work.

Phillip listened intently as Georgia explained to his sister, and hearing of Tommy's dismay, had started to jump up to help with the cord. The two girls so absorbed in their work failed to see Phillip as he arrived, and as Catherine turned with an armful of cord, she slammed straight into him. He collapsed, crying out in pain, and she was suddenly caught between two causes. Georgia looked across at him, angrily, and he cried even more seeing how he had angered her.

'I'm sorry Phillip. I'm busy,' she said shaking her head. 'Catherine, look after him. I've got to go.'

Walter was caught between rushing back to better assist Georgia, and forcing himself to stay where he was to keep Tommy company. Knowing how far it was to the beach, he fidgeted restlessly, and nothing useful to hand, lay down, looking over the edge of the cliff, trying to ensure Tommy that all was well. He talked lightly about the camp and the chicks trying to gain a common ground for some form of a conversation, but the more he mentioned both, the more possessive and resentful Tommy became. He looked up, and despite his perilous predicament, could find nothing polite to reply to his banter. Despite his predicament, he was totally unable to disassociate Walter from the fact that he was German..

'Don't worry. She'll be here soon,' Walter advised him, still trying.

'I'll wait then, shall I?'

'Okay!'

Walter walked away from the edge of the cliff, his latest attempt at comradeship ignored, he decided his presence at the cliff to be more dangerous than not. The more upset Tommy became, the more treacherous his situation became. He was more frustrated with the interminable time it was taking Georgia to get back than irritated at the young man beneath him, but either way he was fast losing patience.

'You still there?' Tommy shouted up.

'I am here,' Walter quickly returned to his supine position, looking down once more. 'Just checking.'

Walter raised his eyebrows.

'Just so you know,' Tommy said, 'I am grateful for this, but just the same, it doesn't mean we're ever going to be friends.'

'That is fine,' Walter laughed ironically at the enmity, shaking his head. 'Maybe we had better just get you safe before we start peace talks.'

'Are you laughing at me?'

'No. Most definitely not.'

'Good!'

'I thought my children were hard to deal with,' he whispered more to himself, 'but this…'

'Children?'

'Yes! Children. I have a little boy and a girl,' he told him, suddenly feeling slightly less alienated.

'Where?'

'At home in Bonn.'

'You have *children*?' Tommy requested affirmation.

'A little boy and little girl! Yes!' Walter repeated, confused.

'Then just tell me this. How can you go to war and bomb and kill other people's children?' Tommy suddenly slammed home the point he had been hedging round.

Georgia had battled her way through the trees, angrily cursing at any obstacles in her way, furious that there was no quicker way to reach the cliffs. She had curled up all the cord she had managed to acquire, and hung it around her shoulder, with a knife tucked into her waistband for good measure. She was in such a hurry that as she approached the crossing at the stream, she tripped and fell over into the water soaking both her clothes and the cord. She looked down at her hand, to find it had snagged against the blade of the knife. She got to her feet shaking the water off her, and looked down at the nick in her hand and sucked hard at the blood that had started to seep through. She bit her lip hard to counter the pain, but weighing up her injury against Tommy's plight, she rapidly battled on.

Walter, anxious about exactly how much time Georgia was taking, and fretful about how long Tommy was going to be able to hold on, decide he had better do something about it himself.

'I am going to see if I can get something to help you,' he shouted down in Tommy's direction.

Tommy's reply, if there was one, was lost between the cliff face and the Walter's

246

journey into the trees.

The branch with which he returned was freshly snapped from a nearby tree, and he stood at the top of the cliff face stripping it of its branches.

'What's happening,' Tommy asked, hearing his approach.

Walter leant over the edge of the cliff and offered the branch down in Tommy's direction.

Tommy looked up desperately as the branch waved above his head. It was a good two feet short of his being able to grab at it, and reluctantly Walter withdrew its offer, and cast it to one side, cussing in his native language.

'Come on, Georgia,' Tommy muttered quietly.

Walter returned with another branch, and though slightly longer, it was still not quite long enough to reach him. He leant slightly further over the edge of the cliff, but just as it looked as if he may have had some effect, a screaming gull launched itself in his direction. In an attempt at avoiding it, the branch slipped from Walter's hands and toppled into the sea below, barely missing Tommy on its descent.

'Don't do that again,' Tommy ordered him.

'I'm sorry!' Walter agreed.

Tommy shook his head, and once more clung to the face of the cliff.

'Wait there. I'm going to hurry her up.'

'Sure. You know where I'll be.'

Walter chased away, leaving Tommy, who looked up, listening to the sound of the receding footsteps. 'Be quick,' he cried, and then softly to himself. 'Be quick.'

Georgia ran towards the landing spot recklessly, and having swerved to avoid running into a tree, ran straight into Walter coming from the opposite direction. She quickly found herself sprawled on the floor.

'Ouch!' she yelped, as the fall reminded her of the injury to her hand. She placed it to her mouth, and sucked at the wound as it started to bleed a little more steadily.

Walter picked her up, his attention split between her welfare, and the whereabouts of the twine. Walter stared down at her hand, and she quickly informed him it wasn't his fault. She handed him the cord and shooed him away. She would catch up with him up shortly.

Phillip was laid on his side. Any animosity between he and Catherine had diminished for the moment. In his effort to jump up earlier, he had strained his wound and a collaboration between the two had been necessary to allow Catherine to do her best to treat it. He had bravely gritted his teeth as his sister had nursed his side. She had replaced the dressing and left it looking as nurse-like as she could. She had commanded him to stay still, which he had more or less obeyed, although he had questioned her constantly about Tommy's welfare, and anything that Georgia might have told her he may have missed. Every time she dared to walk away, he shifted his position to throw more questions after her. She eventually went and sat beside him to avoid him causing any further damage to himself.

'Just look at you,' she laughed.

'What's so funny?'

'So much has changed. Days ago mother would have dealt with your wound and wrapped you up in cotton wool. She would have put you to bed till you were better. Just look at you, now.'

'And just think,' he joined her in a lighter moment. 'We were going to go to Canada because it was safer for us.'

'But for you and your wound,' she said, 'it's really all rather exciting.'

He thought for a second then said, 'Do you like him?'

'What?'

'Edward. Do you… like him?'

'Of course not!' she snapped. 'What on earth would make you think that?' He nodded towards her fingers, which she quickly unfurled. 'You said fingers crossed, that's all.' She sat back, thinking, and found herself smiling.

Walter hurriedly arranged the lengths of twine out on the floor, and started to knot them together. He tested each of the knots, pulling the different lengths against Georgia. He formed a loop on one end that he wrapped around his shoulders, and as fast as was safe, measured out the cord until it seemed that it was long enough to reach down to Tommy. He then formed another loop on that end of the cord, estimating it as roughly the right dimensions for Tommy to be able to slip around his shoulders.

'Are you still safe?' Georgia called down.

'Safe? I'm not going anywhere,' he re-iterated his status.

Walter quickly explained to Georgia what he needed her to do. He handed her the loose end of the cord, and as he set his feet against a solid rock, she gently lowered it down the rock face to just above Tommy's head.

'It's still too short,' Georgia advised him.

Walter stood up slightly, and choosing his footing carefully, eased himself forward until Georgia informed him that the overhang of the rope was at the required length.

'Be careful,' Georgia advised them both with the one command.

Tommy looked up at the loop being offered down and caught sight of Georgia's face. She winked an encouraging gesture of good luck and offered a thumbs-up, and then went about further guiding the rope across and down to him.

The amount of time Tommy had spent hanging off the rock face had been interminable. The sight of the loop of rope descending the cliff suddenly excited him. Despite the danger, and ignoring all warnings, he reached out his right arm and snatched at the offering.

The sudden movement shifted his balance completely. His feet shifted violently, and unable to hold fast with his other hand, his body started to fall away from the rock face.

'No!' Georgia cried from above.

Tommy wildly snatched at the cord just above his head and held his breath.

55

Tommy grabbed at the rope. His fingers just managed to close around the loop of the improvised rope, and with no support, his entire bodyweight now hung like a pendulum.

Walter, less prepared than he might have been reacted instantly on hearing Georgia's scream. He dug his feet into the ground and prepared himself. As strong and agile as he might have been though, he was ill-prepared for the sudden force on his shoulders. He gritted his teeth against the unexpected force exerted on him, and held his breath, praying that his improvised work on the cord would hold.

Tommy had become deadweight, and half expecting to find himself staring up from the floor of the cliff - in pieces. He was amazed to find himself dangling from the rope - albeit only by one hand. His body had naturally fallen away from the face of the cliff, and as the forces of science swung it back, he was just alert enough to grab out. His loose hand caught firmly on a jagged rock, and praying that it wouldn't come loose, Tommy dragged himself in. Straining against his hold on the rope with his other hand, he scrambled to find a foothold, and somehow managed to lodge his feet safely onto a firm footing, where panting like a marathon runner, he finally came to rest.

Tommy hugged the cliff like lichen to rock, and rested, motionless. He had lost all the colour from his face, and Georgia's calls down to him went unanswered for some time. Whether he was truly religious or not did not seem to matter as he let out a short prayer of thanks, and then settled himself, awaiting the next move.

Walter called out, desperate to know what was happening out of his sight.

In a state of total panic, and caught between Tommy and Walter, Georgia charged from one point to the other, and readily relayed the information to both parties as it developed. She clung to the rope at one point in the hope of helping Walter, but the pain from the injury on her hand forced her to drop it. She was glad she wasn't the difference between life and death. However, after a moment of calm, it was established that Tommy was safe. For now.

Walter felt the rope ease slightly, and once Georgia had assured him that Tommy appeared secure, the pair of them set about a new plan of rescue.

Tommy reluctantly released his hold on the rope and watched as it was dragged back up the face of the cliff. He waited, nervously, while it was checked to ensure that all the separate lengths of cord were still holding fast, and finally, it started its way back down in his direction once more. He was instructed not to touch the rope this time, until the loop was well below his shoulders. Tommy had disparagingly replied that he was content to stay where he was for the rest of his life.

Georgia vocally manoeuvred Walter into the correct position, and only when the loop hung by Tommy's waist, did she stop him.

Tommy carefully released one hand from the wall and drew the cord towards him. He grabbed hold of the loop and slipped it over his head, before tucking it under his arm. Then, swapping hands, he did the same with the other arm, and soon the loop was safely lodged under both his arms, and sat snugly under his armpits. He tugged at the rope in front of his chest to ensure it was secure, blew hard puffing out his cheeks, and finally he offered a hesitant thumbs-up with his one free hand to Georgia, who passed on the information.

Walter informed both he and Georgia what he wanted them to do, and further, told Georgia that she should pass on exactly what was happening to him as the ascent took place, pointing out any possible pitfalls.

She nodded.

Walter, leaned back, slowly, and foot by foot, started to edge his way away from the cliff. He dug first one foot then the other into the ground until he was sure he was set firm enough to take the next step, and waited for Tommy to make his move.

Tommy, now feeling slightly safer with the loop of cord under his arms, however makeshift it may be, started his ascent of the cliff face. He looked around him carefully selecting hand and footholds to assist him in his rescue like he had been doing it all his life. He wasn't actually sure whether the constant encouragement from Georgia was a blessing or a curse, but now totally reliant on an unsighted Walter, he realised Georgia's help was going to be essential. He nodded up to her, and she in turn relayed the information to Walter.

Walter waited patiently, his feet now dug into the rear of a large rock that was not going to move with an earthquake. Slowly he fed the cord around him, taking up the strain as Tommy climbed. He was not confident enough to simply drag Tommy up the cliff face, as he was still not overly confident about the knots in the rope he had put together. He was certainly going to need some assistance from Tommy.

Tommy concentrated on the climb as if his life depended on it. The assent was arduous, and before he moved one limb, he assured the three other points were safely implanted onto the rock face. Only then did he trust in the support of the rope beneath his arms. At one point, his right hand slipped, and he was sure if it hadn't been for Walter's support, he may have fallen. Under Georgia's instructions, he settled himself once more, before setting off on his ascent again.

Georgia, in the excitement of watching his progress, was now becoming more of a liability than a help. She shouted instructions, back and forth, several times to the wrong party, and Tommy had to shout up to shut her up, doing his best not to offend her. But if she heard it at all, she paid it no heed. Nor did she shut up, so he started his ascent again, regardless.

Tommy was now making good progress, but an insisted attention to detail meant that he was still some way yet from safety.

'Come on Tommy boy!' he whispered to himself. 'Nearly there!'

Georgia's confused face appeared over the edge above his head, and for what must have been the first time that day, she had not been saying anything. Her face wrinkled, trying to see if she had got it right. It was the same name he had given Walter on the beach.

'What was that?' she asked, her concentration knocked.

'I said… Come on, Dummy,' Tommy blurted. 'I don't want to mess it up this time.'

Maybe that was it, she thought, and suddenly the urgency of Tommy's rescue fully took over her attention once more.

Catherine was once again bored with the task of playing nursemaid to her brother, and playing second fiddle to the excitement farther across the island. She realised that Phillip's feelings were mutual, but despite the fact that he was sporting a particularly nasty wound, she was not overly sure that he might not just be milking it to some degree. He constantly badgered her about Tommy to the extent that she had lost what little interest in him that she had ever had. She had been telling him exactly this when an unusual noise could be heard off into the distance. It was slight, and so delicate that it did not immediately grab their attention.

'I want to go and help him,' Phillip demanded.

'Go then!' she told him. 'It will do you the world of good. But don't come crying to me when your wound turns sceptic and you end up having to have your leg cauterised.' Phillip looked back, horrified. 'Someone will heat up the blade of knife over the fire, and it will be placed on your wound to kill all the germs. It will hurt you for the rest of your life.'

Phillip relented quickly, but after only a moment's brooding, said, 'You go then.'

'Me? Leave you here?'

'I can last till you get back, let me tell you.'

'Fine! I'll go now, then. I'll see you tomorrow.'

'But Catherine…' he started, and then paused. 'Listen!'

'No! You listen!' she answered him. 'I'll tell you…'

'No! *Listen!*'

A combination of careful rope work from Walter, and cautious climbing from Tommy had left the latter only a short distance from the top of the cliff. Georgia, still co-ordinating operations, was ecstatic at his progress. She held out her hand ready to help him over the last leg of the journey.

'Come on!' she vocally encouraged his efforts.

Tommy's feet were now secure on well-founded rocks, giving plenty of grip, and for the moment, breathless, he ignored Georgia's extended hand. Even the any angry gulls had given him a free rein. He fought to catch his breath before the final push, and waited for a moment, allowing both he and Walter a well-earned rest.

Georgia took back her hand, and reluctantly made her way back to allow him to climb over the top when he was ready, and now looked back to see to Walter's welfare. The pair of them looked equally exhausted.

'Right!' Tommy called out, finally. 'Let's go!'

Georgia, not to be ignored, rushed to the edge of the cliff to see the final outcome of the rescue.

'Come on!' she urged, him. 'Not far now.'

251

Walter pulled on the rope, now gathering it into his grasp length by length, and hopefully for the last time, he looped the loose rope round his shoulder.

Tommy, ready to strive for safety, was so close to the top now, he forgot to inform anyone of his movements. He reached up and was just about to grab at what he imagined to be the top of the cliff, when Georgia suddenly leapt up.

'Listen!'

Everyone stopped still.

The faint sound of an engine cut through the air ever so slightly, and Georgia and Walter recognised it instantly.

'It's a plane!' Georgia jumped up and down, and in her excitement, and the need for a better view of the aircraft, ran up the slope colliding heavily with Walter who collapsed forwards, releasing his hold on the rope.

They both watched as the rope fell from his shoulder, and the sound of '*No!*' boomed from the cliff.

Catherine was jumping up and down on the beach, wildly waving her arms. She could not see the aircraft but was certain that her efforts were visible from the pilot's point of view.

Phillip, as excited as his sister, looked up into the sky in the direction from which the sound was coming, and jumped to his feet. Despite a considerable amount of pain, the excitement of imminent rescue fast overtook his need for recuperation, and in a matter of seconds, he was stood beside Catherine, waving just as wildly as she was. They grabbed each other's hands and swung each other around and around in circles, any animosity of the recent hours seemingly lost forever.

Tommy finally scrambled safely over the lip of the cliff, and even had the audacity to produce an egg he had managed to grab during his triumphant, and final ascent. He had not concentrated on anything but his own safety, and had not heard anything but the sound of his own heavy breathing and the scraping of his clothing against the rock face. He smiled back at what he imagined from their smiling faces, was their elation at his eventual safety.

If the pair of them had noted the loss of the rope, it was difficult to tell. Their faces were otherwise employed, and stared expectantly up into the sky, way over Tommy's head.

'Hello!'

'Listen!' Georgia yelled, stopping his talking immediately, and cupped a hand to her ear. Tommy looked further confused, but turning out to sea and following their concerned faces, finally caught up with what had snatched their attention.

The aircraft was no more than a dot in the sky, and though not directly overhead, it was perilously close to the path of the island. The aircraft was flying at such a height that it was not clear to any of the children what type of plane it was. If it was evident to Walter he did not make it clear at this point, but as with the aircraft that had shot down Walter's, it did not make any attempt at revealing that it had seen them.

Catherine watched as the tiny point in the sky passed overhead, and petrified that it might pass them by completely, desperately searched for something else to attract its attention. She looked frantically for any loose wood on the beach, and snatching at it, threw it on the fire, urging Phillip, despite his frailty, to do the same.

It was clear to both Catherine and Phillip that the smoke the fire was pumping out, though admirable for all their efforts, was far from strong enough to attract the attention of Georgia and Walter, wherever they were, much less the aircraft. She stood beneath the silken canopy of the parachute without giving it a second's thought, until having exhausted her visual forage for wood, she looked up in despair, and the great mass revealed its ultimate purpose to her. Large. White. And ample amounts of it.

Tommy, Georgia and Walter stood on the edge of the cliff watching the aircraft disappear into the sky.

'Did they see us?' Georgia asked.

'I don't know!' Tommy answered, looking at Georgia, but his face soured as he saw that she had asked the question of Walter and not him. He looked across at the exalted Walter, who had continued in his waving long after they had stopped

'Were there any markings on the wings?' she continued. 'Were there?' She held her fixed look on Walter.

'I couldn't even see what type of aircraft it was. It was just too far away.'

'But they *could* have seen us, couldn't they?'

Walter looked straight into her hopeful, enquiring eyes, and said, 'Yes. I'm sure they could,' and before any more questions could be asked, placed his hand on Tommy's shoulder. 'Don't you think?'

Tommy broke from Walter's hold and stepped back a pace or two. He stared at Georgia. She still appeared far more interested in Walter's opinion, than she did in his. He looked down and noticed a small amount of blood coming from her hand, but clearly her attention was held firmly elsewhere, so he shrugged his shoulders, and sat down, ignoring the pair of them.

'It's gone,' Phillip informed his sister, pointlessly.

Catherine stared tearfully out to sea at the disappearing aircraft, and it wasn't until Phillip broke her concentration that she too had been bombarded with similar questions to those with which Georgia had flooded Walter. She was in no better a position in which to answer them, and sighed. She swallowed down a large lump in her throat, and more in hope than reality, nodded that of course the aircraft had seen them. Whether it was convincing enough to fool Phillip she wasn't sure.

Phillip pointedly indicated the fire and the charred edges of what was left of the parachute. Catherine looked back guiltily. Her eyes spread wide, and she quickly rushed around grabbing the little of the material that was redeemable, and having placed the charred remains to one side, sat, looking for some form of clemency. Phillip's eyes, magnified through his glasses, could not help but reveal his doubt, and as he shifted his head to look up to where it had once been, Catherine was shrouded in guilt.

'Don't worry,' Phillip consoled her, ignoring the obvious shelter it had provided, and said, 'What were we going to do with it anyway? Make clothes?'

The appearance of the aircraft and its evident departure had quickly overshadowed Tommy's recent plight. Despite his own interest in the appearance of the aircraft, his excitement was mellowed as he was now strangely more concerned in retrieving Georgia's interest in him and not Walter. Convinced which way he imagined the tide to have turned, he left the pair to their conversation and walked away.

A disillusioned Georgia eventually turned her attention back to Tommy, to find him walking away on his own. She considered walking over, but wrongly imagined Tommy's disappointed demeanour to have something to do with the disappearing aircraft. For once, she sat down and sighed. Tommy would have to wait.

56

'Was it one of ours, or yours?' Tommy finally asked Walter, once the excitement had died down slightly. His enmity for Walter should have thawed due to his efforts at successfully rescuing him, but Georgia's reluctance to molly-coddle him, and her partiality to Walter over major decisions had fully removed any gratitude there should have been.

Walter indicated that he had been flat on his back at the time of the 'fly-past', and told him that it really didn't matter whose it was.

'It had to be one of ours,' Tommy sneered. 'After all, we don't want rescuing by 'Jerries,' do we?'

'You are unbelievable!' Georgia was furious. She could not believe his attitude, and verbally flew at him. 'We are all stuck here, and I am convinced you would far rather stay here than be rescued at all.' Tommy turned his head away. 'And as it happens, I don't remember you thanking anyone at all.' Tommy tucked his head into his chest. 'Well?'

'Thank you,' Tommy said into the ground.

'I didn't hear,' she snapped.

'Thank you,' he repeated a little louder.

'You are impossible,' she said, shaking her head. She looked apologetically across at Walter, and said, 'you might have missed it, but he said he's sorry.'

Walter was not overly put out, and nodded. He realised that the pair of them were at odds and suggested that maybe he should go back to check on Catherine and Phillip, and leave them to it.

'I don't suppose Phillip is any the better for having seen that,' he pointed into the now empty sky above them. 'I will see you when you both come back down.'

'Hell will freeze over first,' Tommy snapped.

'Stop it!' Georgia yelled. 'Walter. Go!' she said, and indicated that she was going to stay where she was.

Tommy stood like a spoilt child, refusing to face her. He took a quick glance at Walter's departure, but could not bring himself to say anything more in gratitude. He faced out to sea.

'You really are a one,' Georgia scolded him. 'What is it with you? Do you really not want to be rescued?' Tommy refused to answer. Georgia refused to be ignored. 'Well?'

'It could have been a German plane,' he mumbled.

'And?'

'And yes, I would rather stay here a million years than be rescued by a German ship. I should have thought we all would. Am I wrong?'

'He just saved your life.'

'And I said thank you.'

'Just!'

'It was enough. I'm sorry, but I don't want to spend the rest of my life in Germany and that's that.' Georgia shook her head. 'Besides. I've heard they eat children over there.'

'Ooooh!' Georgia growled. 'Forget it. Just forget it. I'm going back to the others. You can come with me if you want.'

'On the beach?'

'Yes.'

'I've got my own camp. Why would I need yours? I'm fine on my own. Feel free to drop in if you're passing by.'

'The camp is *ours*, not yours. Now grow up,' and with that, she stormed off leaving him where he was.

Tommy watched her as she disappeared into the woods, and lowered his head. 'Grow up. Grow up? I'm fourteen years old.'

Georgia, now slightly more familiar with the terrain had caught up with Walter long before he reached the beach, and could not stop apologising for Tommy's behaviour, almost as if it was her job. Walter quickly dispelled her fears, and told her he was not bothered. He understood.

Georgia called out as they approached the beach to announce their arrival, and also not to unnecessarily scare either Catherine or Phillip.

'How is he? Is he safe?' Phillip demanded, not giving them time to tell him anything. 'Where is he?'

'He's fine,' Georgia assured him quickly, giving him the once over, and then looked across to Catherine to check she was well. 'Did you see the plane?'

Catherine stood sheepishly in front of the fire, and nodded timidly back at her as Walter walked over and sat himself down beside Phillip, who was full of questions about the aircraft.

Georgia stood with her head to one side and stared at Catherine in a distinct, *What have you done?* manner.

'I...' Catherine scrunched her face up, apologetically.

'What?' Georgia whispered. Catherine stepped to one side, still shielding the fire from Walter and revealed the burnt remains of the parachute. 'Oh my!'

'I panicked,' Catherine blurted. 'I don't know what came over me, but...'

'All right!' Georgia assuaged her fears, quietly. 'It's not the end of the world.'

Walter walked over, and Catherine stood to one side fully revealing her crime.

'So that's what happened to it,' he laughed looking up to where it had been tethered. Georgia put her hand to her mouth shocked, not having realised she had missed it in the first place. 'Did you run out of wood?'

'No! I...'

'He's joking,' Georgia calmed her. Catherine scowled at being the butt of yet another joke, albeit from a new source, but finally realised that he was not angry with her, and relaxed slightly.

'There are some pieces left,' she volunteered, pointing across at the last vestiges of the material. 'They might be useful as…'

'Handkerchiefs,' Phillip offered, and burst out laughing.

Catherine, once more supposing she was being laughed at turned angrily, but Georgia chuckling, told her to relax. It was not a personal insult.

Catherine looked across at the three other faces, and soon joined in the laughter. Though only politely, and not totally convinced.

Having survived both his exploits on the cliff face, and the more perilous onslaught from Georgia, Tommy made his way back to the camp. His camp. He carried a substantial supply of eggs, transported inside the suitably adjusted shirt he had amended for the purpose. His previously fraught attempts at fighting off the attack from the owners of the eggs had been under a calmer state of mind, but this time it was much easier in the mood in which he had been. Though more than careful not to put himself in danger on the cliff again, he had been far less patient with the angry birds this time, and a pair of flailing arms had easily cleared a path to his eventual goal, to add to the pile he had already collected on his previous visit.

He put the eggs down to one side, and having returned to the calming influence of the chicks, he ensured that they were both safe and fed. Even if it had last been by Walter. He then started out on a patrol of the camp. He ensured that what few possessions there were, they all were put to one side, and in the place that he had decided they should be, personalising his grounds like an animal leaving its scent. Eventually satisfied, he sat down by the pool, king of his domain.

Still angry with herself over her destruction of the parachute, Catherine had finally been calmed down. Walter had comforted her with the news that she had probably done more good than harm. The smoke created, may well have been spotted by the passing aircraft.

Georgia added that they should all start thinking about building a larger beacon the next day, and added cheerily, 'For the next time.'

At least they now had something to look forward to, and indeed Catherine's misdemeanour may well have turned into gold.

The consolation Catherine had experienced was instantly brought down by Phillip. He had once more had to be treated after his shared escapades with his sister during the visit of the aircraft, and had now been told, in no uncertain terms, that if it needed seeing to again, he would physically be tied to a tree so that he couldn't move until the wound fully healed. The lighter moment shared, he then spoilt everything by demanding more news on Tommy.

'That young man,' Georgia started, still furious with his attitude, 'is totally capable of looking after himself.'

'I told you,' Catherine jumped in, the opportunity to good to miss.

'So what do you think he's doing then?' Phillip harangued her.

'Look! If he is so damned important,' Catherine snapped, her unladylike vocabulary becoming more and more commonplace at Tommy's mention, 'Why don't you go to him, and see if he can put up with you.'

Georgia quietly looked across at the two of them, realising that Tommy had been right. They had indeed split into two camps.

Tommy sat, a lonely figure, silhouetted by the fire against the night's darkness, staring into the ashes of the fire, trying to make out shapes and faces out of the flames.

'It's you and me against the world,' he called across in the direction of the chicks. He stopped and laughed at the ridicule of talking to himself. He stood and walked over to the sleeping youngsters. 'Yes! You and me against the world,' he repeated, picking up one of the baby birds. He stroked it, now feeling much better talking to something with life and breath in it.

Catherine was asleep beside Phillip, who had finally talked himself out. The effort he had expended charging around during the flight of the aircraft had undone all the good that had been done to his wound, and having both succumbed to sleep, the atmosphere was that bit quieter for it.

Walter walked over to the fire and laid more fuel on it, and looked across at a very much awake, and strangely troubled Georgia.

'A... penny for your thought's' he struggled with a saying he had half absorbed during his time in England.

'What do you think?'

'Edward?'

'Yes,' she nodded. 'I still can't believe he's left Phillip here alone for so long. Phillip was the one person who surpassed everything else to him.'

'Alone?' he gestured the four of them.

'To Phillip! Yes. Alone.'

Walter stood, and jumped up and down, stamping his feet and hugging himself against the cold. Georgia looked up puzzled, and still gloomy.

'I'll go and check if he is safe,' he said. 'At least you will all be better for knowing.'

'Not at all. We spent all day with him, and he was so ungrateful, we can only hope that maybe he wakes up with slightly better manners.'

'But he's still on your minds.'

'He's always on our minds. Let him sleep it off. He'll come back in the morning, or at worst, we can go to him then. I'm too tired, and besides, you would scare the life out of him appearing through the dark. Just get some sleep. You've deserved it.'

57

Laid out beside the fire, Tommy, jumped against the sound of a loud hoot from nearby in the trees. He instantly grabbed at the knife lying by his side and looked around him.

'Hello!' he called out, just in case.

He sat up, waiting for whatever it might have been, fondly wishing the night away. He blinked against the dark of the night, and struggled to make out shapes where there were none. He huddled up that bit closer to the fire, and scrunched up his eyes. And just when he thought sleep was not going to be possible, he slept.

The tri-engined, Junkers JU52 aircraft, circled high above the island. The door on the side of the fuselage opened, and a stream of paratroopers dropped through the opening into the night sky. Within seconds, the sky was dotted with a myriad of white chutes, slowly descending towards the island.

The first of the airborne infantry division landed with a heavy thump. They rolled onto their sides, and climbing to their feet, gathered in the billowing material that had seconds before been the canopy above their heads. They reached down to check their chosen weapon, the Schmeisser, MP40, submachine gun, strapped to their side, and then ran across to rejoin the remainder of the division.

The first of the infantry to reach the beach roughly rounded up the three children and herded them into an untidy group.

Three of the division walked up to Walter, stood to attention, and saluted.

Walter, returning the salute, took a weapon from one of the three and angrily shoved his way past an astonished Georgia, and walked away.

The bodies of two huge storm troopers stood over Tommy as he stared back, powerless to do anything. He glared at them, and just as he made an attempt at getting up, the first of the two stamped down heavily onto his chest, pinning him to the floor.

The cries of the other children echoed loudly in the distance, and Tommy struggled, trying his hardest to do something about it.

'Get off me!' he snapped at them, raising his head. 'Get off me, or else.'

The force of the returned slap forced Tommy's head painfully to one side, and the soldier let loose a tirade of words, totally foreign to Tommy. It did not matter. The strength of the words spared him a translation.

The second of the storm troopers stepped forward. As Tommy glared up at him, he drew out a rolled up canvas and waved it in front of his face. Tommy, recognising it as the one he had secreted away, stared back, helplessly.

The soldier drew a dagger from its sheath and held it out for examination. It was similar to Walter's, but had an SS motif embossed into its handle. He smiled at Tommy and let the canvas unroll until the full beauty of the picture was revealed. He shouted something, equally unintelligible into Tommy's face, and as Tommy stared at him, he stabbed at the canvas several times, drawing the blade down and through the material, tearing it into shreds.

The other soldier, now crouched his body directly over Tommy's chest. His foul breath unavoidable, he drew a pistol, cocked it, and pointed it directly at the centre of Tommy's forehead.

'No!!!'

Tommy woke in a sweat, crying out, flapping his arms about him wildly. He looked around frantically, clenching his fists, punching out at an invisible enemy. He rolled over several times before finally coming to terms with his - nightmare, and then sat back, panting.

Unable to return to sleep, and the blood still pumping round his body at a hundred miles an hour, Tommy contemplated rushing back to see to the safety of the others. But almost as quickly as the thought had entered his head, Walter's face returned from his dream, and stopped in his tracks. He wasn't going anywhere.

58

As morning finally broke, Walter was sat crouched by the fire on the beach. He blew on his hands against the early cold, and looked across at the sleeping children. He rubbed his hands together, roughly, and as feeling slowly started to return, he pulled his wallet from his uniform. He opened the slim black leather purse, and withdrew a small photograph. A pretty young lady in her early twenties, and two children. A boy and a girl.

A loud cough from nearby broke him from his reverie. He looked across at the three children, and as Georgia shifted, turning over, he looked back at his family, and kissed the photograph. Leaving it in his lap, he sighed, and looking into the fire, returned to his daydreaming.

'Who's that?'

Walter jumped. He turned to find Georgia stood beside him, wiping her eyes. He did not know if he had drifted off, or whether Georgia had simply crept up on him. He looked up at her, and she nodded down at the photo, still cradled in his lap.

'It's nothing!' Walter quickly put the photograph back inside his wallet. 'Nothing.'

Georgia yawned and stretched, not overly worried about his secrecy, and sat down beside him to get warm by the fire.

'You look happier this morning,' Walter said.

'I don't know what I am yet,' she confessed. 'I was just tired last night. Who knows what today will bring?'

'Edward?'

'I feel bad about leaving him last night. Sometimes he's a pig and deserves it, but things are …'

'Crazy?'

'Crazy.'

'Let's wait till it's light,' Walter advised. 'And see what time they wake up.'

'Best not wake them too soon,' Georgia advised, pulling a face.

They both laughed, and fell into quiet conversation.

Despite the fact that the nightmare was now a part of history, Tommy had once more returned to the cave where his canvas lay hidden. He had not needed to clear a way inside. In the early morning light, he had trouble finding the spot himself. Once he had located it, it was clear that no one had been anywhere near the spot, and even if they had, it was obvious that nothing had been disturbed. He sat himself down for a moment, and thought about exactly what he should do next.

Phillip had now stirred, and whether his injuries warranted his current mood was up for debate, but he threw orders around like they were going out of fashion. Catherine snapped at him to be quiet. Each time she shouted, Phillip would turn over and grizzle at the pain, and she was left, caught between being angry or concerned.

Walter and Georgia returned from a foray for supplies with a meagre supply of food from both the stream and the woods surrounding them. They were not going to get fat on the haul, but it was better than nothing, though Phillip in his rambunctious mood pointed out that nothing, was not too far away from exactly what they had brought back.

'In that case,' Catherine informed him, 'we will share out your portion of 'nothing' between the three of us. Once you are fit again, and you once more become hunter, then you can decide what we have on the menu.'

'But that's not fair!' Phillip complained. 'And don't forget, if it hadn't been for me, you wouldn't know there were fish here at all.'

The debate continued for a while longer, and only the eventual intervention of Georgia brought matters to a head at all. It was finally agreed that if he behaved himself, and both he and Catherine agreed to a truce, maybe he should be entitled to his share of what lay on the platter after all.

Tommy had enlarged his pantry by a considerable quantity. If only man could live by fish and eggs alone, he concluded after a large shoal had visited his stretch of the pool that morning, then he would indeed live a comfortable life. The battle between man and fish was complete for the day however. He sat himself by the edge of the pool, his feet dangling into the water and waited. They'd all be back soon. He was sure of it.

The chicks had all been awake for some considerable time now. Their continual chatter was almost a constant background accompaniment. As the time started to drag, and it was clear that he was to be on his own for some good time to come yet, he decided to spend some of his time in their company. He had never even had a dog at home, much less a younger brother to have to stress over. As he watched the antics of the fledglings in front of him, he wondered exactly what he might have been missing.

'Don't be so angry, my little chick,' Tommy advised one of the youngsters that pecked a little too strongly at his finger. He pushed it gently out of the way to allow him access to one of the less chirpy numbers inside the pen. 'Chicks! Chicks, indeed! You're not chicks. You're gulls. Baby gulls. Gullets,' he threw around a number of options. 'No! It's time you all had names!'

The chicks received the news with the same alacrity that they accepted anything else, and continued to stare back with the same angry faces.

Placated for the time being with the morsels he had been provided, Phillip had quietened. An examination from Walter, and a reapplication of the same dressing, due to the meagre supplies they had at hand, revealed Phillip to be a little brighter in appearance, and certainly a shade darker in his cheeks. He thanked Walter, but it appeared to be no more than just being polite, and he stared back at his sister's less than bothered face.

Georgia, still chief peacekeeper, realised the current truce between Catherine and Phillip was temporary. To try to eke it out that little bit longer, she informed Phillip that if he behaved himself, she would go and check on Tommy and see if she could make

262

him see sense.

His eyes lit up with excitement and as he jumped at the news, all the good that Walter had done to his wound was quickly undone, and he grimaced once more at the pain.

'Will you please stay where you are?' Catherine interrupted, coming to life. 'Every time someone mentions his name, someone comes to harm. Georgia, he is an oaf. If he wants there to be two camps, then so be it. When he…' she indicated her brother, '…is fit and healthy again, he can leave home and go and live with him. Till then, he stays here.'

'And Edward?' Phillip said, uncomfortably. 'What about him?'

'I've just told you. He is…'

'You two will never agree on anything,' Georgia told her, referring to Catherine's constant battle with Tommy. 'So! One of us is going to have to go and see him, to try to see if we can't just sort something out. I somehow don't see that being you?' Catherine sneered and turned her head away. 'Then it will have to be me. Someone is going to have to bring you two back together.'

'Just stop fighting, and one of you go and get him back,' Phillip shouted, 'or I will do it.' Catherine pointed to his bandage. 'I will! You see if I don't. Now one of you, go and do something.'

'Yes, sir,' Catherine threw him a salute.

'We are on a tiny island,' he informed her, as if she were negligent of the fact, 'and the need for two camps is ridiculous. It's not a game.'

'That's it!' Georgia exclaimed. 'That's exactly it. Let's make it into a game.'

'Game!' Catherine countered.

'Yes. Game. You know how independent he can be. There are two camps. Let's find a way to see who can capture the other's camp, and whoever wins, gets to decide…'

'To decide where we should all base our camp,' Catherine said, suddenly caught up in the energy.

The two girls looked to each other excitedly, and even Phillip couldn't help but agree.

'It's a nice idea,' Walter said, but there was a certain amount of doubt in his voice. 'As long as you can get Edward to agree.'

Catherine and Phillip's faces changed like the weather. All the excitement drained, leaving them staring hopelessly across at Georgia.

'Don't be silly. A competition! Of course he'll want in,' Georgia clarified, cheerily.

'That's all very well, but what are the teams going to be?' Catherine asked.

'Us against the Germans,' Phillip called out without any thought to his suggestion. The two girls' faces turned and glared at him. 'I mean… us against Walter.'

'Fine!' Walter agreed, without reacting to Phillip's unintentional rudeness.

'I don't think the numbers are exactly fair,' Georgia pointed out, sportingly, 'Do you?'

'Whatever happens, I want to be on Edwards's team,' Phillip said.

'Big surprise! Well that will keep you away from me then,' his sister informed him. 'So be it. Besides, you are far too ill to be on my ...'

'I think, like Walter says, before we get too excited, we should maybe clear the idea with him,' Georgia said. 'Maybe I should go and tell him.'

'Tell? Suggest, maybe,' Walter, said. 'Just to be safe. Suggest. And maybe you should both go.' Catherine looked over, confused. 'I'll look after Phillip,' he continued.

Catherine looked to Georgia. 'Fine by me. After all. Where else can we go? Home?'

Tommy was sat by the pool, merrily gutting and dealing with the general duties surrounding the fish he had recently caught. He looked very much at home, and could easily have been mistaken for having done it every day of his life. He swept away the guts and threw them back into the pool. The fish he had not set aside for the chicks, he had even – having watched Georgia do so once upon a time – filleted, and laid to one side. He whistled, contentedly, and seemed very much at home in his solitude, when a distant voice distracted him.

'Edward! Edward!' the voice grew as it approached.

Tommy looked up and smiled as Georgia's cheery face appeared. The smile faded some moments later, as Catherine approached, arguing with some plant or other that had decided it wanted to make a lifelong affinity with her clothing.

'No change here then?' Catherine said, marching in as if she had been away for moments only. She marched straight past Tommy to see the chicks, which had cheered up considerably on hearing their approach, and almost chirruped a welcome to order.

Georgia walked across smiling, shyly, and quickly checked him up and down to see that he was none the worse for wear. She looked over at Catherine still ensconced with the chicks, and crouching beside him, quickly offered her hand. Tommy looked to the wound she had sustained the day before. It had now scabbed over slightly, and if it bothered her at all, she didn't show it.

'Friends?' she asked.

Tommy smiled, reluctantly, and gesturing to his own hands with a nod of his head, showed them to be covered in scales and other giblets from the fish. 'No problem. Shake later, yeah?'

Catherine walked across, pointedly checking on the state of the camp, noting the minor changes Tommy had implemented, and seeing the fish laid out, said, 'If you keep this up, when we all get rescued, you might be able to get a job in the kitchen.'

Whether she had meant it as harshly as it had come across, Tommy read it only one way, and Georgia leant across and grasped his wrist tightly to stop him leaping up at her.

'Don't be drawn,' Georgia whispered. 'And remember your promise,' she reminded him about his word not to mention her own connection to Catherine and Phillip with which she had entrusted him. She felt him relax slightly, and then whispered, 'Thank you.'

'I could strangle her,' he whispered back.

264

'We all could, at times.'

'What are you two wittering on about?' Catherine called across, still inspecting the state of the camp.

Georgia settled down to recount the recent news to Tommy, leaving Catherine to amuse herself. She only looked across when Tommy burst out laughing at something Georgia had said, and immediately assumed she was the butt of whatever it was. She scowled across at Georgia, who warned her to behave herself. It was clear Georgia had counselled Catherine long before they arrived to try her best to keep the peace.

Catherine walked away as Georgia and Tommy burst out laughing once more, and as she turned to see what had caused the hilarity this time, Georgia seemed to be recounting her adventures with Walter's parachute. She turned away, but furiously, refusing to be drawn, pretended not to have paid them any attention.

The levity and light nature having run its course, Georgia turned her attention to the real reason for their being there.

'What? Move from here?'

'No! Not move! Just...'

The debate continued.

'I see these guys are still in good fettle,' Catherine called across, interrupting the negotiations.

'No thanks to you,' Tommy pointed out.

'Yes, well...'

'Yes, well, nothing. I've adopted them. Get used to it.' Catherine looked across, jealously. 'And they've all got names now,' he added, successfully putting more space between the two of them.

'But we should *all* have named them,' Catherine barked back, snatching at the bait he held out for her.

'And if you'd all been here, you could all have had your say. But you weren't. So there!'

'What have you called them anyway?' she demanded. Tommy ignored her. 'Well?'

'What have you called them?' Georgia asked excitedly.

Tommy grabbed her excitedly by the shoulder and dragged her across to the gawky chicks' enclosure, and sat down pointing them out to her, deliberately ignoring Catherine's enquiring looks over his shoulder and informed her of his decision.

Phillip was uncomfortable. Both physically, as mentally. Although still missing Tommy, Catherine's absence had restored a few of the manners he had lost during her watch over him. He had finally decided to Walter out of choice as opposed to necessity. He hissed as he turned over to get more comfortable, and reached down to his leg. Walter asked if he wanted him to have another look at it. He tried to brave it out, but the discomfort took over and he decided to accept the offer.

Walter drew back the pad from the wound, and having looked at it, fell silent for a minute.

265

'What is it?' Phillip asked, noting the silence.

'It's - not nice,' Walter was unable to lie. 'It has turned a little nasty, and it has... Well... It needs to be drained.'

'Drained?' Phillip looked back, aghast, and looking down at the wound for himself, noted a certain amount of pus formed around the abrasion. He turned white and looked to Walter for reassurance. 'Am I going to die?'

'No!' Walter laughed. 'It just needs cleaning up, but it will not be nice. I think we will wait until Georgia or - your sister- are here to help.'

'Or Edward?'

'Or Edward.'

Georgia broke through the last of the trees obstructing her return to the beach, and having hopped down, looked directly at Phillip and said, 'I think I've got a surprise for you.'

Phillip looked back, his face pale. Georgia rushed to his side.

Tommy jumped down from the ridge overlooking the beach and walked across like the Prodigal Son. He looked across to Phillip, smiling shyly, then, like Georgia, rushed across, concerned at the look on his face.

Catherine, having taken her time on her journey back, to allow Phillip to eulogise over Tommy's return out of earshot, quickly involved herself in the furore around her brother, wrongly glaring at Tommy, assuming this to be his fault. Nothing had changed.

Phillip lay beside the fire, his pants pulled down slightly to reveal his bare thigh, exposing the wound to its full extent. The wound was there for all to see. A large patch of pus sat fully exposed on top of the wound.

'We are all going to have to be brave,' Walter expertly tried to include everyone in the proceedings. 'The first aid we have is not enough on its own. We are going to have to remove the...'

The sentence was left unfinished as Phillip gripped Georgia so firmly that she yelped. Resuming her coolness, she assured him, 'You'll be alright. We'll all be here to help.'

Phillip did not look as certain as Georgia, but bravely held his silence.

Tommy had removed his belt and doubled it up at Walter's request, and had been told to place it between Phillip's teeth, to enable him to bite down on it, rather than his tongue should the pain be too much to bear.

Catherine's face had looked worse than Phillip's at the explanation, but Tommy sat to his left gripping his hand, whispering comforting words, occasionally exacting a laugh.

Walter sterilised the blade of one of the knives. The tip was now bright red from where it had sat in the fire. He walked across, and Phillip turned away and stared, trustingly, straight into Tommy's eyes, as Walter called, 'Ready?'

Phillip screamed.

Walter dressed the wound as best he could with what little of the dressings remained. Georgia had washed the used bandages several times to allow the changing of the dressings to continue as frequently as possible, and everyone crossed their fingers.

Job done, and Phillip unconscious, sleeping off the worst of the effects of the treatment, the others sat around the fire to recover from the ordeal. The treatment had affected each of them in different ways. Catherine, despite being his sister, had opted against attending the healing, and Tommy had turned several shades of green during the process. So, therefore, Georgia had been left the responsibility as attending nurse to the doctor.

Tommy's return had brought with it a fresh supply of fish. It had not been obtained without a certain amount of alacrity. Georgia had tried everything she knew to swing the deal, and both Phillip's plight, and a personal appeal from Catherine – only given under duress – had brought about the deal at all.

Still much against his will, a meal had been prepared using all the fish he had brought, exhausting all his hard work in one foul swoop. Tommy had made a point about it, but his usually harsh manner was mellowed the more he looked at Phillip's condition.

The meal completed, and Phillip still asleep, Tommy's good manner melted, and he decided it was time to broach the subject of the two camps, and the proposal for the forthcoming games. Georgia mentioned that it was unfair to discuss the games with Phillip out to the world. He had been one of the instigators, and would be more than upset to miss the founding of the first, Inaugural Island Games. The lightness in her voice could not hide the fact that no one there would readily be opting to stay there for the second Island Games, but Tommy remarked that whatever was decided, he doubted Phillip would be fit enough to play to big a part in them anyway.

As Phillip had suggested, Tommy threw in the idea of the children against Walter. Georgia suggested boys against girls. Catherine in her inimitable way mentioned that she didn't care how the teams were divided, as long as she and Tommy were on opposing teams.

'Phillip had one suggestion,' Walter said, finally deciding to enter the conversation. 'I promised I would mention it.' They all looked across. He looked to the ground, shyly, and raising his head decidedly. 'He was sure you would want to be on opposite teams, and he said whoever lost, had to kiss the winner.'

'No!!!' Catherine and Tommy shouted together.

'Yes! Definitely!' Georgia confirmed, hooting with laughter. Walter held his hands up disowning the idea totally. The two would-be recipients of the forfeit looked at each other horrified, and scowled back at Walter and Georgia.

The inevitability of the team captains needed only to be put into words, and Tommy and Catherine were to fulfil those roles. The debate over who should be in whose team also needed no long debate. It was clear, despite the current amnesty between Tommy and

267

Walter that they were never to be teamed up. Catherine, despite wanting both Georgia's guile and cunning on her side – and an option that it be everyone against Tommy dispelled - finally opted for Walter, and Tommy seemed well satisfied with Georgia. Phillip in his slumbered absence was sworn in as the referee.

It had been discussed that still short of a beacon fire, and the island very much unexplored, the two teams were to race around the island in opposite directions, skirting the coast as best possible. The first team to return to their departure point was to be declared the winner.

Further to the basic decision on which camp was to become headquarters, other peccadilloes had been added. Tommy demanded that not only must the new camp be adopted without question, but also the losing team had to serve the winning team for a full two days. Georgia kept her silence at this. It still seemed only days since she had been housemaid to Catherine and Phillip in the relative safety of London. It did not seem too much of a punishment, but she thought she might keep that to herself. Along with that, two days of sitting down doing nothing would simply bore her to death, but whatever! Her competitive nature would not stop her in her effort to beat Catherine.

From Catherine's point of view, two days of having Tommy running at her every whim without being able to say no, was absolutely ideal.

For all the antics the four of them might get up to, Phillip, it had been decided, was going to have to stay on the beach. As furious as he might be at not being able to better join in, he was to be informed that he was to be the referee. They hoped that Phillip might be so thrilled at how important the job sounded, that he might not mind staying where he was. Just in case there was to be a close finish, he would have the ultimate decision as to the winner. Catherine was certain he would fall for it. They would collectively gather up a large quantity of wood with which he would be able to keep warm, and more importantly, keep stoked up. Until a beacon fire was eventually put together, this was their only point of discovery. His role would be bumped up more when he came round again so as not to leave him feeling everything had happened without him.

Tommy thought it worth pointing out that he and Georgia should maybe get a jump-start on the other team. He pointed out that both Walter and Catherine were older than they were. Georgia just managed to save the event dissolving before it even started, by pointing out that they maybe had youth on their side.

Any thoughts of cheating by cutting across the island were dispelled, as both captains were sworn to abiding by the rules. The fact that both teams had a wiser head as a partner somehow eased any tensions on that front. Walter, due to his age, and Georgia, taking into account her professional tendency towards everything.

Despite the excitement as to the start of the games, the inevitable distrust of the other by both of the team captains ensured that nothing was going to happen quickly. The debate over the setting up of the rules, and the oaths taken to abide strictly by them, and the agreement that immediate disqualification would follow the event of failing to do so, took up most of the rest of the morning. Catherine was worried that during the race Phillip may well end up being left on his own for too long. Walter calmed her, promising that they wouldn't leave till Phillip was wide awake, and they had his agreement to do so. He further assured her that in his short time he had been in the air, dangling from his parachute, he had noted that the island was not really that big.

The excitement of the games fresh on their minds, it took Georgia to point out that Phillip was still unconscious. It did not take a doctor to point out that he did not look as if he was coming round any time too soon, and that perhaps the games should be postponed until the next morning. Even under the protestation from Tommy that that was, 'Ages away.'

So, the teams, sat some good distance apart, were left to sort out tactics, and await Phillip's eventual return to the land of the living.

The games were delayed.

A night's delay, and though begged by Georgia, Tommy refused to stay on the beach.

'Even for one night?' Georgia asked.

'Especially for one night,' Tommy reminded her of the prize of the upcoming competition. 'Besides, someone has to see to the chicks.'

'Feed them any more,' Catherine pointed out, and they will be the size of turkeys. They will need wings the size of an eagle to get off the ground.'

Tommy smirked before promising a momentarily roused Phillip that he would return early the next morning.

'I have a race to win,' he said, looking across at Catherine, who scowled back at him for the hundredth time.

59

Phillip had had a rough night, tossing and turning. He had seemed beset with fever, but once more it broke, and with much nursing from both Georgia and his sister, by the following morning he had colour back in his cheeks, and stand-in doctor Walter declared him well on the road to recovery.

'I *can* join in,' he protested, having been informed of the decisions made in his conscious absense.

'Go on then,' Catherine said. 'Get up and prove it.'

'No!' Georgia, Tommy and Walter shouted in unison.

Phillip did, and his decision was made for him. He slumped back down, dejectedly.

The rules established and fully explained, Phillip agreed to abide by them. As Catherine had suspected, once he realised the importance of being the referee, he excitedly promised to do it to the best of his ability. Georgia had readily confirmed, less anyone forget, that the 'Kiss' forfeit had been implemented as he had wanted, and the two of them giggled uncontrollably for some good time.

Catherine and Tommy quickly forged an unexpected allegiance, and turning up at Phillip's side, begged the withdrawal of any forfeit. Georgia was impressed at the association, and was half-way to giving in before the referee put his foot down.

'You both know the rules, and they must be obeyed,' Phillip demanded, and under the proviso that if he winced and whined at his injury that he usually got his way, he put in a splendid performance to ensure the 'Kiss' was now law.

Phillip drew the teams together to ensure all the rules were fully absorbed, and the four competitors, if only pleased to see Phillip back to his old self, obeyed, and listened obediently.

The competitors all shook hands, and the look between Catherine and Tommy was priceless. The meeting of hands was swiftly dealt with, and equally as easily forgotten. They eyed each other suspiciously, the earlier alliance dispensed with, and now stood a good distance apart.

Phillip called the two teams together, and despite the discomfort, raised his arm high into the air, and ensuring that there was no skulduggery, brought both teams back to the starting line.

'On your marks,' he started excitedly. 'Go!'

Tommy and Catherine took off like racing cars, in opposite and prearranged directions, leaving both their teammates lagging in their wake. Georgia and Walter looked back at each other, surprised at the vigour their captains had employed. Georgia made to wave, but Tommy, noticing her absence, returned and grabbed her by the shoulder, and she had disappeared long before Walter could respond.

Catherine stopped, no small distance into the encounter, and called back to Walter who turned up at her shoulder. 'Come on,' she said. 'You don't know how important this is to me.'

'I think I do,' Walter replied quietly, and almost to himself.

'What?'

'I said, I think we should go.'

Catherine looked back strangely, unsure if he had indeed said that, but the urgency of the race overtook the moment, and she pointed forwards.

'Wait!' Walter spoke up, quickly. 'We are going into new territory. Try to be a little more careful. We don't want you tripping over something and becoming our second casualty.'

'Yes! Okay!' Catherine snapped, without really listening, staring incredulously at his delay. 'Now come on.'

'It is not a sprint. Take your time,' he ventured once more, but the words were lost into a back that was quickly disappearing into the distance. He shrugged, and if only to ensure her safety, made off after her.

The excitement of the start of the race, now history, Phillip sat back. His mind span as he thought about the way both teams had charged away. He was sure they weren't going to be long, but excited about news from what they would discover on their travels through the undiscovered country, knew they wouldn't be back too soon. He lay back in the cot that had been hastily put together, and taking his glasses off the end of his nose, tried in vain to clean them on the dirty cloth that had once been his shirt.

His best efforts expended, he finally placed them back where they had come from, and looked down at the watch that had refused to part company with him. Drying out, as might have been suggested at one point, had not had the desired effect, and the watch was now merely a keepsake. The inevitability of his glance at the defunct timepiece only confirmed that he had no way of judging how long they had been gone, nor when he might expect them back. His wound dictated that he was going to have to sit still and wait, however long it took. He stared up at the sky and the gathering grey clouds, and if only for something to do, threw a little more fuel onto the fire.

With a discontented sigh, he snuggled up against the closing change in the weather, and waited.

Tommy had initially opted to cut back through his camp - as it was for the time being - but had been stopped. Georgia, though enjoying the race, had had to reprimand him several times for minor indiscretions. He almost wished he had teamed up with Catherine after all. He was sure she would not have been such a stickler to the rules. He had told her a little bending of the rules would not hurt too much, but she had stopped dead and promised to refuse to go on unless he abided by the rules that he himself had been part of drawing up.

'I almost think you want Catherine to win,' he said.

'I don't care who wins, as long as it's fair.'

'Thanks, team-mate. I might have had a better chance with Walter,' he said.

Georgia looked up, but Tommy couldn't hold her eye. In the ensuing gap in

271

conversation, he realised it was the first time that he had mentioned Walter by name. The slip, if it was a slip, was not missed by Georgia either. She smiled contentedly to herself, and having ensured he follow her amended route, progressed that little bit happier.

The newly formed alliance between Catherine and Walter as a team had by now settled into a far more sedate pace. Walter had explained on the beach that though it was a race, it must also be an exploration. The wise advice had been completely ignored however, the second Phillip had pointed Catherine in Tommy's direction, and blown a kiss. The forfeit.

Thankfully, a combination of a distinct lack in Catherine's general athletic ability, allied with her totally unsuitable clothing for island life, reduced her to a far more sedate pace. Despite her early push to get them as far ahead as possible, her uncanny ability to attract anything plant-like, either thorny or otherwise, had readily thrown any planning right out of the window. Sedate it was going to have to be. Though Walter's insistence at drawing to a halt, to mentally digest anything new they came across, thoroughly infuriated Catherine.

'Come on!' she yelled. 'Don't you want to win? Just think of...'

'Of course. Philli...'

'If I have to – kiss - that... that... Him! I shall... Oooooh!!! Come on.'

Walter nodded, and smiling, followed on behind.

The journey which Georgia and Tommy had undertaken took them past the now almost well-trodden path to the point at which they had first landed. They paused for a moment, remembering how much had happened to them in such a short space of time.

'This way!' Georgia reminded Tommy. 'If we go any further inland it will be deemed as cheating.'

Tommy was relieved. The path they had been forced to take, due mainly to the overgrown terrain in front of them, was strangely sending them in the general direction of the spot where he had left his canvas. Although he was fairly certain *King Solomon's Mines* would be far easier to spot than the entrance to his cave, he almost imagined Georgia to have a hidden aura about her. And there was certainly no point putting that to the test.

'I take it Catherine will choose the camp on the beach if she wins,' Tommy said. Georgia shrugged. 'What will you choose?'

Georgia continued walking.

Tommy stopped, raising his voice. 'Well?'

'I'm on your team. You're the captain. The decision will be yours.'

'But?'

Georgia thought back to the time when the four children were all sat around their first fire, all eating their first fish. Together.

'Let's just win first,' she said. 'If we don't beat the others, we won't even have to

272

decide.'

Tommy was far from happy at her apparent reluctance to stick by him, but having been reminded that the race was still ongoing, he grabbed at her shoulder, and the pair pushed on.

The promised rain seemed to be fast on its way in. Phillip looked up at the larger pieces of the silk from Walter's parachute – that had been spared Catherine's torching – and had been put together into an awning of branches and sticks to form him at least some form of shelter. Though the two competing teams had only been gone a short while, Phillip was beginning to miss their company. He snuggled up, hoping that they had already found something they had missed before.

'A town,! Maybe it wasn't an island after all!'' his imagination flew, but he quickly dismissed the idea.

His mind drifted back to the original campsite, and how simple life had been, realising that if his sister's team were to win, that was going to have to remain a memory. The chicks, which he missed terribly, would have to be transported down to the beach, and life would continue from here.

Shivering, Phillip reached out and threw another of the sticks they had left for him onto the fire. The cold was starting to get to him, and the fire was all he had until anyone came back to tend to his needs.

The wood caught quickly, but did not seem to warm him overly much, and if the wind shifted direction again, as it seemed to do at will, he was going to be cold. Besides, if the wind decided to blow back in the direction of the beach, the rain that was sure to come with it was sure to put out the fire. Phillip stoked the fire as high as he could from his hospital bed, just in case.

The wind, as if sensing his attempt at fighting its collaboration with the rain, duly changed direction, and despite the scant shelter he had been left with, it was not long before the fire was under attack.

He had called out to see if anyone was within earshot, but remaining unanswered, he decided action was the only answer.

The excitement of the race, and everything that went with it had left Phillip feeling far better than he had for some time. The fact that his wound had been both lanced and redressed had had a lot to do with it. He struggled at first to shift his body deeper into cover, but finding that it really wasn't quite as uncomfortable as he had expected, he started to exert himself slightly more than perhaps he should.

In minutes, Phillip had gathered together a small quantity of dryer sticks and slightly larger pieces of wood, and having moved himself back inside the cover of the overhanging branches, had put together a fire of his own. It was no bonfire, but the rain did not seem to be able to penetrate his defences quite so easily, and even if it were only for the efforts he had exerted, he was certainly considerably warmer.

He sat back, his wound reminding him that he may well have overdone things slightly, and slowly his fire grew before him. After some moments he even had to sit back slightly as the larger pieces of wood started to catch, and as the rain started to fall

273

in a far more substantial form, he watched as it attacked what was left of his original fire on the beach.

It had taken little or no time for the rain to take its effect upon the race. Catherine, unconcerned by the arrival of the downpour, had surprisingly hugged the coast as set down by the rules, as Walter had moved further inland, and under cover. He beckoned her to follow him, but she was adamant that they continue. He stopped. Catherine pulled up and looked back angrily.

'Come on. I have to beat him. We can't go that way. It's cheating,' she said, incredibly.

'Edward will do the same.'

'Sure he will!'

'You can't go on in this.' He raised his hand, gesturing to the rain, which was now coming down hard. 'Call it a tie.'

Catherine scowled, but having looked up at the further deteriorating weather, reluctantly walked across to join Walter under cover.

Tommy and Georgia, having made good progress, had needed no encouragement to seek shelter at the arrival of the rain. Rules or not, they had headed inland, and only once they were covered by sufficient foliage to deflect, if not stop the rain, did they stop at all. Georgia shivered, and Tommy put an encouraging arm around her shoulder, and rubbed it to both warm her up, and chivvy her spirits.

'Should we keep going?' Georgia asked Tommy, indicating the ground ahead of them.

Tommy shook his head, shaking water from his hair, only confirming his decision. They would stay where they were for now, and at least wait out the current squall.

60

Phillip was now sat, a lonely figure, the rain rapidly draining what little enthusiasm he had left. His early fervour waned as not only the rain, but the cold took hold. He stared out at the fire on the beach, that was now no more than ashes, and switched his attention to his most recent effort, and hoped that as the rain increased its intensity, it too might not suffer the same fate. He had valiantly ventured slightly deeper into the woods where the rain was failing to break through the cover from the trees above, and returned with a fresh supply of fuel, and though his reserve fire had now built up considerably, he was now really missing the company of the others. His mind shifted to what they were up to, and, one more look at the rain, it did not take a genius to work out that the race must have been postponed.

Due to a lot less cover on their particular side of the island, Catherine and Walter had walked a good way inland to gain any benefit from the overhead cover at all. They stood like drowned rats, not realising until they stopped exactly how wet they had become. They stood and looked at each other and laughed at what the other looked like. Catherine shook her head strongly and water cascaded from where it had soaked the hair on her head. Walter jumped back, as if fearing the droplets were going to make any difference to his already drowned condition. She laughed again, and turning away from Walter, shyly, she continued, further inland.

Walter soon caught up with her, and as they both edged around a large tree blocking their path, they found themselves in a much larger clearing. More still, it was dry.

They both jumped back as several forms of disturbed wildlife took flight, or scampered away to cover. To avoid something furry that did not see her as a threat, Catherine jumped to avoid it, and tripped over one of Walter's feet, and helplessly landed in a heap. Walter laughed, and offering his hands, quickly helped her to her feet.

'Fine! So, maybe the contest does have to be called off, after all,' Catherine agreed with Walter's earlier suggestion. She looked at the state of her clothing, and currently in the dry, dumped herself down on the ground, and lay back, looking up into the treetops.

'I'm sure it's the right thing to do.'

'I know someone who won't so readily agree.'

'I'm surprised you've given up so easily.'

'Let him freeze. Georgia wouldn't go on in this, I'm sure. And, as both members of the team have to get back, the race would be null and void anyway.'

Walter found a dry spot of his own and dumped himself on the floor, impressed at the apparent thaw in her demeanour, and together they both looked around at the spot in which they had ended up.

Tommy and Georgia had likewise continued their pursuit inland, as the weather dictated, and shelter for them too, had fast overtaken the game. Tommy looked around, trying to work out their logistics, but was clearly lost and looked across to Georgia, who looked equally non-plussed.

'Well?' Georgia asked.

'God knows!' Tommy cussed, and blushed as Georgia smirked at his blasphemy. 'Buggered if I know,' he further mimicked a voice he would have heard in the markets of London in what was now a previous lifetime, causing Georgia to roll around in laughter.

'Stop it,' she scolded him, merrily.

'You do realise I've just lost to Catherine,' Tommy pointed out. '*And* you know the forfeit.'

'I shouldn't worry about losing.'

'Worry! She wouldn't give up.'

'Give up! Are you joking? Catherine hasn't got any duck in her.' Tommy looked confused. 'She doesn't operate well in water. And don't forget, she may be older, but she is still a girl.'

'A girl. She's more of a man than I will ever be.' Georgia hooted with laughter again. 'Anyway. That would make it a draw!' Tommy shouted happily. He danced around, delighted at the currently unconfirmed result.

'We mustn't be too long,' Georgia pointed out. 'Phillip will be...' She looked across to where she could see the rain pouring. 'Oh my! Poor Phillip!' She turned to run back.

'Wait!'

'He'll be soaked.'

'He's got the fire,' Tommy pointed out, far from enthusiastic in his argument. 'Just rest for a moment, anyway! Until the rain stops. Then I'll come with you.'

Georgia, slumping to the floor, lay back listening to the rain falling, and jumped as a spot of rain penetrated the roof of the trees overhead. It landed directly on the point of her nose. She shook her wet head where it had failed to dry, spraying Tommy, who sat beside her, thoughtfully.

Tommy leapt away, and lay in a new spot, facing her, listening to her, humming contentedly. He moved his head gently from side to side in time with the tune, but suddenly called out, 'Quiet!'

'Don't you like my singing?' Georgia asked, laughing.

'No.'

'No?' she sat up, angry at his response.

'No. Not that. Just listen.'

They both sat quietly listening, trying to push the sound of the falling rain to one side.

'Voices!' Tommy said, straining to hear. 'Voices!'

As the rain showed no signs of relenting, Walter suggested he go back and rescue Phillip. Catherine protested, loudly. Whether it was her maternal instinct, or that she did not wish to be left alone was arguable, but Walter's decision was certainly delayed as she argued her case.

'Hey!' Tommy voice yelled out from the dark.

Catherine jumped, startled. Tommy laughed at her, and a slightly less impressed, Georgia appeared.

'You could have given me a fit,' Catherine flew at Tommy, who drew back and sheltered behind Walter as she tried to get her hands on him.

Eventually, having chased him round for a minute or two, the energy drained out of her. She stopped and seeing Georgia, walked over to give her a hug.

'Got you!' Tommy sneered, playfully.

'You gave up then,' Catherine managed to get in first.

'Just came to find you. Didn't want you to get too wet.'

'Anyway, we were way in front of you two, so technically we were the winners.'

Tommy and Catherine started a pointless debate, and Georgia and Walter stepped back to allow it to fight itself out to a pointless draw.

'I think we should have been a team,' Georgia suggested to Walter. 'I think we would have walked it.'

'I'm the winner,' Catherine declared.

'Fine!' Tommy relented somewhat surprisingly. 'So be it. Where do you want the kiss?'

'The what?'

'The kiss. The forfeit.' He puckered his lips and advanced on Catherine who looked back at him, horrified.

'No! Wait! Maybe you *were* slightly ahead.

'Then you owe me a kiss,' he retorted quickly.

'A draw!' she spluttered.

'A draw?'

'A draw.'

'Yes! A draw,' Georgia interrupted the debate. 'A draw. No winners. No losers. Agreed?' Walter nodded his agreement, and as much as the two of them had been enjoying the display, they both looked to Tommy and Catherine to finally bring the battle to a conclusion.

'Agreed,' Tommy murmured.

They looked to Catherine.

'Agreed.'

'No kiss, but shake hands,' Georgia tried to eke out some form of agreement between the two.

The pair stared at each other and reluctantly held out a hand.

The shake done, the pair of them wiped their hands on their clothing as if they had landed in something quite unsavoury.

'But...' Tommy started.

'But nothing,' Georgia said with her arms folded.

'This doesn't decide which camp we are going to use.'

'Yeah!' Catherine said.

'Yeah?' Georgia quizzed her. 'You have never said, 'Yeah' before, ever.'

Catherine stood, embarrassed. 'It's him,' she pointed at Tommy. 'He must be rubbing off on me.' There was an awkward silence.

'Yeah!' Tommy quickly put in.

'Oh my goodness! I'm turning common,' Catherine said, looking perplexed, and shook her body as if she were covered in ants.

The hilarity continued as the three others rolled around laughing at Catherine's antics. The angrier she became, the more they laughed, and only clap of thunder deep into the distance finally brought them to their senses.

'Oh, my goodness!' Georgia spoke what everyone else was thinking. 'Poor Phillip!'

'I'll go back,' Tommy blurted.

'You'll get lost. Georgia go!' Catherine decided.

'And what? You sit here and wait?' Tommy questioned her.

'There are worse places to sit,' Georgia informed them, and everyone looked around at the surroundings. 'Far worse.'

Phillip was seated by the now burgeoning fire, looking back out across the beach. The thunder had been short, and he had only been frightened for a short while. The rain had now slowly started to relent, and higher up into the sky, the sun was fighting hard to make an appearance. He heaved a lonely sigh, fed up with his solitude, and awkwardly reaching for another piece of wood, was about to throw it angrily onto the fire when he heard voices.

Still not fully convinced they were alone on the island, and despite the pain, he carefully crouched down behind a bush. Just in case.

The four competitors returned en masse to the beach and looked dejectedly at the sodden ashes of the fire there.

'Phillip!' Catherine looked up nervously.

'Phillip!' Georgia echoed.

'Phillip!' Tommy.

'Over here!' Phillip poked his head out of the spot where he had taken cover.

They all rushed across, noting his slightly improved state, and as a group, almost dismissing him, surrounded the smaller fire, trying to rid themselves of any water that had penetrated their clothing on their travels.

His welfare eventually sought and tendered, he looked up keenly. 'Well?'

'Well what?'

'Who won?' he demanded.

'It was a draw,' Catherine informed him blandly. Phillip physically shrank before their eyes.

'Don't worry,' Georgia told him.

'But the kiss?' he stressed.

'A draw is a draw,' Tommy said, and looking across at the less than amused Catherine, said, 'she demanded a kiss, and I had to drive her away. But like I say, a

278

draw is a draw.'

'Oh, ha, ha! You wish!'

'Didn't she Georgia?' Tommy said. Georgia nodded playfully to Phillip.

'Georgia! Really Phillip,' Catherine told him in no uncertain terms, 'I would rather kiss a snake.'

'I go and see if I can find you one, shall I?'

The laughter finally concluded, and once they had all settled, they rested beside the fire. They recounted the race to the bemused Phillip who lapped up every word, and the excitement at the suggestion that they all move into a new camp was almost too much for him. For the sake of his recuperating body, he had then to be virtually tied down to stop him jumping up and getting away immediately.

61

Many days had passed, and the new camp now had a settled look to it. Any thoughts about loyalty to old campsites were quickly forgotten. Tommy was more than satisfied, and moreover, the further away from the spot where he had hidden his canvas the better. It did not even warrant checking on any longer. Trips away from the new camp were no longer necessary as they had just about everything they needed nearby.

Georgia's worries about a beacon fire had quickly been rectified, and after a much delayed exploration of the island, the most suitable spot had been quickly decided upon. The island had not provided any large mounts on which to set it, but the spot they had chosen was close to the new camp, and certainly as high as the island was prepared to allow.

What the new camp had done for spirits in no time at all, the enmity Tommy held for Walter was still going to take a little longer to mend. Walter had tried his best, but Tommy was still far from receptive. They kept a respectful distance, and on Tommy's part, the pair of them were at best, on a nodding relationship.

The camp was in what had turned out to be a large clearing which was sheltered on two sides, providing plenty of cover. The stream – which seemed to cut straight through the island - ran close by and they now had an almost larger, deeper, fish bearing pool.

The trees that grew overhead were heavy in both branches and leaves. The cover they provided seemed best able to keep out all but the strongest of the weather, and though it had not yet been tested to its fullest, it seemed to be by far the most suitable, weatherproof spot on the island. The only downside was that even on the sunniest days, the camp was more likely to be in the shade.

Georgia had pointed out, she would rather be in the dark and dry, than in the open and wet. Catherine added that the darker it was, the less she would have to look at Tommy's ugly face, and an appropriate answer had started a quarrel out of nothing, which nonetheless ran its course.

A large fire burned in the middle of the camp. The girls had occupied one side, with Tommy tucked away on the other. Phillip had insisted on joining Tommy and had made his pitch beside him for his forthcoming convalescence. Walter had found a spot of his own nearby, both neutral, though available to both parties if required.

The chicks had now gained in both strength and size, and Tommy - having moved them safely across - had made them a new, much larger enclosure. It had initially been put together in a hurry to enable them to be brought across at the first opportunity, but what it lacked in quality, it more than made up for in size.

The new pen was a accumulation of sticks and mud, and though almost shanty in its design, between them, the chicks and Tommy seemed most satisfied in its design.

Walter had offered to assist Tommy at one point, but his offer had been flatly refused. While it held together, Tommy was accepting the plaudits alone.

Jobs shared out as equally as seemed fit, if only after an initial debate, the chicks were now prominently Tommy's property and concern. Phillip, despite light duties, and a pig-headed stubbornness to stick by Tommy's side - if not just an excuse to keep away from his sister's clutches – had lost a lot of his initial concern over the chicks, but promised he would certainly see no harm came to them. Georgia fussed over them when she was allowed, but Catherine's love affair with them had dissolved when Tommy had named them without her input. She thought Tom, Dick, Harriet and Daisy were silly names anyway, and had constantly badgered him about exactly how he knew what sex the birds were in the first place.

Tommy told her *It was nothing to do with her, so there*! It was only when she had suggested that as soon as they were big enough, they would be on the table for dinner, that she was banned from any contact with them at all.

The supply of fish, both for their own consumption, and for that of the feeding of the chicks, had made for long spells in the pools up and down the stream, though Tommy had by now become equally as adept at the job as Phillip had once been. Walter had asked to help, but Tommy, now an old master at the task, informed him that his talents might perhaps be better employed elsewhere.

The revolver and the bullets, as had formerly been agreed upon, had been kept apart, and still remained in two different charges. Walter suggested that maybe they should perhaps unite the two and hunt for a different variety of diet.

A meeting had been organised, as everything now seemed to have to pass a vote to proceed, and it was agreed that Tommy and Walter would go, together, to hunt the next morning.

The union agreed upon, Tommy was to be entrusted with the loaded weapon. In truth, despite his lingering suspicions about Walter, he was not overly adamant about it. As hunting went, he knew he had not even been overly at home with a catapult, and his previous history with live ammunition spoke for itself. But still, the thought of handing across the live weapon to… It just didn't seem right. He would keep possession of it, at least until a prospective target was agreed upon. Food was imperative. Even with Georgia's limited time in the kitchen at home, she - with a begrudging hand from Catherine - had tried just about every possible way to prepare it differently with what they had available to them, but it still ended up tasting like fish.

First light. Tommy held the revolver tightly in his right hand with the clip holding the bullets in the left as he and Walter marched off together. Walter had handed over the magazine containing the bullets but had urged Tommy not to put them into the gun just yet. He could have mentioned the safety clip on the revolver, but he thought better of it, and decided that for everyone's sake, the revolver and the shells were best kept apart for now.

They walked in relative silence, both for the sake of disturbing any prey they might happen upon, and early attempts at conversation between the two coming to a relative halt, as Walter's initial questions had been greeted with only grunts from his co-hunter.

After the previous few days, roaming the island, the two hunters approached the spot

281

at which they had agreed was the place best likely to contain their prey. They had all heard sounds of animals careering off into cover during their initial search of the island, but it was agreed that it had probably been nerves, and that it was likely that there was nothing larger than rabbits here. So, rabbits it was.

The rabbits, like those in Rabbit Wood, so long ago, were out in force, and the two hunters drew back carefully, and quietly, not to disturb them. A poignant moment passed without audience as Tommy nervously handed across the weapon and the magazine to Walter. He took them both and loaded one into the other, and if he noted the poignancy of the moment, he kept it hidden. He looked at Tommy, and with a nod of the head, gestured towards the prey. Tommy smiled apprehensively, and pointed across at a large rabbit sat up, chewing happily on fresh vegetation.

The three children at the New Camp had only heard the one shot, and despite a newfound trust in Walter, they could not but wonder what had happened, or who had fired at what. They waited in silence.

Walter appeared and they all shrank back slightly until he held a large rabbit up in front of him, and a grinning Tommy appeared over his shoulder.

'One rabbit?' Catherine scolded them.

'They wouldn't queue up once they heard the first shot,' Tommy said. 'We can go back. Don't worry.' He held the revolver into the air. 'But we aren't going to last long if every bunny costs us a bullet. We may just *have* to get used to fish.'

They all sat around the fire, sucking on the last of the bones, ensuring nothing had gone to waste, and collectively mulled over a better method of hunting rabbits. Georgia had mentioned loosely about snares, but she did not elucidate on how she had come about the information. Their appetites freshly assuaged, the mention of a rabbit emerging from a burrow and slipping its head through the loop of wire or the like, and ending its life some time later under strangulation was not easy listening for any of the youngsters. Catherine screwed up her face at the explanation, so Walter promised he would try to see if he could work his way around the task with what they had available. He nodded across at what remained of the cable that had once been part of the parachute.

'I will help you,' Tommy promised edgily, to which Walter nodded.

'Strangulation?' Catherine asked once more, for clarification.

'I'm sure they aren't overly pleased at being shot,' Georgia informed them.

'I used to prefer it when food came from the kitchen,' Phillip concluded, and they all agreed, silently.

Catherine sat back, far from bloated, but nonetheless fed, and sighed.

'What?' Tommy asked.

'We finally have a beacon ready to light, and yet we've seen hide nor hair of any rescue whatsoever.'

'Maybe we should build an airstrip,' Tommy taunted her. 'We will need one after all the aircraft they have sent out to search for us. Better still! Let's build a harbour to land all the ships that we've been spotted so far. Maybe we could even build you a boat?'

'A raft!' Phillip yelled. 'We could build a raft!'

Catherine looked at him and tutted, but then, and maybe only for lack of anything better, looked across to Tommy, then Walter. 'What about it? A raft?'

'Nice idea,' Tommy said, taking on the question, 'but we are on an island, not in the middle of the docks.'

'So that's that then,' Catherine flared, and another row erupted, the strain showing, as everyone let loose in the ensuing fracas.

Walter sat out of the now heated debate, and started scratching out something in the dirt in front of him. Georgia having had enough of refereeing the current conflict, looked across to him, and almost in despair, went over to see what he was doing.

'What's that? she enquired.

He looked up at her approach, and quickly brushed out what he had done and dismissed it. 'Nothing!'

A scathing lunge from Catherine, just missing Tommy's head, spared Walter having to fend off further questions, and he and Georgia watched as they took off in pursuit in yet another scuffle.

'Look at them. Romeo and Juliet,' Walter said. Georgia looked puzzled. 'Don't worry.'

'No! Do worry!' Phillip called from nearby.

'Fine!' Walter walked over and settled beside Phillip, joined by a transfixed Georgia. 'Two families, both alike in dignity.'

'Dignity?' Georgia questioned.

'Living in similar conditions, maybe!' he gestured to their current surroundings, and continued, paraphrasing, 'On this fair island, where we set our scene.'

Walter carried on, further condensing and distorting the original story and characters into Catherine and Tommy, to an engrossed audience until he had managed to put across his point.

'Poisoned!' Phillip sighed.

'That is how the real story ended. I just…'

'These two? Lovers?' Georgia burst out laughing, and her point was further compounded as Tommy ran past them hotly pursued by a raging Catherine.

'Maybe not,' Walter declared, though both Georgia and Phillip saw what he had been getting at.

'Anyway,' Georgia said, relentlessly, 'What *were* you scratching in the dirt?'

Walter took a sharp stick and once more started to scratch out a design in the dirt. Catherine stopped in her tracks noticing them huddled together, and not wanting to miss out on anything, ceased her current pursuit of her foe and joined them. Finally, a returning, and equally curious Tommy, united the group.

'Phillip's raft,' Walter said, returning to his earlier reference, and as they all looked on, he scratched, rubbed out and re-scratched out further designs without anything really taking ultimate shape.

'Fantastic!' Tommy exclaimed. 'What if…'

Ideas flew around with everyone putting in their oar, trying to add or modify any design that came about, and too many cooks evidently spoiled the broth, and nothing came about. But the idea had been mooted, and everyone was positive.

'We are safe here anyway,' Phillip pointed out. 'Do we really need to build a raft at all?'

'It was your idea, Catherine reminded him.

'Yes. But having seen those,' he pointed to the various designs in the dust, 'I'm not quite so keen now.'

'Maybe we should all design a raft. We can decide whose is best,' Georgia ventured.

The suggestion of an open competition had each of them hurriedly scrambling around for their own space with a stick with which to begin their own designs.

'Finished!' Phillip raised his head from his plan, and having completed his first, chivvied the others to hurry along with theirs. He scrambled to his feet and limped across to peer over the shoulders of the others. 'Hmmm!'

The combatants finally all sat back, content in their work.

'Well?' Catherine said.

'Who is the winner?' Phillip demanded.

'Well, actually…' Tommy started.

'You are not the judge,' Catherine blurted. 'We all have to decide together.'

Georgia nudged Walter, referring to his Romeo and Juliet scenario earlier in the day. He smiled back.

The rough designs were barely discernable in the dirt, and there was no likelihood of a general agreement, but despite no clearly outstanding design, the judging had to be observed, and as a group, the drawings were adjudicated.

The main dispute emerged when Catherine walked straight past Tommy's design without even stopping to look at it. It was at this point that it became clear the winner was never going to be agreed upon, and it was only as Georgia suggested that it didn't matter which they chose, as long as they at least tried one, that calm was eventually restored.

'Anyway, I think Walter should decide,' Catherine, said. 'He has at least been to University.'

Walter independently pointed out the various faults in structural design in each of the raft's plans as best he could in the dusty ground, and, in spite of the various protestations from the relevant designers. 'The only way we could decide would be to try them out,' he declared.

'But we are barely able to build one, never mind five,' Catherine disputed. 'The only way we can try all five is if we made…'

'Models!' they all exclaimed together.

284

62

The excitement of the upcoming event had even brought Phillip out of himself, and due to a combined effort to gather the relevant materials together for him, he was able to join in without doing himself too much damage.

The five individual parties split up and went off to their own areas of construction, and furtive glances over the shoulder at each other revealed the seriousness with which the competition was being taken.

Twigs, small branches, and the use of reeds as a device for binding the pertinent pieces together were now the order of the day. That, and the inventiveness of five individual brains. Such was the intensity of the competition, even Phillip's moan about his inability to keep the pieces of his raft together – because of his age - rousing the help of Walter was rebuked. A slightly over-competitive sister quickly pointed out that competition was competition, and even the usually affable Walter was sent scurrying back to his own model. Phillip was left to his own devices. Even Georgia ignored Phillip, and keeping her head down, continued with a craft of her own.

The advent of night brought about a cessation to the temporary docks, and the five competitors, far from congregating around the fire - as was the norm - kept their distance from one and other, keeping their models under lock and key, fiercely proud of their work. What would otherwise have been a chatty night, tired eyes soon turned into an early one. Chatter was reduced to a bare minimum. 'Good nights' were offered and received, but even under the suspicion of designs being stolen, eyes were shut long before they normally would have been.

The sun rose and as the reduced daylight just managed to fight its way into camp, four suspicious heads raised themselves and looked around, cagily. Walter, too, was caught up in the event, but he took the proceedings slightly less seriously. Though only slightly.

It was Walter that wisely insisted that they all took a breakfast of sorts before anything else happened. But once again, the food was taken back to the personal docks for consumption, where final adjustments were made, and models prettified for the upcoming race.

'I'm bound to lose,' Phillip squeaked pathetically from his quarters. 'I should be aloud to start further up the course. And I'm the youngest.'

'It's your side that is hurt, not your hands,' his sister reminded him bluntly. 'And you haven't been too young for anything so far, so just get on with it.'

'But ...'

'You are supposed to be Huckleberry Finn. Build yourself a raft.'

'Georgia!'

'You heard your sister.'

The day had blossomed as if commanded by the organisers. The sun shone brightly, any wind had died, and the stream flowed with a gentle wake promising fair travel to all who took to its waters. Conditions could not have been more perfect.

The parade, as the individual crafts were brought down to the stream, could not have been bettered by a royal procession. Everyone eyed the others' rafts suspiciously as they were brought down to the agreed starting point.

All five of the rafts differed to some considerable degree, but in general, the sizes were similar and close to a foot or so in length. The lack of ideal materials may have hampered any professional numbers being presented, but one certainly wouldn't have dared suggest it to any of its owners. Phillip had tried his hardest to make his number a little bit bigger than the others, hoping that size really was important, but the lack of any form of reliable string or binding - the cable from the parachute having been banned deciding it could be put to better use - had meant all rafts were more or less uniform in design.

All seemed to be progressing well as the starting point was approached, until a row erupted as Catherine bumped slightly into Tommy. His accusation that she had tried to make him drop his raft because, *hers was rubbish,* was curtailed by the suggestion from Georgia that if they didn't both shut up, they would both be disqualified, and not be able to compete at all.

They were quickly separated, but it did not stop any competitive rivalry. They continually sneered at each other as they proceeded to the starting point.

All the rafts were placed carefully on the edge of the bank by the river as the rules were meticulously scrolled through once again. Just to be sure. The competitors were to stand in the stream, side by side, and hold the various rafts until they floated in the water, and only at the agreed count, would they all be released. Together. The winner was to be the first raft to complete the course, which finished as the stream dropped a foot or so into the flat pool below them further down the stream. If none of the rafts happened to be intact at that point, the raft that had progressed the farthest along the stream until it had finally fallen apart would be declared the winner. The winner would be excused duties for an entire day. The limited work that Phillip in fact contributed, in the excitement, was overlooked, and so, the rules stood.

Walter, with his trouser legs rolled up to the knees, walked out into the stream and stood in the middle. It had been predestined that Catherine and Tommy would stand either side of him, as Catherine had already stated that she was sure Tommy had had a battering ram fitted to his raft to stop her winning. Tommy had told her, never mind a battering ram, he had tried hard to have torpedoes fitted.

Ultimately, Georgia would stand next to Tommy, with a shaky but resilient Phillip stood beside his sister.

The water ran between their legs towards the finishing line that appeared to be positively miles off into the distance, and there was a sudden hush as the owners and their rafts became one. Five eager faces looking downstream.

'One, two…' Tommy announced.

'No, wait!' Catherine shouted. 'Not you! Let Walter do it.'

'Anyone,' Tommy said. 'As long as we start it before I turn grey.'

'Attention then!' Walter said. 'On the word three. One, two…'

All the boats were held floating on the water.

'…Three!'

All the rafts were released together, and as one, took off downstream in a flotilla.

Five soggy bodies leapt to the side of the stream to follow the race from there, cheering them along as they went.

'Go on, Huck!' Phillip yelled. 'Right on down the Mississippi.' Watching carefully, he cheered on, but the smile on his face turned upside down as his craft sailed straight into a protruding rock. He watched, awestruck, as the inadequate bindings unwrapped in front of him, and the twigs and sticks fell apart, drifting off like a shipwreck.

Phillip glared across at his competition, pleadingly, almost demanding another shot. He sadly wasn't even going to get any sympathy. Indeed, the remaining competitors unanimously cheered its demise as the race was now down to four, and ignoring him totally, they chased off in pursuit of their own craft.

Phillip's loyalty to his raft was fleeting, and similar to that of him and his sister. Hearing the excitement of the others, he quickly decided to switch his allegiance to another number.

The four remaining rafts jostled for position on the seemingly endless stream, in which they appeared to be making so little progress, and they were cheered on enthusiastically. Georgia's raft seemed to have found a spot in fast water and started to draw clear of the other three. She screamed in excitement, jumping up and down. The three remaining craft appeared to have been left in its wake, and their owners now appeared as downcast as their vessel. She ran on ahead of them elatedly, only to look back to them in horror, as her craft appeared to have suddenly stopped, dead in the water.

'It's run aground,' Tommy shouted joyously as if he had been at sea all of his short life.

'That's not fair,' Georgia moaned.

'Fair is for hair,' Catherine shouted, and like Tommy and Walter, rejuvenated in their fresh hopes, moved her out of the way to follow what was left of the race.

Walter's craft, which appeared to be the sturdiest of the three remaining runners, seemed to gain in confidence as it started to take up the lead. His face shone equally as much as Catherine and Tommy's. He called out for it, and as it pulled ahead of Catherine's charge, she yelled angrily at the foul tactics.   'No, Walter!'

Walter ignored her protestations, smiling like the *Cheshire Cat*, only to adopt the same disillusionment as Phillip and Georgia, as his chances of being the owner of the winning raft, died in front of him. His raft had passed Catherine's with a certain alacrity, and taken off triumphantly, only to catch an errant wave that had appeared from nowhere, and sent it fiercely off course. For all his advantage of age, university education, and the sturdier design, he had to watch, awestruck, as his raft spiralled out of control, only to end up lodged against the large bank of mud on the opposite side of the river. Nature had even decided that a particularly boat hugging stick should stick out into the stream, further blocking its way , and sadly that was where it was going to stay.

Walter blew frantically through his lips in its direction, as if its force would traverse the expanse of the stream and break it free from its hold. But it wasn't to be.

'Ha ha!' Tommy exclaimed.

'Out of the way, Walter,' Catherine said, dismissing him, and carelessly pushed him to one side.

'Two left,' Phillip called excitedly. 'Come on Edward!'

'Are you sure you are my brother, Judas?' Catherine spat at him as she looked back over her shoulder.

Phillip smiled mischievously.

The support was now split. Phillip called excitedly for Tommy's craft, whilst Walter, to level the numbers cheered for Catherine. Georgia in her tactful way, and loyalty torn between the two, cheered them both along.

The two remaining craft jostled for position as they progressed towards the finishing line. Both of the owners were impressed at the way their craft had managed to hold together. They urged them along vivaciously, but slowly, and to the horror of the owners, the two survivors started to veer towards each other.

'Don't you dare,' Catherine yelled, as if Tommy had somehow orchestrated the manoeuvre himself.

With the finishing line only yards away, Catherine's raft moved ahead ever so slightly and crossed in front of Tommy's, blocking its path. It refused to give up its line, and as the two boats crossed the line, it was clearly Catherine's race, by a nose.

Catherine, far from ladylike in her manner, charged triumphantly into the water in pursuit of her winning craft. With no due care or attention, she splashed her way over towards the spot where the water fell the foot or so into the pond beyond. She stepped out and down to recover it, and as her foot settled upon a submerged rock, she slipped, lost her balance and fell headlong in a huge splash and disappeared below the water.

Tommy laughed hysterically despite his loss, but it seemed forever before Catherine eventually emerged, soaked to the skin. Everyone joined Tommy in his laughter, but despite her bedraggled state, she held out the remains of her now desolate raft and declared, 'The winner!'

Georgia helped her ashore, and tried her best to arrange her hair, as much as the water, and the various remnants of the pond that had attached to it would allow, and gave her a congratulatory hug.

'You cheated,' Tommy said clutching at straws, as he looked across at her victorious pose. He walked after her declaring the race a draw, but Catherine put fingers in her ears and tunefully 'La La La'd,' totally ignoring his protestations on her victorious walk back to the camp.

Walter, Georgia and Phillip now followed on behind, deflated.

Walter and Georgia were going through a post-race examination of their model rafts, discussing the pros and cons of each. Phillip with nothing to show for his exploits just sat there, offering advice where he thought it appropriate. Tommy walked across trying to make a case for his efforts to the trio, when Catherine walked past with a twig held out in his direction.

'Your craft I believe,' she said, and smirked.

'I was robbed,' Tommy answered.

'Robbed! You weren't worth pilfering.'

Georgia quickly stepped between the two, confirming the result and telling them both to learn to live with it. One gracious in victory, the other sporting in defeat.

'There you go,' Catherine said. 'Be sporting.'

Georgia growled at her, reminding her of the meaning of the word gracious, and leaving their quarrel to one side, pointed out there was something to be said for all of the rafts in the post race debate.

'I won. I don't care.'

'I bet you don't,' Tommy said.

'And I believe I have a day of being waited on, hand and foot.'

'No change there then,' Tommy added, and opening up the conversation, declared, 'and besides, I would rather spend the rest of my life here than set one foot on a raft designed by you.'

'That can be arranged.'

Walter ignored the banter and sat restructuring different pieces of wood in a number of ways.

Tommy looked across, concerned. 'What's up?'

'Just playing,' Walter threw away the work he had put together. Tommy picked it up and put it back in front of him. 'No. Really. I was just ...'

'Make it work.'

Walter, amazed at Tommy's interest, started to show him what he had been doing, and slowly found he was holding court.

63

The completed prototype model of the raft they had all agreed upon, sat in front of them.

'We're safe,' Phillip said, smiling at the individual faces, receiving nothing in reply.

'This is a model,' Walter explained the obvious, and we are a million miles from making a real one.' Phillip's face dampened.

'But it *is* a beginning,' Georgia said, as she sat behind Catherine, unconsciously plaiting her hair, urging the others along to raise their spirits.

'This has been put together using shredded reeds and pieces of plant we have come across here. The only substantial rope - cord - that we have, is what was attached to my parachute. That is nowhere near enough for a raft for one of us, let alone five.'

'But a good start,' Georgia once more interjected. 'A very good start.'

'We need more rope, we find more rope,' Tommy urged them all. 'We've got nothing else to do.' He noticed Georgia's plaiting, and continued, 'You could knit us some.'

'It's called plaiting,' Catherine threw back at him.

'Then plait. Plait like you've never plaited before.'

'We probably don't even have enough wood to build anything suitable,' Walter advised reasonably.

'We live in a bloody forest,' Tommy cursed. 'We'll find the wood. Girls, you find something to…'

'Plait!' Catherine said.

'…Plait,' he concurred.

Assuming the role of safety officer, Tommy informed his quorum that aside from the dangers of falling from the cliffs around the coast, inland, they had nothing to fear. There were no animals that they had to avoid. Except for Phillip, everyone had crossed the island back and forth several times, and but for the natural fear that night brought about, they were all safe. They appeared to have food and water for the foreseeable future, and apart from being shipwrecked, they had everything they needed.

'Except?' Catherine foresaw a stumbling block.

'Except rope.' he informed them. 'We have actually got enough wood to build an ark with, but nothing to hold it together. Walter and I can get all the wood, but girls, you've gotta find something to – plait – to tie it all up.

'It will take ages,' Catherine complained.

'We've got ages.'

The five volunteers resolutely agreed to pool their resources in an attempt to find solutions to their worries. But as Tommy and Walter walked off on their first forage for suitable wood, the girls sat down and sighed. Walter stopped and looked back.

'What?' Tommy demanded, suddenly short of his workmate.

'What on earth are we really supposed to use?' Catherine spoke for the pair. 'Wood? It's everywhere. Rope! Tell us what to search for, and we'll work till we drop.'

'Just try!' Tommy demanded, and grabbing Walter, the pair marched off.

Georgia grabbed Catherine's hand, and clueless, the pair clasped hands, and walked off together.

The entire collection of knives on the island was of little or no use at all where timber felling was concerned. The suitable lumber was going to have to be that which did not need heaving right across the entire length of the island, or that which had fallen through natural causes.

The initial pieces of wood that had been brought back were of every shape and size due to its availability rather than it fitting the bill. The pieces that were surplus to requirement were quickly handed over to Phillip, who during his slow recovery, had insisted upon light duties, and he would use them as firewood.

Tommy and Walter, far from everyday farm folk, had bound rags around their virgin hands to stop the forming of blisters. With Phillip already down, they could ill afford another body down. The dressings were not foolproof, and Walter suggested quality, not quantity, and Tommy, already feeling the strain of the work, readily agreed.

Despite the relative safety on the island, Georgia had decided, for all the added stress, that it was probably safer to have Catherine by her side than let her wander off alone. They would search together. It would certainly take longer, but in the long run... Catherine, despite her relatively short period of time on the island, had still only recently adjusted to the wildlife and all of its ins and outs. She still needed to be tended on nearly every occasion, and delighted in Georgia's decision, following her like a magnet.

'Promise me you won't tell anyone,' Catherine said, 'but I haven't got a clue what we're looking for.'

'Only if you promise you won't tell anyone that I haven't got a clue either.'

'We've got nothing else to do. Anyway! We can't be the first people to be stranded. Let's think what Robinson Crusoe might have done.'

Georgia looked back, impressed, and proud of Catherine's resilience, gave her a hug, and they walked on.

The wood was stacked up like a bonfire, and Phillip had done his best to sort out what had been brought back into some semblance of order, but he had been commanded not to even try to lift anything that looked remotely heavy. *Anything that looks like it may be too heavy, you leave it alone*, Walter had insisted. He had nodded obediently, but not wanting to appear useless, he struggled as best as his sleight body would allow.

Tommy and Walter sat by the fire exhausted, sharing stories, as the girls, having provided a light meal, sat on the far side examining the possibilities of making anything useful out of what they had brought back. They fiddled and fussed over various pieces of plant, and toyed and muddled with anything suitable, trying to plait or knot together something that might be offered as something to show for their day's efforts.

Phillip, feeling useless had slunk away and sat with the chicks. They seemed no happier for his company, but he had fed them so he felt at least for that moment, they owed him their company.

Much of the following week was taken up in similar pursuits, and apart from an expedition in the form of a hunting party one morning, the camp had been turned into a builder's yard. The girls had triumphantly concocted some form of binding from a mixture of reeds they had found down by the stream, and although it had seemed fairly lightweight, Catherine excelled herself. As much of a surprise to herself as everyone else, she had managed to strengthen it with the introduction of a concoction of mud and other substances she had somehow dug out of the stream. Indeed on drying out, it seemed to fit the bill substantially, and the girls were now able to work away merrily, and on equal terms.

The continued search for anything close to the correct pieces of wood they might need, and the necessity to methodically search the entire island had brought Tommy and Walter close to the spot where Tommy had hidden his plundered swag from the gallery. He had not been back for some time, having satisfied himself that if it had lasted this long undiscovered, it would last a lot longer. On reaching it ahead of Walter, even he had trouble spotting the exact spot behind which lay the entrance to the cave. He quickly removed anything that looked as if it might be in any way useful before Walter arrived, and he mentally patted himself on the back as Walter walked straight past without so much as a second glance. Tommy quickly led him away.

Phillip was totally absorbed in the raft making, and recounted the story of Huckleberry Finn on countless occasions to anyone who would listen to him. He had even got round to calling Tommy, Tom Sawyer, and it took some time for Tommy to relate to hearing the name Tommy again as he had fully immersed himself in the persona of Edward Burrows, and now no longer flinched at the mention of the name Edward.

'Look at him,' Georgia said to Tommy in the midst of one of Phillip's narrations. 'If this doesn't work, it will break him.'

'If this doesn't work, it will break me, never mind him,' Tommy confessed. 'So we'd better make it work.'

'Of course,' Georgia nodded vigorously, but her face did not breed confidence.

With so much cord and twine needed, the girls had tried in vain to teach the boys the art of plaiting. But for all their efforts, it appeared to be a craft more suited to girls, and it seemed easier for the pair of them to get on with it on their own, rather than waste any more time trying to convert the boys. Catherine wasn't overly sure that the boys simply weren't trying, just to get out of it.

Phillip had retired to bed as Tommy returned to a soulful Walter, and dumped himself on the floor in a useless heap.

'What's wrong?' Walter asked him.

'What's right?' Tommy sighed. Walter looked across, concerned, and threw another lump of wood onto the fire. 'That could be our mast you've just toasted there.'

'Perhaps!' Walter laughed. 'What is wrong?'

Tommy looked across to check the two girls were engrossed in conversation of their own, and reluctantly opened up.

'We,' he indicated the three other children with himself, 'were all, by some strange coincidence, thrown together aboard a ship, bound for some strange country or other.' Walter nodded, comprehendingly. 'We also, by some means or other, ended up inside a lifeboat as castaways, for what seemed like weeks, but was probably just – days. By some small chance in a million, we were thrown up on this godforsaken island in the middle of nowhere, and have to be thankful that we were saved.' Walter nodded again, a good listener. 'We were safe.' Walter shifted his position, keeping concentration as Tommy continued his narration. 'By some strange fluke we met you, and we have all somehow come to live together, under – not exactly the best of circumstances.' He straightened himself up. 'Now, having somehow survived the perils of the sea in a made to measure lifeboat, specially built for the purpose, found food, water, and safety, we now all want to submit ourselves to fresh perils out there in the open sea on board a raft that is going to be made of sticks.' He pointed across to the wood, which was still stacked according to size. 'Why would that be?'

'For them!' Walter pointed across at Phillip and the girls.

'Them?'

'Yes. Them!' Walter sighed. 'That you are all here is somehow...' he struggled for the right word. 'Providence,' he continued. Tommy frowned. 'It was foretold. It was meant to be. Preordained.' Tommy still looked confused. 'Er - There is no going back.' Tommy's eyes widened. 'No. I mean... we cannot change the past.' Tommy relaxed slightly. 'What we are doing now is something we *have* to do. It is a hope. It is a reason to get up every day, yes?'

Tommy thought for a moment, and then nodded, 'Yes.'

Walter leant back, and taking a wallet from his uniform jacket, pulled out the photo of his children from inside. He thought for a second, and then offered it to Tommy, realising some short time ago it would have been thrown straight onto the fire. Tommy accepted it and unusually showed a growing interest in both it, and Walter's life, and the pair talked quietly into the night.

The following morning Tommy and Walter worked busily, sorting through the wood they had salvaged. They quickly and sadly determined that much of the wood they had gathered was useless for building purposes, and realised it would soon only become fodder for Phillip's fire. They looked across at the large pile of wood they had decided to keep, and debated which of the pieces ought to go where. Some of the pieces were far too long, and nothing short of an axe was going to do anything about that, so a second seeding of the wood was undertaken.

'I've got more splinters from that piece of wood, than from all the other pieces put together,' Tommy gestured to a freshly rejected log that he was sure he had dragged the entire length of the island. 'And now it's no good.'

'I'll burn it for you,' Phillip shouted across.

'I could have got you something far more suitable from just over there,' Tommy ranted, his effort destined for the fire regardless.

'You can content yourself that you brought it back just to stop me getting cold,' Catherine called across.

Tommy's reply was mumbled, and probably the better for that.

The girls had stuck rigidly to their task and had produced a fair supply of binding. 'Wope', as Phillip had named it. He told them that rope made out of weed had to be called 'Wope' and the name had been adopted. He busily frustrated the girls in their efforts, and as each piece was laid to one side, he picked it up and stretched it as tightly as he could.

'Stop testing everything we do to see if you can find fault. Go and do something else,' Catherine reproached him. Phillip moved away and clutched at his side. 'And you can pack that in. Besides, you are very nearly fitter than I am now.'

'Behave, the pair of you,' Georgia tried to stop the clash, and then informed her that if the strapping could not take a trial from Phillip, there was no way it would survive a seagoing journey. Catherine conceded, and a smug Phillip walked away putting the latest piece through its paces, whistling victoriously.

'That boy!' Catherine growled. 'The sooner we get home, the sooner we can get back to normal.'

'Let's hope we all can,' Georgia confirmed. 'Let's hope we all can.'

Catherine looked up, having realised she wasn't the only one going through periods of depression, and coming to terms with the fact that they were going nowhere until they had built the raft, muscled down to her work once more.

Walter had fully opened up his heart to Tommy in their now frequent fireside chats, and Tommy had unusually absorbed everything he had revealed. But despite the softening in their association, and an unspoken understanding that anything said between the two would remain that way, Tommy did not feel able to reveal anything more about his past than he had revealed to any of the others there. He had many times thought about his past, the death of his father, his escape, and his new identity. He was often so content with his lot, that it was only on rare occasions - and at times when he cussed himself for doing something wrong - that he even thought of himself as Tommy. He even found that he now referred to himself as Edward, but was still surprised, his true identity had survived the test of time this long.

No! Just for the time being, he decided it was better to keep it that way.

'Come on slackers,' Phillip brought them both back to the present. 'It won't build itself, you know?'

Walter rose, and held out a hand for Tommy, which he grabbed, and was dragged to his feet.

Phillip watched, impressed. 'Good! Now get on with it.'

'Fine by me,' Tommy agreed, 'but someone has to feed the chicks. You do that.'

'Fine by me, too.'

The raft, as it was, was slowly beginning to take shape. The various lengths of un-honed timber had been laid out on the ground in the desired shape a combination of the five minds had agreed upon. Catherine had informed them that as her raft had won the model race, surely the design ought to be hers. But level heads, and more so, Walter's age, finally won the day, and the main bulk of the design was eventually his.

Walter had laid out the lengths of twine they had managed to salvage from the parachute beside the wood they had selected and provisionally put together. He and Tommy walked around the raft, and pointed out the joins that would need the strongest support. They selected, and then laid the suitable lengths of twine on the ground beside the raft, and once it was depleted, turned their attention to the girls' efforts.

The hand-made contributions from the girls had been carefully amassed, but left to the side of the collection of the wood, and would only be used where the stress on their efforts would not be so reliant. It was also pointed out that the longer it was left to dry out, the stronger it might become.

Walter was crouched over one corner of the raft surveying a possible joint. He shook his head pessimistically, but said nothing. Georgia laughed as Tommy and Phillip dipped and dodged from side to side, turning their heads from right to left, tutting, giving their own personal views on the structure.

'Well?' Catherine asked Walter, the organ grinder, ignoring the views of the two monkeys.

Walter sighed, and shook his head. 'We haven't got the tools to make this safe enough to...'

'...set out to sea tonight,' Tommy swept the conversation along, without bringing the enthusiasm down.

'Yes! Like he says,' Walter concluded. 'There is nothing to stop us trying. We are however still short of wood.'

'But we have plenty here,' Phillip pointed out, indicating the multitude of logs and branches that lay around, freshly abandoned.

'It is not the right wood.'

'But we're surrounded by the stuff,' Tommy added, almost unnecessarily.

'What about the wood from the fire we have ready to use for the beacon?' Catherine asked. 'Have we checked through that?'

'That's already the beacon,' Tommy pointed out.

'But we won't need it once we've set sail. We don't want to come back here. Can't we use that?' She looked to Georgia for help. 'Surely it makes sense?'

Georgia raised an interested eyebrow.

Walter nodded, concurring.

'But the beacon?' Phillip complained. 'What about if we need to light it before we have the raft made?'

There was an uncomfortable silence as the two options were weighed up.

'We do both!' Catherine jumped in, gesturing with her arm. 'Replace any of the wood we need from the fire, with all the useless stuff we have around here.'

Georgia, convinced, smiled proudly, almost as if her star pupil had just been presented to the world.

'Brilliant!' Tommy exclaimed, surprising everyone.

Phillip refused to hold Catherine's eye, but out of the corner of his eye, he was sure she was poking her tongue out at him.

64

Once Catherine's idea of at least examining the wood from the older beacon, and the better of it had been brought down for use on the raft, excitement grew.

Phillip suggested that they should light what was left of the old beacon fire immediately. What possible harm could it do? Once they were aboard the raft, they wouldn't be coming back anyway. If it was lit, it could be seen from much farther away, and any passing ship could come in to rescue them. Then they wouldn't need the raft anyway.

'It's a good idea,' Tommy started to explain. 'But what if we light it, and use up all the wood on the island too soon? What do we do then? If anything goes wrong?'

'What if we set off on the raft, and any rescuers come to the island and we have gone?' Catherine added to the quandary.

'We can leave you here, just in case,' Phillip told her, angry that plans were not working out quite as simply as he had thought they might be.

here was an uncomfortable silence. Walter looked away, chewing on his lip.

'Well?' Tommy asked him quietly.

'Let's just finish the raft first,' Georgia interrupted. 'If it's ready to set sail, we can think about it then. What do you say?'

The problem may well have been dispelled for the time being, but there were certainly questions to be answered.

The girls, almost inseparable now, worked like there was no tomorrow. They had collected every reed and piece of grass that looked as if it might plait, and there was now a substantial amount of Wope.

Walter and Tommy were so engrossed in the composition of the raft that Phillip – virtually fit and ready to take up duties once more – found himself being ignored. He had badgered the two boys to allow him to help, but had been shunned, and the two girls seemed far happier in each other's company, so he was now at a loss as to what to do with his time. He had spent some moments with the chicks, but already fed, they too seemed better occupied, so he walked off to see if he could do anything to the beacon.

Phillip wandered aimlessly through a small plot of trees, kicking sulkily at anything that got in his way. Fed up, he slumped down onto a pile of leaves, and brooded, petulantly. If no one wanted him, then here was as good a place to be as any. He looked lazily ahead of him, at nothing in particular, and found himself staring at a straight length of wood that he was certain would put him in good stead with both Walter and Tommy. It may even gain himself some credence from his sister. It was a large piece of wood and definitely a job for two, but despite the occasional twinge in his side, and not wanting to have to share the glory of the discovery, he decided the job was his.

He fought gallantly with the piece of wood, and as much as it wanted to remain part of the forest, and his body told him it was the wrong move, Phillip had other ideas.

297

Though his body reacted to the strain, he was not going to give in, and finally, after a valiant struggle, the hefty branch came loose, and Phillip stood back victorious.

The task of freeing the wood done, he now had the job of getting it back to New Camp. He heroically fought his way through undergrowth barely suitable for rabbits, much less a young boy, and at one point, he was certain he was going to have to concede and seek assistance, when suddenly the branch gave way, and he triumphantly broke out into better ground.

Georgia and Catherine both looked up at his approach, and Georgia rose to help him.

'I'm fine,' he insisted, and Georgia sat back down.

'Some help here,' Catherine snapped at Georgia, ignoring Phillip totally.

Phillip breathed in deeply, and summoning all his strength, recommenced his journey.

Walter was stood by the raft, engrossed in its design, and half-heartedly waved at Phillip's approach.

Phillip was annoyed that nobody really cared about his discovery, and currently, Tommy did not even appear to be there at all.

Determined to make a point, and almost exhausted from his efforts, he decided he was going to leave the wood with Walter, and as far as he was concerned, it was positively the last help he was going to offer anyone until the end of the war.

Summoning all his remaining strength, he heaved the stump of the branch into his arms, and started on the final part of his adventure.

Just as the branch seemed comfortable in his arms, and he would finally be able to set aside both it and all his worries, he stepped forward onto a small rock that shifted under the considerable weight of him and the branch, and his ankle gave way.

His foot shot violently to one side, and his leg gave way. Helplessly, in an attempt to break his fall, he released his hold on the branch, and as it fell to one side, he landed in an untidy heap.

'Ow!' Phillip yelled out in pain.

Walter, Georgia and Catherine rushed over to his side, and helped him to his feet.

'I'm okay,' Phillip assured them, angry that it had happened in front of an audience, and brushed himself down.

'You're so clumsy,' Catherine goaded him.

'I thought you might want this,' he pointed down to his gift. 'It's…'

Phillip stopped short. As he looked down at the wood he had brought back, he stared in disbelief at where it had come to rest. The branch had fallen heavily to the floor, and the stump had crashed its way straight through the fence of the chicks' enclosure.

All four heads looked urgently to the occupants.

Three of the chicks - though in truth only Phillip and Tommy could actually put names to them – were loose, and ran round unsure what to do with their freedom. Phillip checked on them, and desperately turned to Catherine. 'Where's Harriet?'

In the sudden confusion, Walter quietly bent down and picked up a small, motionless, feathered body in his hands, and turned it over.

Phillip shoved Catherine out of the way, and looked down into Walter's hands.

'Oh dear!' Walter sighed.

'Fix her, Walter,' Phillip demanded. 'Please! Like you did me.'

Walter turned away from Phillip and fiddled with the limp body. He turned it over in his hands once more, gently rubbing it, and slowly looked up disconsolately, and catching Georgia's enquiring stare, gently shook his head. Phillip caught the slight shake and fell to the floor in tears.

Georgia, passing on the task of herding up the remaining trio to Catherine, rushed across to his aid and hugged him.

'Edward! He's going to kill me,' he mumbled through tears, and breaking from her grip, slumped to the ground.

'It was an accident,' Georgia shouted in an attempt to pacify him.

'What was an accident?' Tommy enquired, returning with another large piece of timber. He immediately caught the distress in Phillip's face.

'I'm so sorry,' Phillip yelled as he noticed him, and as Tommy looked down at the three remaining chicks - playing havoc at Catherine's vague attempt at rounding them up - he rushed off, inconsolably.

Tommy dropped the wood, caught between following Phillip, and discovering the reason for the apology. He looked across at Georgia, who seemed to have tears in her eyes, and then to Walter.

Walter slowly held out Harriet's limp body in front of him.

Tommy slowly walked across as everyone looked to see how he would react. He took Harriet's body in his hands, and after a quiet moment stroking her, laid her on the ground, sniffed strongly, and walked away.

'Don't you dare hurt him,' Catherine screamed.

Tommy ignored her.

The old campsite offered no signs of welcome. Seemingly long since deserted, it turned its back on its visitor. Phillip slumped down beside the disused fire, sorting through what was left of the ashes, but it was pointless, and simply served as a place to be alone.

Tommy, correctly having guessed where he might have gone, walked up behind him, quietly.

'It was an accident, I promise,' Phillip cried. 'I am so sorry. I didn't mean it. Don't you believe me?'

'We've had worse. Your wound? My adventures on the cliff?'

'But I've never killed anything before.'

'The fish? The rabbits?'

'But they weren't pets. And these were yours. I'm so sorry.' He burst into tears once more, and Tommy sitting down beside him, chatted quietly and comforted him.

Tommy returned with Phillip some time later. Catherine looked up quickly at the pair of

299

them, but noticed Phillip looked none the worse for wear. He had cried himself out, but could still not stop apologising. On seeing the others once more, he offered up his apology to them also.

'We must bury her,' Georgia said, respectfully. Tommy nodded.

'Beside the stream?' Phillip asked. 'Please!'

'Beside the stream,' Tommy confirmed.

'And can we make a cross?'

'If we are hoping to complete a raft, I think we can manage a cross,' Walter told him. 'Come on.'

Phillip rushed across to help him.

The children stood reverently behind Walter, who was scooping out the last of the earth from a hole he had somehow managed to dig out beside the stream where they had raced the rafts. He stood and brushed the loose earth from his hands, and stood back to look at Tommy.

Tommy picked up Harriet's body, and deferentially brought it forward. He looked down at her, and sniffed, swallowing hard. He tried to stand up, as if to say something, but was quickly overcome, and had to hand the body across to Walter. He stood back.

Walter, as much caught up in the event as the children, knelt on the ground, and delicately placed Harriet inside the grave.

The children huddled together, and Phillip's tears were accompanied by equally loud sniffs from the girls. Even Tommy wiped a tear that was forming in his eye, and they stood, speechlessly, until Georgia asked if perhaps someone should say a prayer.

They looked bashfully at each other with nothing immediately forthcoming, and eventually all eyes turned to Walter. He stepped forward and ushered them all to the side of the grave. He closed his eyes and dipped his head, and they all followed suit. He spoke in a quiet voice, and each child opened their eyes as he spoke lightly, in German, and seeing that he was in prayer, closed their eyes as he continued.

A short while later he concluded the prayer with an, 'Amen,' and once more they followed suit. They stood back and Tommy bent down. He picked up a handful of the earth that had been piled up beside the grave, and scattered it on top of Harriet, and slowly, each of the funeral party did likewise.

They eventually stood back, and as Walter filled in the hole and patted down the earth, Catherine handed over the cross they had all put together. Tommy planted it at the head of the grave, and after a final moment's silence, they all made their way back to the camp.

65

It was now some days later, and the raft was slowly beginning to take shape. The main frame had been strapped together to the best of their ability, but everyone wanted to attach more and more to it, imagining that the more wood there was, the better it would float. Walter had assured them that that was fine, but pointed out that the more wood they attached, the more cord they would need to use.

After his unfortunate involvement with Harriet, Phillip was resigned to doing nothing. He considered himself to be a bad omen, and didn't mind reminding anyone that cared to listen. He steered clear of any duties involving the raft, and everyone was so worried with his withdrawal, that Tommy had to demand his assistance in getting some fish for everyone's dinner. The purpose of the expedition was not for food, but the fish they managed to catch while Tommy reinvigorated Phillip's spirit, were indeed a bonus. He was better now. Well, nearly.

Walter, mainly due to his age, and an unmatched respect for having attended university, had been duly elected skipper of the raft ahead of its launch. Catherine had decided that the authority from Captain downward should be decided upon age, and that being the case, Tommy might even consider saluting her.

The salute Tommy offered her suggestion was not quite what she had expected, and it was quickly agreed that all tasks should be perhaps be shared out equally amongst the crew as a whole.

It was dark and the children were sat quietly around the fire chatting when Walter walked across, sombrely. He sighed as he warmed his hands over the flames.

'What is it?' Georgia asked.

'I can't tell you.'

'Walter! What is it?' The children huddled together, concerned.

'We have spent so long over the raft, I haven't got the heart to tell you.'

'What?' they all demanded in unison.

Walter looked across, solemnly. 'I think it's ready.'

With that, he jumped out of the way as the quartet jumped to their feet and danced and spun each other around, cheering, whistling and hooting in excitement.

'Wait!' he shouted, as a rejuvenated Phillip rushed around gathering together various items. 'It has to go through trials first. We don't go anywhere until then.' Phillip stopped temporarily, but the excitement was too much to keep him grounded for long, and he ran off again, unrestrained.

'Calm down,' Catherine said, not for the first time trying to assert some discipline on her brother, although she looked equally excited. Phillip dropped everything, and seeing her face, rushed over and grabbed her hand and dragged her across to look at the finished raft. Walter shrugged at Tommy and Georgia who looked equally excited, and almost as desperate to follow them.

'I suppose you both ought to go and check it over,' Walter said to them.   Tommy snatched at Georgia's hand and they hurried across the camp. Walter followed behind at a more sedate pace to allow them all to share the moment together.

'We'll have to be careful in the dark,' Phillip informed them, standing in the centre of the raft. 'We won't know which way we are going until morning.'

'I have told you once. We are not going anywhere until we have taken the raft on several trial runs,' Walter cooled his ardour.

'But you said…'

'I did not say anything of the kind.'

Phillip deflated visibly in front of them.

'What he means,' the ever pliant Georgia said, 'is… I don't know. What do you mean?'

'Do you want to put your trust - your lives - in something we have almost thrown together?

'But it's ready,' Phillip said, thumping his foot down on the raft. One of the smaller pieces of wood beneath the stamp creaked noisily. Phillip froze.

'There you go,' Walter said. 'I should have kept quiet until the morning, but I thought we all needed some good news. Tomorrow! We can start trials on it tomorrow. Till then…'

'Till then?' Georgia repeated. 'What? Go to sleep?'

'I think we are all too excited to go to sleep,' Catherine informed him on everyone's behalf.

'We cannot do anything until morning,' he advised. 'Anybody with a better idea, I am open to suggestions.'

Walter sat by the fire and waited in vain for some of the enthusiasm to die down, but it took some time, and stories of expectant voyages aboard the raft, encounters with pirates and brigands, and imminent rescues carried on deep into the night. Phillip seemed to be in mid-flight running round and round when suddenly there was a lull in proceedings. On closer inspection, sleep appeared to have overcome him, and he was finally curled up, fast asleep. Catherine made to move him, but a firm, hushed, 'No!' from everyone so as not to risk waking him up, encouraged her to leave him exactly where he was, so she sat back.

As excited as they all remained, Walter talked them through a variety of trials and safety tests the raft would have to be put through, to ensure nothing fell off too soon, and certainly before any thought was put to setting out to sea for good.

'Too soon! I would rather it didn't fall off at all,' Tommy ventured.

'Then I will have to be hard on her.'

'You?' Tommy queried.

'I don't want to endanger anyone's lives until I know she is fit to sail.' Tommy looked suspicious. 'Oh! You think I want to go off on my own? Leave you all here?

No. I just thought as the oldest one here, I should…'

'It's not that,' Tommy said apologetically. 'I just want to help.'

'It's all right. You can tie me up now if you want. To make sure I don't steal it during the night,' Walter laughed.

'No,' Tommy smiled. 'No need for that.'

'Let him do it all,' Catherine said to Walter, indicating Tommy. 'If he floats off never to return again, then it won't all be a total loss.'

'Fine by me. I'd sooner encounter sharks.'

'Give them my love.'

'Why don't we all try to get to sleep?' Georgia suggested. 'I am sure morning will not get here any sooner by sitting up.'

They all settled down.

'Walter? Are you still there?' Tommy asked through a laugh.

'Still here,' he answered, equally amused.

'Go to sleep, both of you,' Georgia warned them. '*Good night!*'

Whether the original idea for the raft had been for a much smaller model, or that not enough thought had been made as to exactly how far they would need to move the finished craft upon completion, was soon obvious. Perhaps it had been that it had always been a pipe-dream in the first place.

The five craftsmen stood and surveyed their finished monster, and no matter in which direction they looked, the path to the coast did not appear to be any closer than any other. Nor in fact, did any combination of moves make the raft any the lighter.

'We should have built an aircraft,' Tommy said. 'We wouldn't have had a runway for that either.

'That's not very helpful,' Catherine said, seeing the dismay in the others' faces.

'But practical nonetheless.'

'We either take it apart and rebuild it, or we drag it,' Walter informed them, angry that hr hadn't envisaged this problem. 'Either way it will take…'

'Forever,' Phillip shouted, and ran off. The others watched him disappear, but on this occasion felt just as downbeat as he did, though nobody made to take off after him.

'Forever is right,' Georgia sighed, and as she slumped down, the others joined her.

Forever, in fact, was the best part of three long days and nights. A partial deconstruction had been necessary. The whole craft had needed to be carefully transported, before reassembling with cord they had miraculously managed to save, and new Wope to replace that which had needed to be cut to enable the deconstruction to take place at all. The newly erected craft finally sat beside a sea that lapped up onto the shore, and everyone sat back, exhausted.

The delay of the launch date, and the loss in time it had incurred, had not been all bad. The weather had now taken a turn for the better, and an agreed full nights rest had been insisted upon before anything else took place. Tempers had been stretched to their very limits, and at times, certain repaired allegiances were put to the test, until at last, one sunny morning, they all stood ready to put, 'Harriet' - the agreed name for the raft - through her paces.

Walter rolled up the legs of what was left of his uniform trousers, and stood in the shallows waiting to drag the raft out onto the sea for its maiden voyage.

Tommy was reluctant to stay ashore during the first sea trial, but after much persuasion from Georgia, had eventually agreed that perhaps Walter should indeed take the first outing.

'Besides, Landlubber!' Catherine goaded him. 'We don't want you sinking it just yet.'

Tommy scowled at her.

Despite its considerable size, though it seemed much smaller now with the sea as a background, the construction suddenly looked decidedly rickety. Any reservations anyone had about the future success of the raft were kept to themselves, so Walter, watched by an enthralled audience, dragged *Harriet* forward until the sea gently lapped against her bow.

Everything appeared to be going well. *Harriet* moved resolutely out onto the water, and as buoyancy took effect, she had passed her first test. She floated.

The tide pushed *Harriet* back towards shore, and unexpectedly, she snagged on a gnarled piece of wood jutting out angrily from the shore, almost refusing to let her go.

Catherine, catching everyone unawares, and without a second thought to her own safety, leapt into the water. She launched herself onto the rear of the raft, hoping her momentum might shift it from its mooring.

So stuck did *Harriet* appear to be, that Walter's attention was currently elsewhere, and only once he had fully cleared the obstruction did he fully realise that Catherine was there at all.

The release from its hold on the island momentarily unsettled the boat, and Catherine, far from steady on her sea-legs, firstly wobbled, then fell to her backside in the centre of the raft.

'It must be quite sturdy then,' Tommy nudged Georgia, before he had really taken in what had just happened..

Catherine sat where she was, in the centre of the boat and looked up at Walter. 'Well?'

'Are you okay? Nothing broken?' Catherine looked around the raft. 'Not Harriet. You?'

'I'm fine!' Catherine smiled back, contentedly.

'I must get you ashore,' Walter said, and turned to look back towards Georgia, Tommy and Phillip, now some distance away.

Catherine noted the dismay in Walter's face, and looked back for some comfort from Georgia on the shoreline. It was only at this point that she noted the almost undisguisable sight of envy on Tommy's face, and quickly turned her worried visage into one of glee.

Two experimental paddles that had been roughly put together, lay on the surface of the raft. Walter signalled that Catherine should pick one up. He took the other, and somehow, balanced on opposite sides of the raft, the two started a hesitant series of strokes through the water.

Georgia led a series of loud cheers from the shore, echoed by Phillip, and soon, Tommy, having been caught up in the excitement, cheered along with them.

Walter shouted anxious instructions in Catherine's direction, desperate for her safety, but it was unnecessary. Somehow, between the two of them, and be it more luck than judgement, the raft seemed to be under control.

'To shore!' Walter yelled.

'To sea!' Catherine shouted back. 'Let's test her out.'

Short of throwing her off the raft, there was very little Walter could do about it, and Catherine did not look overly out of place on board.

Walter now resigned to her company, instructed Catherine, as best possible, and soon, incredibly, they seemed to have mastered some sort of control of the craft. Between the two of them, they began to put *Harriet* through her early paces. They swapped positions several times, paddling on opposite, then the same side of the raft, each time coming to grips with navigation, and discovering what the oars would allow them to do.

After some time, the pair finally steered *Harriet* back towards shore.

'My turn,' Tommy shouted from the shore.

Just as the raft seemed under control and heading for shore, it caught an awkward wave, drawing it back out to sea.

'You're doing that purposely,' Tommy shouted, wrongly assuming this was due to clever boatmanship and not because of the swell of the sea.

'Be careful! Don't go out too far!' Georgia shouted.

'Bye bye! See you in England!' Catherine called, and waved heartily as the raft drifted out a little further to sea.

Georgia smiled and continued waving, but suddenly saw what the crew of the raft had not. At the rear of the raft, one of the main bindings had started to come loose, and unbeknownst to those aboard, one of the larger structural pieces had started to edge its way loose.

'Look out!' she shouted to them.

But Catherine was having far too much fun and screeched continuously, provoking Tommy. Georgia shouted again, and Tommy finally cottoned on to her concern. He too jumped up and down, pointing to the rear of the raft, But this only egged on Catherine all the more. As she almost danced a jig, she stumbled slightly, and put her foot behind her to gain her balance. What had been there, moments before, had now come apart, and as her foot gave way, she collapsed backwards.

Walter watched the whole thing in what seemed like slow motion, and swiftly leapt to grab her hand.

305

But it was too late.

Catherine put out a hand to stop her fall, but as the raft shifted, she missed grasping hold of anything at all. As she lost her balance, she stared at the water that was considerably choppier now than it had been by the shore, and appeared to be coming closer by the second. Her legs gave way, and as she cried out, helplessly, she toppled and fell headlong into the sea.

Walter was caught between diving from the raft to save Catherine, and trying to keep what was left of the raft together. They had both dropped their paddles, and the raft was fast drifting out of control. He looked off the edge of the raft towards Catherine, and crouching down, flapped his hands in the water, trying to manoeuvre it in her direction to allow her to climb aboard.

Tommy had had no such concerns. Quickly stripping off the majority of his clothing in what seemed like a second, and finally clad only in his under-shorts, he dived straight into the sea and swam out frantically towards her.

Catherine started to panic. The sudden cold of the sea-water shot through her body, and struggling to come to the surface, she struck out for shore. She waved her arms, no stranger to swimming, but as she tried to kick out with her feet, the length of what was left of her dress caught round her legs, binding them together, and she froze. She looked around helplessly, but as her mouth opened to scream, nothing came out. An ill-timed wave washed over her head, and as the water entered her mouth, she started to sink.

Tommy stretched out, his arms fighting the water between Catherine and him. He kicked his feet wildly, and just as her head disappeared beneath the waves, he grabbed at her hair and drew her head back to the surface. Kicking his feet furiously, treading water, he just managed to get his arms under her shoulders. Turning onto his back with Catherine's unresponsive body on top of his, he somehow managed to steer them both back in the direction of the shore.

Catherine, opening her eyes, snatched herself free from Tommy's hold, and struck out hysterically with her arms. Her closed hand struck Tommy squarely on the nose, and instinctively, he released his hold on her.

Tommy impulsively clasped at his nose, but somehow managed to keep his mind fixed on the job in hand. He shook the pain from his head, and shouted at her.

Further adding to problems, Catherine's body now seemed to seize up. Tommy, thinking quickly, grabbed at the material on her shoulder. He reached down with his feet to see if he could stand up, but he was clearly still too far out, so before she started to panic again, Tommy reached out and started swimming towards shore with just the one arm, holding firmly onto her with the other.

Walter, helplessly watching the rescue from afar, frantically tried to steer the remainder of the raft safely back to shore.

Tommy finally heaved Catherine's body onto dry land, where she struggled, now hitting out in wild panic. Georgia and Phillip arrived quickly, and leaving Tommy to his own devices for the moment, started to rub furiously at Catherine's body in an attempt at getting some feeling back into her limbs. They too had to avoid her flailing arms, but as she stared into Georgia's face, her resistance gave way, and in seconds she was sat in a heap, sobbing furiously.

Georgia now rushed over to see if Tommy was okay. He seemed far less affected by the cold of the sea, and though shaking from his encounter, managed to get himself to his feet, and brushing off a caring arm, walked across to see what was left of Catherine.

Catherine was crying cold tears, and her body shivered uncontrollably. Phillip now fussed over both of them, but Tommy held out his hands to her and she grasped them gratefully as he helped her to her feet.

'You okay?' he asked her.

'Fine,' Catherine lied through chattering teeth. Tommy put his arms out and she fell into them and nestled her head into his shoulder crying once more. She hugged him like she might never let go, and Tommy whispered soft words in her ears. Georgia walked over to relieve him, but Tommy shook his head at her approach. She smiled sweetly and grabbing Phillip by the shoulder, encouraged him to go with her to help Walter.

Walter, having struggled with the quickly disintegrating raft, had by now, managed to get it to shore, where Georgia and Phillip did their best to help him to drag it safely onto dry land. Once there, they left it to its own devices, and the three bodies rushed back to the aid of the two drowned fish.

66

The eventual debrief on *Harriet's* performance, and an examination of her remains was to be left until much later in the day. The five dejected islanders sat around a now roaring fire, and conversation was at a minimum.

Catherine and Tommy were now much healthier for the warmth of the fire, but several items of their clothing still hung on sticks nearby until they were thoroughly dried out.

'So we've had it?' Phillip opened his case for the opposition.

'Maybe just a slight hiccup?' Georgia mediated.

A debate ensued with opinions swaying firstly one way, then the other. Tommy was strangely quiet, allowing the conversation to flow back and forth keeping his thoughts to himself. Walter, still shaken over Catherine's misadventures, insisted that he give the raft a thorough examination before anyone decided anything. He started to get to his feet.

'No!' Georgia said, indicating Tommy and Catherine. 'Not now. It can wait. There is no benefit in doing anything now. Sit down. All of you.'

'It was all my fault,' Catherine apologised to the assembled company, seemingly taking the weight of the world upon her shoulders.

'Don't be silly,' Georgia protected her. 'If it hadn't been you, it might have been…'

'Me!' Tommy said. 'It might have been me.'

'I was going to say, all of us. And besides, the fault was neither of yours. It was the raft's fault. It didn't matter who was aboard it.

'I will have to recheck the bindings,' Walter said.

'You don't have to check anything,' Tommy informed him. 'No one is going anywhere on it. Not now. Not ever.'

Walter shrugged, and sat back down.

Tommy climbed to his feet, and taking his items of clothing from the fire, started to walk away. He checked in his pocket to see that the lighter was still there, and leaving the others to it, quietly disappeared.

Georgia was the first to notice Tommy's prolonged absence. Everyone was absorbed in their own thoughts about the day's events, and she seemed to have been the only one to notice quite how quiet he had been. She thought about taking off after him, but wondered if she were simply being over motherly. One look at Catherine as she shook, still far from warmed through, and she realised her interests were better occupied where she was. Tommy would have to take care of himself for now. She caught Catherine's eye, but her enquiry was ignored as she simply moved closer to the fire, and scrunched herself into a slightly tighter ball.

The moon lit the sky, and a myriad of stars filled the firmaments. Tommy sat quietly beside the remains of the raft, staring at it. It lay, undisturbed, exactly where Walter had left it earlier. The thrill and hope of the quintet was no longer there. The raft was no longer anything more than a pile of sticks.

After a few more moments, lost in thought, Tommy rose and walked across to *Harriet*. He slowly walked around the frame of the raft, idly kicking at several of the points where the bindings still held, and bending down, picked at the work the girls had spent countless hours plaiting together. They shredded with little or no effort, no longer affording any resistance. He kicked at the structure once more, and as still more debris fell to the ground, he stood back before starting to walk away.

After only a few paces, Tommy stopped and looked back at it. His mind returned to Catherine, struggling in the sea. He saw her helpless face, and the tears she had shed upon rescue. He fingered the lighter in his pocket for the hundredth time, and now took it out. It wasn't going to happen again. Of that he was sure.

A small fire, quickly put together with a handful of mercifully dry sticks and leaves, started to gain strength. Tommy added more and more fuel to the fire, and slowly, the smaller pieces of wood started to catch.

As sparks started to fly from *Harriet*, and a steady fire now overtook her body, Tommy sat back and watched her demise totally unmoved by his actions.

For all the care Catherine was going to need over the next couple of days, Tommy had been gone far too long for Georgia's liking, and she was now unable to leave him alone any longer. She left with the same casualness that Tommy had, and fortunately there was no inquisition into her departure. She walked off in the same direction in which he had, and guessing that he had gone back to the raft, to lay to rest any ghosts of the day, followed the same route.

She smelt the smoke long before she saw him, and rushed down to see what was going on.

Tommy stood over the burning raft, and despite hearing footsteps, he did not turn to see who it was. Georgia stopped by his side, flabbergasted.

'What have you...?'

'We could all have died,' he answered, before she had even finished the sentence. 'We could all have died.'

'But you can't. We...'

'What? Did you really think we were going to rebuild her and try again? Did you think I would let any of us get on board something like that again?'

'So you decided, for all of us?'

'I did what needed to be done.'

Walter arrived, accompanied by Catherine and Phillip, and the trio stared at the fire.

'What have you done?' Catherine asked, rather than yelled.

'You nearly died.'

'I...' the sentiment robbed the words from her. 'I...'

'But now we're stuck here,' Phillip said.

'You wouldn't have got any further than there,' Tommy pointed out to sea, reminding them exactly how far the raft had travelled before coming to grief. 'Is that what you wanted?'

'But I can swim. I would have been all right.'

'If you could swim all the way back to England you wouldn't need the raft in the first place.' Phillip fell silent, his protest brought to an abrupt halt.

Tommy sat down by *Harriet's* shell, and looked into the flames. He calmly repeated exactly what he had said to Georgia, and then fell silent.

'He's right!' Walter announced, further explaining how he had never intended any of the children to have climbed aboard the raft until she was fully seaworthy. Her sea-trials had failed.

'But we could have...' Phillip started.

'No we couldn't,' Catherine finalised. 'No we couldn't.'

'Then we are all here until someone finds us,' Catherine said, as the last of the flames on *Harriet* started to die out. 'Is that it?'

'Unless you wake up and find God has given you wings overnight, then that's about it,' Tommy said. He climbed to his feet, and slumped off back towards camp, followed closely by the others.

'Thank you,' Catherine whispered as she walked past him on the way back. 'For everything you did for me. That was really sweet,' and before he could react, she walked off, without once looking back.

67

Some days had passed and Walter and the children, having worked their way through various temper tantrums, guilt complexes, and general disillusionment, had settled down to the fact that, barring a miracle, and certainly for the near future, they were all stuck where they were. The beacon, it had been decided, should be lit, and should burn constantly - short of them stripping the woodland bare - and the camp had now spread out slightly more. Rotas had been agreed upon, and somehow been kept to, and boredom was now the only major issue.

Tommy was stood by the 'Larder,' as Catherine had insisted on calling it, checking on supplies. One of the chicks, Daisy, squawked noisily behind him.

'You be quiet and behave yourself,' he warned her lightly, 'or you'll end up in here for dinner.'

Daisy squawked all the louder for his counsel, and he pointed a warning finger in her direction.

'You've got me talking to myself,' he chastised Daisy, and crouched down beside her.

Daisy reacted angrily, jumping up and down, furiously waving her wings.

Tommy watched fascinated.

'Come here,' he shouted to the others. 'Quickly!'

They all rushed across hurriedly from their various duties, and mustered beside him.

'Look!' he told them, and picking up Daisy, threw her gently a few feet into the air. She hovered momentarily, and then fell to the ground with a thump.

'I think it is a cat that is supposed to land on its feet,' Catherine advised him, 'not Daisy.'

'But didn't you see. She beat her wings. They can fly. They are old enough to fly.'

'Well good luck, mummy duck,' Catherine said, the first to decline that particular duty. 'They are all yours.'

'Remember!' Walter warned him. 'Once they fly, they may well leave for good.'

Phillip groaned at the idea.

'Well, they're hardly prisoners,' Tommy said. 'Sure, they would never have survived without us…'

'Without you,' Georgia laid the majority of the praise where it was due.

'…but I think we are going to have to let them go.'

'No!' Phillip yelled. 'I don't want them to go.'

'One day, every bird has to fly the coop,' Catherine said. 'Even Daisy.'

'Yes! They can't be looked after forever. It just isn't fair,' Tommy told Phillip.

'But!' Walter pointed down at the three chicks. 'They are going to need to be a little bit stronger than that. So they won't be going anywhere too soon.'

Tommy grabbed at Dick, and as he pecked angrily at his hand, he threw him up in the same manner he had Daisy.

Dick flew with the same enthusiasm that Daisy had, but landed in a equally useless heap. He struggled to get to his feet, but having done so, shook his feathers and took off to join his kin, squabbling angrily.

'Yes. I think you may have a job on your hands there, just yet,' Georgia said. 'Good luck.'

Over the following number of days, Tommy and Phillip, though taking their task seriously, were a source of constant amusement, alternately casting one of the chicks to the other in an attempt at strengthening their wings. The early shaking of the wings on Daisy's maiden attempt at flight had been a fluke. Indeed, the chicks had had to be moved to a softer landing ground for their lessons, as despite all their bird like qualities, they still tended to nose dive, and showed far more interest in the ensuing reward of a feeding session than the continued pursuit of flight.

'I should start padding their feet,' Catherine advised. 'If they fall on the floor any more, they are going to start developing blisters.'

'Ha ha!' Tommy sneered back.

'Maybe they've been grounded,' Georgia put in.

'That's it!' Tommy declared. 'From now on, all flying lessons will be in private.'

Tommy had now even lost the encouragement of his wingman, Phillip, who since the loss of the raft, seemed to lose interest in most things, if an improvement was not instant. Georgia had offered to assist him, but Tommy had decided to take on the task as his personal challenge, and had politely declined the offer.

'Are you sure they are not penguins?' Catherine added to her previous recommendation.

'You wait and see.'

'Don't be too long,' she said. 'I may be an old woman by then.'

The days seemed to drag on and on, and once Phillip had withdrawn from the flight programme, it was only the on-going battle between Tommy and Catherine over the chicks' progress that seemed to raise spirits at all. Any mention of escape from the island inevitably led back to the raft and all that went with it, so that subject was carefully avoided.

Sat around the fire, the mood was weary, and conversation was at a minimum as monotony settled in once more. Phillip was enduring a more than usually strong bout of the blues.

'We are all bored,' Catherine reminded him. 'We are all in the same position.

'You're not missing your birthday,' he mumbled.

'I'm not what? Speak up if you're going to speak at all.'

'Your birthday!' Georgia said.

'When is it?' Tommy asked.

'It's the…'

'It doesn't matter when it is, or was,' Catherine said. 'We don't know what the date is anyway. Nobody has kept a record. I don't even know what day it is, much less what month. It's just been forever. That's all.'

'But it could be your birthday,' Georgia said. 'Let's celebrate.'

'His birthday is months away,' Catherine mumbled in a couldn't care less voice. 'It could of course be Christmas. Does that mean we are all going to sit around and sing carols?' The others looked back, beaten. 'We don't know when it is. Nothing good happens here to any of us any more. Get used to it.'

'Then you won't be interested in watching my youngsters fly tomorrow?' Tommy announced, trying to lighten the mood.

'They're ready to fly?' Georgia exclaimed.

'When?' Phillip asked, quickly forgetting the possibility that it may have been his birthday.

'Tomorrow,' Tommy decided on the spot. 'Tomorrow!'

'But they can't even get off the floor. The rubbish you feed them, I'd be surprised if they could get off the ground if you put a propeller on them,' Catherine laughed.

'Then don't come. They'll be glad to see the back of you.'

'And I them.'

'They *can* fly,' Phillip said. 'Really! I've watched them.'

'Really!'

'Yes. Really!' Walter added. 'I also have watched the effort that has been put in, and I will be happy to watch them. Tomorrow?'

'Tomorrow,' Tommy confirmed.

'Don't forget we probably messed up the raft through rushing things,' Georgia said to Tommy when he was on his own. 'Don't do it too soon. Not just to prove Catherine wrong.'

'Too soon? She's not all wrong. They are becoming dustbins. It is time they were given the chance to join the others. I've seen other young birds flying from the cliffs. It may be just the right time to let them go. We're stuck here, but *they* don't have to be.' He rose and walked her over to the chicks. 'They're a big part of us, but sadly another something we have to come to terms with. They are going to have to go.'

'I wish we could go with them,' she bemoaned quietly.

'So do I,' he concurred.

'Well! Who knows? Maybe we'll all wake up with wings.'

The excitement in the change in routine was slightly overshadowed by the thought that the chicks would no longer be part of their lives. If they did what they had all supposed they would, they would fly away, and for all the care they had been shown, out of their lives.

Though the chicks had largely been ignored by at least three of the party, and Phillip for a good deal of the time, the thoughts of their leaving affected everyone. Tommy had told Phillip that he would have a word with Georgia to see if she could hunt down any

313

more mother gulls, and maybe they could start with a new batch of orphans in no time at all.

'Orphans!' Tommy repeated, reminding himself of his father's departure. 'Orphans!'

Several times during the evening, one or another other of them walked across to wish the chicks their own farewell, or perhaps just using them as listeners to another of their gripes.

As morning dawned, Tommy was far less keen to see them off than he had been the previous night, and he now wondered if he had just offered the spectacle as a form of one-upmanship to Catherine. He spent a long time petting them, and despite their illustrious time together, they still pecked at him irritably as if he had only just found them, and complained furiously at being picked up again.

'Maybe I should have called you Catherine,' he informed Daisy as she chewed at his finger. 'And who knows? Maybe that way, I wouldn't miss you after all.'

He smiled, though sadly, realised the time was fast coming to say goodbye, perhaps forever.

Though it was Tommy who had truly adopted the chicks, and certainly had the major say in all things chick, the decision about their eventual emancipation was decided by everyone together. They had decided that they should be released from the cliffs where they had been found, beside their original landing spot. How long ago had that been? How many birthdays had been missed?

Walter pointed out that perhaps they should eventually let the gulls loose a little way back from the cliff itself. He pointed out that if any of the three needed had second thoughts, the fall from there might not be so far. Hopefully the sound of all the other gulls flying around would alleviate that problem, but it wouldn't hurt, just in case.

It was agreed.

68

The party of five shared the transportation of the birds to their departure point, and nobody escaped a sharp reminder that, despite the kindness shown to them, they were still wildlife, and they were passed from person to person as each of their carers nursed wounds received from ungrateful pecks.

As they neared the landing spot, Tommy took hold of Daisy, Walter held Tom, and Georgia took the final fledgling, Dick, from a very grateful Catherine who though upset at their imminent departure, would probably miss them the least. They stood at the cliff face and after a short farewell ceremony, raised their charges into the air, and waited impatiently.

Catherine was urged to hurry the count along, and she counted, 'One! Two!' and then, after a slight hesitation, 'Three!' At the command, 'Go!' they all threw their charges high into the air.

They stood, huddled together in a group and watched, concerned, as the three fledglings valiantly flapped their wings. Just when it appeared that the three were about to plunge downwards, and require a good deal of First Aid, first Dick, then his brother, and finally Daisy started to battle gravity, and slowly, they started to rise into the air.

Suddenly, they too started to believe in their own ability, and it soon seemed as if all the other birds along the cliff had united in a chorus of encouragement. As their grounded audience watched carefully, they started to circle, slowly at first, teasing the air, and supposedly without as much as a backward glance, away.

The launch complete, and as their sponsors thought they had seen the last of them, the three birds turned sharply and flew back towards the cliff, and as if experimenting landing for the first time, clumsily crash-landed at their feet.

The spectators joyously spun around wildly at their charges' success, grabbing the chicks and throwing them back into the air once more.

The trio quickly joined the other birds in the air, and after a shaky start, united with them in their aerobatics. Walter and the children looked up in admiration and cheered their continued success until the chicks no longer seemed dependent on them. All apart from Tommy, who was indulging himself in a moment of his own. He had lost his children to the big wide world, and he now stared blearily out to sea.

Tommy blinked and looked up once more to the sky, to clear what he imagined were tears from his eyes, causing him a certain amount of blurred vision. He imagined he had seen something in the distance, far out to sea, but could not quite believe it. He wiped at his eyes to further check he was not seeing things.

'Come here!' he shouted, but was ignored as the others continued to cheer at the flypast. 'Come here. Quickly!' he yelled more urgently. The others stopped at the stress in his voice and walked across.

'What?'

'Look!' He pointed down, away from the air display, and back out to sea. 'Look!'

Five pairs of eyes stared out in the direction he had indicated. The eyes started to stretch wider and wider at the sight.

'A ship,' Phillip whispered, and then, 'A ship!' loud enough to pierce the tissue on the eardrums.

The joint excitement at the news of what they could now all see for themselves, married together, and any further interest in the chicks' departure disappeared with them.

'Smoke!' Georgia yelled. 'Smoke!'

'Stay here,' Tommy shouted, and was about to run off when he stressed, 'and wave your arms till they fall off. I'll see to the fire.'

And with that, Tommy rushed off inland, closely followed by Walter.

Tommy and Walter madly threw any wood they could lay their hands upon into the depths of the fire, which though it had continued to burn since it had first been lit, had diminished slightly as the days had gone by. As belief in rescue had dwindled, the interest in the beacon fire seemed to have dwindled with it. Nonetheless, it was still alight, and just needed encouragement.

Tommy and Walter stared into the flames as the new fuel caught, and all too slowly for its stokers' liking, the smoke started to gain both strength and volume.

'Is it ours, or yours?' Tommy asked failing to stifle the insensitivity of the question.

'It does not matter. It is safety. It doesn't matter whose it is.'

'You're right.' Tommy stood tall and held out a hand. Walter looked at the gesture and grasped it firmly. 'You're okay.'

'You are not too bad yourself.' He dragged him towards him and hugged him lightly, rubbing the hair on his head. 'Now. Go back and join the others.'

'But what about you?'

'Don't worry. I'll be along in a minute.

Tommy paused for a second, and then quickly took off.

Catherine, Georgia and Phillip continued jumping up and down frantically, and to their delirious delight, a small boat was lowered from the ship, complete with crew. They stopped waving and hugged one another in disbelief. They looked back for Tommy and Walter, but secure in the knowledge that they would not be too far away, they started waving once more.

Tommy ran from the fire, thrilled at the sight of the ship, but as he rushed back he suddenly applied the brakes and pulled up sharply. He looked ahead and then behind him, considering two options open to him. He bit down hard on his lip hard, and turning away from the route to the landing spot, ran away, deep into the woods once more.

Walter, having dressed the fire, walked across the camp gathering together various items of clothing, and started dressing himself in what remained of his uniform. He brushed it down, and donned it as if he were on parade. He paused and then looked around to check he had everything he needed.

Tommy took far more time than he wanted to track down the entrance to his cave. The opening had overgrown to such an extent that he had to dig deep with his hands to confirm that there was a cave behind it at all. He hurriedly scraped away all the good work he had put in to hide it in the first place, until finally, the small opening revealed itself once more. Despite their imminent rescue, he looked carefully over his shoulder to confirm that the canvas was to remain a secret, and that he hadn't been followed.

The parcel containing the canvas lay, undisturbed and mercifully, dry. The variants in weather, fortunately for Tommy, had not penetrated the cover he had prepared. He picked up the parcel, and with no thought to repairing the face of the cave, tucked the canvas back into what remained of his trousers, and but for the several layers of dirt on them, it sat there comfortably as if he had never removed it in the first place. He checked himself over quickly, and then, with somewhere better to be, and without wishing so much as a farewell to the place he had spent so much time in, made off to return to the others.

The boat-party, from the ship now anchored some good way off, did not appear to be making for the spot where the three of them watched. The small launch seemed to be making for a spot further along the coastline. Phillip looked in panic to both Catherine and Georgia, but they did not seem to share his worry.

'Come on!' Georgia yelled, and joined by Catherine, they took off along the top of the cliffs.

Phillip took one more look out to sea to ensure the boat had not changed its mind, and looking round, realised he had a lot of ground to make up, and he hurried along behind them. He, like his sister, and Georgia, had never seen a German ship before, or indeed, a German naval uniform. It had merely been considered that the craft was British. Whoever it really was, it didn't seem to matter. They were saved.

Tommy, equally as negligent in naval matters, quickly arrived at the spot where they had first seen the rescue party, seemingly moments ago, to find the others gone. He would however have had to have been struck stone-deaf not to have heard their voices further along the cliff. He looked out to sea to discover the reason, and hurriedly followed the racket.

69

The launch came ashore on the beach at which Walter had originally set up camp, and the crew quickly disembarked. There was little evidence left to substantiate that anyone had been there at all, as it had been stripped bare once the main camp had been set up.

Several naval personnel of various ranks stood, looking up the beach, and stood speechless, rifles hung loosely at their sides as the bedraggled figures of Catherine, Georgia, and Phillip approached at speed. They stopped in front of them, and stared into their faces as their breath slowly returned to their heaving chests.

'Well, what have we got here,' the leading officer said.

'They're ours!' Phillip yelled, and grabbed his sister in a hug, nearly knocking her off her feet. 'They're ours.'

Catherine and Georgia stood straight, trying to arrange the remnants of what was left of their own clothing into some semblance of order, then stood proudly, and almost to attention.

Phillip, beaming, and seeing the girls attempts at smartening themselves up, tried to drag his unkempt hair into some shape for the sake of appearances, and thrust out a hand and said, 'How do you do. My name is Phillip Belvoir.'

Catherine, no longer able to restrain herself, launched herself at one of the younger sailors and hugged him. 'We're safe!' she exclaimed. 'We're safe.'

Georgia held back.

'Hey!' Tommy called from much further away, attracting their attention. He rushed down, but approaching the beach, suddenly slowed his pace to a walk. As the still astonished naval staff on the beach looked over at his approach, he stopped. The appearance of authority suddenly filled him with a fear he had not felt for an age. Certainly since they had arrived on the island. He stood silently for a second, thinking, then decided, offered his hand, and said, 'Edward Burrows.'

The officer in charge of the launch struggled to ascertain any of the gabbled information that was being thrown at him, and the others in the crew stared on in continued disbelief.

'They're just kids,' one said to the other. 'Just look at the state of them.'

Walter had worked his way back to the beach and despite his conversation with Tommy, it had not escaped his notice that the ship had been an Allied vessel. He was dressed as he had been when he had parachuted in, and but for two or three items that they had utilised elsewhere during their captivity, he looked very much the same figure they had first happened upon. He walked out from behind a tree, shouted down, and started to raise his hands into the air.

One of the armed crew, his attention snatched away from the children, reached down and raised his rifle. Walter slowly reached down to a holster at his side, slowly withdrawing the revolver for submission. As he stepped forward his foot caught awkwardly on an exposed root, and clumsily he slipped and stumbled. As he did so, the hand holding the revolver reached out to help him regain his feet, and a shot rang out.

Walter regained his balance, and stood staring at the children. He dropped the revolver harmlessly onto the ground and reached to his chest. He took his hand away and looked at the dark red smear across it. He breathed in and choked slightly as fluid started to build up in his lungs. He looked once more to the children and dropped to his knees before finally crashing forward onto the ground.

'No!' Tommy cried, and casting aside arms that had been placed around him, rushed forward, pushing his way past the others. He shoved past the guard who was removing a smoking rifle from his shoulder.

'He'd better be all right,' Tommy turned and stared at him violently, and then rushed on.

Walter's body lay limply on the floor. Tommy collapsed by his side and grabbed him firmly by the lapels, drawing him up to him. 'Wake up, Walter! Wake up!'

'Make him better! Make him better!' Phillip cried from the beach, and breaking the hold of the crewman stood behind him, rushed off in their direction.

Tommy was crouched over Walter, furiously beating at his chest, as Phillip arrived at his side.

'Make him better,' Phillip repeated, desperately.

'Wake up, Walter!' Tommy yelled at Walter. But though neither of them possessed any medical knowledge, it was clear his final breath had exited his body.

Tommy was pushed to one side, and an unidentified adult examined the body. He quickly checked for signs of life, but the evidence was negative, and he stood up next to Walter's dead corpse, and confirmed to the others, 'He's dead.'

Georgia collapsed to the floor, and Phillip had to be held up by an equally distraught Catherine.

The crew of the launch looked on, further perplexed. Tommy looked back, tears running down his cheeks like a stream, and yelled, 'Murderers!'

'Search his body for identification,' the officer in charge instructed another of his crew.

Tommy listened to the order with incredulity.

'You leave him alone!' Tommy stared at the party coming forward, and turning round, collapsed on top of his body. With a certain aptitude, and before the search party arrived, he slipped his hand inside Walter's tunic, and carefully withdrew his wallet. He deftly pocketed the purse, and his task complete, returned to the now immobile face. He considered removing Walter's dog-tags, but he realised they were the only official identification Walter possessed, and he left them where they were.

The urgency to retrieve the children and return them to the safety of the ship was paramount. But the emotions at Walter's demise were far from done with.

'What's going to be done with him?' Tommy demanded.

'Come on, son!' one of the crew ignored his demand, and tried to drag him away.

'What's going to be done with him?' Tommy repeated, snatching himself away.

'He'll be buried at sea,' another, calmer voice announced from behind them.

A furious debate ensued and the four children quickly detached themselves from their rescuers, and stood back, glaring at them.

The officer in charge of the launch had ascertained from the children that no one else was on the island, but a further launch had been sent across, and a search party organised.

The children ardently refused any immediate offer of return to the ship, and begged that Walter's body remain on the island. The initial refusal had resulted in Phillip snatching away from caring hands, and defiantly running away. Tommy ensured them that he would hide away and it would be impossible for any sort of search to find him unless they agreed to their demands.

A frustrated officer, not wishing their rescue vessel to spend any more time at anchor than it had already, had had to give in to their mandate, and it was finally decided that Walter's body was to be interred on the island after all.

Walter's resting place lay beside that of Harriet and the cross they had constructed for her. An agitated officer hurriedly organised the burial, and the children stood in a line circled by a naval party and full respects were paid and a short prayer said.

The grave was filled in and a sturdier, larger cross, put together by one of the crew had been erected and placed at the head.

The children were left to pass their short and final respects over the grave, whilst the rest of the island was searched.

Any shared words for Walter were whispered, and a quiet 'Amen,' from each of the children at their departure was spoken through a flood of tears, and they were then marshalled back to the waiting transport to carry them back to safety.

Bonn 1950

There was a loud knock at the front door to the small house in Kaiser Strasse.

A pretty, fair-haired lady in her mid-thirties, her hair swept back into a tight bun, rose from a chair in the living room, and walked across to answer it.

She brushed herself down to straighten her clothing, and fighting off the efforts of her two children, just managed to get to the door first. She opened the door, to be greeted by a young dark-haired man, bearing a handful of assorted envelopes.

'Good morning, Frau Muller,' he said. 'I am sorry to bother you, but I have a letter you have to sign for.'

'Not at all! Please! Come in.'

She dispatched her two children, and led the postman through to the living room. She walked across to a bureau, picked up a pair of glasses and perched them on the end of her nose. 'Now. Where do I need to sign?'

'Just here,' the postman offered her a notebook.

She signed the document and duly turned to return it to the postman, who was engrossed, looking at an oil painting hanging over the fireplace.

'It's pretty isn't it?' she said.

'It's startling.'

The oil painting was framed, and showed St George sat on a rearing stallion confronted by a fire-breathing dragon. Below it, and spread out along the mantelpiece, lay a wallet, a small photo of her two children when they were younger, and various other papers that had been inside.

She signed for the letter, and bade the postman 'Good morning.'

EPILOGUE

The front door to the apartment closed noisily, shutting out the customary bitter cold of the Montreal night. A pair of shoes stamped heavily on a rough mat inside the door, scattering several small clumps of snow that had refused to give up their hold outside across the floor. The tall, uniformed officer blew on his hands, as the warmth of the room started to take its effect on his body. Removing his coat, he hung it clumsily on a hook beside the door, and set to cast his jacket onto the sofa, thought better of it, and opted to better drape it over the back of a wooden chair, set tidily beside a polished wooden table. A small metallic brooch, displaying: R.C.M.P. - The Royal Canadian Mounted Police - surrounded by maple leaves, hung carelessly off the lapel, currently ignored by its owner.

'So! Did you catch me any criminals today?' a gentle voice called from a hidden room.

'Not today! Just a heap of paperwork,' he replied, yawning, and stretching out his body, made towards the voice.

'Anyway - Officer Tommy Adams!' the voice called proudly, as if it were the first time she had greeted him in his role. 'I have had a letter, and we are set to have guests.'

'Georgia, if we have any more visitors, we will...'

Georgia strolled into the room, halting his short journey, grabbing her husband's hand, and rolling into his arms.

'It's from England.' The middle-aged officer straightened up, and looked across eagerly. 'It's from Lady Catherine Belvoir. And Phillip! They're both coming over to see us.'

'I'll have her arrested at the airport,' Tommy announced without a thought.

'Don't you dare, Tommy!' Georgia growled playfully, holding him at arms length to fully demand his attention, and her face, breaking into a smile, added, 'now give me a hug.'

'Only if you let me arrest her,' he offered her a compromise.

'Give me a hug!' she demanded, refusing to let up.

Tommy wrapped his huge arms around her shoulders drawing her into him, and as she snuggled into him, he kissed her head.

'Mmmmm!' she cooed. 'I do love you.'

'I'm still having her arrested!'

The End

322